May you find intrigue
and inspiration in
these pages.

John Elland

The
THIRD TESTAMENT

John Eklund

iUniverse, Inc.
New York   Bloomington

The Third Testament

iUniverse books may be ordered through booksellers or by contacting:

iUniverse
1663 Liberty Drive
Bloomington, IN 47403
www.iuniverse.com
1-800-Authors (1-800-288-4677)

ISBN: 978-1-4502-2503-8 (pbk)
ISBN: 978-1-4502-2504-5 (cloth)
ISBN: 978-1-4502-2505-2 (ebk)

Library of Congress Control Number: 2010905198

Printed in the United States of America

iUniverse rev. date: 7/14/2010

In memory of Tony Woewucki (July 12, 1922–March 16, 2002)

Chapter 1

A Pleasant September Sunday

"Thou art Peter, and upon this rock I will build my Church, and the gates of hell shall not prevail against it ..."

As I would come to realize, Christ's words to Peter, establishing the Church, are unequivocally the most important words in the entire Bible. Therefore, it is only fitting that they are the words that begin my story.

I was in my usual Sunday morning spot, the second to last pew in the back of St. Mary's church, when Father Tom began the gospel reading. Reciting Matthew 16, the young, introverted priest spoke in a way that seemed much stronger and clearer than usual. His voice was baritone and echoing and easily reached every parishioner in every corner of St. Mary's. Normally, it had a meek, nasal quality, almost like a shy Jimmy Stewart with a sinus infection. Something was definitely different.

Maybe he started using a new nasal spray or switched antihistamines, I thought as I sat dreamily gazing upward at the beautiful domed ceiling of the cathedral. Sweat slowly dripped down my fifty-seven-year-old wrinkled brow as I gazed.

St. Mary's was packed with people and it was very warm, if not sweltering. The air conditioning obviously was not working. That was no surprise, for St. Mary's was an old church, strong on charm but weak on modern amenities. The heat did not bother me, though. I was too engrossed in thought to care. In a circuitous manner, I began reminiscing about my daughter, Ellen, in her youth. Years before, she had had her own experiences with nasal sprays and antihistamines. They were memorable experiences—experiences that exemplified all of the joys and trials of child-rearing. Thinking about them, I could not help but smile.

1

Ellen suffered from allergies when she was in grade school. Each fall, during ragweed season, her nose would turn red, matching her watery eyes. The poor thing was forced to carry a box of tissues with her everywhere she went. Thankfully, antihistamines helped to take the edge off of her symptoms. The dilemma for her was picking out which antihistamine to use. It was a comical dilemma. Although sweet as sugar and cute as can be, Ellen was a precocious and particular child. She was exceedingly choosy about her medications, always looking for one that was just right and accepting nothing less.

"Dad, this one just isn't working for me," she would say in as authoritative a tone as a young girl with pigtails could. "It must be an inferior brand."

"Sweetheart, why don't you give it a couple of more days?" I would reply in an encouraging manner. "Sometimes these things take awhile to kick in. Sometimes you just have to be a little bit patient. Things will get better."

"But I can barely breathe," she would retort in overly dramatic fashion, often followed by a forced cough. "I can tell that I'm getting worse. Can't you?"

"You sound all right to me," I would say. "I think you'll be fine. Actually, I think you may be making a bigger deal out of this than you should. You know it is not good to exaggerate. You remember the story of the boy who cried wolf, don't you?"

"I'm not exaggerating," she would fire back obstinately, with arms crossed. "My nose is completely stuffed and my lungs are tight. In fact, I think I may start to wheeze at any moment."

She never once wheezed, but she knew that wheezing was a cause for concern for parents. She was clever that way.

Every autumn it was the same routine. One year, her doctor gave her four different prescriptions before she finally found one to her liking. It was expensive, if not amusing. Between the multiple different prescriptions and the need for refills, we were constantly running back and forth to the local corner drugstore—so often that the pharmacist got to know us on a first-name basis. Not only did we pick up the antihistamines there, but we also stocked up on Hall's cough drops, Visine anti-itch eye drops, and boxes upon boxes of Kleenex. The whole affair was like an episode from a sitcom. Fortunately, Ellen seemed to outgrow her allergies over time.

Ellen outgrew her allergies, and poor old Henninger's Drugstore went out of business. That may be more than just a coincidence.

The memories of Ellen's prescriptions and the now-defunct drugstore reminded me that I needed to stop by Walgreen's pharmacy. Walgreen's had left an automated message on my answering machine the day before: "Thank you for using Walgreen's pharmacy. Your prescription is ready for pick-up at

Walgreen's pharmacy. Your prescription is ready for pick-up at Walgreen's pharmacy. Your prescription is ready ..."

The way the woman on the recording changed the inflection in her voice when she said "Walgreen's pharmacy" was certainly annoying. Her tone in the first part of the message was unremarkable, but then she paused, without good reason, and blurted out "at Walgreen's pharmacy."

Do they hire professionals for jobs like that? I wondered.

It was never long before my mind would begin to wander at church. I would often fall into a stream of consciousness, filled with loose associations, or I would pass the time making checklists of things to do. Following my usual routine, I started making a checklist outlining the rest of my day.

First, I'll go to pick up my blood pressure medication at Walgreen's. While I'm there, I'll buy more Hershey's with almonds. Whoever first decided to combine chocolate with almonds was a true genius. That unknown, divinely inspired soul made the world a much better place. Really, what did Einstein ever do for society that could compare with the pure joy of eating a 31 Flavors chocolate-almond ice cream cone? And what did da Vinci ever create that could compare with the magnificence of a chunk of dark chocolate almond bark? Later, I'll meet Jerry to watch the Bears game ...

The Chicago Bears were 2–0, and although it was early in the season, there was realistic hope that they would not end up being a total embarrassment. Being a pragmatist, I was not asking for a repeat of the glorious 1985 championship season, the year they lost only once and clobbered the New England Patriots 46–10 in the Super Bowl. One simple playoff win would suffice. It seemed like it had been forever since they had actually won a game in the playoffs. Even making it to the playoffs was a rarity for them. The years of futility were frustrating, but I kept coming back for more nonetheless. It was sometimes hard being a Chicago fan.

When the game is over, I'll go back home and order some gifts for Ellen on the Internet. I'll spend my evening working on a lesson plan for this week.

I was employed as a professor at a small local Catholic college, and Sundays were the days I worked on my lesson plans. The upcoming week, I was scheduled to lecture on Norse mythology, with an emphasis of discussion on its influence on modern culture. I enjoyed the Norse myths immensely. They had a primitive charm to them. Although in general they were not nearly as popular as the Greek and Roman legends, a few Norse tales definitely merited discussion. I already knew what the first day's topic would be.

I'll start with the story of how mistletoe became associated with kissing. It is one of the major focal points of the Norse tradition and is a story that the class should enjoy.

In my opinion, the epic story of the mistletoe is one of the greatest myths ever told. Although written in simple terms, it compares favorably to anything in the Greek, Roman, or Asian genre. The story revolves around the tragic death of a Norse god named Balder. He was the god of light and springtime and was the most beloved of all the beings in the vast Norse universe. Because of the long winters they endured, the ancient Norse people placed a great emphasis on light and springtime, and Balder was a Christ-like figure to them. According to the legend, Balder had a dark and unsettling dream one night; he dreamed that he was going to die. Word of Balder's sinister premonition spread throughout all of Asgard, the golden kingdom of the gods. The other Norse gods were so disturbed by his dream that they had every creature and every object in heaven and on earth promise to do no harm to Balder. So great was the love for Balder that every creature and every object in heaven and on earth unreservedly agreed. The mountains and the seas, the giants and the dwarfs, the stars and the moon, the trees and the beasts, the fish and the birds, the frigid ice and blazing fire—all made a sacred vow to protect the creator of light and bearer of spring.

It seemed that with the litany of solemn pledges, Balder was safe. Yet there was one dire omission: the gods of Asgard neglected to ask the mistletoe, thinking that it was too dainty and weak to cause anyone harm, especially a powerful god from Asgard. The oversight was a tragic one. Several days after Balder's ominous dream, Loki, the Norse equivalent of Satan, tricked Balder's unsuspecting blind brother, Hoder, into shooting an arrow at Balder's heart. At the tip of the arrow was the neglected mistletoe, magically strengthened by Loki's evil. Hoder took the arrow with the deadly tip, pulled back the bowstring, and let it fly toward his beloved brother. Hindered by his lack of sight, Hoder knew not what he was doing; he was an innocent victim of Loki's evil. When the mistletoe struck, Balder fell dead immediately and was condemned to spend eternity in the underworld.

The gods of Asgard were stunned and horrified. Throughout the entire universe there were cries of unbridled grief. The wailing of those saddened was heard day and night. Weeks passed, but the mourning continued, with no foreseeable end. Faced with such hopelessness, the sorrow-filled gods sent a messenger to confront Hel, the queen of the underworld, and plead for Balder's return to the world of the living. Hel agreed to allow Balder's return, but only if all things, both living and lifeless, would weep for him. All things wept, except for Loki, who disguised himself as an old crone and refused to shed one tear. Because of Loki's wickedness, the god of light remained in the land of the dead. With Balder gone, the heavens and the earth were left in darkness and cold. Three bitter winters came in sequence with no summer in between. Hope and happiness faded away, becoming distant memories. All that was once good became tarnished with evil, and morality disappeared.

It remained that way until the mythical universe eventually came to its cataclysmic end.

The end of the cosmos was called Gotterdammerung, the Twilight of the Gods. In the final days, the gods of Asgard fought one last great battle against the frost giants and hellish creatures of the underworld. All perished in the battle. Odin, king of the gods, was devoured by a giant wolf, and Thor, the mighty god of thunder, succumbed to a serpent's poison. Despair and desolation were ubiquitous. The heavens burned with fire and the land sank into the sea. The Norse gods were no more.

Because the innocent mistletoe had caused so much grief and suffering, the Norse people decreed that mistletoe should never again be associated with death or sorrow. It became a custom for warring Norse tribes to declare a truce, should they happen to meet under the mistletoe. Over the centuries, this peace-related custom eventually evolved into the love-related custom of kissing under the mistletoe.

My stream of consciousness continued as the Mass went on.

After the mistletoe introduction, I'll spend the rest of the lecture focusing on how J. R. R. Tolkien used themes from Norse myth throughout the epic Lord of the Rings.

I began reciting the lecture in my mind:

In Norse myth there were nine worlds: Muspelheim, Nilfheim, Darkalfheim, Midgard, Jotunheim, Vanaheim, Alfheim, Asgard, and Gimle. Some of the worlds were occupied by gods, some by giants, some by elves, and some by dwarves. Man lived in Midgard, or as Tolkien would say, middle earth. Magical rings played a very important role in the old Norse legends. There was one cursed ring, in particular, that would bring doom to whoever wore it …

My train of thought was broken, as it was time to rise and receive Holy Communion. With my hands clasped, I reverently walked up to the priest to receive the Host, but I walked right past the bearer of the wine cup. I had never found it sanitary to share a wine cup with hundreds of other parishioners, even if it is the Lord's cup. Wiping the rim with a cloth just did not do it for me.

After communion, I headed for the door.

It was a beautiful September day, perfect for football. I got in my car, drove to Walgreen's, where I picked up my blood pressure medication, and then headed for Al's Pub, where my good friend Jerry and I went to watch the Bears' games. Meeting Jerry after Mass in fall was my Sunday routine. I had been doing it for many years. Back in high school, Jerry and I used to go to church together. He had since become an agnostic. Losing his faith, he no longer prayed to God, and he never attended Mass. In general, he viewed religion with skepticism, if not cynicism. Yet despite his loss of faith, he made it very clear that he was not an atheist.

"You really have to be a pompous fool to be an atheist," he would say.

Jerry was no fool; he was just a doubter. That is really what an agnostic is—one who believes that it is impossible to know if God exists; in other words, a doubter. An atheist arrogantly believes that God does not exist. Atheism goes far beyond simple doubting. I had always felt there was something evil about being an atheist. It seemed to me that a good-willed, logical person would at least contemplate the possibility that there might be a supreme being and show enough respect to not outright deny his existence.

Jerry and I had been friends for over fifty years. He and his wife, Joyce, had me over for dinner at least once a week. Ever since my wife, Tina, died eleven years before, Jerry and Joyce had been like family to me. Moreover, they treated Ellen like she was their own daughter, and I could never adequately express my gratitude for that.

"Over here, Fred!" shouted Jerry as he waved to me from across the dimly lit main hall in Al's Pub.

Al's Pub was an inviting, old edifice that in many ways resembled an Alaskan Yukon lodge. On the roof of the pub was a stuffed Kodiak bear encased in glass. Inside the pub's sturdy doors were high, wood-beamed ceilings and two cozy fireplaces. The walls were a rustic wood, and several of the windows had beautifully handcrafted stained glass. Jerry was sitting on a bar stool near the giant television screen in the pub. He was a large man, and the stool almost seemed too small for him. Despite the discrepancy between his size and the stool, Jerry, in all other ways, looked perfectly at home in a sports bar. With his rotund build, gruff voice, poorly groomed mustache, and jovial nature, he was the epitome of a middle-aged football fan.

"Hey, Jerry, what's new?" I called out as I made my way past the large, central stone fireplace adorned with a giant mounted moose head. "It looks like the game is about to start. Do ya think the Bears will make it three in a row?"

"Even a blind pig finds an acorn, so anything is possible," he quipped.

"That's right; anything is possible," I replied with a chuckle.

I sat down on the stool next to Jerry's and reached for a menu. Jerry grabbed a basket of peanuts and popcorn that was sitting on the bar and slid it between us.

"What's Ellen been up to?" Jerry asked. "Has she found a new man yet?"

"She's seeing a couple of different guys but nothing serious. I'm not in any rush to see her married off anyway."

"True, true." Jerry nodded in agreement. "But she'll need to get married for you to get those four grandkids you hope to have."

"I do look forward to someday having grandkids," I conceded. "Four is a good number, but five may be even better. You know, with five I could field the starting lineup on a basketball team."

"That's a good point," Jerry said with a wink and a smile. "Very well thought out."

"I just want to make sure she has met the right guy," I said. "That's why I'm in no hurry."

"I hear ya," Jerry said, his eyes moving rapidly to the television screen. "Hey, here's the kickoff."

The game began, and Jerry and I settled in and cheered for our Bears. We each had a couple of drinks—beer for Jerry and root beer for me. In addition to the drinks, Jerry had a double cheeseburger with fries, and I had a slab of Al's famous barbecued ribs. We ate and talked and watched the action. It was a good game. The Bears were playing the Minnesota Vikings, who were also undefeated. Both teams were fighting hard. The Bears had their ups and downs. They were losing by a field goal at halftime but led, 9–6, at the end of the third quarter. It seemed like the Bears were beginning to take control, until their quarterback, Rex Grossman, threw a costly interception early in the fourth quarter that was taken back for a touchdown by the Vikings. The Monsters of the Midway battled back but were never truly able to regain momentum. Things looked really bleak when the Vikings went ahead 16–12, with little time left in the fourth quarter, but then Grossman redeemed himself by connecting with wide receiver Rasheed Davis on a twenty-four–yard scoring strike, with 1:53 left in the game. Jerry and I and about forty other enthusiastic fans in the pub jumped up and shouted when Grossman threw the winning touchdown. Popcorn and beer flew everywhere, but no one, not even Al, seemed to care. It was a fantastic way to finish. The Bears were 3–0, and I was feeling great.

"I just love football in September," I said to Jerry. "The start of each new season brings new hope and excitement. The rush from each victory is incredible."

"Yeah," Jerry replied. "That usually lasts one or two weeks, and then the Bears get clobbered, and you spend the next month clinically depressed because you realize how crummy the team really is."

"Spoken like a true Chicago fan," I lightheartedly gibed.

"Hey, I just tell it like it is, my friend," Jerry retorted.

Jerry and I parted ways, and I went home to work on my Norse myth lecture. Sitting in front of my computer, I pensively gazed at the waving American-flag screen saver and contemplated the task at hand. Soon enough, I started putting together a PowerPoint presentation. I had used some of the slides in the past, but many were new. I usually tried to do something unique in each academic year, instead of just giving the same lectures over and over again. That kept it interesting for me and, I hoped, it also kept it interesting for my students. The Balder myth had always been one of my favorite lectures. I started with the title slide "Neglecting the Mistletoe." In previous years I had spent a lot of time focusing on the details of the myth. This time, I wanted to be more dramatic and less detailed. I had come to realize that the drama kept the students' attention much better than the details. I contemplated focusing on the pitiful state of Balder's brother, Hoder. In many ways, he was the most tragic figure in the myth. I jotted down a few theatrical sentences as they entered my mind:

> Blind to the light that his brother provided, Hoder was an innocent victim to Loki's evil. How horrified he must have been when he found out that he'd shot the fateful arrow. What anguish the gods of Asgard must have felt to know that the long, dark winter would never come to an end because they had neglected the mistletoe.

At 9:00 PM the phone rang. It was Ellen. I had been expecting her call; she called me every night. Whether early or late, she always called to check up on her old man.

"Hi, Dad."

"Hi, sweetheart. What's new with you?"

"Nothing much. I saw that your Bears won today. Did you and Jerry have a fun time celebrating?"

"We sure did," I said. "How about you? What did you do this afternoon?"

"I worked out this afternoon. I know you think I'm crazy training for this triathlon, but it should be fun, and besides, I burn so many calories working out that I can pretty much eat what I want."

"I'm just amazed at the amount of energy you have. You certainly didn't inherit that from me. I get tired just thinking about all of the exercise you do."

"I'm just trying to get in shape, Dad."

"Get in shape? What are you talking about? I can't imagine anyone being in any better shape than you are. You don't need to get in shape. I'm the one who needs to get in shape. I'm getting older and uglier with each passing day."

"That's not true, Dad. You look as good as ever," she said. "You're a younger, taller, and thinner version of Anthony Hopkins."

"Are you trying to say that I look like a gangly Hannibal Lecter?" I jested.

"Oh, Dad," she said. "You're something else."

Ellen and I talked for about fifteen minutes and then said our good nights.

I spent another hour working on my lecture before getting ready for bed. I then said my prayers and turned off the bedside table lamp next to the picture of Tina holding Ellen as a baby. It had been a good day, and I felt that pleasant, peaceful, tired feeling that sometimes comes right before sleep. It was not long before I drifted off into the Land of Nod.

Chapter 2

DREAMS OF A FRIEND

IN THE DARKNESS of the night, I woke suddenly from my sleep and for a brief moment was confused as to where I was. After orienting myself, I looked over at the clock on the bedside table and saw that it was 3:00 AM. I had been dreaming, which for me was very strange, as I almost never dreamed. I guess everyone dreams, so I should really say that I almost never remembered my dreams—at least, I had not for many years. When I was a child, I would remember my dreams all the time, but as I grew older it seemed I would pass the night without recalling anything. That is how things were up until Tina died. Then I had nightmares. The nightmares went on for several months, and they can only be described as horrible. I still remember them, though I would rather forget. In the nightmares I would see her skin progressively get replaced by grotesque black tumors. I would reach out my hand, as if to try to pull her away from the evil that was devouring her, but stretch as I might, I could never quite reach her. I so wanted to help her in the most urgent way, but I just could not reach far enough.

"Stretch!" I would cry out.

"Please help me," she would call back, her eyes wide with fear.

My efforts were futile. Again and again, they were futile. The black tumors kept getting larger and larger until finally, she was gone. Each time I would awaken in a cold sweat with a feeling of utter panic. They were indeed horrible dreams. Thankfully, they eventually stopped.

This dream was different. It was a good dream. I dreamed that I met a very dear old friend that I had not seen in a long time. He was a friend from my youth, a period of my life that I had stored away deep in the corners of my mind, a happy period, a time when my troubles were few. I met my friend in front of the little Tudor-style cottage that had been my childhood home, a home I had not been to in many years. He was waiting for me on the front porch and walked out to the sidewalk to greet me as I approached. He acted as if he had been expecting me.

"Welcome, Fred," he said, extending his hand. "It is good to see you." His manner was warm and comforting.

"It's good to see you, too," I replied, shaking his hand as a gentle breeze went by. The tone of his voice and the firmness of his grip were oh-so-familiar. In fact, everything was so familiar and so vivid. It was very unusual. I had had vivid dreams before but never like this. The vividness was astounding.

There we were, on the street where I used to live. The street was lined with elm trees, which arched in such a way as to almost make a canopy over the road. Sadly, those trees are all gone now, wiped out by Dutch elm disease, decades ago. Yet in my dream they were so real. My father's car, a dark green 1952 Chrysler Imperial, was parked in the driveway. I recalled reading the license plate number—MTZ563. The letters and numerals were distinctly clear in my mind; it was like I had just read them yesterday. That's not all: a little red squirrel scampered across the neatly manicured lawn as my friend and I spoke. It was the squirrel that my mother used to feed in our backyard. It had a big round belly from all the food it ate. The squirrel looked just the same as I remembered, yet it was so many years ago.

My friend and I talked for hours in my dream; at least it seemed like hours. We reminisced about our youth. It was actually much more than just reminiscing. Minute by minute, I saw more and more people and places— people and places I never thought I would see again. Across the street was Charlie Davis, my overweight and immodest bygone neighbor. Shirt off, he waved to us as he pushed his manual lawn mower around his front yard. To the immediate west was Betty Murphy, the old widow who used to hand out boxes of raisins instead of candy at Halloween. She smiled brightly in our direction as she pulled weeds from her rose garden. Walking along the sidewalk was Tom Erickson, the town drunk. To my surprise, he actually looked sober for once. Normally, he would stagger and sway while talking to himself. A few houses down were the Thompson twins. Wearing T-shirts, shorts, and no shoes, they were happily playing fetch with their dog, Ruffy. And then there was Mildred O'Shaughnessy. An avid golfer, she was hitting plastic golf balls off a tee next to her driveway.

It was like I had jumped in a time machine and returned to my past. Thinking about it brought on the strongest sense of nostalgia that I had ever felt.

"Oh, to be home again," I softly murmured in the darkness of the night. The sentimental sensation made me smile. There I was, lying in my bed at three o'clock on a Monday morning, smiling ear to ear. It was a good feeling, a very good feeling. It was as if I had taken a magical vacation, a trip back in time.

My friend was a friend in the truest sense of the word, and it was so nice to be able to talk to him, albeit only in a dream. I even told him about the terrible emotional struggle I had after Tina's death. I had never been able to talk about that with anyone—not Ellen, not Jerry, not anyone. After telling him about my struggles, it was almost as if he had been there with me all along.

As I lay there in the dark, I ran through every aspect of my dream in an effort not to forget. I recalled how we walked while we talked. We did a lot of walking. We walked along the block where I used to live, passing the old community house where I'd had Saturday morning pancake breakfasts with my family. We walked past my junior high and high school. We walked past the pizzeria where I had my first job. We walked past St. Catherine's, the church where I was baptized and received my First Communion. We walked through Memorial Park, stopping briefly in front of the solemn statue of the Unknown Soldier to pay tribute, as had always been my custom. I saw so many things. There were so many memories. I woke up just as my friend turned to walk away.

Dreams, by nature, tend to diverge from reality and may even approach the abstract. This dream was certainly no different. There was one aspect that seemed particularly bizarre. In my dream, I knew I was talking to a very dear old friend—someone I had known for years; someone I could easily consider a best friend, which raised the mystifying question: if this was my very dear old friend, why couldn't I recognize his face? It was not the face of anyone I had ever met and certainly not of any friends I had ever known. In addition, I could not recall his name.

How curious, I thought. *I have a dream of a dear old friend whose face I cannot recognize and whose name I cannot recall. Yet it was so vivid, and the friendship seemed so real.*

I stayed in bed for another ten minutes, pondering the events of my dream, chalking them up to neural processing, or brain housekeeping, or some such process. I then got up to get a glass of water before promptly falling back to sleep. When my alarm went off at 5:30 AM, I turned over, reached out toward the bedside table, and hit the snooze button. Ten minutes later I did the same thing. That was my typical morning routine. Some mornings I would sit up in bed and grumble about how early it was before I'd actually get up and start getting ready for work.

On the morning after my strange dream, I skipped the grumbling and jumped into the shower. The hot water and steam poured over me, gradually waking me up. While I stood there under the reviving spray, my thoughts returned to my mysterious old friend. It began to unnerve me that I could not recognize his face. It seemed as if it had to be someone I had known very well, but I just couldn't place it.

It definitely was not Jerry.

"It wasn't Joe, either," I said aloud. Joe would have been the logical choice because I hadn't seen him in years.

Jerry, Joe, and I were best friends, growing up. People used to call us the Three Musketeers. We went to school together, up until college. Then I went to St. John's University in Collegeville, Minnesota, and Joe and Jerry both attended Northern Illinois University in DeKalb. Despite being separated, we remained good friends until after college. At that point, Joe went to medical school and got in with a pretentious group of friends. Jerry and I were not really sure what happened after that, but Joe seemed to really change. We suspected that he might have gotten into drugs, but we had no proof. Joe started calling us less and less, and he seemed to go out with his new friends more and more, often to exclusive clubs. By his fourth year of medical school, we stopped hearing from him altogether. There was a rumor that he'd been arrested for drunk driving. We also heard that he was almost expelled from medical school for writing a spoof that was highly degrading to women. He'd titled it "The Double X Chromosome Syndrome—The Most Prevalent Genetic Illness." In the spoof he cited things like PMS and other "hormonal-related mood swings" as proof that being female is a mental illness. The Joe we had known growing up would never have done anything like that. The Joe we had known was a really good guy. He would have never deserted his friends.

Jerry took Joe's desertion particularly hard. Jerry's parents died when he was in high school, and Joe became his surrogate family. For a time, they were inseparable. Unfortunately, people change, and so it was with Joe.

The friend from my dream did not look or sound like Joe. He did not act like Joe.

He could not have been Joe. Why can't I remember his name?

My shower ended, and I got dressed and started what turned out to be a very ordinary day. By six o'clock that evening I had completely forgotten about my strange dream. A busy day at work can do that to a person, especially a busy Monday.

Chapter 3
A Trip to the Doctor's Office

BEFORE I KNEW it, Thursday had rolled around. I had been dreading Thursday for some time because I had a doctor's appointment in the afternoon. I had nothing against doctors. In fact, my father was a doctor. It was just that I had always been a bit of a hypochondriac, and I seemed to have no problem thinking of all sorts of horrible things that the doctor might find wrong with me. A little medical knowledge can be a dangerous thing, and I'd picked up enough knowledge from my dad to know that almost any symptom can potentially be associated with a severe, deadly illness. Even if the likelihood of that deadly illness was infinitesimal, it was still enough to provoke my anxiety, and I did not deal well with anxiety.

I never went to the doctor until after Tina got sick. Tina was diagnosed with melanoma at age forty-four. She had a mole on her leg that started to change color. We really did not think too much of it at first, but when it continued to change, she decided to see her internist. Her internist sent her to Dr. Montgomery, a dermatologist, who thought it looked like nothing serious but said that Tina should have it removed, just in case. Well, a week later we got a call that it was actually very serious. I can still remember the words Tina spoke in a panicked voice: "The doctor said I have melanoma."

The memory of how she looked at that very moment will forever be etched in my brain. She was as pale as a ghost, and her face was motionless. I had never seen her look so frightened. I was frightened, too. Tragically, our world came crashing down. In a mere eight months the cancer had spread to her liver, bones, and lungs. It spread so fast that we could not believe what was happening. It was a nightmare. We did everything we could to fight it. Tina underwent four different experimental therapies, but her tumors just kept growing. With each new therapy, we held out hope that "this one will be the one to really help." We were fooled several times. She would often seem to get more energy after starting the experimental drugs, leading us to believe that they were working. We thought that if she was feeling better, it must mean the tumors were shrinking. In reality, none of the therapies worked. Near the end, she developed hideous black nodules all over her skin, visible reminders that the cancer was devouring her. There was no escaping the suffering.

Tina became weaker and weaker as the cancer continued to spread throughout her body. She was in near-constant agony from the tumors in her liver and bones. The narcotic pain medicines she took made her want to sleep all of the time. One of them made her vomit profusely. No matter how much medication she took, the pain still persisted. There was never a waking moment where she was comfortable. She either slept or suffered—there was no in between.

Eventually, the melanoma spread to her brain. That was the most frightening of all. She developed seizures that would strike without warning. One moment, she would be talking to me, and the next, she'd be unconscious on the floor. It was truly terrifying. At times, it seemed she was about to stop breathing. I would panic and call 911. There was nothing else I could do. I felt so helpless.

Over time, the tumors in her brain altered her personality. She just was not the same person. It broke my heart to see the woman I loved endure such abject misery. I prayed and prayed for an end to the suffering. The end indeed came—Tina died on March 16 at 6:25 AM, with me at her bedside. I held her hand as she took her last breath. For the rest of my life, I will never forget that day or that moment. Tina was my soul mate, and I have not been the same since.

Becoming a widower was not easy. I can only thank God that Ellen was already grown up when her mother passed. It was bad enough that I lost my wife but to know that my only child had lost her mother was hard for me to take. I was determined that Ellen would not experience anything like that again for a long, long time. For the first time in my life, I became concerned about my own health. I was more fair-skinned than Tina, and I'd certainly had my share of childhood sunburns, so I thought I should get checked out by a doctor to make sure that I did not have melanoma. That was when I made an appointment with Dr. Stevens, a local internist whose office was just two minutes from where I worked. When Dr. Stevens examined me, he did not find any signs of melanoma, but he did diagnose me with high blood pressure.

"You are under a lot of stress," he said. "You need to try to relax."

Easier said than done, I thought.

I never did get the hang of relaxation. My blood pressure just seemed to get higher and higher with time. I tried different diets and exercise, but nothing seemed to help. It was not long before Dr. Stevens started me on blood pressure medication. I did not like having to take pills but was resigned to the fact that I had no other choice.

Dr. Stevens was a very personable physician. He seemed to be hardworking, caring, and compassionate and was not elitist in the least. I got the sense that although he was an MD, he was not a wealthy man. In some ways he reminded me of my father—my father also was an internist. He worked long hours but made a very modest wage, as far as physicians go, due in large part to the fact that he did not perform very many procedures. Doctors get paid not so much for what they know as for which procedures they do. My father had a hereditary condition called "essential tremor," which caused his hands to shake. That precluded his doing any finely detailed procedures, which in turn precluded his earning a good wage.

A colleague of my father's used to tell this story: "There was a man from Nashville whose uncle was a brilliant landscape artist. The uncle painted with vibrant colors in his youth and middle years. His paintings were full of life. They were truly glorious. As he grew older, however, he developed cataracts and suffered from poor vision. His world became gray. He began to paint with lifeless tones, and his work lost its vibrancy. His paintings just were not the same as they had been years before. Well, one day the uncle underwent cataract surgery. Within a short period of time his vision was restored. The old man once again painted with vibrant colors. Life returned to his artwork. Around the same time as his uncle's cataract surgery, the man's two-year-old son developed an infection. The man didn't think his son's infection was serious, but he took him to the family physician just to be sure. The family physician obtained a blood sample from the son and gave him a shot of antibiotics. The blood sample later showed that his son had a deadly bacterium. Had the antibiotics not been started right away, his son would have died.

"The man's uncle had his sight restored by a skilled physician who performed an intricate procedure for a fee of five thousand dollars. It was well worth the price. The family physician performed no procedure but saved his son's life. He was also monetarily reimbursed. The fee for the office visit that day was forty dollars."

It never bothered my father that he made much less than his colleagues. He just enjoyed taking care of patients. Dr. Stevens was of the same mold.

When I got to Dr. Steven's office I checked in with the receptionist and sat down in the soothing, blue front-office area to wait. I was about twenty minutes early for my appointment. To pass the time, I flipped through several magazines without actually reading any of the articles all of the way

16

through. When I finished skimming *Sports Illustrated*, I picked up a copy of *Contemporary Life* magazine. An article on page fifty-eight piqued my interest. It was on Medjugorje, the small town in Bosnia-Herzegovina that astounded the world a quarter-century ago. In 1981, several children from that remote village began seeing apparitions of the Virgin Mary. She spoke only to them, and only they could see her. The apparition of the Blessed Virgin instructed the children to deliver a message from Christ to the people of the world. She encouraged prayer, promoted peace, and called for the conversion of atheists. The children who witnessed the apparition were thoroughly scrutinized and put through a panel of intricate psychological tests, but neither science nor psychology could account for their claims. Soon after the apparitions began, there was a profusion of purported miraculous healings in Medjugorje. *Contemporary Life* magazine retold the story, with an update of the recent events in the small, southeastern European village. Reading about it stirred my memory.

I recalled my father telling me stories of how his grandmother, my great-grandmother, had been deathly ill as a child. She had contracted rheumatic fever during a particularly long and cold winter and was slowly slipping away with each passing day. The local doctor, or whatever the equivalent of a doctor was at that time, said there was nothing he could do to help her. Eventually spring arrived but despite the thaw, the little girl's condition continued to worsen. As a last-ditch, desperate attempt to save their only child, her parents sold everything they owned to finance a monumental journey. They took her to a small village in France—Lourdes—that had become famous throughout the world. People had reported miraculous healings associated with the spring water there, and it was their last hope. Although her parents were not overly religious people, they were encouraged by the stories they had heard. Barely conscious, the little child almost did not survive the arduous trip. She grew weaker with each day of the journey. The situation looked grim—very grim—but something special happened that day they arrived in Lourdes. After being immersed in the spring, my great-grandmother regained consciousness. Her eyes fluttered open for the first time in weeks, and she spoke to her parents. She told them she was thirsty. It was a miracle. Over the course of the next several days, she grew stronger and stronger. Her parents were overjoyed. They had every reason to be. By the grace of God, my great-grandmother survived the rheumatic fever and lived a full ninety-one years before she passed of old age.

"Fred Sankt!" the nurse called my name, breaking my train of thought. "Hello, Mr. Sankt. Come right this way," she said. "How are you today?"

"I can't complain."

She led me to a scale, where I was weighed. "One hundred seventy-five pounds. You've gained five pounds since we last saw you."

"I wasn't as active as I would have liked to have been this past summer," I said. "I plan on trying to get out and walk more."

Next, she led me into the exam room, where she took my temperature and pulse. Then came the moment of truth—she checked my blood pressure. I think I held my breath the entire time. I was sure it was going to read high. Just the anxiety of going to the doctor's office would seem to be enough to make my pressure shoot through the roof.

"One-thirty over seventy," the nurse said.

I started to breathe again. That was the best reading I had had in over six months.

"Wait here, and the doctor will be with you shortly."

"Thank you," I replied.

I waited another thirty minutes before there was a knock on the exam room door.

"Hello, Fred," Dr. Stevens said in a pleasant tone. "How are you?"

"I'm well, Dr. Stevens. My blood pressure reading was pretty good today."

"So it was," said Dr. Stevens, looking at the nurse's notes on my chart. "That's excellent. Have you had any side effects from the medication?"

"No, none at all," I replied.

Dr. Stevens then began asking me an entire checklist of questions: "Any headaches, visual changes, fevers, chills, sweats, chest pain, shortness of breath, cough, abdominal pain, diarrhea, constipation, blood in your stool, pain or burning when you urinate, back pain, arthritis, weakness, numbness, tingling, or weight loss?"

I truthfully answered no to the entire list.

"How about anxiety or depression?"

I paused briefly before I answered. "No, I'm doing just fine, Doctor."

"Good."

He then started to examine me in his scrupulous manner. He looked into my ears and mouth and shined a light in my eyes. He listened to my heart and lungs and pressed firmly on my abdomen. He then began looking over my skin. Once again, I held my breath as he checked for suspicious moles.

"Looks good, Fred. You've got a clean bill of health. Keep up what you're doing. I'll see you back in six months."

"Thank you, Doctor. That's good news."

I had survived another trip to the doctor without adding to my paranoia. My feelings of worry and dread quickly abated, and I looked forward to getting back to my usual routine.

Chapter 4
OCTOBER 7

OCTOBER 7, 1972, was one of the best days of my life. It was the day I married Tina. I can still remember how she looked that day; how happy we both were; how wonderful it was to be in love. For the first few years after she died, I had a really hard time, emotionally, on our anniversary. The sense of loss was overwhelming. Each October, sadness would fill my heart, and I would sink into a depression, forgoing food and all pleasurable activity. However, as the years passed, I tried to focus on the positives, and there were many positives. Even though, in the grand scheme of things, Tina was only with me for a short time, I thanked God for each and every precious moment—every hug, every kiss, every warm hello, every laugh we laughed, and every smile we smiled together. Not many people are fortunate enough to experience what we had—it was truly magical. We were truly blessed.

It is said that God created man and woman in his image. Indeed, Scriptures read "male and female he created them." Over the years, I thought a lot about that statement. Most of the people I knew interpreted "the image" as a physical description. I, however, believed otherwise. To me, the image of God was not a physical one but spiritual. I believed that Scriptures' statement about the image of God was intended to describe the beauty and wonder of a holy union—the holy union of man and woman, the sacrament of marriage. It was the spiritual union, not the physical features of man, that resembled God. In my heart and in my soul, I felt that way about our marriage. It was the nearest thing to heaven I had ever known.

Another anniversary had arrived. It was Saturday, October 7, and just as I got out of the shower in the morning, the phone rang. It was Ellen. I had sensed that she would call. Actually, it was not so much that I sensed it; it was that I knew it.

"Good morning, Dad," she said with a cheerful voice.

"Good morning, sweetheart."

"I tried to call you earlier but there was no answer," she said. "I thought that maybe you had gone out for your walk."

"No, I didn't walk this morning. You must have caught me while I was in the shower," I said. "You're up early for a Saturday."

"Yes, I have a lot I want to get done today, so I set my alarm. I've already been on a six-mile run, and I'm planning on going biking later with Jack."

Ugh, Jack, I thought as soon as I heard his name. *Of all of the single men in the world, why him?* Just the mention of the name Jack was enough to make me cringe. *He's such a narcissist. I don't get how Ellen can stand being around him. Ugggh!*

Jonathon "Jack" Murphy was one of the young men Ellen was seeing. He worked in the business world and had an outgoing personality. Like Ellen, he was into fitness. He had a chiseled body but unfortunately seemed to be a little bit in love with himself. In truth, at times I found him to be downright obnoxious. He was always trying to make himself look more important. On more than one occasion I felt like reprimanding him, but I kept my mouth shut because I did not want to make waves with one of Ellen's friends. I did, however, take every opportunity I could to mention the Sankt family golden rule: "It's nice to be important but more important to be nice." Not surprisingly, he never seemed to catch on.

For whatever reason, Ellen enjoyed spending time with Jack but, thankfully, was in no way crazy about him.

"You sure do have a busy day," I said, acknowledging her plans without making any mention of my disdain for Jack.

"What do you think I should bring to Jerry and Joyce's tonight?" Ellen asked.

Jerry and Joyce had invited us over for dinner at 6:00. They invited us over every October 7.

"I know they love your cheesecake," I replied.

"But Dad, you hate cheesecake. I was thinking of trying something new. I was planning on baking a pecan pie."

"I think that's a great idea," I said.

Pecan pie was Tina's favorite dessert. She would bake it on special occasions when Ellen was a child.

Ellen and I talked for a while. Neither of us actually brought up the fact that it was the anniversary of the day that Tina and I were wed. We didn't have to—we each knew what the other was thinking, and besides, neither of us wanted to cause the other to become emotional. Emotions have a way of making people feel out of control. Emotions are paradoxical. They can be truly wonderful—even the saddest emotions can make us feel alive; can make us feel a reality that is otherwise absent—yet the fear of losing control is so strong that the natural human reaction is to suppress emotions and not let others see them. And this is what Ellen and I did: we suppressed them; we hid them from each other. It seemed safer than facing our fears.

After I got off the phone with Ellen, I walked upstairs to the bedroom. I opened the door to the closet and reached for a large, gold-colored box on the top shelf near the back. The box had a thin layer of dust on its cover, having remained undisturbed for quite some time. I gently brushed off the dust and carried it over to the wing-backed chair next to the window that overlooked the backyard. I then opened the box and pulled out the first of three old photo albums. Each of the albums contained pictures of Tina and me. They had been perused so many times that their bindings were beginning to wear. Just seeing them caused me to sigh.

The first album had pictures from before we were married. There were a lot of pictures of us with all of our friends from college. We looked so young. I had a lot more hair back then. Tina looked absolutely beautiful. I could not believe she picked out a guy like me. There was one picture of the two of us together at the carnival. Tina was holding a floppy, gray, stuffed elephant I had won for her. The sun was shining brightly, and we were both smiling ear to ear. I remembered that day. We were so carefree. We were so in love.

We were truly happy.

As I sat there, I wished I could return to that moment, if only for a while. As I looked through the pages of the album, there were so many moments to which I wished I could return.

The second album made me smile a melancholy smile as I lifted it out of the box. It was our wedding album. We'd had a small wedding. It was mainly just family and a few close friends, but it was perfect. Jerry was my best man. I remembered how eloquent he was when he gave the best-man speech. Our parents were so proud that day. Tina's mom cried, which of course made Tina cry. They were happy tears. I came to a picture of the two of us dancing together. Tina was in her beautiful white-satin gown. Her hair was exquisitely styled, swept up on top with loose tendrils falling gently down her neck. She looked like a movie star. I was wearing a black tuxedo with tails. We were gazing into each other's eyes. It was a moment of sheer enchantment.

"That was our first dance as husband and wife," I whispered sadly.

Staring at the picture for quite some time, I sighed and sighed again. Then, with rasping voice, I started softly singing an old song from a long-forgotten musical. It was a song that I often sang when I was feeling blue.

"Who can I turn to when nobody needs me?" I gently crooned. "My heart wants to know, and so I must go where destiny leads me …"

The last album contained an assortment of pictures, ranging from Tina's childhood to photos taken just before she became ill. I flipped through the album as I sat in the chair.

We had some really great memories.

I tried not to let my emotions get the best of me as I looked at them, but it was hard. Even after eleven years, it was still hard.

The albums were not the sole contents of the box. At the bottom of the box was a small, gold-colored envelope. The color of the envelope almost matched the color of the box, so if someone did not know it was there, it would be easy to overlook. It appeared battered, though it had only been handled a few times. I picked it up slowly and stared at the frayed edges.

"Should I open it?" I asked myself in a soft whisper.

The question seemed so difficult for such a simple task. It was a featherweight envelope, but it many ways it carried the weight of the world.

"Should I?" I whispered again.

After a moment's pause, I opened it. Inside was a lock of Tina's hair. It was a beautiful, rich auburn color. I poignantly grasped it in my fingers for a few seconds, allowing the floodgates of my emotions to open wide, before I put it back in the envelope.

The phone rang. It was Jerry.

"Good morning, Fred. How are you?" he asked with an upbeat voice.

"I'm good, Jerry, and yourself?" I replied, trying to pull myself out of my melancholy mood.

"Can't complain. Do you and Ellen have any special requests for dinner tonight?"

"We'll eat whatever you guys fix," I said.

"Well, I was thinking about barbecuing out in the backyard. I thought I'd get one more use out of the grill before I store it away for the winter."

"Barbecue sounds great to me, Jerry, and I know Ellen sure won't argue with that. Is there anything you would like me to bring?"

"Just a big appetite," Jerry quipped.

"You can count on that," I said, feeling better as I anticipated the evening. "I really can't wait."

"Hey, how'd your appointment go with the doc this week?" Jerry asked.

"It went really well," I said. "My blood pressure is finally under good control. Everything else checked out fine. He gave me a clean bill of health, so now I can go out and enjoy life to the fullest."

"That's fantastic, old man!" Jerry exclaimed. "You and I can look forward to being a couple of grouchy old bums together. Someday, we'll tell stories to your grandkids about how tough we had it in our day. We'll exaggerate like crazy, of course. We'll tell 'em how we had to walk ten miles back and forth to school in the dead of winter when the wind chill was negative seventy degrees Fahrenheit and the snow was piled up twelve feet, and how we had to work an eighty-hour workweek just to barely pay the bills. We'll tell them how there were no computers and how if we made a mistake when we were writing something, we'd have to start all over from scratch. We'll be just like my grandfather was. You remember Grandpa Rex, don't you?"

I remembered Jerry's Grandpa Rex well. He was a true character. Not a day in his life went by when he didn't go out of his way to make someone laugh. He had a marvelous sense of humor—marvelous and mischievous. There was one time back in the 1960s when he pulled a particularly funny prank on a gullible local newspaper reporter. The prank involved the use of "Russian" tennis balls. Grandpa Rex and his best friend, Ben McCarthy, were avid tennis players. They liked to play year-round but were too tight with their money to join an indoor club. Determined and rugged, they routinely shoveled the snow off the outdoor courts in winter and played in the freezing cold, wearing ski caps, sweats, and gloves. No courts had nets up at that time of the year, so they brought their own. Realizing that regular tennis balls did not bounce well in the frigid air, they purchased white rubber balls from K-Mart to play with, which worked out quite well. They would sometimes stay out in the cold, hitting balls for several hours. It was certainly an unusual sight—two old men outside in January, in Chicago, playing tennis. Word got around, and one day a female reporter from the *Daily Herald* called Grandpa Rex and asked if she could meet him and Ben out in the cold to take pictures and do an interview. Grandpa Rex agreed with delight and instantly began to scheme. He carefully inscribed CCCP, the insignia for the Soviet Union, on the tennis balls. At that time there was a great fear of and fascination with Soviet Russia, and Grandpa Rex knew that the CCCP inscription would create a big splash. The tennis balls looked so authentic that the reporter didn't even question their validity. Later that week, on page two of the *Daily Herald*, there was a picture of Grandpa Rex and Ben McCarthy. Right next to their picture was a close-up photo of a round white ball with the inscription CCCP. Grandpa Rex laughed louder than I'd ever seen him laugh when he saw the picture and read the story about the Russian tennis balls, which he had claimed were shipped to him from northern Siberia.

"How could I forget Grandpa Rex?" I chuckled. "If we model his behavior, my poor future grandkids will have a complex."

"That they will," Jerry chuckled in reply.

It was nice to be able to joke with Jerry. It was nice to have a clean bill of health. A mind free of troubles is a wonderful thing.

After talking with Jerry, I went for a walk. I first drove to Mayslake Forest Preserve in Oak Brook and then started walking down one of the dirt paths. I enjoyed taking walks out in nature and took them as often as I could. The fresh air and rustling of the trees relaxed me and allowed me to gather my thoughts. The outdoors was my sanctuary.

The day was a particularly nice day for a walk—pleasantly warm but not hot and just the right amount of humidity. A few of the trees had begun to show a hint of their autumn hues. Otherwise, it could have passed for a midsummer's day.

As I approached the spring-fed lake on the south side of the preserve, I came upon several people who were out walking their dogs, taking advantage of the near-perfect weather.

Dogs are such funny animals, I thought as I walked. *They are so loyal and friendly to their human owners but will viciously snarl at other dogs that happen to come along.*

I had to smile as I saw a little black-and-brown dachshund growl at a yellow lab that was strolling by. The yellow lab's paw was larger than the dachshund's head, but that didn't seem to faze the little dog one bit.

Mayslake Forest Preserve, a ninety-acre plot of land sitting in the middle of one of Chicago's most prestigious suburbs, was the one-time home of coal magnate Francis Stuyvesant Peabody. Peabody acquired the land in 1919 and immediately began construction of the thirty-nine–room Tudor Revival mansion that prominently adorned the estate. The mansion was constructed just north of an idyllic, natural spring-fed lake, and Peabody named the land Mayslake as a tribute to his wife and daughter, both named May. Unfortunately, Peabody died of a heart attack at age sixty-three, just after the mansion was completed. His grieving family decided they did not want to live there and sold the land to the Franciscan Order of the Friars Minor in 1924. As a memorial to Peabody, a replica of St. Francis of Assisi's famed Portiuncula Chapel was erected on the estate, the only one of its kind in the entire United States. The Franciscan monks prayed in the chapel and used the mansion as a retreat house for nearly seventy-five years before they sold the land to DuPage County. Ever since that time, the bucolic estate has been open to the public. It is one of the true hidden gems of the Chicagoland area.

As I walked along, I admired the row of magnificent homes that lined the southern border of the nine-acre lake. Although not as grand as Peabody's colossus on the northern end of the lake, they were impressive mansions in their own right.

How nice it must be for the children who grow up there, I thought. *Everyone should have it so good.*

I knew people, however, who would look at those homes and say the exact opposite. "No one should have it so good," they would grumble. I did not feel that way at all. I was never one to take a disdainful stance toward the wealthy. Rather, I simply appreciated the grandeur of the architecture.

There is nothing wrong with constructing something majestic, and those homes are definitely majestic.

Although I found nothing wrong with the privileges of wealth, I certainly thought it was nice that Peabody's estate was open to the public and was being put to good use. The First Folio Theatre Company held Shakespearian plays on the grounds of the estate each summer. People would come with picnic baskets, blankets, and citronella candles and enjoy the theater under the stars. In many ways, the picnicking ensembles resembled a much smaller version of Ravinia, the renowned suburban music festival that took place on summer evenings in the northern suburb of Highland Park.

In the colder months, the First Folio company moved indoors and put on a variety of performances inside Peabody's mansion. The mansion itself was still undergoing renovation, and there were reportedly plans to expand its usage.

It would make a fantastic haunted house, come Halloween, I thought as I walked along.

Reaching the end of the lakeside path, I turned around and headed back east until I came to a narrow trail that led through a wooded area to an open field. A babbling brook, lined with tall cattails, transversed the field. I walked alongside the pastoral brook for several minutes until I came to a small wooden footbridge. I stopped for a moment on the footbridge and looked downward at the shallow water passing underneath.

Tina loved this spot, I thought as I watched the water pass by.

Tina had discovered the charming little bridge several months before she died. She came back with me on several occasions to admire it until she got too sick. It was one of the few places where she found peace during her difficult struggle.

There is definitely something about flowing water that soothes the soul, I mused.

After my brief stop at the bridge, I continued on the trail toward the chapel—the best part of the entire preserve. It was a small and simple four-walled structure, yet it was awe-inspiring. On the front of the chapel was a vibrant mural depicting a glorious vision of heaven. The roof of the chapel was adorned with an ornate steeple, complete with a statue of the Blessed Virgin holding the infant Jesus and topped with a botonnee cross. It was not at all something you'd expect to find in a suburb of Chicago.

Standing in front of the exquisite replica, I felt a closeness with God.

"Lord, bless the poor in spirit," I whispered as I looked up at the beautiful mural. I then began to recite the Prayer of St. Francis, word for word, from memory.

On the way home from my walk, I stopped at the market to pick up a bottle of Zinfandel from Australia to bring to Jerry's later that evening, thinking it would pair well with the barbeque. When I got home, there were two messages on my answering machine. The first was a telemarketer trying to sell timeshares in the Bahamas, and the second was Ellen, with a list of ideas of what I should wear to the barbecue. She was always trying to give me fashion advice.

She enthusiastically said, "Your blue button-down shirt goes well with those new khaki pants, or you could wear the green polo with the gray shorts and deck shoes. Make sure your socks match whatever you are wearing. But don't wear those off-gray socks that you love so much. They're fraying and should be thrown out."

I could not help but chuckle after listening to the message. "That's my little girl, trying to take care of her old man."

Ellen picked me up for dinner at 5:30. I wore the blue shirt and khakis she had suggested. It was simple and comfortable, and she seemed pleased.

"You look so nice, Dad," she said as she gave me a kiss on the cheek.

"So do you, sweetheart."

Ellen was a beautiful girl. As the Irish would say, her bright blue eyes smiled, and her auburn hair glistened in the sun. She looked just like her mother, and more than that, she had the same youthful love of life that her mother had had. Her petite frame was filled to the brim with vim and vigor. I was glad that Ellen's personality turned out more like her mother's than mine. I had always been more of the pensive, philosophical type; more of a thinker than a doer. Tina was the opposite. She'd lived life to the fullest and brought joy to those around her. Hers was a better way to live.

"Let me use your bathroom before we head over to Jerry and Joyce's," Ellen said as we were preparing to depart.

"No problem. I'll be waiting by the front door," I said.

While she was in the bathroom, I slipped a hundred dollars' worth of twenties into her purse. Ellen worked as a pediatric dentist. She had just started to establish a practice and was living from paycheck to paycheck. She was proud and independent and would not knowingly accept money from me, but I had my ways.

I knew Ellen would eventually be very successful at what she was doing. Although I had never seen her work, I could not imagine anyone better at dealing with frightened young kids than Ellen.

If she can't make them smile, then no one can, I thought as I waited.

Within a few minutes, we were on our way. Jerry and Joyce had a modest but nice home, a brick-and-stone bungalow that had been remodeled several times. Joyce was not thrilled with the house when they'd moved in; she fully believed that one day they would relocate to a better place. As time went on, however, she decided she loved the location and did not want to leave. She still did not care for the house, though, and therefore had lots of work done. She enclosed the entire front porch, making it a handsome structure with mullioned windows and a pecky cypress-wood foyer. She also added on two rooms to the back of the house. By the time she was done, it looked nothing like the house they'd originally bought.

Joyce met us at the door when we arrived. She was a vibrant woman in her early fifties who was always smiling. She had perpetually rosy cheeks and could have easily passed for a young Mrs. Claus, not solely based on her looks but also on her warmth and hospitality.

"Welcome, guys," she said. "Follow me out back. Jerry's already out there, busy at the grill."

Jerry and Joyce had a large backyard, perfect for barbecuing. They liked to cook out as often as they could during the warm months and were very good at it. We had a nice time at their place that night. The chicken they prepared was delicious, and the pecan pie could not have tasted any better. After dinner, Jerry made a toast to Tina and me. It was simple but elegant, and it was the only mention of our anniversary the entire evening. Jerry could be a barbarian at times, but he also had the ability to be quite graceful when he wanted to. He had a gift for knowing just how to say and do what was appropriate.

That is a gift I wish I had.

By the time I got home that evening, it was already late. I quickly changed clothes and got ready for bed. I called Ellen to make sure she got home OK, and then I said my prayers. Feeling very tired, I turned off the bedside lamp next to the picture of Tina holding Ellen as a baby and immediately went to sleep.

I woke suddenly at 3:00 AM, breathing deeply as if I had been running. "Another dream," I said to myself as I sat up in bed.

It was déjà vu—another dream and another 3:00 AM awakening. "How strange," I whispered in the dark.

It was indeed strange—two dreams in less than two weeks. I was not at all accustomed to dreaming. Yet what puzzled me the most was not simply the fact that I was dreaming but the profound vividness of the dreams. They both seemed so real—and that was not all they had in common. My friend from the other dream was in this one also, but the circumstances were drastically different. In this dream, I was standing in front of the office building on

66 North Dearborn in Chicago. It's a building that I often passed when I lived downtown, but I had not been there in many years. The building was burning—black smoke poured through its broken windows. The continuous fountain of smoke blended with the dark night sky as it drifted upward. Several stories up, I could see bright orange flames. The flames were not brilliant, like a bonfire, but were sinister and frightening, crackling with fury. I could hear screams from people trapped in the building. They were calling for help and sounded so desperate. It was terrible. Compounding the misery, the burning building created a horrible stench in the air. It was the stench I remembered most vividly when I awoke from the dream; I felt nauseated from the stench. It was the oddest sensation. I smelled nothing, but the memory of the stench made me feel like I needed to throw up.

In my dream, I was the only person on the street outside. It was like an episode from *The Twilight Zone*. There was no one on the sidewalks, and although there were cars parked along the streets, there was no traffic. Not one single car or truck passed by. I could hear the roar of sirens in the distance, but no help ever came. I started shouting in my dream. "Someone help! Someone please help!" I called out into the night air, but no one answered. My shouts simply echoed down Dearborn Street. It was like I was alone in a surreal urban canyon.

As time passed, the screams from the people trapped in the building became louder and louder. They were high-pitched shrieks that pierced the night, sounding almost inhuman.

"I've got to do something," I said aloud. "I've got to help them."

The problem was that I did not know what to do. My heart was pounding as I continued to call out into the smoke-filled night. "Where's the fire department?" I shouted. "Why hasn't someone called the fire department? Help! Someone please help! Call 911!" Call out as I might, no help arrived. I could hear the sirens in the distance, but the fire trucks were nowhere to be seen.

In my dream, my heart raced ever so rapidly, and I began to panic. To make matters worse, my voice grew hoarse from shouting. The situation seemed hopeless. In frustration, I dropped to my knees, turning my head to the sky, as if in search of divine guidance. It was at that precise moment that I saw movement down the street, far in the distance. A figure was approaching from the north. He walked slowly toward me, his silhouette coming in and out of sight as the smoke in the air temporarily obscured my view. As the figure got closer, I could see that it was my friend from my previous dream.

"Please hurry!" I called out to him. "We have to do something. This building is burning, and there are people trapped inside. No one is coming to help them."

"You can help them," my friend said to me with an air of calm. "You can help them, and you will help them."

The words "and you will help them" were the last thing I remembered before waking up.

Chapter 5
THE THIRD DREAM

WHY AM I having these dreams?" I asked myself when I woke up later that morning. *Why?*

The lack of a logical explanation bothered me at first until I reminded myself that dreams are not supposed to be logical. Dreams are not supposed to make sense. No one really knows why we dream. Science tells us that dreams are an important component of the formation of memories, but that still does not fully explain why we dream what we dream. I spent much of the day thinking about it, if for no other reason than I had little else exciting going on at work. Not only that, remembering my dreams was a novelty to me—it happened so rarely. Perhaps people who frequently recalled their dreams would not have made a big deal out of it. To them, it would have just seemed routine.

Back when Tina was alive, we had a neighbor, Mrs. Duerf, who talked about her dreams all of the time. To her, dreams were an extension of reality and were as much a part of everyday life as brushing her teeth and kissing her spouse good night. Her world was a different kind of world, and she liked to share it with everyone she met. Not a day went by without a tale of her previous night's REM escapades. The list of interesting people she met and extraordinary places she visited in her dreams was unending. She always gave some profound explanation for everything she dreamed. I thought she was a little wacky, to say the least, but Tina found her stories intriguing.

Mrs. Duerf was very old and died a few years ago. She had many casual acquaintances but few relatives and even fewer friends. I was one of only a handful of people at her wake. It seemed that the other people at the wake had the same opinion about her that I did. Shortly after I arrived at the funeral home, one of our neighbors came up to me and said, "She was really a nutty old gal, wasn't she."

"She sure was," I said with a reaffirming nod of the head. "She sure was."

As batty as I thought she was, though, I will always remember her fondly because of something she told me shortly after Tina passed. It was early in April 1995, and I was in the process of cleaning out Tina's things from the house. I was simply exhausted, and the work I was doing could not have been more depressing. One evening, out of the blue, Mrs. Duerf came over to bring me a cake she had baked for me. It was an old Creole recipe. Everything she did was related to the Creole culture in some way. She was from the French Quarter in New Orleans and lived like she was still there. She spoke with an accent and tried to throw in a French phrase every now and then. When I opened the door in answer to her sturdy knock, she smiled brightly and said, "Bonjour, Fred. How are you doing?"

Out of politeness, I invited her inside. I thanked her for the cake and started a safe conversation about the weather. When I finished commenting about the recent heavy rain, she asked me again, "Fred, how are you doing?" This time, her tone was not that of a warm greeting but of a sympathetic neighbor.

Although I told her I was coping well, she must have been able to see the pain in my eyes. I'll never forget what she told me.

"Fred, listen to my words," she said. "You were blessed by God. You were blessed by God with a soul mate, and when you're blessed with a soul mate—a true soul mate—that person never leaves you."

When she started in with her monologue, I thought to myself, *Please stop.* I was tired and extremely irritable and had no patience with listening to the grating, albeit good-intentioned, ramblings of a crazy old lady. I prayed she would stop, but she continued on.

"Fred, when you go to sleep at night, and you toss and turn in your bed, you are taking a long journey. That journey is a difficult journey, filled with fear and anxiety. You see horrible things on that journey—things that make you cringe; things that make you want to run and hide. But you do not run. And you do not hide. Rather, you face your deepest fears and bravely continue on. Why do you continue on? Why do you continue on when you're faced with such barriers? Because at the end of your journey, when you're in your deepest sleep, you find a place of peace. You find a special sanctuary, a piece of heaven. Fred, when you are in your deepest depths of slumber, you find yourself reunited with your soul mate, and there is no pain; there is no suffering; there is only the love that brought you together. Every night, Fred, you two are together in a perfect place. The love never leaves; it never fades; it burns brightly in that deep sleep. The nightmares are just part of the journey, Fred. They're just part of the journey."

I had never told Mrs. Duerf, or anyone else for that matter, that I was having nightmares. She just knew. She could see it in my eyes and in the way I carried myself. She was an eccentric old lady who just wanted to help by telling me a story. The crazy thing is that her story actually did make me feel better.

As the day wore on I decided that I had wasted too much time thinking about my dream from the night before. It was time to put it out of my mind. I would not have made any more of it, except for the fact that I had an even stranger dream the next night.

"Hello, Fred," a voice called out to me in my dream. It was the voice of my friend, the friend whose face I could not recognize and whose name I could not recall.

"Hello," I called back as I made my way over to where he was standing.

We were near a great lake in a place I had never before visited. It was certainly not any lake in the Midwestern United States. It was surrounded by rocky cliffs to the east and to the west. We stood along the shore, alone. The day was deeply overcast, save for a few spots where the rays of sun broke through the clouds and brilliantly illuminated the water. A strong breeze was blowing inland. It was a warm and pleasant breeze. There was no sign of civilization anywhere. The only sound came from the undulating sea. The waves rolled in, singing a peaceful lullaby as they crested. It seemed so real.

"It is time," my friend called out to me.

We both paused after he said those three words. They were only three simple words, but they seemed to grip my soul. It was almost as if I knew what was going to come next but was not ready to face it.

"It has been two thousand years, Fred—two thousand winters, two thousand springs, two thousand summers, and two thousand falls. Generations have passed. Empires have risen and fallen. There has been great glory and deep despair, strife and jubilation, love and loss, life and death. Men have known truth and tyranny and good and evil. The world has seen the birth and death of countless saints and sinners. This is what we call history. It is a history of so much more than just dates and names. Dates and names are simple facts. Too many look upon history as a compilation of singular events and simple facts to be memorized, then forgotten. They see nothing more. St. Petersburg, Leningrad, but then St. Petersburg again—was this just a simple fact? A change in names? No, this was truth. The truth in history unlocks the doors of the mind, and only through those doors will freedom of will lead to freedom of the soul. It has been two thousand years, Fred, and now the season calls for change. It is time."

"I know," I replied. "But how can I possibly ..."

"You can and you will," my friend reassured me. "Fred, you believe. This much I know. You believe like we believed. I can see into your heart. I have been with you when you recite the creed. While many others who surround you simply speak words, yours is truly a profession of faith. That faith will guide you. It will guide your hand, Fred. You will not fail. It is his will."

"But I am not a writer!" I exclaimed.

"You are his chosen writer," he retorted with an air of calm and confidence.

"Why me?" I asked. "There must be others who are much better suited for this task. I stutter and stumble over my own words. I've never been able to express what I really want to say—never. Why me?"

"Fred, when you walk alone along the dark path in the middle of the seemingly endless night, you will encounter the hooded stranger. He will ask you the question he asks of all those who pass. It is a question of merely six words: 'Do you know who I am?' These are the only six words that he will speak. Oh, there are a great many who think they know the answer, yet so many falter when faced with the question. So many succumb to his wicked ways. But you, Fred, will not falter. The Lord knows you will not falter. Do you know what your reply will be? You will look the demon straight in the eye and say, 'Do you know who *I* am?' You will speak only this and nothing more. He will then see what you cannot see now. He will then know that which man's greatest logic cannot explain. The fruits of the victory at Calvary were passed along to God's people, and a mere two thousand years cannot erase that fact. So when you ask the question 'Why me?' I say, 'Why should it be anyone other than you?'"

Again we paused and listened to the waves crash against the shore. The wind had picked up, and now it seemed as if the clouds were racing across the sky.

"Do you believe in Christ?" my friend asked me. I was taken aback by his question.

"Of course I do," I replied.

"Then feed his sheep."

"Do you believe in Christ's Church?" he questioned again.

"Of course I do. You know I do."

"Then feed his lambs."

"Do you love God?" he questioned me a third and final time.

I was troubled by this inquisition, but I answered him simply. "Yes, I love the Lord."

"Then write the story of his people. Make this your covenant with him—to record the events of his people over the past two thousand years, to write the Third Testament."

I took in a deep breath and let it out slowly. Turning away from the rolling sea, I looked my friend straight in the eye and said, "If this is his will, then it shall be done."

Chapter 6

Who Am I?

Sunday rolled around again, and I went to Mass. After the lector read passages from the Old Testament and from the Acts of the Apostles, Father Tom stepped up to the podium and began the Gospel reading:

> When they had finished breakfast, Jesus said to Simon Peter, "Simon, son of John, do you love me more than these?" Peter said to him, "Yes, Lord, you know I love you." He said to him, "Feed my lambs." He then said to him for a second time, "Simon, son of John, do you love me?" Peter said to him, "Yes, Lord, you know that I love you." He said to him, "Tend my sheep." He said to him a third time, "Simon, son of John, do you love me?" Peter was distressed and said to him, "Lord, you know everything; you know that I love you." Jesus said to him, "Feed my sheep. Amen, amen, I say to you, when you were younger, you used to dress yourself and go where you wanted; but when you grow old, you will stretch out your hands and someone else will dress you and lead you where you do not want to go." Jesus said this signifying by what kind of death Peter would glorify God. And when he had said this, he said to him, "Follow me."[1]

The Gospel reading was undeniably similar to the conversation I'd had with my friend in my dream. It seemed like an amazing coincidence that the priest would have that exact reading the very week. Yet I was getting used to the unusual. I had been thinking about my dream quite a lot. Unlike the two

---

1   Adapted from John 21:15–19. The New American Bible. Washington DC, 1970.

previous strange dreams, I could at least rationalize why I'd had the third one. I had long believed that the Church should try to incorporate modern events into its readings and teachings.

The last readings were from two thousand years ago. Has nothing important happened in two thousand years? I questioned myself. Certainly, there has not been anything as monumental as the coming of Christ, but the Old Testament doesn't have anything that monumental either. The Old Testament is a story of God's people and is filled with the teachings of the prophets. In the last two thousand years, there may not have been what we would call "prophets," but there have been many saints and spiritual leaders who have greatly impacted the world. Just as in the Old Testament, the last two thousand years have been filled with countless inspirational writings calling people to the path of God. These writings are a treasure to the Church. Should these writings be neglected at Mass? In addition to that, the Church has officially authenticated numerous miracles. Were these events not important? Was the story of God's people in the last two thousand years any less important than the story of his people in the two thousand years preceding the coming of Christ?

Given my background as a professor, and even more so my deep personal interest in modern theology, I had toyed with the idea of writing a Third Testament of sorts for quite some time. I had planned on including stories of the major saints, like Saint Patrick and Saint Francis, and of the great miracles, like Guadalupe and Lourdes. In addition, I had planned on including extensive excerpts from the works of the most prominent Christian theologians, like Augustine and Aquinas. At the very least, I had planned on writing a book for children that I imagined would be similar to the illustrated children's Bible stories that I used to see in the waiting rooms of dentist's and doctor's offices—when displaying such things was not yet politically incorrect—except instead of having stories from the Old Testament, it would have Christian stories from the last two thousand years.

As I sat there in the cathedral, listening to Father Tom's sermon, I decided that after I retired, I would begin to write such a book. I had never before written a book, but it seemed like it would be a perfect retirement project.

If only I could draw, I would even do the illustrations.

- - - - - - - - - -

On Monday morning, I went to work and lectured to my freshman class on Charlemagne and Christendom. It was a beautiful day, and the students were still in their "weekend mode." I could tell that they had absolutely no interest in hearing about Charlemagne or the Holy Roman Empire. Students being students, this happened from time to time. By experience, I found that

I could regain their attention by doing something other than lecturing, such as telling a joke or playing a quick game. Given their level of apathy, I decided to take a break from my lecture and play the game "Who am I?"

"OK, guys," I said. "I know it's nice outside, and no one wants to concentrate on Charlemagne, so let's do something different for a minute. Let's play a game. OK?"

"OK," the class said in monotone unison, without even the slightest hint of enthusiasm.

"Come on. It won't be that bad," I said. "I'm going to give you some characteristics of a person, and you have to tell me who that person is. The first one of you to answer correctly will get ten points extra credit."

When I mentioned extra credit, everyone took greater notice. I found it amusing that students always seemed to be much more motivated to get extra credit than they were for their regular assignments. *Year after year, kids never change*, I mused. "OK, let's begin," I said. "Just call out when you know the answer. Are you ready?"

"Yes," they answered.

"Who I am?" I began, loudly and clearly. Looking around, I saw that I now had everyone's attention. "I am a notable figure from the Bible ..."

"Jesus Christ!" shouted one of the students from the middle of the room, cutting me off. I saw that it was Rick, a portly young man who had already established himself as the class clown, even though it was early in the academic year.

I chuckled and said, "No, not Jesus Christ, but kudos to you for knowing that Christ is a notable figure from the Bible. I'm surprised; that's a big accomplishment for you, Rick."

Rick smiled, pleased that he had placed himself at the center of attention.

"Now may I continue?" I said. There were no further remarks, so I proceeded. "In the midst of a great war, I came to three shepherds and proclaimed that the war would soon end, but that because of the evil of man, a new and greater war would begin, heralded by a strange light in the sky." I paused briefly to see if there were any early guesses.

"Can we answer more than once?" one student asked.

"No," I said. "You can only answer once. If, in the end, no one knows the answer, then I'll give half-credit for any repeat guesses." There were no takers, so I continued. "Standing before the three shepherds, I further prophesized that an evil nation would spread terror everywhere, and that a great and holy man would be struck down because of the evil."

"Elijah!" one of the male students from the back of the room shouted out.

"No, it's not Elijah," I said.

"Isaiah," another student answered.

"No, not Isaiah either."

"Oh, well, those are the only prophets I know," the student said, provoking the laughter of the rest of the class.

A smile broke out on my face, and I continued. "Encouraging the shepherds to pray for sinners, I promised that in the end, the evil nation would be converted, and the world would be saved." I looked around the room. "Any guesses?" I asked.

"John the Baptist?" answered a woman with thick glasses.

I shook my head.

"How about John the Apostle?" another student asked.

"No, not John the Apostle," I said.

Then there was silence. The classroom was filled with blank stares.

"Really, there are no other guesses?" I said. "I didn't realize this was that hard."

"Give us a clue," a deep-voiced male student said.

"What kind of a clue?" I asked.

"Was the prophet in the Old or New Testament?"

"New Testament," I said.

"I've read the New Testament several times, and there is no such prophecy," a bold young woman sitting in the front row insisted.

"I didn't say that the *prophecy* was from the New Testament, just the person," I said.

The class now looked very confused.

"Has anyone here ever heard of Fatima?" I questioned in a half-mocking tone.

"Aha, the Virgin Mary," several students answered in unison, finally putting together the pieces of the puzzle.

"Yes, the Virgin Mary," I said. "Since you all seemed confused, let me explain. In the year 1917, Mary appeared to three shepherd children in Fatima, Portugal, and proclaimed that World War I would soon come to an end, which it did in 1918. She warned, however, that if man did not mend his ways, a second more horrible war would erupt, heralded by a strange light illuminating the nighttime sky. On January 25, 1938, the night sky was illuminated over much of Europe by an unusually bright display of the aurora borealis, and World War II started soon thereafter. She further proclaimed that Russia would spread evil throughout the earth, but that peace would return if the world, including Russia, was consecrated to her Immaculate Heart. In the year 1984, Pope John Paul II officially consecrated the world, including Russia, to her Immaculate Heart, and soon thereafter, the foundations of Soviet Russia began to disintegrate. Her final prophecy involved the attempted assassination of a holy man. This prophecy was not fulfilled until years later, when a man employed by the Communists tried to murder Pope John Paul II. The assassination attempt occurred on May 13, 1981, exactly sixty-four years to the day from Mary's first visit to Fatima. In St. Peter's Square, in the presence of seventy-five thousand onlookers, Pope John Paul II saw a little girl carrying a picture of the Lady of Fatima. Just as he bent over to recognize the girl, two shots rang out. The shots came from the assassin's gun and were aimed at the Pope's head. Had he not stooped, Pope John Paul II would have been instantly killed. Two more shots were fired and he was hit, but the wounds were not fatal. The good pontiff survived the assault and later credited the Mother of God with saving his life. He took the bullet that had pierced his flesh and placed it on the crown of the statue of the Blessed Virgin that stands on the grounds of the Cova da Iria in Fatima. It remains there to this day as a symbol of heavenly truth."

"That's cool," said a poorly shaven male student with long black hair.

"Yeah," said Rick, this time not in jest. "Let's play some more."

"No," I said. "That's it for games for today. Let's get back to the lecture. It is time to learn about Charlemagne and the Holy Roman Empire."

My plan was successful. For the rest of the period I had the class' undivided attention.

Chapter 7

Evil in the Hearts of Men

ON MONDAY AFTERNOON, when I came home from work, I sorted through the mail, paid a few bills, and then sat down to relax and watch television. I was looking forward to the Bears game later that night. It had been a long time since the Bears were last on Monday Night Football, and there was a lot of excitement around town. They were playing the Arizona Cardinals in Arizona and were trying to remain undefeated. It was all any of the local news stations were talking about.

Feeling content, I sat back in my La-Z-Boy chair, ate some dark-chocolate–covered almonds, and sipped ice-cold water as I watched the pregame news reports. Except for food and bathroom breaks, I made no plans to move from that chair for the rest of the evening. I even kept my cordless phone by my side so I would not have to get up if anyone called.

At about 6:00 PM, there was a loud knock at my door. *Who could that be?* I was not expecting company. I knew both Jerry and Ellen were still at work, and they were the only ones who visited. "Probably a Jehovah's Witness," I said to myself.

I hit the mute button on the TV, got up from my chair in the family room, and walked toward the door. Before I could reach it, there was another loud knock. I looked through the door's peephole and saw that it was a sheriff. *Why would a sheriff come to see me?* I quickly opened the door and asked, "How may I help you?"

"Are you Frederick Sankt?" the sheriff asked in a stern tone.

"Yes, I'm Fred Sankt. What is this about?" The look on the sheriff's face and his tone of voice had me worried. *Something must have happened.* My heart began to race. *Oh, please, God, tell me that Ellen is OK.*

The sheriff handed me a large manila envelope. "You've been served by the circuit court of Cook County," he said.

"*What?*" I asked in disbelief. "For what?"

"Mr. Sankt, I suggest you get an attorney." He offered no further explanation or comment.

I stood there, stunned. "This must be a mistake," I said. "I'm no criminal. I've done nothing wrong." My heart was pounding and my hands began to tremble as I opened the envelope and removed the summons. I read the first page:

Sylvester Jones, Plaintiff, vs. Frederick Sankt, Defendant
Summons

To Mr. Frederick Sankt:

You are summoned and required to file and answer to the complaint in this case, a copy of which is hereto attached, or otherwise file appearance, in the office of the Clerk of the Court. You must file within thirty days after service of this summons. If you fail to do so, a judgment by default may be entered against you for the relief requested in the complaint.

Thomas, Thomas, and Hughes, Attorneys at Law
Nicholas Hughes
Attorney for Sylvester Jones

"Sylvester Jones," I said to myself. "I know that name ... but from where?" I quickly turned to the second page and continued reading. The summons was nineteen pages in all and much of it was in legalese. Still, I understood enough to know why I was being sued. In short time, I remembered distinctly who Sylvester Jones was.

About two years earlier, I had been involved in a car crash while on my way to work. It was December, and the roads were slick. There wasn't any ice, but there had been a mix of rain and flurries the night before. I had a bad head cold at the time and debated whether or not to call in sick. I decided to tough it out and go to work, but I was running late. I felt rushed, so I was driving a little over the speed limit. About thirty seconds before the crash, I vividly remember looking down at the speedometer to see that I was going 40 mph on a street where the limit was 35 mph. The stoplight was green as I approached it, but it turned yellow when I was approximately fifty feet from the intersection. I was close enough that I thought I'd make it through without any problem, and I believe I would have—except that the car in front of me stopped abruptly. I hit the brakes but not in time. I skidded into Sylvester Jones' car. There was very little damage to our vehicles, just some dented fenders, but Mr. Jones was irate. He got out of his car and started swearing at me. He was a giant of a man with dark black, protruding eyes, and I was intimidated. I apologized, telling him that I never expected him to stop so suddenly. At that point a maroon Buick pulled up behind us. A man got out of the car and introduced himself as Eddie Simpson, a former police officer from Cincinnati. He said he saw the entire thing and that I had been speeding. He had a cell phone and called the police.

As soon as the officer arrived, Sylvester Jones started complaining of neck pain. I could not believe what was happening; it was like a nightmare. I felt miserable, standing out in the cold. My head was throbbing, and my throat was so sore that I could hardly speak. I was certain that I had a fever. I just wanted to go back home and go to bed. *Why didn't I just call in sick this morning?* I thought. Thankfully, the officer was very professional and recorded each of our stories in an efficient manner. We then exchanged insurance information and went on our way. My insurance eventually covered Mr. Jones' car repairs. The total bill was less than two hundred dollars. I had not seen or heard from him since—at least, not until I was served the summons.

Sylvester Jones, I now learned, was suing me for chronic neck pain that he claimed interfered with his ability to work and function normally. I was accused of driving recklessly, and the summons listed Eddie Simpson as a witness.

"I thought this was settled two years ago," I said incredulously.

I looked out my window. *Did any of my neighbors see the sheriff come to my door?* I wondered. I felt embarrassed and had a terrible feeling in the pit of my stomach. I felt like a criminal, like I had something to hide. *Did I do something wrong? People drive five miles over the speed limit every day, and they certainly don't all stop as soon as the light turns yellow.*

Sylvester Jones had stopped abruptly and unexpectedly in front of me, and I'd applied my brakes as soon as his brake lights came on, but the road was slick.

I sat back down and read through the summons again. I just could not fathom it. My mood sank deeper and deeper as I turned each page. *Where am I going to find a lawyer?* I wondered.

Jerry must know of some good lawyers, I surmised. He worked as a police officer so I figured that he'd have some suggestions. I dialed Jerry's number.

"Jerry, I can't believe it. I'm being sued!"

"Sued? Sued for what?"

"Do you remember that car accident I was in a couple of years ago?"

"Do you mean the little fender-bender at the stoplight on First Avenue?"

"That's the one. Well, the guy I hit is suing me for pain, suffering, and loss of wages. He claims he is having chronic neck pain from the crash and that he is unable to work."

"What?" Jerry exclaimed. "That's outrageous! When did you find this out?"

"Just now," I replied. "A sheriff knocked on my door and handed me the summons. I'm in shock. I need to find a lawyer, Jerry. Do you know of any good lawyers?"

"Fred, most of the lawyers I know are arrogant SOBs. They aren't worth the powder to blow them away. I've heard of one guy, though, named Jacobson— he's supposed to be very sharp. I'll ask around the office to see if anyone has more information."

"Thanks, Jerry, I'd appreciate that."

Jerry came over later that evening and looked through the summons with me.

"Thomas, Thomas, and Hughes," Jerry said with a grim expression. The look on his face when he read the names told me something was wrong.

"What are you thinking, Jerry?" I asked. "What is it about Thomas, Thomas, and Hughes?"

I could sense Jerry's reluctance to answer my question. He paused and stumbled through his words, eventually saying that he had heard of the Thomas, Thomas, and Hughes law firm. It was a well-known firm with a reputation of having aggressive lawyers.

"What do you mean by aggressive lawyers?" I asked.

"Fred, I don't want to scare you, but ..."

"But what?" I asked, now clearly concerned.

Jerry looked me straight in the eye and said in all seriousness, "The Thomas, Thomas, and Hughes firm is known for attacking defendants' personal funds."

"What does that mean?" I asked.

"It means that they sue for above and beyond what a defendant's insurance will cover. They sue for ridiculously large amounts of money. They take people's homes and their savings."

The summons did not specify an amount; it only stated that it was in an amount greater than fifty thousand dollars. "They would try to take away everything because of an accident?" I asked in disbelief. "It was an accident. It wasn't like I intended to do any harm. That's preposterous!"

Jerry looked at me solemnly. "They've done it before. They do it to doctors all of the time."

"But I'm not even rich," I said. "Why would they target me?"

"They don't know that you're not rich," Jerry explained. "All they know is that you live in a nice home in a nice part of town."

Jerry was right. I did live in a nice home in the village of Riverside, but I was not rich. Tina's family, however, was wealthy. After we got married, her family helped us pay for our home, a classic Victorian that bordered the Des Plaines River. It was the only home we ever owned.

"They'd take my home?" I asked, my head spinning from the shock. I felt like someone had taken a dagger to my heart.

Tina and I loved Riverside, a historic town—Rockwellian in many ways—designed by Frederick Law Olmsted, the architect who designed Central Park in New York. Instead of planning the community in a grid fashion, as are most other cities, Olmsted planned the streets to follow the area's natural contours. The gas-lantern–lit streets wound in and out between a forest of trees, leading to Riverside's soubriquet: "A village in the forest." Olmsted had impeccably good taste. A classic clock tower adorned the village hall, which looked like it belonged in nineteenth-century England, and a charming water tower sat in the center of the village. It was unlike any other water tower I had ever seen in Illinois.

Tina and I became enchanted with Riverside long before we moved there. The first few years after we were married, we lived in an apartment in downtown Chicago. We did not own a car because we really had no need for one at the time. Yet there were days when we felt like escaping the hustle and bustle of the busy downtown area, and so we would, on occasion, catch the train to Riverside, where we'd walk along the river, admiring the old mansions that lined the street along the river path. After our walks we would sit in the library and read leisurely. The library was marvelous. It was a handsome stone structure with stained-glass windows and cozy chairs that overlooked the Des Plaines River. It was an easy place with which to fall in love.

Moving to Riverside was one of the best things that ever happened to us. Tina and I were overjoyed to own a home in the town we loved. Our dreams were fulfilled, but we could never have fulfilled those dreams without help. I definitely could never have afforded to move there solely on my salary. I sometimes struggled to just pay the taxes. I had thought about selling the house in the past, but it was where Ellen had grown up, and I just could not do it.

"What should I do, Jerry?" I asked.

"You need a top-notch lawyer," he said. "Just before I came over, I called over to the office to get Robert Jacobson's number—the guy I mentioned earlier. He's supposed to be the best." Jerry handed me a slip of paper with the phone number.

"I'll call first thing in the morning," I said, sighing deeply. Then, looking

Jerry straight in the eye, I asked a rhetorical question, "This is really bad, isn't it?"

Jerry could see that I was distraught. "Fred, hang in there." He then gave a single nod, the type of nod given between friends who share an exclusive understanding. He spoke the name I had not heard in a decade: "Victor Petrov."

I stood silent for a moment and then sighed deeply a second time. Nodding in acknowledgment, I replied, "Victor Petrov."

Chapter 8

THE PLANNING BEGINS

I WAS DEFINITELY shaken up by everything that happened. I had never been sued, and the information Jerry gave me about possibly having my personal assets attacked really had me frightened, to the point that I became somewhat irrational. I ran through the crash scene in my mind, over and over again. I obsessed about it.

"Oh, why didn't I call in sick to work that day?" I asked myself. "Why didn't I just stay home?"

I was convinced that I was going to lose everything I owned. It was a thought that caused me great anxiety. The more I ruminated about it, the more panicked I became. I could think of nothing to calm me down. I dealt poorly with stress; I was certain that one day it would cause me to lose my mind.

- - - - - - - - - -

Later that night, the phone rang; it was Ellen. Within seconds, she realized something was wrong. "Are you all right?" she asked. "You sound down."

"Sweetheart, I received a little bad news today. I'm being sued."

"Sued!" she exclaimed. "For what?"

"Do you remember that car accident I was in two years ago, when I slid into the back of that car at the intersection?"

"Yes, I remember," she replied.

"Well," I said, "the man whose car I hit is suing me for pain and suffering."

"That is ridiculous!" she said, clearly upset. "The fenders were barely even dented. How could he be seriously hurt? And that was two years ago. Didn't your insurance cover the costs? I thought everything was settled with that."

"Yes, the insurance covered the crash costs at the time," I said, "but the man is now complaining of continued pain and suffering. He says the pain is keeping him from doing work. That's why he's suing me. It'll be OK, though. This type of thing happens all of the time. I spoke with Jerry this afternoon, and he gave me the name of a really good lawyer who will handle this."

I did not tell her about Jerry's theory that I was being targeted because of my address, nor did I plan on ever telling her that. I definitely was not going to mention the possibility that the law firm handling Sylvester Jones' case intended to go after my personal assets.

"Dad, this is terrible," she said. "I'm so sorry. When are you going to see the lawyer?"

"I'm going to call him first thing in the morning. I'll see him as soon as possible."

"I'll go with you when you go," she offered. "That isn't something you should have to do alone."

"No, sweetheart, I'll be OK," I insisted. "There's no reason for you to miss work. Really, it's not a big deal."

"Dad, I'll be there with you," she said. "Big deal or not, I'm going to be there."

Ellen's persistence forced me to concede. I didn't want to disagree too strongly—she might suspect there was something else wrong. Furthermore, I wasn't doing a very good job of hiding the fact that I was frightened.

"Dad," she said, "this is going to be OK. Tomorrow, I'll come over and make you dinner. Call me as soon as you've talked to the lawyer."

"Thanks, sweetheart," I replied. "I'll give you a call tomorrow."

I went to bed after I hung up the phone, but I couldn't sleep. My thoughts were racing. I turned on the television, hoping to take my mind off of things, but it ultimately led to more frustration. Catching the end of the news, I discovered that my agonizing over the summons had caused me to miss one of the most remarkable comebacks in Chicago Bears history. Down 20–0 at halftime, the Bears rallied to beat the Cardinals 24–23 in unbelievable fashion.

"That figures," I grumbled.

Once the news ended I flipped through the channels, but there was nothing that interested me, and my ruminations continued in merciless fashion. I kept the television on, hoping that the background noise would help distract me, but it did not. Tossing and turning, I simply could not fall asleep.

"This is ridiculous," I said aloud after a couple hours of frustration. "I'm driving myself insane."

Shaking my head, I smiled and chuckled at my own paranoia, for sometimes there is nothing left to do but laugh. I knew I was being excessive, but unfortunately, I could not control my fears.

I'd make a lousy Jedi, I mused. The Jedi were mythical knights from the George Lucas *Star Wars* movies. They derived their power from controlling their emotions and risked seduction from the "dark side" each time they let their emotions get the best of them.

"Control! Control! You must learn control." I recalled the famous line from the second movie in the *Star Wars* series. *I feel so out of control*, I thought.

Sighing in frustration, I turned off the TV and looked for a book in the small bookstand in the corner of my bedroom. Although I rarely read for pleasure, I frequently received books as gifts. On the top shelf of the bookstand were a few books that I had received the previous Christmas. Because I was a professor at a Catholic college, most of the books I owned had some connection with religion. I quickly glanced at the titles. One was *The Da Vinci Code* by Dan Brown—the only book I'd received that I had actually read. Although I did not in any way support Brown's attack on Christianity, I still found the book interesting. It certainly made for some good classroom discussions. Brown popularized the subject of Mithraism, which happened to be one of the religions on which I taught.

"Mithraism is an incendiary subject," I whispered as I held *The Da Vinci Code* in my hands. "It is a subject that has caused a lot of confusion for a lot of people."

Mithras was a pagan sun-god, symbolized by the bull. Initially venerated by the ancient Persians, he later was worshipped by other peoples, including members of the Roman military. Over the course of time, the followers of Mithras borrowed greatly from the Christian tradition. They claimed that Mithras was born on Christmas Day to a virgin mother and had twelve disciples. They further claimed that he sacrificed himself to redeem mankind. In a bizarre variation of the Communion cup, the Mithraic cultists believed that they could achieve salvation by drinking the blood of a slain bull.

There were many who alleged that Christianity borrowed from Mithraism, as the worship of Mithras predated Christ. What they didn't take into account was that the Christian traditions did not appear in the Mithraic ceremonies until centuries after the Resurrection of Christ. It wasn't Christianity that borrowed from Mithraism but the other way around.

"So many are misinformed," I murmured. "So many are just idiots."

Next to *The Da Vinci Code* was the entire *Left Behind* series. I hadn't read any of the books in the series, but I intended to. Several of my colleagues had highly recommended them. Looking at the sixteen thick volumes, I shook my head. *Nope, I'm not going to start that.* Although I was sure the series would be interesting, I wasn't quite ready to take on such a time-consuming endeavor.

Next to the *Left Behind* series was Joel Osteen's book, *Your Best Life Now: 7 Steps to Living at Your Full Potential*. Inspirational books, in general, did not appeal to me, and I quickly skipped over it.

The last book on the top shelf of the bookstand was *God and Ronald Reagan: A Spiritual Life* by Paul Kengor. I had always been impressed with Reagan's faith and with his hope-filled "city on the hill" vision of America. Unbeknownst to many, Reagan was a deeply religious man. He was raised in rural Illinois by a devoutly Christian mother, and from the very beginning was taught good Christian values. He carried those values with him throughout his life, and frequently turned to Scripture for guidance, especially during the most difficult times of his presidency. For the most part, Reagan kept his personal beliefs private, but from time to time his sentiments would leak out into the press. I recalled reading once that after John Hinckley Jr.'s assassination attempt in 1981, Reagan professed his belief that he was saved by divine Providence for an important future role and subsequently, he dedicated what time he had left to God.

The Gipper … hmm.

Rapidly skimming through the book, I surmised that it was a good hagiography of our fortieth president. Intrigued, I brought it back to bed and began reading. Unfortunately, I did not get very far. I read the first paragraph four times in a row, but nothing registered—I just could not concentrate. The negative thoughts just kept coming.

"Lord, please help me," I prayed as the hour grew late. "Please, Lord, help me through this."

The insomnia was exasperating. I was simply exhausted, and it was about 2:30 AM before I finally fell into a restless sleep.

When I awoke the next morning, I felt like I'd had a nightmare, but the nightmare was real. After grumbling to myself far longer than usual, I got out of bed and took a shower. Thankfully, my shower helped to calm me down somewhat. I convinced myself that I was being irrational.

Jerry is probably wrong, I thought. *Why would this lawyer go after my personal assets? I've never heard of that happening to anyone. In any case, it was just an accident. No one is going to try to take away my house and car because of an accident. Jerry must be wrong. The worst-case scenario is that my insurance will have to pay out some money, and my rates will go up. That's what insurance is for, isn't it? Accidents do happen. I'll be fine.*

Later that morning, I took out the slip of paper with the lawyer's number and dialed the phone.

A secretary answered. "Jacobson Legal," she said. "How may I help you?"

"I need to make an appointment to see Robert Jacobson regarding a legal matter," I said.

"Are you an established client of Mr. Jacobson's?" she asked.

"No," I said, "but I need a lawyer."

"What is this in regards to, sir?"

"I'm being sued," I explained. "I was just served with the summons yesterday."

"What is your name, sir?" the secretary asked.

"Frederick Sankt," I replied. "The last name is spelled S-A-N-K-T." I gave her a summary of the details of the case. After speaking with her for a few minutes, I found her to be quite sympathetic. She displayed patience and went out of her way to try to be supportive. Perhaps that was part of her job—making potential clients feel better, or perhaps she was simply a kindhearted person. Whatever the case, I appreciated it.

"One of the lawyers from our office will be contacting you this afternoon, Mr. Sankt," she said. "Don't worry about a thing. We deal with cases like this all the time."

At about four o'clock that afternoon, the phone in my office rang. As promised, it was a lawyer from Jacobsen Legal, who arranged an appointment for the following week.

- - - - - - - - - -

The next days passed by ever so slowly. Ellen and Jerry were very supportive, but I still had a rough time. My irrational thoughts returned, and I continued to have difficulty sleeping. The threat of losing everything had me so worried. From the time I got up in the morning until the time I eventually fell asleep each night, I constantly ruminated about the lawsuit. I incessantly reassured myself that I had done nothing wrong and therefore was at no risk of losing everything, but it seemed to take all of my concentration and energy just to keep myself from being in a state of panic.

One evening I sat down in front of my computer and stared at the screen. "I've got to do something to take my mind off of this," I said out loud. I got on the Internet and checked my e-mail. There were no new messages, only junk mail. I then went to the *Chicago Tribune* site to read online articles about the Bears. That was normally one of my favorite pastimes. Some nights, I would spend up to two hours reading about the team and exchanging predictions with other fans on the Chicago Bears Fans message board. My love of football, however, was not enough to get my mind off of my troubles. I sighed deeply in frustration. I just wanted to feel relaxed; I just wanted to feel content, but my thoughts were racing. I tried playing computer solitaire but found no solace.

"Oh, Lord, please grant me peace," I prayed.

I sat for a moment, holding my head in my hands. It was so quiet that I could hear the second hand on the clock. Tick, tick, tick, tick, tick—it went on and on and on. It was maddening. I began to feel sorry for myself but was determined not to give in to the lure of self-pity.

"Victor Petrov," I whispered, shaking my head with eyes closed.

As it always had, the name stirred my spirit.

Lifting my head out of my hands, I looked forward, took a deep breath, and probed my mind for anything that would distract me from the anxiety. For a moment my thoughts were blank, but then I recalled the dream I'd had the week before.

"The Third Testament," I whispered to myself.

Maybe … just maybe I should.

"The Third Testament," I said again, my voice louder.

Unlike my other attempts at distraction, the concept of a "Third Testament"—a modern Christian Scripture, a continuation of the story of God's people—caught my attention.

It has been two thousand years.

"It is time," I mumbled, recalling the words of my friend. As seconds became minutes, and I thought about it more and more, I finally picked up the Bible and started flipping though the pages of the Old Testament.

"Exodus, Joshua, Samuel, Ezra, Nehemiah," I read aloud. "The Old Testament is simply a history of God's people. Psalms, Proverbs, Song of Songs, and the prophetic books—these are simply a compilation of inspired writings from the times before Christ."

As the wheels in my brain began to briskly spin, I asked myself: *If we so honor the historical records and inspired writings that occurred before the coming of Christ, why do we almost completely disregard the records and inspired writings that occurred after his death and Resurrection?*

Before I knew it, the anxiety of the lawsuit was lessened, and my focus was redirected toward the idea of writing a Third Testament. I performed a quick search of the Internet to see if anyone had written anything resembling a Third Testament. I found a couple of books with that title, but their content was completely different from what I had in mind.

What should I include in a Third Testament? I wondered. Feeling inspired, I came up with four key components:

1) It needs to be a history of the Church and its teachings.

2) It needs to be a story of the greatest saints and most notorious sinners.

3) It needs to be an anthology of spiritual writings.

4) It needs to be a record of the miracles of the past two millennia.

Instinctively, I started typing a list of ideas on the computer:
-A story of God's people—Christians—encompassing the last two thousand years
-A history
  -Martyrs/Christian persecution
  -The conversion of Rome
  -Council of Niceae
  -The fall of Rome and conversion of the barbarians
  -The spread of Christianity
  -The threat of militant Islam
  -The Holy Roman Empire
  -The Eastern Schism
  -The Great Schism
  -The Reformation
  -Thirty Years' War
  -The plague
  -The second Islamic threat
  -The Church and science
  -Christianity in the New World
  -The French Revolution
  -Missionaries/the global Church
  -The Communist threat
  -Vatican II council
  -Legacy of charity

-The lives of the saints (the saints are the prophets of the modern era)
  -Martyrdom of the apostles
  -Saint Leo the Great
  -Saint Augustine
  -Saint Patrick
  -Saint Gregory the Great
  -Saint Wenceslaus
  -Saint Thomas Becket
  -Saint Francis of Assisi
  -Saint Thomas Aquinas
  -Saint Catherine of Siena
  -Saint Juan Diego
  -Saint Ignatius of Loyola
  -Saint Teresa of Avila
  -Saint Martin de Porres
  -Saint Bernadette Soubirous

-Saint Maximilian Kolbe
-Other important Christians
    -Mother Teresa of Calcutta
    -Pope John Paul II
    -Reverend Billy Graham

-The devil's minions
    -Nero
    -Attila the Hun
    -Octavian
    -Frederick II
    -Voltaire
    -Darwin
    -Hitler
    -Marx
    -Lenin
    -Stalin

-A Book of Inspiration
    -Psalms
        -"Amazing Grace" by Newton
        -John Newton's other works
        -"A Mighty Fortress Is Our God" by Martin Luther
        -"Pagne Lingua" by Thomas Aquinas
        -"Canticle of the Sun" by Saint Francis of Assisi
        -"The Lorica" by Saint Patrick
        -"On Eagles' Wings"
        -"O Come, O Come, Emmanuel"
        -"The Lord of the Dance"
        -"Be Not Afraid"
        -"The Battle Hymn of the Republic"
    -Inspirational Christian writings
        -"On His Blindness" by Milton
        -The works of John Donne
        -"Spiritual Exercises" by Saint Ignatius of Loyola
        -"Dialogue of Divine Providence" by Catherine of Siena
        -The works of Saint John of the Cross
        -The sermons of Jonathan Edwards
        -The works of Saint Theresa of Lisieux
        -"Footprints"
        -The works of C. S. Lewis

-The story of William Booth and the Salvation Army
-The Flanders Ceasefire

-Miracles
    -The Glastonbury thorn
    -Constantine and the cross of light
    -Saint Peter and the Huns at Mantua
    -Saint Michael at Mount Gargano
    -Saint Patrick's cures
    -Saint Francis' stigmata
    -Saint Anthony's sermon to the fish
    -Guadalupe
    -Oberammergau
    -Lourdes
    -Fatima
    -Dunkirk

I brainstormed for a couple of hours and then went to bed. Thankfully, the Third Testament idea did temporarily take my mind off of my troubles. Unfortunately, when I woke up the next morning, my state of irrational panic returned. Much to my chagrin, thoughts of despair plagued me throughout the day. The ruminations were merciless. It was incredibly frustrating.

Jerry called later in the day. He could tell that I was stressed and did his best to calm me down. "Fred," he said, "I've been talking to the guys at work, and they all think this is going to turn out in your favor. You shouldn't even worry about it."

What he said may have been true, but I worried nonetheless. My anxiety was a curse. I knew that I was being irrational, but I simply could not control my fear.

Chapter 9
THE LORD IS MY SHEPHERD

IT HAD BEEN a brutal week, and I was in need of a change of scene. Thankfully, that change came quickly. Saturday, October 21, was the day of Ellen's triathlon. The triathlon was held at the Land Between the Lakes in western Kentucky. I hit the road on Friday evening and headed to Kentucky to give my support. It was an eight-hour drive, most of it down boring I-57. Notorious for its dearth of natural features, I-57 was a strip of highway that spanned almost the entire state of Illinois in a north-south direction. It was lined entirely by cornfields and had no change in elevation whatsoever along its seemingly endless course. Reluctant to deal with such a long stretch of monotony, I decided to split up the trip. I spent Friday night in a hotel in Effingham, Illinois, a four-hour drive from Chicago. Effingham was easy to pick out from the otherwise uniform landscape surrounding I-57 because on the eastern side of the highway in Effingham stood a giant 198-foot white cross. Inarguably, the cross seemed out of place along the busy road, but it was intended to serve as a beacon of hope to the fifty thousand travelers estimated to pass the site each day. Newcomers to the region would sometimes confuse Effingham's roadside cross with its more famous counterpart in southern Illinois, the giant cross at Bald Knob in Alto Pass. Often photographed, the cross at Alto Pass was a beautiful structure that served as a national symbol of faith in God. It stood high atop a 700-foot hill and could be seen over an area of 7,500 square miles. Although not as tall as the Effingham cross, it was much more majestic.

I awoke very early Saturday morning in Effingham, long before sunrise, and started back down I-57. I made two stops prior to my final destination in Kentucky. The first was to see the cross at Bald Knob. It required a minor diversion from my route, as Bald Knob was closer to the Mississippi River and Missouri than it was to Kentucky. It was a worthwhile diversion, though, because the cross atop the hill was an inspirational sight. Surrounded by blazing autumn hues and highlighted by the bright, early morning light, the magnificent cross dominated the region. I was moved by its grandeur and briefly knelt to say a prayer. *Lord, please help ease my stress*, I prayed as I looked up at the giant cross. *Please help me gain control over my anxiety.*

The second stop—a frivolous one—was in the town of Metropolis, Illinois. Metropolis was the self-proclaimed hometown of Superman, and it had a Superman festival each summer, along with several shops and museums dedicated to America's greatest fictional hero. The town even had a giant Superman statue in front of its City Hall. I parked my car in the center of town and got out for a photo opportunity. The stop didn't take me too far off course, as Metropolis was just across the Ohio River from Paducah, Kentucky. In no time, I was back on the road and arrived at the triathlon start site in Grand Rivers, Kentucky, just before the 10:00 AM start time. I easily picked out Ellen, as she was wearing all-red swimwear, except for a purple swimmer's cap. She was standing next to Jack.

"Hi, Dad!" she called out, waving to me as she saw me making my way over to where they were standing. "You didn't have to come all this way. Once the race starts, you probably won't even see me." She gave me a hug and a kiss on the cheek.

"Hello, Mr. Sankt," Jack said.

For most of Ellen's friends, I would say, "Call me Fred," but for Jack, "Mr. Sankt" was just fine.

"Good luck today," I said.

"Thanks, Dad," Ellen said. "I can't wait to get started."

"I can't wait, either," Jack said, hopping up and down and rolling his head back and forth like a boxer before a fight. "Let's get this thing going."

Just at that moment, a horn sounded, indicating that the event would soon begin.

The triathlon consisted of a one-mile swim, a twenty-mile bike ride, and a six-mile run. It sounded like torture to me, but then again, I had never been into long-distance racing. As Ellen and Jack made their way to the starting point, I picked up one of the course maps that the organizers were handing out. On the map were red stars that indicated areas along the route where tents were set up for refreshments and stands for viewing. Ellen was right; I was not able to see her throughout most of the race, but I did catch glimpses of her, here and there. My eyes widened with excitement when I did. Inherently taciturn, I did not shout out or wave but cheered silently in my heart.

The race lasted several hours. The small crowds that gathered at different sites along the course were enthusiastic and very supportive of all of the contestants. It was good to be a part of it. Really, the entire event turned out to be better than I would have ever imagined.

Smiling brightly, Ellen met her goal—she finished the race. Still somewhat out of breath, she gave me another big hug when it was all over.

"Oh, Dad, I'm so glad you could be here," she said. She was truly beaming.

Jack was disappointed that he had not finished in as good a time as he'd expected. "I think I must be coming down with something," he said. "I did much better during my training sessions."

Typical Jack, I thought.

That evening the three of us met for dinner at Patti's 1880 Settlement in Grand Rivers, the purported home of the best pork chops in the world.

"We used to come here all the time when I was a kid," said Jack as we waited for the server to take our order. "It was my family's favorite restaurant. I guarantee you are going to love the food." Jack was originally from Murray, Kentucky, and only moved to the Chicagoland area after college. He still had the slightest hint of a southern twang in his voice. "I'm so hungry, I could eat everything on the menu," Jack said.

"Me, too," said Ellen.

"It was sure quite a day, wasn't it?" I said. "You two must be exhausted."

"We are, but it feels good," Ellen said. "Although physically I feel drained, mentally I feel so exhilarated that I could stay up all night."

"I'm going straight to bed after dinner," said Jack. "We've got a long drive tomorrow. I dread it."

"Seven to eight hours is a long time on the road, especially when you have to work the next day," I said.

"Especially when it's the most boring strip of highway on the planet," Jack added.

"It really is a long drive and a long day," Ellen said. "Dad, I can't believe you're planning to make all of those stops."

"Where are you stopping, Mr. Sankt?" Jack asked. To my surprise, he seemed genuinely intrigued by my plans.

"Well, I'm getting up early to head down to your old neck of the woods. I'm going to an area just south of Murray to locate a slip of land I own."

"I didn't know you owned land in Kentucky," Jack said. "What made you decide to buy land down here?"

"I didn't buy it," I said. "My parents bought the land in the 1950s, a half-acre plot just a mile from Kentucky Lake. They thought that one day the area would be developed, but it never was. I inherited the land from them and have been paying taxes on it for years. I guess I'm hoping for the same thing they hoped, and that's why I haven't sold it. In any case, when I was about ten years old, I used a magnifying glass to burn a sign of our family name, and I nailed the sign to a tree on the property. I'm just curious to see if I can find it. I haven't been there in over forty-five years. For all I know, all of the roads may be overgrown. If I recall correctly, the last time I was there, they were gravel roads."

"Sounds like quite an adventure," Jack said.

"The whole day is going to be an adventure," I said. "After that, I'm going to catch Mass in Paducah, Kentucky. If I time it perfectly—and I mean perfectly—I'll make it just in time for their 11:00 AM service. Then, I'm planning to head north past Golconda and stop at Garden of the Gods before finally heading back home."

"Garden of the Gods is nice," Jack said. "Have you ever been there?"

"No," I said. "But I've seen pictures. I'm really looking forward to it."

"It's probably the most scenic spot in Illinois," Jack said. "It's doesn't compare to some of the scenery in Kentucky or Tennessee, but I think you'll like it."

"What time do you think you're going to get home, Dad?" Ellen asked.

"I'm guessing around 10:00 PM," I said. "I'm OK with the long day, though. It kind of reminds me of my college days, when my buddies and I would take road trips to watch the football team play away games. I remember one time in 1969 when St. John's was playing in the Mineral Water Bowl in Excelsior Springs, Missouri. It was about a ten-hour trip, and we only had the weekend to do it, but we had a blast."

"The Mineral Water Bowl?" Jack snickered. "What kind of a bowl is that?"

"It's for smaller schools," I said. "St. John's actually has a great football tradition. Their coach, John Gagliardi, is the winningest coach in the history of college football. No one hears about them down here in Illinois because they're a Division III school, but they get a decent amount of press up in Minnesota."

"They probably get the press in Minnesota because the state's other football teams are so bad," said Jack. "The poor locals have no one else to root for."

"That may be true," I said with a grin.

I enjoyed our outing that evening. I was feeling much more relaxed than I had earlier in the week, and even Jack's obnoxiousness did not bother me. It helped that Patti's did, in fact, have the best pork chops in the entire world.

- - - - - - - - - -

On Sunday I got up early, as planned, and headed toward Murray. Using old maps and a compass, I was able to locate the plot of land my parents had bought. The gravel roads were barely usable, but I managed. Parking in a dirt patch alongside the road, I got out of my car to look for the sign I had made, but it was nowhere to be seen. I walked a hundred yards in each direction, but I couldn't find it.

Maybe the tree fell in a storm and was carted off, I thought. *Or maybe the wooden sign simply decayed in the elements over the years.*

I looked closely at the tree trunks for any remnants of a sign, but I didn't see any. I then looked to see if there were any old stumps along the road but again came up empty. Finally, after over thirty minutes of searching I gave up.

"Oh, well," I said to myself. "At least I located the property." I was about to leave when something caught my eye several feet above my head. "What is that?"

Looking closely, I discovered the sign I had been searching for. The letters SANKT were still distinctly clear. I had initially missed it because I had been searching at eye level. I had not considered the fact that the tree had grown taller over a forty-plus year period. "Well, I'll be darned," I said. "After all these years, there it is."

I was pleased that I had found the sign. It brought on a feeling of nostalgia for my youth. I took out my camera and snapped a photo for remembrance and then headed back to my car.

Following my plan, I went to Mass at St. Francis de Sales in Paducah, a charming little church in the center of town, where I prayed with conviction. Even though I was feeling much better, I still had the lawsuit on my mind. I prayed that my lawyer would tell me that it was no big deal and that I would be fine.

Once I hear those words from a lawyer, then I'll be OK, I reasoned.

After Mass I drove northeast passed Golconda to Harrisburg, Illinois, the home of the Garden of the Gods. The Garden of the Gods Recreation Area was considered by many to be the crown jewel of the Shawnee National Forest. It consisted of a series of sandstone cliffs and rock formations with such colorful names as Camel Rock, Noah's Ark, Mushroom Rock, Fat Man's Squeeze, Devil's Rock, Anvil Rock, and Tower of Babel. I parked my car and took the quarter-mile observation trail adjacent to Camel Rock. There were several points along the trail that gave spectacular views of the recreation area. I took out my camera and snapped a few photos of the Camel Rock formation, which was aptly named because it truly did look like a camel's head and body, including several rocks that passed as humps.

This place is really beautiful, I thought as I looked out at the fantastic fall foliage and rock formations. *And the crisp autumn air is perfect.* Feeling content, I snapped a couple more photos before deciding that it was time to leave. *It's going to be a long drive home, but I'm really glad I made the trip.*

Turning around, I was instantly startled by the sight of something moving along the rocky path, and I almost dropped my camera. It was a slithering rattlesnake, only six feet from where I was standing. I knew that southern Illinois had its fair share of snakes, and I knew that rattlesnakes liked to sun themselves on rocks, but I was not prepared to come in such close contact with one.

The snake began to rattle its tail and made itself into the shape of an S, indicating that it was about to strike. My heart began to pound, and my hands quivered. I immediately turned to take a different route back, but my plan was thwarted by another snake slithering along, several feet to the right.

"Oh, boy," I said. "This is going to be a problem."

My only exits along the trail were blocked. I had only one other option, and I had to act quickly. I instantly started to traverse the rocky outcropping in the middle of the trail but did so with great trepidation because I knew that snakes were likely to be there also. "Lord, please guide me through this," I prayed.

Traversing the rocks was by no means difficult from a physical perspective. It simply involved small steps up and down. It was, however, difficult from a psychological perspective. The steps up did not bother me, but each step down was a dangerous endeavor because I could not see what lay underneath the rocks.

If there's a rattlesnake coiled below, I'm done for, I thought.

Instead of just stepping down, I took small leaps so as to land farther from the underside of the rock. They were literally leaps of faith. After leaping down from four consecutive rocks, the pounding of my heart grew faster as I saw yet a third snake, just feet to my left, slithering out from underneath a sandstone ledge.

"I hate snakes," I said aloud as I made a quick jump. "I need to get out of here."

The day had turned out to be much more of an adventure than I had bargained for. Looking around, I was shocked that there were not any other people in the area. Garden of the Gods was a popular site, and it was a beautiful autumn day. There should have been swarms of people. *Maybe everyone is home watching football,* I thought.

There were several cars in the parking area, so I knew there must be others there, but I did not see them. The feeling of isolation made me even more nervous.

If a snake bites me, there will be no one around to help, I lamented as I continued on along the rocks.

The anxiety of the situation was taxing, but thankfully, my attention was soon redirected. Gazing upward, I saw a bald eagle flying high above. It was a majestic bird, soaring freely, and it stood in stark contrast to the deplorable slithering snakes on the ground. I had always been fascinated by American bald eagles and felt fortunate to have spotted one. It was not that long ago when eagles were on the endangered species list. Because of the efforts of the U.S. Fish and Wildlife Service, they were just beginning to make a comeback. I was pleased that they were.

Not only are eagles beautiful creatures, but they symbolize the virtues of America, virtues that provide hope for the world—a world in certain need of hope.

Having reached an open area of flat rock that was devoid of crevices, I decided it was safe to take out my camera and snap a shot of the magnificent bird. The sun was shining brightly overhead, and there was a scattering of fluffy white clouds, so I anticipated that it would make a fantastic picture. I took three or four shots, some with the zoom lens and some without. I then put my camera away and continued onward, sighing as I walked up to yet another rocky step-down.

"Just two more to go," I whispered. I was several feet from the main trail, a wide, shaded dirt trail that was not likely to harbor any snakes. Being so close to the end brought on a feeling of exhilaration, and I made up my mind to make the last two jumps in quick succession.

"The Lord is my shepherd," I said as I leapt from the first rock. "I shall not want," I said with a sigh of relief as I leapt to safety from the second.

- - - - - - - - - -

Tuesday finally came, and I drove with Ellen to see Mr. Jacobson at the law office. We checked in at the secretary's desk.

"Hello," I said, "I'm Fred Sankt, here to see Mr. Jacobson."

"Good morning, Mr. Sankt," the secretary said pleasantly. "Have a seat. Mr. Jacobson will be with you shortly."

After about a fifteen-minute wait, a tall gentleman in an expensive-looking suit came out to greet us.

"Hello, Mr. Sankt, I'm Robert Jacobson." Mr. Jacobson had a New York accent. He looked very successful and carried himself with an air of confidence. His hair was slicked back, and his tie was knotted tightly. Nothing was out of place. Ellen and I followed him into his office.

"Have you ever been sued, Mr. Sankt?" he asked.

"No, sir, I haven't," I replied.

"Have you had any other traffic violations?"

"Only a few parking tickets," I said with a smile.

Mr. Jacobson did not smile in return. He went over the summons and explained in greater detail why I was being sued. He then asked me for my side of the story. His manner was terse, and he cut me off on more than one occasion. With all of the interruptions, it took me close to an hour—a brutal hour—to get through everything.

I was already feeling nervous. He then asked a question that sent me into a state of panic. "Do you have asset protection?" he asked.

"What do you mean by asset protection?"

"Mr. Sank," he said, mispronouncing my name, "the Thomas, Thomas, and Hughes firm is going after your personal assets—your home, your car, your life savings. Just last month, they put a lien against a physician's home and had his wages garnished. They do this sort of thing all of the time. The physician lost everything, but it was his own fault because he was stupid not to have asset protection."

I could not believe it. For several days leading up to the meeting with Mr. Jacobson, I had been telling myself that my deepest fears were completely irrational, and then, within a matter of minutes, I found out the terrible truth—my fears were very real indeed. Even though Mr. Jacobson confirmed the seriousness of the situation, it still didn't make any sense.

Can the legal system in this great country of ours really be that screwed up? I thought. *Would they really take away a man's home because of a traffic accident? This is surreal.*

I then recalled the disheartening fact that I was dealing with the same legal system that frequently let hardened criminals go free and not infrequently put innocent people behind bars. My heart sank. "But what is asset protection? How do I get asset protection?" I asked.

"There are a number of ways to get asset protection," Mr. Jacobson explained. "The easiest is to transfer all of your savings and possessions into your spouse's name."

"My wife is dead," I said. "She passed away several years ago."

"Well, that doesn't help, does it," he said coldly. "You can hide your savings overseas, but that is tricky to do, and it doesn't protect your home. You could also put your home in your daughter's name, but that would involve a substantial gift tax."

I was in a state of shock. I could tell that Ellen was as well. I felt so bad that she had to hear all of it. "That just doesn't seem right," I said. "I have to try to hide my assets like I'm some sort of criminal? For a traffic accident that happened two years ago? I didn't do anything wrong. Where's the justice? Is there no justice?"

"Justice has nothing to do with it, Mr. Sank," the lawyer said. "This will be decided in a court of law, not a court of justice. I'm going to do everything I possibly can to make sure you keep your assets, but I can't make any guarantees."

"There really is no justice," I said.

"No, Mr. Sank," he said, mispronouncing my name a third time, "there is no justice. That's why it's important to have a good lawyer."

That concluded our meeting. Mr. Jacobson said he would be contacting me in the next several weeks to schedule the deposition. He also referred me to another lawyer in his office who specialized in asset protection.

Ellen expressed her displeasure as we walked outside to the car. "Oh, Dad, this is terrible," she said. "Maybe we should find another lawyer. He seemed so cold."

"Sweetheart, he may be cold, but according to Jerry, he's the best there is. He seems to know what he is talking about. I've got to win this case, and I believe he offers me the best chance."

Chapter 10
The Depth of Despair

The lawsuit against me was a terrible burden. The threat of losing everything I owned was enough to drive me insane. It seemed that my anxiety level could not go any higher. After meeting with Mr. Jacobson, it seemed that things could not get any worse. Yet things are not always as they seem. I thought I had trouble. I thought I knew stress. I thought that I was carrying the weight of the world. But nothing could compare to the devastation that was about to enter into my life.

The anchors on the evening news reported that Wednesday, October 25, was a beautiful fall day—but not for me. They said that the sun luminously lit the bright blue sky—but I did not see it. They said that the leaves on the trees glistened in the sun, their red and orange colors brilliantly pleasing the eye—but all I saw was black. On Wednesday, October 25, God asked me to bear a cross that no man should have to bear.

The tragedy started at 9:43 AM with the ring of a phone. It was Ellen. She sounded as if she was crying.

"Sweetheart, what's wrong?" I asked.

She hesitated a moment before she replied. I was not prepared for what I was about to hear. "Dad," she said in a faltering voice, "I have melanoma."

The words she spoke stopped time. The words she spoke shattered my world. All of the hardships I had faced throughout my life paled in comparison to the anguish brought about by the words "I have melanoma." A wave of nausea came over me. My hands began to tremble. My legs felt weak beneath me.

Please, Lord, no! I prayed before I spoke. "You have melanoma?" I repeated in disbelief as the adrenaline began to pump through my veins. "How can this be? Has a doctor told you this?"

"Dad, I had a mole on my leg that started to itch a few weeks ago," she explained. "I didn't want to mention anything because you were so stressed out with the lawsuit. I went to see a dermatologist last week, and he removed the mole. He called me this morning and told me it was melanoma, and that I need to see a melanoma surgeon and an oncologist."

"Why do you need to see a surgeon and an oncologist?" I asked, panicking. "Was the melanoma that deep?" I had learned enough about melanoma after Tina was diagnosed to know that the deeper the melanoma goes into the skin, the worse the prognosis. The deeper it goes, the more likely it is to spread.

"Dad, it was very deep," she said. "I'm really frightened."

I was more than frightened. I was horrified. After going through Tina's illness, just the mention of the word melanoma caused me to break into a cold sweat and gave me an ache in the pit of my stomach. *Oh, dear God, what if it has spread*? I agonized. I knew that if it had spread, it would mean almost certain death within a matter of months. "When do you see the surgeon?" I asked.

"I see the surgeon on Tuesday," Ellen said.

"Tuesday!" I exclaimed. "Was that the soonest they could get you in?"

"Yes," she answered. "When I first called the surgeon's office, they said the next available appointment was in three weeks, but the dermatologist called the surgeon directly and got me in to see him on Tuesday."

Armageddon!

Our entire world had crumbled in the blink of an eye. I did not know how we would go on. The thought of Ellen's having cancer was too much to endure. The anxiety was paralyzing. I found it hard to work. I found it hard to even breathe. The uncertainty was the worst part. Waiting to meet new doctors and not knowing what they would say was excruciating on my nerves. Ellen's appointment with the surgeon was five days off—five days of pure hell. I was not able to sleep at all for the first three nights. I stayed up watching television but never really paid any attention to what I was watching. I could not focus on anything at all. My mind just raced. I had never been a drinker, but given the circumstances, I seriously considered taking a shot or two of alcohol to calm my nerves. I was not able to eat, either. The sight and smell of food brought on a wave of nausea. In essence, my existence had, in short time, become an unbearable form of psychological torture. I prayed so hard for a reprieve from the agony. I prayed harder than I've ever prayed before.

"Please, Lord, let this turn out OK," I prayed. "Please, Lord, don't take my little girl from me."

Tuesday finally came, and we met with the surgeon. To my surprise, Jack offered to take off work to accompany Ellen, but Ellen declined his offer. She appreciated his support but did not want him to see her distressed. She did, however, agree to let me accompany her. It was just the two of us in the consultation room when Dr. Atandijian entered. A short, heavyset man with a dark black mustache, he wasted no time. Dr. Atandijian sat down across from us and began to go over the details of the case. Speaking with a thick Middle Eastern accent, he said that he would need to repeat surgery in the area where the mole had been removed so he could take a wider margin. He would also remove some lymph glands from Ellen's upper thigh.

"Before we do anything else," he said, "we need a CAT scan to make sure the melanoma hasn't spread to your liver or lungs."

Ellen had the CAT scan on Wednesday, and she had an appointment to see the oncologist on Friday. I had been scheduled to see the lawyer about asset protection on Friday, but I rescheduled so that I could accompany Ellen.

"The lawsuit seems so meaningless now," I said. I bargained with God. "Take my money and my home. Take everything I have. But please don't take Ellen."

I was a complete wreck as Ellen was getting her CAT scan. I spent much of the day pacing back and forth and doing all of the things that people do when they are nervous. I hyperventilated. I sighed incessantly. I rationalized over and over that things would be OK. I looked up melanoma statistics on the Internet to reassure myself that most cases of melanoma do not spread, and that most patients live normal lives after their melanomas are removed. I was hopeful that I would find other reassuring information. At the same time, I was fearful that I would run across statistics that would exacerbate my anxiety. In the end, I broke even. I uncovered about as much reason for hope as I did for concern.

On Wednesday evening, Ellen and I went to Mass at St. Mary's. We were both in desperate need of relief from the stress, and we looked to find that relief at church. We went to pray mostly for ourselves but also for our deceased loved ones. It was All Soul's Day, the day that Catholics from around the world remember their faithful departed. Ever since Tina died, we never missed Mass on the Feast of All Souls. Being at St. Mary's seemed to help ease our tensions a little bit. We really had no control over the stressful situation we were in, but by going to church, it seemed like we were at least doing something. I had always believed that the worst part about stress is the feeling of helplessness—the feeling that there is nothing you can do to fix whatever situation you are in. Going to Mass and praying to God diminished that feeling of helplessness.

Ellen and I were not the only ones feeling despondent that evening. St Mary's parish was at least three-quarters full with mourners. Most of the people were parishioners we recognized from Sunday services. There were, however, a few faces that were new to us. In particular, there was a middle-aged woman in the pew in front of us who caught my attention. She was there by herself, holding a rosary in her hands and praying intently but not participating in any of the songs. When it came time for the greeting, she turned around, shook our hands, and said, "Peace be with you." I could instantly see that she had been crying. Her teary, dark brown eyes were filled with sorrow. The woman's sadness moved me. The pain in her eyes was so evident. Her emotions were almost palpable.

She looks so miserable, I thought.

There was no doubt that the woman was grief-stricken over the loss of someone very dear to her. It was sad to see that she was there all alone. Feeling dejected and vulnerable myself, I had a great sense of empathy for her. I replied, "Peace be with you," and nodded my head to acknowledge her pain.

Every week at Mass I would routinely greet those sitting in my vicinity. I would always say "Peace be with you," almost instinctively, without really thinking about what I was saying. My blessing to this woman was different. Never before had I felt such sincerity in the blessing as I did that night. Emotions can affect a person that way. In my heart, I believed that her blessing also was sincere.

I said a prayer for the sad woman. "Almighty God, Lord of Mercy, grant her peace and ease her pain." It was one of many heartfelt prayers I said that evening. My only hope was that my prayers were being heard.

Ellen and I spent the next day anxiously awaiting the visit with Dr. Gudmundson, the oncologist. Dr. Gudmundson worked in the same office as the surgeon, and we knew he would have the results of the CAT scan when we went to see him. I was so nervous that I could have exploded. Yet the anxiety was the only thing that kept me going. I was in a state of constant exhaustion from lack of sleep, and I had lost ten pounds in just one week from not eating. I tried to hide it all from Ellen.

"Pull yourself together!" I told myself. "God will see us through this."

On Friday morning I accompanied Ellen to Dr. Gudmundson's office. After dealing with Tina's illness, I had developed a great appreciation for oncologists.

An oncologist is very much like the Wizard of Oz, I thought. *People with great problems travel to see him, with unrealistic hopes and presumptions. They expect the oncologist to solve their problems and give them good news. Unfortunately, in the real world, there is often little an oncologist can do to stop the spread of cancer. People often come away disappointed and disillusioned. Still, oncologists nobly take up their patients' crosses and try to help them in any way they can, even if they have no magical solutions. For that, they deserve praise and admiration.*

Dr. Gudmundson was exactly what one might imagine an oncologist to be. He was a distinguished older gentleman with white hair. He wore a long white coat with a stethoscope draped around his neck. He sat down across from us, and when he spoke, his voice was deep but gentle. "Ms. Sankt," he said, "you had CAT scans earlier this week. I would like to go over the results with you now."

I did not like the sound of what he said. I knew if everything was OK, he would have just said that the CAT scans looked fine. There was a gnawing feeling in the pit of my stomach; I felt sick.

The doctor took a deep breath, exhaled, and then said, "The scans show that the melanoma has spread."

With those words, tears began to fill my eyes.

"You have multiple small tumors in both of your lungs and a relatively large tumor in your liver," he said. "Your bones may also be involved, but we will need to get a PET scan to be certain. We also need an MRI of your brain. Melanoma has a tendency to spread to the brain, so it is important that we look there." The doctor then paused to give us a chance to digest the information he had just delivered.

"Dr. Gudmundson, what is the prognosis?" Ellen asked. "Is this something that can be treated?"

I could see the look in Ellen's eye. She was panicked and desperate. I was so frightened to hear what Dr. Gudmundson would say next. I knew the prognosis for metastatic melanoma; Ellen knew it, too.

The prognosis is dismal, I thought. *Once a tumor has spread, there is nothing that can be done.*

Despite her words, Ellen was not really asking for a prognosis; she was begging for a ray of hope. She was begging that he would say something positive. I feared that Dr. Gudmundson would start listing dreary statistics. Fortunately, he did not. The wise old doctor had a good bedside manner.

"Ms. Sankt," he said, "I can't predict how long you have to live. Only God knows that. Statistics are available to try to predict a patient's life expectancy, but they are just numbers. Everyone is different. Each individual is unique, and statistics don't account for that. What we need to do now is to get the scans and the MRI, and then start treatment. There are several different treatment options that I'd like to discuss with you." Dr. Gudmundson explained that the standard therapy for melanoma, a drug called interleukin-2, was very toxic and was not particularly effective. "In all my years of practice, I've never seen a patient respond," he said. "I've read in the medical journals about patients who have responded, but all I've seen is patients getting very sick from the treatment."

He went on to say that there were several promising investigational drugs, and he suggested that Ellen enroll in a clinical trial. "I have a couple of the experimental drug trials available here at my office," he said, "but I suggest that you also go to the Chicago Cancer Institute for a consultation before choosing any treatment. They have excellent doctors there who specialize in melanoma." He gave us the name of the physician at the Chicago Cancer Institute, Dr. Sherman Greenspan. "Talk to Dr. Greenspan and see what he has to offer," Dr. Gudmundson said. "In the meantime, we will order the PET scan and MRI. I know that you must feel overwhelmed by all of the tests, but once you are done with these, you shouldn't need anything further until after you've started therapy." He then looked Ellen straight in the eye. "Keep your chin up. We're going to fight this."

We appreciated Dr. Gudmundson's kind words of encouragement, but they could not negate the fact that we had just received the most dreadful news imaginable. I had lost my wife to melanoma, and I came to the realization that I was going to lose my only child, too.

Why couldn't it have happened to me instead? I thought. *Lord, please take me instead of Ellen. She is so young and has her entire life ahead of her.*

Ellen cried all the way home from the doctor's office. Although I did my best to hide it, I was utterly devastated. I tried to be strong and reiterate Dr. Gudmundson's words—"We're going to fight this"—but it was hard. I didn't know what to say. I could think of no words that could make the situation better.

Chapter 11
THE BOOK OF MARTYRS

THE NEXT SEVERAL days were like I was in a dense psychological fog. My head was buzzing, and I was dazed. I still couldn't sleep, and I had no appetite. Jerry and Joyce tried to be supportive, but nothing and no one could cut through my despair. I felt so terrible for Ellen, but I also felt sorry for myself. Seeing my only daughter suffer was the worst thing imaginable, but for Ellen's sake, I was determined to remain strong. I did everything I could think of to keep myself from completely going insane. I rationalized over and over again, but it was to no avail, for in my heart I knew my rationalizations were themselves irrational. The melanoma could not be beaten. That was the sober fact. There was no escape from it. My gut instinct was to hide, but there was no place to hide. Trying to be logical, I told myself that I should try to stay active and try to stay positive, and I did the best that I could. Each afternoon I would force myself to go to the forest preserve after work, just to get outside and collect my thoughts. It took all of the energy that I had just to make myself go. It also took a lot of faith.

"I can't give into despair," I would repeat over and over again. "I must hold on to hope. Have faith. Never lose faith. With the Lord, there is a way. There is always a way." I did a lot of praying as I walked along in the cold. I also did a lot of bargaining and begging. "Please, Lord, grant us a miraculous redemption. Please give us hope. I'll do anything. Just give us something to be hopeful for. Please!" Day after day, I walked and prayed.

One day as I was walking, a raven flew down from the trees and walked beside me. It seemed to come out of nowhere. It landed just three or four feet from where I was. With the exception of eagles, I did not like birds. Even though I loved animals in general, I found most birds to be ugly creatures. This raven was particularly ugly—a beady-eyed black bird with a sinister appearance. It followed me for several yards along the path. I kicked at some small stones to see if the noise would startle it and cause it to fly off, but it did not flinch. In an odd manner, its presence disturbed me. Behaving as it did, it brought to mind Edgar Allen Poe's melancholy poem:

> And the Raven, never flitting, still is sitting, still is sitting, On the pallid bust of Pallas just above my chamber door; And his eyes have all the seeming of a demon's that is dreaming, And the lamp-light o'er him streaming throws his shadow on the floor; And my soul from out the shadow that lies floating on the floor, Shall be lifted Nevermore![2]

"Poe understood," I whispered to myself. Poe indeed understood the torment that comes with the loss of a loved one. Each day after my walks in the forest preserve, I would stop by to see Ellen. As often as I could, I would bring her pastries from her favorite bakery but, like me, she was not eating well. She obviously was depressed; she had every right to be.

I usually did not stay at Ellen's for too long. Many days, she would have Jack or other friends over, and I did not want to intrude. Still, I wanted her to know that I was there. After my visits, I would go back home, even though I hated to go home. Home was supposed to be a place to relax, a warm place where a man could escape his troubles. Yet for me, home was no longer a place of warmth; it was a place of emptiness. It was a place where my dark thoughts would time and again get the best of me. Thankfully, Jerry came to visit quite often. He usually showed up a little after seven and stayed until about nine o'clock. We passed the time in front of the television, watching *M.A.S.H.* and other mindless reruns. The lighthearted old shows helped to temporarily keep my mind off my troubles. Unfortunately, the diversion was only temporary. After Jerry left, I'd go up to the den and sit in front of my computer. I spent most of the time searching melanoma Web sites on the Internet to see if anyone had any "miracle cures." I searched all of the major cancer center Web pages. I searched for melanoma clinical trials. I read testimonials from melanoma patients on the Web. I even searched for herbal medications. I read page after page. My eyes were so blurred from exhaustion that it was hard to read at all, but I went on. Most of what I read did not sound encouraging, and the things that did sound encouraging were of questionable integrity. Dr. Gudmundson had warned us about looking things up on the Internet.

"Beware of what you read. There's a lot of quackery out there," he said. "If something sounds too good to be true, it likely is too good to be true."

---

2   Adapted from URL: http://en.wikipedia.org/wiki/The_Raven. Downloaded 1-31-09.

Search as I might, there were no miracle cures to be found. It seemed like every path led back to the road of despair. There seemed to be no cause for hope. It felt as if I had truly hit rock bottom, and I began to lose faith.

Has the Lord forsaken us? I wondered. In my darkest moments, I believed that he had. Although I did my best to fight it, the sadness in my life was clearly taking a grievous toll on me. I woke up each morning and cursed the start of the day, and I went to bed each night with a feeling of utter dread. There was never a moment of peace; there was only pain. My life continued on that way, minute after minute, hour after hour, and day after day. It truly seemed as if the misery would never end.

Then, late one evening, something most unexpected happened. Without rhyme or reason, my mood suddenly changed in a dramatic way—a way I'll never forget. I was sitting at my computer in the den, reading about the dismal prognosis of stage IV melanoma, when I thought I heard a knock at my front door. I looked over at the clock and saw that it read 11:45 PM.

Who would knock on my door this late at night? I wondered. I listened carefully, but there was no further knocking. *It must have been the wind*, I decided. Still, it had sounded like a knock, so I went to the door and looked outside. There was no one there. I opened the door and stepped onto the front porch. It was a calm, cool night, and there was no wind. The trees were perfectly still. There was no movement anywhere; no sign of squirrels or birds. There were no cars passing by. The gas lantern-lit streets of Riverside were perfectly quiet.

I must be going crazy, I thought. *I must be hearing things.*

I went back up to my desk and sat in the leather chair, shaking my head in disgust. "This is insane!" I said aloud. "It's shameful. I'm driving myself crazy, and I'm certainly not doing Ellen any good." I took a deep breath and exhaled slowly. *I've got to get out of this psychological fog! I've got to start doing something positive for Ellen. I've got to turn this ship around.*

Then it happened—the dramatic change occurred.

Pounding my fist on the desk, I uncharacteristically erupted, "Dr. Gudmundson said we were going to fight this. Well, we should fight!"

Just like that, my mood of despair turned into a strong conviction. Although unexpected, it was a welcome change. Anything would have been better than the despair, even denial and delusions.

Wrapped up in a rush of newfound energy, I continued to talk to myself out loud.

"I don't care how far we have to travel or how much money it is going to cost, we are going to fight this melanoma!" I said. "We'll go to Europe if we have to. We'll go to China if we have to. We'll see twenty different doctors if we have to. We'll see herbal specialists if we have to. We'll find a way to beat this. We won't give up, no matter what!"

I then looked at the Bible that was sitting on my desk and prayed, "Please, Lord, God Almighty, I will do whatever you ask … I will do anything. Please let us win this fight."

It was late, but amazingly, I was not tired. I didn't feel like going to bed. It was like I was in a manic state, and driven by the mania, I got up from my desk and began to pace. I walked back and forth for a full thirty minutes, my thoughts racing the entire time. Then, searching for something else to do, I turned to an unlikely pursuit—a pursuit that would change my life in immeasurably ways. I opened up the file on my computer that contained the outline of *The Third Testament*, the outline that I had put together just a few weeks before. Even though I was severely sleep-deprived, my sensorium was heightened, and the thought of a biblical Third Testament deeply intrigued me. It seemed like such a novel idea. At the same time, it seemed like such a crazy idea. Yet at that point in my life, I was comfortable with crazy.

Staring at the outline, I impulsively decided to start writing but was not sure where to begin. *It is such an enormous task. There is so much to include.* The enormity was mind-boggling, but inexplicably, I was determined to start.

I'm going to do this. Even if it takes me decades to complete, I'm going to do this. It is such a remarkable idea. I can't believe no one else thought of it before. I've got to do this!

After several minutes of frenzied contemplation, I managed to regain a modicum of focus, and resolved to proceed in chronological order.

"I'll start with the fate of the twelve apostles," I said to myself. "That is the most logical conclusion—to pick up the story of God's people where the New Testament left off."

In surreal fashion, I then typed the title of the first section, "The Book of Martyrs."

Just as the Old and New Testaments were divided into books, it is only appropriate that the Third Testament should also be divided into books.

With that thought, I looked up at the clock and saw that it was 1:17 AM. And I looked at the calendar and saw that it was November 17. I'll never forget that date and that hour, for it was the moment in time when my unlikely journey into authorship commenced.

Before I knew it, my fingers were busy at the keyboard. Simply enough, I began "The Book of Martyrs" with the story of Saint Peter. Although I had never written anything before, it felt so natural to begin. There were many events involving Peter that I could have chosen to write about, but I was determined to focus on things that impacted modern society. I also was determined to focus on things that seemed biblical—things that everyday

Christians would logically have included in the Bible, were it not already written. I therefore started with the account of Peter's vision of Christ carrying a cross into Rome—the story that prompted the founding of the Church of Domine Quo Vadis, a historic church that still stands to this day outside of Rome. After a brief introduction, I wrote:

> Peter, formerly called Simon, son of John, was a direct witness of the Risen Lord. In the courtyard of the high priest, fear and weakness of faith made him deny Christ three times. After the Resurrection, he thrice proclaimed his love. He proved his love by traveling to distant lands, fearlessly preaching God's word. With all his heart, he tended God's sheep and fed His lambs. He did this for all of his days. And when he was done, Peter was martyred, just as Jesus had prophesized. In accordance with the Lord's plan, his martyrdom occurred in Rome.

> As the leader of the Church on earth, Peter was targeted by Nero during the great persecutions. Day after day, he was hunted like an animal, certain to face torture and death if caught. Upon urging from his devoted followers, the Lord's disciple made plans to flee the great city so that he could continue his quest to spread the word of God. But then one night he had a dream that brought about a change of heart. In the dream, he encountered Christ carrying a cross toward the city of Rome. When he saw him, the fisherman, although old and frail, dropped instantly to his knees in awe and said, "Domine, Quo Vadis," or "Lord, where goest thou?"

> With a sad, but sweet voice, the Lord looked straight at Peter and said unto him, "I go into the city of the seven hills to be crucified."

> Bewildered, Peter said unto him, "Lord, art thou being crucified again?"

> And the Lord said, "Yes, Peter, as thou has deserted my people, I am being crucified again."

> Christ was to bear the cross again because his foremost disciple was forsaking his duty.

> It became undoubtedly clear to Peter what he must do. The disciple awoke from his dream with conviction in his heart. He was determined to fulfill his destiny. He would remain in Rome to die a martyr.

As I wrote about Peter's encounter with Christ, I recalled Henryk Sienkiewicz's version of the event. Sienkiewicz was a Polish novelist who lived in the late 1800s. One of his most famous works was *Quo Vadis*, written in 1895, which was very popular around the world. MGM made an epic movie based on his work in 1951, before Hollywood became completely overrun by secularists. The movie starred Deborah Kerr and Robert Taylor and was nominated for eight Academy Awards, including Best Picture. I saw it on TV when I was a teenager and became intrigued by it, so I went to the library and checked out the book.

Sienkiewicz told the story much better than I, I thought, recalling the well-written work. *I wish I had skills as an author, but I'm a novice. I'll just have to do the best that I can.*

The fact that I had absolutely no book-writing experience made authoring *The Third Testament* all the more crazy, but I really did not care. *I'm sure I'll hone my skills over time*, I rationalized.

Continuing on, I wrote about Peter's crucifixion:

> It was not long before Nero's henchmen discovered the apostle's whereabouts, and Peter was imprisoned and tortured. For nine months he was kept in a squalid dungeon called Tullian Keep, chained to a column. Nero was certain that through physical abuse he could force Peter to deny Christ. Yet crow as the cock might, there would be no denial this time. The Rock of the newly founded Church would not be broken. Because he held firm to his convictions, Simon Peter, son of John, was crucified in the Neronian Gardens in the year AD 67. Believing that he was not worthy to die in the same manner as his Master, Peter requested to be hung upside down on the cross. His request was granted, and he died with his head facing the earth.

It is written:

> "As the last hour of the apostle approached, Peter gazed out over the eternal city, the city of madness, the throne of the world, where the Beast reigned. He lifted up his eyes and said: 'O Lord, Thou didst command me to conquer this city, which rules over the world, and I have subdued it. Thou didst command me to found thy capitol in it, and I have done so. Now, O Lord, it is thy citadel, and I am going to thee, because my work is done.' He then looked out at the temples and cried: 'You will be the temples of Christ.' And he looked out at the people who swarmed before his eyes, and said: 'Your children will be the servants of Christ.'

"Now no one there present, not merely among the soldiers digging the pit in which the cross was to be planted, but even among the faithful, could divine that the real ruler of that city stood amongst them; that Caesars would pass away, that waves of barbarians would come and go, that ages would vanish, but that this old man would forever hold their uninterrupted sway, and that this persecuted Church, for which the old man lived and died, would triumphantly stand, in Rome and around the world, eternally."[3]

As the seconds became minutes and the minutes became hours, I became more and more immersed in my work. The words just flowed, and they kept my mind from sinking back into the sea of despair. I wrote of Saint Thomas and his journey to evangelize far away in India. I wrote of Saint James and how the Pharisees had hurled him from the pinnacle of the temple because of his unwavering faith in the Son of Man. I wrote of Saint Jude and his mission to the city of Edessa, where he carried the shroud of Turin. I wrote of Saint John's vision of the Apocalypse, experienced at age ninety-six while on exile in Patmos, and how the vision inspired him to transcribe the Book of Revelation. I described the martyrdoms of all of the apostles. I then wrote about the early Church and its many struggles. Foremost among the Church's struggles was the tyranny of the Roman emperor Nero, the man who started the great persecutions. From the very first time that I conceived of the idea of a Third Testament, I knew it would have to include a section on Nero—and a prominent section at that.

A Third Testament without Nero would be like the Old Testament without the pharaohs, and the New Testament without Herod. In truth, the story of Nero is more important to Christian history than are the stories of the pharaohs and Herod. Nero was as biblical a tyrant as there ever was.

I was deeply intrigued by the fact that Nero was considered by many to be the Antichrist. His immoral behavior certainly supported the theory. He was indeed a miserable beast who despised Christianity.

Driven by avarice, jealousy, and lust, Nero murdered his own wife, mother, and brother; he did so without remorse. As horrible as those acts were, he did worse. Finding sexual gratification in torture, he repeatedly masqueraded as a wild animal, raping both male and female prisoners—innocent and helpless prisoners.

---

3   Adapted from Henryk Sienkiewicz. *Quo Vadis, A Tale of the Time of Nero.* New York: Thomas Y. Crowell Co., 1905, pp.492–495.

The depth of his depravity was unfathomable, I thought as my mind became completely occupied by my new project.

Nero's most notorious act of tyranny involved the torching of Rome. At the time of Nero's reign, Rome was an old city with wooden edifices and narrow and crooked streets. The avaricious emperor dreamed of a new monumental Rome, which he conspired to call Neronia. In the year AD 64, he purposely set the city on fire so that he could justify rebuilding it on a grander scale. The consequences were dreadful. Rome burned for six days and seven nights. Three-quarters of the city was consumed, and thousands died. As the flames engulfed Rome, Nero ascended the tower of Maecenas and, to the accompaniment of his lyre, sang of the ruin of Ilium.

Thus came the saying, "Nero fiddled while Rome burned," I mused.

Needing a scapegoat, Nero blamed the Christians for the great fire and subsequently ordered the first great Christian persecution. He had the followers of Christ tortured and murdered in droves. Some were torn apart by dogs, others were crucified, and others were set on fire to illuminate the night. It was the diabolic fervor with which the evil emperor carried out the persecutions that led many to believe he was the Antichrist.

Regardless of whether he was the spawn of Satan, he was, at the very least, a pawn of Satan, I reasoned. *Few men in history have done as much to undermine the Church as he.*

I wrote:

> The beast began by having self-acknowledged Christians arrested. Then, on information gathered through the use of torture, large numbers of others were condemned. The emperor of Rome, the most powerful man on the face of the earth, made it his quest to eradicate the people of God and destroy the fellowship of the Holy Spirit. Driven by sheer madness, his cruelty knew no bounds. Countless Christians were tortured and killed under Nero's command. Saint Peter was crucified, and Saint Paul was beheaded. Death was followed by cruel death. It was not long before those closest to Nero began to realize that the emperor was possessed by abject and absolute evil. Many of the citizens of Rome came to pity the Christians. Many were moved by their great faith and courage. Many found the tyranny of Nero abhorrent. Yet many others, hearts filled with hate and swayed by the devil, took pleasure in the merciless onslaught. Nero's madness was but the unfortunate beginning of the Christian persecutions. Emperor Domitian was no less brutal. Satan's influence in Rome was ever so strong but so was the faith of the people of God. Because of this profound faith, the Church would survive; Nero would not.

In the end, Nero failed in his quest. His reckless ambitions bankrupted the empire, both morally and financially, and the citizens of Rome turned against him. Instead of glory, the avaricious emperor ultimately found only ridicule. His demise was ironically appropriate. For a man who loved the arts, his fall from power was dramatic, and his death theatrical. I briefly described his demise in *The Third Testament*:

> With Rome in turmoil, Nero set off to Greece, where he performed as an actor and played his lyre. He believed that the arts were all he had left. His irresponsible behavior so infuriated the masses that in the year 68, he was overthrown. The Roman senate declared him an enemy of the state and sentenced him to death. Nero, consumed by his own avarice and madness, had utterly failed in his quest to destroy the Church, and the devil abandoned him. Powerless and forsaken, he took his own life. On the ninth day of the sixth month of the sixty-eighth year, Nero stabbed himself in the neck with a dagger. His last words uttered were these:

> "Jupiter, what an artist the world is losing in me."

> With those final words, the reign of the beast was over. By the grace of God, the Church endured his wrath, and the fellowship of the Holy Spirit continued on.

Surviving Nero's reign was one of the first and worst obstacles that the Church has ever had to overcome. After I finished writing about him, I decided that his story should be the first story of my book. I believed it was absolutely necessary to emphasize Satan's historical opposition to the Church in order to aptly recount the saga of God's people.

It is impossible to understand what it is to be a Christian without first understanding the evils that Christians have endured—and continue to endure.

My long evening was still not done. Just before the break of dawn I wrote about one of the greatest events in the history of Christianity—the Assumption of the Blessed Virgin Mary into heaven. The Assumption occurred at Gethsemane, in the valley of Josaphat, in Judea. A glorious event, it was uplifting to write about, especially considering I had spent most of the night writing about martyrdoms and the Antichrist.

The story of the Assumption began in a similar manner as the story of the birth of Christ—with a visit from an archangel. Several years after Christ ascended into heaven, Saint Gabriel the Archangel was sent to Ephesus by

God to tell Mary of her approaching departure from the earth. He said to her:

> "Hail, holy woman. The time has come. In answer to your prayers, you shall return to heaven with your Son, into true and everlasting life. And you shall be exalted, for every gift has been given to thee by the Lord."

As recorded in the ancient manuscripts, Gabriel said only this and nothing more. He then bowed his head to her and disappeared into the light.

Heeding the archangel's message, Mary traveled to Jerusalem to spend her last days there. In a miraculous manner, the apostles, too, came to Jerusalem from their various locations on earth, summoned by the Holy Spirit to honor the Mother of God. Together with the apostles, Mary once more visited the holy places of the city, including Mount Calvary, where her beloved Son died. She then retired to a poor cottage in the countryside, to prepare for her departure from this world.

Within three days, Mary fell into a peaceful slumber. By the order of Saint Peter, the apostles brought her body to a tomb at Gethsemane, in the valley of Josaphat, and waited there for a sign from God. On the Lord's Day, Jesus, accompanied by a host of angels, came to assume the body and soul of the woman who bore him. The presence of the Lord awoke Mary from her slumber, and, by the power of the Holy Spirit, she ascended with him into heaven above. As she ascended, a brilliant light lit up the sky, and the Lord called out:

> "Let thy heart rejoice and be glad, for thou art the queen over all things, and every soul that calls thy name shall find mercy, both in this world now and that which is to come."

The apostles were in awe as they watched Christ and Mary ascend upward. Dropping to their knees, they bid Mary a joyous farewell, saying:

> "Blessed art thou among women, and blessed is the fruit of thy womb."

Inspired by God, Saint Gregory of Tours, an early historian, was one of the first to record a description of the Assumption. He did so almost fifteen hundred years ago. Prior to him, the story of the Assumption was passed along only though oral tradition or in obscure apocryphal works. It was Gregory's description that largely led to the Church's recognition of the event. In the 1960s, Pope Pius XII officially made the Assumption Church dogma, and today, Christians from around the world celebrate the Feast of the Assumption on August 15. Thanks to Saint Gregory, in many nations it is a national holiday. Given the importance of his contribution, I included a translation of Gregory's description at the end of my work. I wrote:

> "The Apostles took up her body on a bier and placed it in a tomb; and they guarded it, expecting the Lord to come. And behold, again the Lord stood by them; and the holy body having been received, he commanded that it be taken in a cloud into paradise, where now, rejoined to the soul, Mary rejoices with the Lord's chosen ones."[4]

After I finished writing, I took a deep breath and exhaled slowly. For the first time in several weeks, I felt a sense of calm. I fell asleep soon thereafter and slept well. The next day was Saturday, and I did not awaken until 11:00 AM. I spent the entire day with Ellen, and her spirits seemed to have lifted. She, too, had found the conviction to fight the dreaded disease.

---

4   URL: http://members.tripod.com/~maryimmaculate/marian8.html. Downloaded 1-7-06.

Chapter 12
THE FIGHT BEGINS

ONCE THE INITIAL shock from Ellen's diagnosis began to wear off, we moved forward with our lives. There were good days and bad. The "good days" were not necessarily good in the true sense of the word, but they were good because they were manageable. Fear and anxiety were still very much present, but they were no longer overwhelming. It helped that Dr. Gudmundson prescribed a new investigational therapy for Ellen. As he explained it to us, the drug sounded promising, and we again found hope. It was so nice to have hope— and so unexpected—because we had previously believed that all was lost.

Hope is one of God's greatest gifts, I decided.

We also met with Dr. Greenspan, who prescribed a more aggressive approach, but it really did not sound any better than what Dr. Gudmundson had to offer. Ellen decided to go with Dr. Gudmundson, and I supported her decision.

- - - - - - - - - -

I spent all of my free moments writing for the next couple of weeks. Although my mania had worn off, I nevertheless found refuge in my work. Writing became my respite from the cruel world.

I know it is absolutely crazy, but this Third Testament idea does seem to ease my mind, I thought. *Maybe it's because I've completely lost my mind; maybe I really am delusional to think I can do this. No matter; whether or not I'm insane, it's good to have something to occupy my thoughts.*

In keeping with my plan, I continued recording the history of the early Church. As much as possible, I tried to focus on things that molded Christian tradition. Looking at the historical timeline, I considered several topics: Luke and Mark, the authors of the Gospels; Joseph of Arimathea and his evangelization in England; Mary Magdalene and the mysteries surrounding her; and the martyrdom of Saint Paul. After some deliberation, I decided to begin with the account of Mary Magdalene and the miraculous red egg, the event that launched the tradition of painting eggs at Easter.

Ever since The Da Vinci Code *was published, there has been a lot of interest in Mary Magdalene,* I thought. *Unfortunately, most of the interest is focused on scandalous myths and not on the good that she did. That is not a surprise, given the media in this country.*

Although I was a professor of religion, I was certainly no expert on Mary Magdalene. I therefore had to do a little research before I could start writing. I turned to the East, to a source outside of Catholicism, for information about her. In the ancient Eastern Orthodox manuscripts, Mary was depicted not so much as a repentant sinner but as a pious woman of high social standing. According to the manuscripts, after Christ's death and Resurrection, she traveled around the world, evangelizing, just as did the apostles. One of her stops was in Rome, where she confronted the emperor, and told him of Christ's many great deeds. Holding up an egg, symbol of new life, she described how Christ rose from the dead. At first the emperor did not believe her, but then came the miracle. I wrote:

> Now, Mary Magdalene was a woman of wealth and therefore was admitted to the court of Tiberius Caesar in Rome. Tiberius Caesar was curious to understand why a woman of her social standing would be preaching to the crowds in the streets about a crucified Nazarene. At the time of Easter, he arranged a meeting with her, and she told him the story of Christ's life and death. Tiberius Caesar listened with fascination. Mary told him how the Son of God went about doing good: curing the sick, mending the lame, casting out demons, and preaching to the masses. She told him of his commandment, "Love thy neighbor as thyself." She told him how Christ was condemned by the Pharisees out of jealousy and fear. The great Caesar listened most intently when she told him how his appointed servant, the procurator Pontius Pilate, washed his hands of the matter and delivered Christ to the Pharisees to be murdered on a cross. Then, in an effort to explain the miraculous Resurrection, Mary picked up an egg from the dinner table at which they sat. She held the egg in her hand and ardently detailed how Christ rose from his tomb. Instantly, Tiberius Caesar's fascination turned to disdain. He was a well-learned man who did not believe in such things

and was insulted that a woman would speak such "folly" to a man of his rank. He censured her. With eyes wide and voice raised he exclaimed:

"A man can no more rise from the dead than the egg in your hand turn red!"

The emperor of Rome intended to say more, but he suddenly stopped, for he was distracted. He intended to go on a tirade and denounce Mary, but he did not. Instead, he bowed his head in awe, for before his very eyes, the egg in the hand of the woman turned red, as testimony to the truth she spoke.

I'd bet most parents don't even know why they have their kids paint eggs at Easter, I thought as I wrote about the red egg. Tina and I certainly didn't know when we raised Ellen. It seems like this should be something that they teach in Sunday school.

After completing the passage about Mary Magdalene and the Easter egg tradition, I went on to write about Saint Paul, Saint Luke, and Saint Mark. Gathering what information I could from the various religious texts in my possession, I briefly described their paths to the knowledge of God. I then wrote of Joseph of Arimathea, bearer of the Holy Grail, and of the sacred thorn he planted at Glastonbury—a thorn that miraculously flowered during the Christmas season. I was particularly intrigued by Joseph's story. It was known that he journeyed to England after Christ's death and Resurrection. Yet many believed that Joseph journeyed to England years before and that he even brought Jesus to England in his youth. The latter belief inspired Blake's famous poem "Jerusalem," one of my all-time favorites, which I included in the book:

And did those feet in ancient times
Walk upon England's mountains green?
And was the Holy Lamb of God
On England's pleasant pastures seen?
And did the Countenance Divine
Shine forth upon our clouded hills?
And was Jerusalem builded here
Among those dark Satanic mills?
Bring me my bow of burning gold!
Bring me my arrows of desire!
Bring me my spear! O clouds unfold!
Bring me my Chariot of Fire!

I will not cease from mental fight,
Nor shall my sword sleep in my hand
Till I have built Jerusalem
In England's green and pleasant land.[5]

Incessant in my work, I wrote about the martyrdoms of Ignatius of Antioch, Polycarp, and Justin. Of the three, Ignatius was the most renowned, in large part for the zeal with which he embraced martyrdom. Prior to his death in the Roman Coliseum, Ignatius said:

> "The only thing I ask of you is to allow me to offer the libation of my blood to God. I am the wheat of the Lord; may I be ground by the teeth of the beasts to become the immaculate bread of Christ."[6]

Inspired by Ignatius' words, I included several passages from the Acts of Martyrs, the official records of early Christian martyrs made by ancient notaries, in *The Third Testament*.

I then wrote of the trials and tribulations of Saint Valentine. Valentine's story was a noteworthy one. A skilled physician and devoted bishop from Terni, Valentine was imprisoned and sentenced to death by the evil Roman emperor Claudius for violating Claudius' ban against marriage. Valentine was targeted because he had knowingly defied the emperor by presiding over the wedding ceremonies of countless couples. During his time in prison, Valentine converted the jailer and the jailer's blind daughter to Christianity. By the grace of God, he cured the daughter of blindness, and the two became good friends. I wrote:

> In the third century, during the reign of Emperor Claudius II, there lived a saintly bishop in the village of Terni named Valentine. He was a devout follower of the teachings of Christ, and he dedicated his life to doing good. He converted pagans, preached God's message of love, and prayed for the poor. Of all of his good deeds, Valentine was best known for his service to the sick. The finest of physicians, Valentine dressed the wounds of those injured with medicinal ointments, and stayed with the infirm during times of need. Many lived, whom others felt would surely die, because of the saintly bishop's care. Word spread far and wide of

---

5   URL: http://en.wikisource.org/wiki/Preface_to_Milton:_a_Poem. Downloaded 1-31-09.
6   URL: http://www.americancatholic.org/Features/SaintOfDay/default. asp?id=1171. Downloaded 1-8-06.

his remarkable skills as a healer, and even the staunchest pagans came to seek his aid.

Valentine often tended to those who suffered the wrath of Emperor Claudius, who had earned the title "the Cruel." Claudius was undeniably cruel. He had a heart of stone and a fiery temper. He loved no one and sought only personal glory. He tortured and murdered those who did not serve him to his liking. He had a particularly strong hatred of Christians and persecuted them with great fury.

Much as Claudius was "the Cruel," Valentine was "the Compassionate." No man or woman in all the empire demonstrated more caring than the bishop of Terni. He stood in stark contrast to the ruthless emperor.

It was only a matter of time before Valentine himself would come to experience Claudius' wrath. Under Claudius' rule, Rome was involved in many bloody and unpopular military campaigns. Frustrated by his difficulty in taking men from their homes to be soldiers, Claudius outlawed marriage. Although celibate himself, Valentine viewed marriage as a most sacred union. Valentine refused to heed the emperor's order and continued to preside over the weddings of young couples. Word of Valentine's deeds spread quickly, and men and women throughout the empire journeyed to Terni to be wed by the good bishop. Word also spread to Claudius, who, infuriated by Valentine's insubordination, had the bishop arrested and brought to Rome to be executed.

Valentine was imprisoned in a dark dungeon and was not allowed visitors. His only human contact was with the jailer who brought him food and drink. For the first several weeks of the imprisonment, the jailer did not speak a word to the bishop. He only left the food and walked away. One day, however, the jailer broke his silence.

"Are the tales true? Can you heal the sick?" the jailer asked.

Valentine was surprised that the jailer had spoken to him, and at first did not respond.

"Can you heal the sick?" the jailer emphatically asked again. "I must know."

Valentine answered him, "Only God can heal. I am but a humble servant of the Lord."

"My only daughter has lost her sight. She suffers in a world of darkness. Will you ask your God to help her?" the jailer pleaded. "I can offer you nothing in return but will be forever grateful."

"Take me to her," Valentine responded.

The jailer, in secret, brought the bishop to see his daughter. The pagan woman, though blind, had a warm heart and joyful spirit. Valentine was moved by her youthful love of life. The saintly healer knelt in prayer and said:

"Lord Jesus Christ, God of Light, illuminate this house and all those who dwell within it. Let them come to know your great love and compassion."

Valentine's words, though spoken softly, were clearly heard in heaven above. With the help of the Holy Spirit, he restored the woman's sight. That very day the woman went out into the fields and, for the first time, saw the beauty of the world. The fields were filled with yellow crocuses, and the woman marveled at their brilliant color. She was moved to tears. "Oh, the flowers that I saw today!" she exclaimed to her father. "I simply do not have words to describe their splendor."

The jailer and his daughter were overjoyed. They converted to Christianity, and at the end of each day they worshipped with Valentine in his prison cell. It was not long before the jailer's daughter and the bishop became close friends. She brought him bread, and he taught her how to read. As the weeks passed, they came to spend more and more time together. The woman no longer visited solely at the end but also at the beginning of each day. She willingly forfeited the brilliance of the summer sun for the time spent reading by candlelight. The awareness of this sacrifice saddened the bishop. One day, Valentine said unto the woman, "Child, do not waste your days in this world of darkness. You are young. Go out and live. Do not come here to this dungeon."

Despite Valentine's request, the woman continued to come to his cell, day after day. She begged Valentine to let her help him escape, but Valentine stubbornly refused. He said, "If you set me free, you and your father will be hunted, just as I was hunted. You would have to hide in the shadows. That is no way to live one's life. I could never let that be."

Months passed, and the day of Valentine's execution finally arrived. On the fourteenth day of the second month, in the year AD 270, the saintly bishop was beaten and beheaded in Rome, under the order of Claudius II. Just hours before his death, the bishop of Terni left a farewell package for the jailer's daughter. It did not reach her possession until after he was gone. With tearful eyes and cheerless heart, the woman sadly unwrapped the twine that bound the box. Inside was a beautiful yellow crocus, more vibrant than she had ever before seen. No one knows how it had come into Valentine's possession, for it was the winter season, and no flowers were in bloom. More than that, the bishop had been constantly confined to his cell and had no access to flora. Grasping the flower, the woman looked to heaven and smiled. Her heart was instantly warmed, and her tears of sorrow turned to tears of joy.

The crocus was not the sole content of the box. Accompanying the yellow flower was a letter. In the letter, the bishop encouraged the young woman to follow the path of God and to live a life filled with love and compassion. He told her not to mourn his death but to think of him when she saw the flowers of the spring. He thanked her for the time spent with him during his long and bitter confinement, and he promised that they would see each other again in heaven someday.

The farewell letter, written in the twilight of life, was brief in words but abundant in sincerity and kindness. At the very end, the good martyr signed it simply, "From your Valentine."

It's too bad more people don't know this story, I thought. *So many see the day as nothing more than a time to exchange Hallmark cards and heart-shaped candy boxes. Our secular society has even dropped the "Saint" from Saint Valentine's Day. That is a shame.*

After completing the section on Valentine, I wrote of the great emperor Constantine and the magnificent cross of light that changed the course of history:

The first three centuries of the Church were marked by turmoil. Gnostics spread false teachings of Christ throughout the ancient world. They proclaimed that the creator of the world, the God of the Old Testament, was a dark and cruel deity, forever at war with the pure and spiritual God of light, depicted in the New Testament, from whom Jesus originated. The Gnostics arrogantly believed that they alone were privy to a secret knowledge of the divine. They even created their own false gospels, which contained blasphemous stories of the Lord. In response to the false teachings, the early Christian bishops began to develop official lists of inspired writings, called canons. These canons, rooted in truth, laid the foundation for the New Testament.

The greatest source of turmoil for the early Christian Church was the Roman persecution. The injustice that began under Nero and extended under Domitian continued on for generations. Many holy men and women were tortured and murdered under the order of the emperor of Rome. Some had their eyes and tongues gouged out; others had their feet sawed off. Some were thrown to wild beasts; others starved to death in dark dungeons. These good souls were martyred because, of their own free will, they chose to follow Christ, the King of kings, rather than blindly follow an earthly king. They dedicated their lives to helping the sick, the poor, the orphans, the widows, and the victims of war, plague, and famine. They gladly gave themselves to those in need rather than pay homage to the pagan gods. For this they suffered, but in their suffering, their faith grew stronger. It was this profound demonstration of faith that led countless numbers of Roman subjects to convert to Christianity.

The worst of the Roman tyranny took place in the eastern half of the empire. By the beginning of the fourth century, the Christian converts in the East were reaching large numbers, and the Eastern emperors laid plans against them. In the year 311, the hard-hearted Maximinus Daia called for a large scale bloody persecution of the children of God. Maximinus was a fanatical idolater and tyrant. He sought to abolish the Church and put in its place a heathen organization of high priests and magicians, whom he deemed would be of equal rank with the governors of the provinces. Maximinus demanded that all things Christian be destroyed and that all those professing faith in Christ be put to death. Yet shortly after he gave the order, something strange and unexpected occurred. The bloodthirsty monarch utterly reversed his command. The idolater's change of heart puzzled many, until it was learned that Maximinus Daia did not act of his own free will but had been coerced by the new leader of the Western Empire, the great general Constantine.

Constantine, born in Macedonia, was the son of Constantius Chlorus, leader of the Western Roman Empire, and Helena, the pious daughter of an innkeeper from Drepanum. Although himself a pagan, Constantine long admired the great faith of the martyrs and showed deep sympathy toward the Christians. When his father died at York in the year 306, Constantine was hailed as emperor of Rome by his loyal troops. However, the general's claim to the throne did not go undisputed. His brother-in-law, the avaricious tyrant Maxentius, boldly challenged him for control of the empire, and a bitter conflict ensued. Like Maximinus, Maxentius despised the Christians and sought to eradicate them from the face of the earth.

In the fateful year 312, the conflict between Constantine and Maxentius reached its climax. Realizing that there was no hope for peaceful negotiations, Constantine led his army through northern Italy to the outskirts of Rome, where Maxentius had treacherously established a stronghold. As he approached, fear swept across the great city, and the citizens of Rome prepared for the worst. On the twenty-eighth day of the tenth month, an epic battle took place near the Tiber River. The momentous struggle was fought by opposing factions of the Roman legions at the Milvian Bridge. It was a confrontation that would define the destiny of the world. As Constantine's forces advanced upon the infamous stone bridge, they found themselves outnumbered by ten to one. Faced with such incredible odds, Constantine prayed for divine assistance, but instead of praying to the pagan gods of Rome, he prayed to Christ, the God Almighty. He dropped to his knees and looked up to the heavens. With earnest prayer, he called on God to reveal his truth, and stretch forth his right hand in guidance. The Son of Man, Risen Lord and Savior, heard his plea. The King of kings responded to the fervent cry from the ruler of men, and Constantine's prayers were answered with a mystical vision. The vision appeared to him on the eve of the great battle. In this vision, Constantine saw a brilliant, shimmering cross of light emblazoned on the setting sun. The cross, symbol of the Resurrection and the Way, lit up the entire sky. Constantine could not believe his eyes, but his men also saw the brilliant cross. As they looked closer, they saw that the shimmering cross bore an inscription. The inscription read:

"In hoc signo vinces," or "In this sign you will conquer."

In answer to Constantine's plea, God indeed stretched out his right hand in guidance, and the sign granted miraculously delivered an outmanned army from certain annihilation.

Constantine's vision diametrically changed the course of battle. After seeing the vision, the inspired general ordered that the Greek monogram for Christ, Chi Rho, be marked on the shields of all of his soldiers. Bearing the symbol of the Lord, Constantine's army won an overwhelming victory, despite seemingly insurmountable odds. Maxentius was killed; his body was swept into the Tiber River during retreat, and Constantine became the undisputed leader of the Western Empire. Having conquered "in the sign of Christ," Constantine credited the victory at Milvian Bridge to the Son of man, and ordered the end of all Christian persecution within his realm. In the year 313, the Edict of Milan officially ended the persecution and provided for the return of confiscated properties to their rightful owners. After three bitter centuries, the Christian people were finally free.

Eusebius, the renowned historian, described the event:

"He saw with his own eyes the trophy of a cross of light in the heaven, above the sun, and bearing the inscription, 'in hoc signo vinces.' At this sight he himself was struck with amazement, and his whole army also, which followed him on the expedition, and witnessed the miracle."[7]

Constantine's vision had such a profound effect on the spread of Christianity that I decided that it was only right to name one of the books of *The Third Testament* after him, "The Book of Constantine."

Continuing on, I wrote of the Arian heresy and the Council of Nicaea. The Arians believed in Christ but denied that he was equal to God. In the year 325, a council of bishops from around the world gathered in Nicaea to discuss the controversy. They concluded that Christ was of the same substance of God. The Nicene Creed was established at the council:

We believe in one God, the Father Almighty, maker of heaven and earth, and of all things visible and invisible, and in one Lord Jesus Christ, the only begotten Son of God, begotten of the Father before all worlds. Light of Light, very God of very God, begotten not made, being of one substance with the Father, by whom all things were made, who for us

---

7   Adapted from Rosemary Ellen Guilley. *The Encyclopedia of Saints*. New York: Checkmark Books An Imprint of Facts on File, Inc., 2001, p. 82.

men and for our salvation came down from heaven, was incarnate by the Holy Ghost of the Virgin Mary and was made man; he was crucified for us under Pontius Pilate, suffered, died and was buried; and the third day rose again according to the Scriptures, and ascended into heaven, sits at the right hand of the Father, from thence he shall come again with glory to judge the living and the dead, of whose kingdom there shall be no end. We believe in the Holy Ghost, the Lord and Giver of life, who proceeds from the Father and the Son, who with the Father and the Son together is worshipped and glorified, who spoke by the prophets. We believe in one holy, catholic, and apostolic Church. We confess one baptism for the remission of sins, and we look for the resurrection of the dead and the life of the world to come. Amen.[8]

The creed proclaimed that Christ was not created or made, but was one being with the Father. The truth of the Son of man's divinity was upheld in Nicaea, and, to this day, the followers of Christ profess the Nicene Creed at Mass.

The Creed is as biblical as any of the passages from the Old or New Testaments, I concluded.

- - - - - - - - -

One afternoon while I was busy at work, the doorbell rang. It was Jerry.

"Hello, Fred," he said.

"Hi, Jerry, come on in. Would you like something to drink?"

"No, thanks, I'm good."

We both sat down.

Jerry sighed and then asked, "How's Ellen doing?"

"She's doing OK. She recently started therapy with Dr. Gudmundson. We're both hopeful."

"Does the therapy have a lot of side effects?" Jerry asked.

"No, it really doesn't," I explained. "It's not chemotherapy, so it doesn't cause a lot of vomiting. It's an experimental drug that they are using to try to shrink blood vessels. Dr. Gudmundson is really excited about it. He says the tumors can't grow if you choke off their blood supply. It makes a lot of sense if you think about it."

"That sounds promising, Fred. How are you holding up? You look a lot better than you did just a few weeks ago."

---

8   Adapted from URL: http://en.wikipedia.org/wiki/Nicene_Creedhttp:// en.wikipedia.org/wiki/Nicene_Creed. Downloaded 3-7-09.

"I'm doing OK. I'm staying busy, and that helps keep my mind off of things. It also helps to know that Ellen has started therapy. I can't tell you what a relief it was to settle on a treatment. For a while, we didn't know if she should get treated by Dr. Gudmundson or Dr. Greenspan. The therapy that Dr. Greenspan had at the Chicago Cancer Institute was a lot more aggressive but would have caused a lot of side effects. The therapy she is on now really has no side effects, and it sounds just as promising as what Greenspan had to offer, if not more promising. Anyway, Dr. Greenspan rubbed us the wrong way. All he seemed interested in was getting another subject for his study. Talking to him made us feel a little like a guinea pig. We're very happy with Dr. Gudmundson."

"I'm glad to hear things are going OK," Jerry said. "I hadn't heard from you in a while so I wasn't sure how you were holding up."

"I'm sorry I haven't been all that communicative as of late," I said. "I've been so incredibly busy. I've been going with Ellen to all of her appointments, and when I'm not in a doctor's office, I'm talking with lawyers about the lawsuit. I come home each night and just try to relax."

"I understand completely," Jerry said. "I'm really just glad to hear you're doing OK."

We were both silent for a moment.

"Fred," Jerry said, "about the lawsuit … I've done a little research."

Even though I had been spending a lot of time on the phone with lawyers, I really hadn't been concentrating on the lawsuit. My mind was occupied with Ellen's plight. Still, I knew that the lawsuit presented a serious problem, and the thought of it still filled me with great angst.

"What kind of research?" I asked.

"Well, I looked into Sylvester Jones' background. He's definitely not an upstanding citizen."

"What do you mean?" I asked. Jerry had me curious.

"He's been tried for a couple of felonies, but he's never been convicted. He's a con man. During the late 1990s, he ran a scam ripping off elderly widows and widowers. He tricked them into sending him money in return for bogus insurance. Dozens of innocent and trusting elders sent him their hard-earned savings and got nothing in return. The cops eventually caught on to Jones' scam, but, as is too often the case, he got off on a legal technicality. He's also been linked to inner-city gambling and prostitution, not to mention petty theft. He's been arrested in six different states. Yet for one reason or another, he has stayed out of jail. He's a sleazeball, Fred. He's a real sleazeball."

"He's a sleazeball who's trying to take away my home and life's savings," I said. "Those lawyers that are working for him are sleazeballs, too. Do you see their ads on TV? They're on all the time. 'Have you been the victim of a motor vehicle collision? Has your doctor been negligent in your care? Have you sustained a work-related injury? Make sure you get the compensation you deserve!' Their ads make me sick. I've stopped watching TV, they bother me so much."

"That's my point," Jerry said. "I think these guys are crooks. I'll bet you that Sylvester Jones isn't even injured."

"I'd like to believe that," I said, "but he has doctors' reports documenting that he has pain."

"I thought about that, so I spoke with a friend of mine who's an emergency room doc at Memorial. He explained a lot to me. There are no laboratory tests for pain. There are no x-rays or scans that show pain. The doctors say he has pain because Sylvester Jones tells them that he has pain. They have no way to prove or disprove it."

"You think this is all a scam?"

"I'm sure it is, and I'm going to prove it."

Jerry's theory certainly caught my attention. All along, in my heart, I believed that I was the victim, not the perpetrator, and Jerry's discovery substantiated that belief. In some ways, I felt vindicated. The lawsuit had been like salt in a deep wound, and now the sting from that salt was lessened. Instead of feeling ashamed, as if I had done something wrong, I felt angry that I was being swindled by a crook and his rotten lawyer.

Chapter 13
HAPPY HOLIDAYS

In Flanders on the Christmas morn
The trenched foemen lay,
the German and the Briton born,
And it was Christmas Day.

The red sun rose on fields accurst,
The gray fog fled away;
But neither cared to fire the first,
For it was Christmas Day!

They called from each to each across
The hideous disarray,
For terrible has been their loss:
"Oh, this is Christmas Day!"

Their rifles all they set aside,
One impulse to obey;
'Twas just the men on either side,
Just men—and Christmas Day.

They dug the graves for all their dead
And over them did pray:
And Englishmen and Germans said:
"How strange a Christmas Day!"

Between the trenches then they met,

Shook hands, and e'en did play
At games on which their hearts were set
On happy Christmas Day.

Not all the emperors and kings,
Financiers and they
Who rule us could prevent these things—
For it was Christmas Day.

Oh ye who read this truthful rime
From Flanders, kneel and say:
God speed the time when every day
Shall be as Christmas Day.[9]

—"A Carol from Flanders," Frederick Niven (1878–1944)

The Christmas season came and, as might be expected, my battle with depression grew harder. Despite feeling miserable on the inside, however, I did my best to hide the sadness and for the most part was successful. There were many days when the hope of Dr. Gudmundson's therapy was all that kept me going, but I concealed my struggle so well that no one noticed. There were other days when I purposefully tried to stir up my anger over the lawsuit, because anger was an emotion I could deal with better than sadness. Then there were days when I felt nothing but emptiness. Those were the worst, but I went about my business as usual in a professional manner.

To me, each act of emotional concealment was critical because I knew I needed to appear strong for Ellen. As is typical of families in times of strife, Ellen and I started to spend more time together, and I wanted to avoid doing anything that would contribute to her sorrow. At the same time I wanted to cherish every moment I could, for I did not know how many more we would have together. Sometimes it was difficult to balance the two, but at other times it came naturally.

One weekend, we made plans to focus on Christmas. Although I felt no holiday cheer, Ellen insisted that we try to lose ourselves in the spirit of the season.

"I want Christmas to feel how it felt years ago," she said. "I want us to do all the things we would usually do."

---

9   W. Reginald Wheeler, ed. *A Book of Verse of the Great War*: Yale University Press, 1917, p. 111.

I was willing to do anything that would make her happy and therefore supported her proposal.

"We'll hit all of our usual spots," I said.

Simply enough, we started with some Christmas shopping. Cash in hand, we headed over to the local mall where we encountered all of the stereotypical sights and sounds of the Yuletide season: colorful lights, ringing bells, giant inflatable snowmen, singing plastic reindeer, and Salvation Army representatives on every corner. Yet there were no crèches, no angels, no stars of wonder, no Wise Men, and certainly there was no mention of Christ.

"Happy Holidays," a politically correct greeter at Target said to Ellen and me as we entered the store.

"Merry Christmas," we replied in return.

"The dechristianization of America," Ellen turned to me and said. "It seems to be getting worse every year."

"True," I said. "I find it sad that the American public is trying to distance itself from its Christian roots. People seem so quickly to forget that this country was founded on Christian principles and that those principles are what made this country great."

"At least there are a lot of good people out there who are trying to fight it," Ellen said. "I heard a good line on the radio the other day—the radio host was quoting a famous patriot ... I can't remember his name. He was the one who said 'Give me liberty or give me death.'"

"Patrick Henry."

"Yes," she replied. "Patrick Henry. I wish I could remember how the quote goes. It was really powerful."

Smiling, I recited the quote from memory: "'It can not be emphasized too strongly or too often that this great nation was founded, not by religionists, but by Christians, not on religions, but on the gospel of Jesus Christ.'"

"I should have known you'd know it," she said, rolling her eyes playfully.

"Well, I *am* a professor of religion and history," I said with a wink.

My smile and wink and Ellen's playful eye roll were in no way natural. They were simply the expressions we would have expected from each other, had we not been in the situation we were in. Having to fabricate our cheer was not easy, but things could have been worse. Truth be told, Ellen was feeling relatively good and was in the best spirits I had seen her in a while. Although she had every right to be depressed, she was determined to go on with her life, even if it was a life in serious jeopardy. After spending all of Thanksgiving in tears, she'd pulled herself together and focused on making the best of Christmas. It temporarily brightened my spirits to see her coping so well.

Thank the Lord she is doing OK, I thought.

After shopping at Target, we drove downtown to Chicago, where we ate lunch at the legendary Walnut Room of Macy's, formerly Marshall Field's, on State Street. The Walnut Room was a very popular spot around the holidays. The ornate walls were covered in imported Russian wood paneling, and there were carolers caroling, store workers dressed as elves, and happy children everywhere. In the center of the room was a beautiful forty-five-foot Christmas tree adorned with old-fashioned, handcrafted ornaments. The room epitomized the Christmas spirit.

"This place brings back so many fond memories," Ellen said. "I remember when I was five years old, and we came here with Mom. Both of you took off work that day to see me perform in a kindergarten reenactment of the Nativity story. I played the role of a shepherdess and had only one line, but I was still so nervous to speak in front of everyone's parents. I was thankful that you and Mom were able to come. After the performance, we headed downtown to eat a late lunch. It began to snow as we entered the city, and I kept saying that the snow must be a sign that Santa was here. When we walked into Marshall Field's, I was mesmerized by all of the sights and sounds. And then seeing the giant tree ... I felt like I had taken a trip to the North Pole. It was wonderful."

"I remember that day, too," I said. "It really tickled your mom and me to see you so excited. As we drove through downtown Chicago, you kept saying, 'The lights are so beautiful. They're so beautiful.' And your eyes almost popped out of your head when you saw the giant Christmas tree here."

"Christmas as a five-year-old certainly is magical," Ellen said. "That was probably my most memorable Christmas season ever. Not only was it the year we first came here, but it also was the year that I picked out my treasured antique Saint Nick figurine, the one Mom bought for me from the Community House's Santa's Workshop. It was also the first year you took me to Long Grove."

"Long Grove," I said. "It's been a long time since I was there. What a marvelous town. I wonder if it is still as charming as it was back then."

"I was there just last year with a couple of friends," Ellen said. "It's still the same. The red-brick sidewalks and quaint little shops make you feel like you're in a Norman Rockwell painting. The old covered bridge is still standing, and the little country church with the tall white steeple is still there also. It's really a bustling place around the holidays. They have horse-drawn carriage rides and live reindeer each weekend in December. The day I was there, carolers were decked in Victorian garb, singing in front of the village tavern. It was really nice."

"It sounds really nice," I said. "We'll have to go back there sometime."

"We definitely should go back," Ellen agreed.

At that point a man in a long black coat, accompanying a woman with a bright red sweater, walked past our table. The man was carrying a shopping bag that depicted a scene from the movie *It's a Wonderful Life*—the scene at the end of the movie with George Bailey singing "Hark, the Herald Angels Sing" with his family in front of the Christmas tree.

"Dad, didn't someone compare you to George Bailey once?" Ellen asked.

"Yes, a long time ago," I said with a smile, this one natural. "Your mother must have told you that."

"She did," Ellen said. "That's quite a compliment."

"It may have been the nicest compliment I ever received," I said, "except it wasn't intended as a compliment."

"Really? How so?"

"Well, it's sort of one of those situations where you had to be there to understand, but I'll try to explain. It was 1975, and I was at a commencement dinner from graduate school. We had a small class of graduates; there were only about twenty of us. Professor McGill, the head of the graduate program, emceed the dinner. He had a wonderful sense of humor and could really work a crowd. One by one, he told witty anecdotes about all the graduates, and he had everyone laughing. But when he came to me, all he could come up with was a George Bailey comparison. He said, 'Ever see the movie *It's a Wonderful Life*? Well, ladies and gentleman, I give you George Bailey.' He said it in a way that sounded funny, and everyone chuckled, but I think many of the attendees did not know why they were laughing. Sure, I was even thinner then than I am now, but I didn't really look like Jimmy Stewart in any other way."

"Sounds like he was trying to make light of your boy-next-door personality," Ellen said.

"That makes the most sense, but I was never really sure. In any case, even though Professor McGill was just trying to be funny, I still thought it was nice to be compared to George."

"You could do worse."

"No doubt," I agreed. "Now I just wish I had a guardian angel looking after me like George did."

She smiled playfully. "You mean an angel second-class, like Clarence from the movie?"

"I think I'd need more than a second-class guardian angel to help me out," I said with a chuckle.

Ellen leaned back in her chair, her eyes scanning the room as she took in the holiday scene. I could see that she was feeling nostalgic. I know I was.

"Look at the man at the table to our right," said Ellen, discreetly tilting her head in that direction. "Doesn't he remind you of Father Bob?"

I glanced to the right and saw an overweight gentleman with white hair and a white beard. "He sure does," I agreed.

Father Bob was the pastor of St. Mary's Church years before Father Tom came along. Sadly, he died when Ellen was still in grade school. He was a kindhearted man, filled with spirit, and all the kids loved him.

"I remember how each Christmas Eve we would drop off our gifts for the family sponsorship program before attending Mass," Ellen said. "Father Bob was always dressed as Santa Claus, which was perfect because he looked just like him. You and Mom would tell me that we were bringing the gifts to Santa so he could distribute them to the family we were sponsoring."

"Yes, I remember," I said. "Then after Mass, we would go to the Old Swedish Smorgasbord for dinner. Do you remember that place? It closed down a long time ago. I recall that the food wasn't that great, but it was our tradition."

"I remember," she said.

"You would always be so excited when we finally got home. Your mother and I used to worry that you wouldn't fall asleep, but no matter how excited you were, you always did."

"I remember driving home after dinner; how the entire block would have luminarias lining the street. That's when my excitement started to skyrocket," Ellen said. "It was beautiful. It's a shame that custom faded away, but I guess people were afraid of fires."

"I suppose that's why it fell out of favor," I agreed, "but you're right—it really was something to see the entire street lined with candles."

Ellen and I enjoyed reminiscing during our lunch together at the Walnut Room. After we finished eating, we headed to St. Gregory the Illuminator Church on Diversey Avenue. It was our annual tradition to stop by the church to pay our respects to the victims of the Christian Holocaust. St. Gregory's was an Armenian church that was established in the year 1915. My family had been going there since shortly after its establishment. Although both of my parents were devout Catholics, my grandmother on my mother's side of the family was Armenian Orthodox and narrowly escaped death during the Christian Holocaust of World War I. My grandmother was very proud of her heritage and always reminded me that Armenia was the first nation in the history of the world to adopt Christianity as its official religion. She married my grandfather, a devout Catholic German, in 1921. In deference to him, she agreed to have her children and grandchildren raised Catholic, but she made us promise to never forget the 1.5 million Armenians and Assyrians who were brutally massacred by the Ottoman Turks during World War I—murdered solely because they were Orthodox Christians.

"You know, your great-grandmother and great-grandfather are the reasons I became a professor," I said.

"Really? How is that?"

"Both of them were involved in major historical events during World War I," I said. "As you know, your great-grandmother barely survived genocide at the hands of the Muslim Turks in 1915. Well, your great-grandfather's brush with history was no less impressive. He partook in the legendary Flanders cease-fire of 1914."

Ellen looked perplexed. "What was the Flanders cease-fire?"

"It was a remarkable event, a truly remarkable event—one that proved that there is hope for humanity." Clearing my throat, I proceeded to eagerly relate the story of the miraculous cease-fire. "In the early winter of 1914, the Germans were engaged in a fierce battle with the British and the French in the Belgian province of Flanders. Focused on victory, both sides were strategically entrenched in eight-foot-deep ditches. They doggedly fired upon each other from their muddy lairs. The sounds of cannons roared day and night, interrupted only by human cries of agony. There was seemingly no end in sight. Then, all of a sudden, there was a change.

"As Christmas Day approached, the German soldiers put up small Christmas trees, lit with candles, outside of their trenches. In the spirit of the season, they began to sing carols in their native tongue. Seeing the trees and hearing the familiar songs, the British and the French troops also began to sing, and a spontaneous truce resulted. Signs were lifted on both sides, calling for a cease-fire. It was not long before the previously bitter opponents sang in harmony together. Miraculously, soldiers left their trenches and met in the middle of no-man's-land to shake hands and exchange gifts. They took time to bury their dead and then played a soccer match. For a precious moment, in the midst of the horrible war, there was peace and goodwill."

"I didn't know that Great-grandpa Alfred was in the army," Ellen said.

"He was in the German infantry," I said. "The cease-fire saved his life. Just a few days after the cease-fire your great-grandfather was wounded in battle. He could barely walk, and he soon found himself surrounded by British soldiers. They were about to open fire upon him but at the last second, they received an order to halt from a British sergeant, who had befriended your great-grandfather during the cease-fire. Instead of being killed, your great-grandfather was mercifully taken prisoner and after the war moved to England, where he met your great-grandmother, who had come to England with her family as refugees from Turkey. They instantly fell in love, got married, and eventually moved to Chicago. I'm surprised your great-grandpa never told you the story because he loved to tell stories."

"I don't remember his ever telling me about the war, but he did like to tell me stories. He used to always tell me about our ancestors and how we were descendants from royalty," Ellen said.

"I know," I said with a sigh. "Not just any royalty, either. He claimed—

without any proof, mind you—that we were direct descendants of Charlemagne, although he referred to him by his German name, Karl the Great. He would go through our entire lineage, generations and generations, and have an anecdote about every one. Your great-grandfather could really be a character at times."

"I remember that he had all of these little sayings," Ellen said.

"That he did," I agreed. "'It is nice to be important,' he would say, 'but it is more important to be nice.' That was one of his clichés that I've always tried to live by."

"Me, too," Ellen said.

"In any case," I continued, "with such strong family connections to World War I, I grew up a huge World War I history buff. I read countless books about the war and the people who were affected by it. I found it fascinating. My interest in history grew over time, and soon enough, I became a professor."

"It was Providence that you did because I can't imagine your doing anything else. You were made for that job."

"I do love my work," I said. "I'm blessed in that regard."

After a thirty-minute car ride through the city, Ellen and I arrived at St. Gregory's. The old Armenian church was decorated for Christmas with pretty blue lights and wreaths with red bows, but our visit there did not conjure up warm feelings of Christmas. Rather, it brought out feelings of sympathy. To me, the church was a somber reminder of the holocaust that had taken place decades ago. Although I was not a part of it, I remembered my grandmother's pain and shared in it.

Over one and a half million innocent people senselessly massacred, I thought. *And they've been all but forgotten by the majority of the world.*

Opening up the door to the church, Ellen and I solemnly went inside where we knelt in a pew and said a brief prayer in remembrance of the holocaust victims. At the front of the church was a small altar adorned with an icon of the Blessed Virgin holding the infant Jesus. Mary wore blue garments covered with a red shall. On her head was a golden crown, signifying her role as Queen of Heaven. The Christ child was on her lap, dressed in yellow. He was holding up his right hand, as if he was blessing the world. Admiring the icon, I reached into my coat pocket and pulled out a locket that my grandmother had given to me when I was very young. The old wooden locket contained the same icon, and I always brought it with me whenever I visited St. Gregory's.

"Keep this in remembrance," I recalled my grandmother saying when she handed me the locket. "My father gave it to me before he was taken away by the Muslim Turks, and now I give it to you."

I loved my grandmother very much. The locket was the sole possession that I had to remember her by. There were no pictures; they were lost in a basement

101

flood when I was a young man. To me, the locket was a treasure, and I held it close to my heart. It had so much meaning for me; it was a symbol of both love and sadness, two emotions that I had become quite accustomed to.

"I've haven't forgotten," I whispered as I grasped the locket in my hand, "and I never will."

Ellen and I were only at St. Gregory's about fifteen minutes before we turned to leave. It had been a long but good day, and we were ready to head home. I took one last glance at the icon on the altar before making my way to the exit. On the way out the door, I silently prayed, *Lord, please bless us, and please bless all those who suffer.* Then, I slipped two hundred dollars into the church's donation bin, sighing softly as I did.

Chapter 14
THE MIRACLE OF DUNKIRK

"WHAT ABOUT DUNKIRK?" asked Tom, the brightest student in my Religion and History class.

"What about Dunkirk?" I echoed, questioning the rest of the group.

"Dunkirk was just a product of British wartime propaganda," said Katie, a young feminist and one of my most outspoken students.

"Perhaps," I said.

"I think Medjugorje and Fatima would be better examples," said Chris, a serious student with thick-rimmed glasses who took religion to heart.

"Definitely," agreed Arthur, a less serious and more boisterous version of Chris. "Medjugorje and Fatima are the best examples of miracles in the twentieth century."

"It's hard to argue with Medjugorje and Fatima," I said, "but let's stick with the topic of Dunkirk for a while."

Although my Religion and History class was small—only eight students—it was often livelier than my larger classes and was the sole element of my job that still captured my interest during my period of depression. In everything else, I just went through the motions, which was easy to do, having taught for so many years. Our topic of discussion that day was the Venerable Bede and his famous work, *The Ecclesiastical History of the English People*. Written in the year 731, it was a history of England, covering the time of Julius Caesar to the date of its completion. It was considered by many to be the most important and accurate reference on England's early period. Throughout the work, Bede, a Northumbrian monk and careful scholar, commented on numerous miraculous events, recording them in the same way he recorded the dates of battles and the deaths of kings. In reading his work, it was evident that the meticulous historian accepted miracles as commonplace. *Not a surprise, considering he was a devout monk*, I thought.

With Bede's acceptance of miracles as a focal point, I posed the question to the class: "If modern-day history was recorded by devout Christian believers instead of pure secularists, which twentieth-century historical events would be deemed miraculous?"

Tom's Dunkirk proposal was the first answer to my question.

"Why did Tom suggest Dunkirk?" I questioned the group.

"Because Winston Churchill called Dunkirk a 'miracle' as a means to rouse the spirits of the British people," Katie blurted out.

"Is that why you brought up Dunkirk?" I asked Tom.

"No," he unequivocally answered. "Although Churchill did say that Dunkirk was a miracle, that is not why I brought it up. I brought it up because what happened there was truly inconceivable."

Pleased with Tom's response, I cleared my throat and prepared to launch into a long discourse. "Dunkirk is a coastal town in northern France, situated across the English Channel from Britain. During World War II, the Nazis had the entire British army trapped there. As you know, at the onset of the war, the Nazi military marched through Europe with unprecedented velocity. Equipped with legions of heavily armored tanks and swarms of Stuka dive bombers, they brought terror to all who stood in their way. Their onslaught began in 1939 with an unprovoked invasion of Poland. Then, in just a few short months, they ran practically unopposed through Norway, Denmark, Holland, Luxembourg, and Belgium. Luxembourg fell in just one day, and Holland in just four. Even heavily fortified Belgium only lasted twenty-eight days.

"To the Christian world, the ease with which the Nazis spread their evil was startling. Understandably so, the people of Europe lived in constant fear—fear of death and fear of Hitler's tyranny. In an effort to help their beleaguered allies, the British sent their entire army to the Continent to try to halt the advance, but they lacked the resources. In May 1940, the Nazis escalated their aggression and invaded France. Although self-confident, the ill-prepared French were no match for the Nazi war machine. Their munitions were outdated, and their defense plans were inept. They lost battle after battle, completely overwhelmed by the blitzkrieg—the lightning war. With the meek French Resistance collapsing quickly, the situation for the British was grim. Armed only with rifles and light artillery, they had no effective defense against the powerful Nazi tanks that rolled over the French countryside. Seeing that they could not win without tanks of their own, they ran in full retreat toward the coast. They were desperate to escape; they were desperate in general. The British knew if their army were to be destroyed, then there would be no stopping Hitler. The stakes were ever so high. Not only was the British Empire at grave risk but the Church itself. As Winston Churchill said, 'Upon this battle depends the survival of Christian civilization.'

"By late May, the Nazi tanks were fast approaching from the east, and the Nazi air force, the Luftwaffe, was mercilessly dropping bombs from above. Even if the Luftwaffe could have been held at bay, a rescue was impossible because the waters of the English Channel were too shallow for large military transport vessels and were much too rough for small vessels. There appeared to be no hope left. Anticipating the worst, the British leaders announced that the nation should prepare itself for dreadful news. Many readied themselves for surrender. General Sir Edmund Ironside lamented, 'This is the end of the British Empire.'

"On the beaches of Dunkirk, the forlorn British servicemen dropped to their knees in prayer. It was all they had left to turn to. To them, it seemed that the hour of doom had truly come. Then, miraculously, a series of unlikely events unfolded. First, Hitler called off his tanks. To this day, no one knows why. Then, a dense fog rolled in, and the English Channel became as still as a mill pond. The fog was totally uncharacteristic of the season, and the waters had never before been so placid. Because of the heavy fog, the Luftwaffe was grounded. The helpless men on the beaches could not believe their good fortune. But that was just the beginning. They had yet to witness the true miracle. In the heavy mist, they could barely make out a remarkable sight on the horizon. When they did, they rubbed their eyes in disbelief. What they saw approaching from across the English Channel was the strangest armada in the history of the world. You see, the British leaders had put out a plea to their people for assistance to rescue the soldiers trapped in France, and the good citizens of England responded with bravery and faith. Boats of every shape and size came from across the Channel: transport ships, motor boats, fishing smacks, river cruisers, trawlers, barges, yachts, lifeboats, and paddle streamers. Many of the boats had previously only sailed on the Thames and were not fit for a rough sea voyage. But by the grace of God, they successfully made the journey on the quiet sea. Because of the unusual armada, over three hundred thousand British soldiers were saved, over ten times the number that the most optimistic estimates had predicted."

As I spoke, the students listened intently. They hung on to every word.

"The skies remained fogged and the water calm, just long enough for them to complete their mission," I added. "The timing of the uncharacteristic weather was perfect; it was providential. It is said that the same Lord Almighty, who centuries before had parted the Red Sea, had again intervened, halting the Nazi advance in order to preserve his Church."

"That's a lot to chalk up to chance alone," said Chris.

"Yeah!" Arthur enthusiastically agreed.

Katie remained silent.

"There's actually more to the story," I said. "Just before the miraculous rescue, the people of England came together in a National Day of Prayer, led by the Archbishop of Canterbury. Throughout the entire country, Christians poured into churches to pray for their sons, husbands, and fathers. School classes were interrupted and pubs were emptied. The unity of faith was remarkable. There had never been anything like it, before or since."

"A nation prayed, and a miracle occurred," Arthur said. "That sounds like something Bede would have written about."

"True," Tom and Chris blurted out in unison.

I glanced over to Katie to see if she had anything to add—she almost always did—but she continued her silence.

"What else would you include on the list?" I questioned.

"Pope John Paul II," answered Liz, a sorority girl by looks but a true scholar nonetheless and one with the faith of a child. I was impressed by her answer.

"Tell the class how the life of Pope John Paul II could be construed as a miracle," I said.

"Well, first of all, his pontificate fulfilled a prophecy by Padre Pio, the great twentieth-century mystic from San Giovanni Rotondo," she said. "Decades before he was elected pope, John Paul met Pio, who told him that he would become pope and also told him that he would suffer an assassination attempt. 'I see you in a white robe stained with blood,' Pio said.

"Not only that," she continued, "but John Paul's election as pope was a miracle itself. He was the first non-Italian pontiff in over four hundred years. Given the troubles in the world at the time, he was the perfect man for the job. Divine intervention, perhaps? I think it likely was. As pope, he traveled the entire world—more than all the other popes combined—fighting for human freedom, morality, and the sanctity of life. He galvanized the anti-abortion movement, and he took a particularly strong stand against the Soviet Union and Communism. The Berlin Wall would have never fallen, were it not for him. Catholicism would have sharply declined, were it not for him. He certainly changed the course of history, and I have no doubt that he will one day be called Saint John Paul the Great."

"Very good," I said to Liz. "I think it's fair to add that one to our list. Anyone else?"

There was no answer. "All right, I have one for you," I said. "What do you think about the acquisition of Jerusalem by the British in World War I?"

The students just looked at me with blank stares.

"Most people wouldn't think of that as a miracle, but if you consider the circumstances, you could argue for it," I said. "Does anyone want to try to read my mind and tell me what I'm thinking?" Everyone stayed silent, even Tom, so I began to explain my rationale.

"When most people think of World War I, they think of Germany, France, Britain, and trench warfare, or they think of the Bolshevik Revolution in Russia," I said. "Yet perhaps the most monumental event to occur in World War I was the British reclamation of the Holy Land from the Ottoman Empire. Prior to the reclamation, Jerusalem had been in Muslim control for over six hundred years, dating back to the Crusades. No one ever dreamed it would return to Christian hands, and had it not been for divine Providence, it may never have. Yes, modern scholars tell us that by the beginning of the twentieth century, the Ottoman Empire was on the decline. Yet when the British engaged the Turks in battle at the beginning of World War I, they suffered nothing but defeat. The modern day Mohammedans proved to be as stalwart as their ancestors. The course of battle did not change until General Edmund Allenby took command of the British forces."

Pausing for a second, I raised my eyebrows so that my eyes were exceptionally wide and said, "Here's where one can argue that the hand of God was in play. You see, Allenby was a devout Christian who carried the Bible with him everywhere he went. Not only that, he also was a Zionist—he believed that the establishment of the state of Israel was a necessary step in the path to the Second Coming of Christ. Allenby used passages from the Bible to guide his military decisions and, in doing so, routed the Ottoman army. Driven by nothing but his faith in God, he accomplished something that Richard the Lionheart and all the other crusaders had failed to do."

The students' eyes were now wide also.

"What makes the story really interesting," I continued, "was that the decisive battle to free the Holy Land was fought in a place called Mediggo. Does anyone know the English name for the town of Mediggo?"

I looked at each student in the group one at a time and each one gave a gentle shake of the head—until I came to Tom, who was subtly smiling.

With a deep voice, Tom answered confidently, slowly enunciating each syllable for added stress. "Ar-ma-ged-don."

Speechless, the rest of the group seemed amazed by his answer and turned to me for confirmation.

After a brief dramatic pause, I said, "Yes, Armageddon. Armageddon, or Har-Magedon, means 'Valley of Mediggo.' In true biblical fashion, the Zionist quest was fulfilled because of Allenby's triumph on the fields of the Lord."

I was very impressed that Tom knew the answer and was even more impressed with his next display of knowledge.

"Those of the Baha'i faith believe that the battle at Mediggo in World

War I was the same battle described in the Book of Revelation," Tom added. "They believe that Allenby's victory fulfilled Saint John the Apostle's ancient prophecy."

"True," I said.

"Wow," said Arthur. "The twentieth century was a very biblical century."

"Yes, it was," I said. "If looked at in a Christian way, instead of a purely secular way, it was perhaps the most biblical century since the time of Christ."

"That is awesome when you think about it," said Chris. Several other students made similar remarks.

I could not help but smile. The students were all good kids, and their interest and enthusiasm was contagious. "Is there anything else you would add to our list?" I asked the group. No one answered, so I prepared to make a statement of dismissal. However, as soon as I opened my mouth, I was unexpectedly interrupted.

"I think the Ipatiev House should be included," said Vladimir, a usually introverted young man with a Russian accent.

The Ipatiev House? I thought to myself. I had never heard of it. Looking around, I could tell that none of the other students had heard of it either.

"What is the Ipatiev House?" I questioned.

"It is an isolated military compound, hidden deep within the Ural Mountains in Russia," said Vladimir. "It is where Czar Nicholas and his family were brutally murdered by Lenin and the Communists."

"How is that a miracle?" Katie chided, rolling her eyes.

"Let him explain," I said, giving Katie a look of displeasure.

Taking a deep breath, Vladimir held it in for a moment but then expelled his breath and answered. He spoke timidly at first but gained confidence with each word. "Czar Nicholas was the head of the Russian Orthodox Church," he said. "He was a good man who loved his family and loved God. His execution marked the triumph of Communism over Christianity, and the Ipatiev House was the site of that triumph. Decades later, in celebration of the collapse of the Soviet Union, a group of Christian workers erected a cross where the Ipatiev House once stood. At the onset of their work, the sky was covered with dark clouds, and a heavy snow was falling. But then, miraculously, the clouds suddenly parted, allowing a brilliant ray of light to fall directly on the cross. The light circumscribed a halo, and no snow fell on that area. The snow was still coming down heavily everywhere else but not over the illuminated cross. The local villagers believed—and still do believe—that the brilliant halo was a sign from heaven."

I was surprised that Vladimir spoke without being called upon—that was a first. I wanted to encourage him to speak more, but looking at the clock, I saw that we had run slightly overtime, so instead, I simply thanked him for his contribution and then dismissed the class.

- - - - - - - - - -

Winter break was in a few days. As usual, Christmas came and went very quickly. Next up was January, the coldest and bleakest month in Chicago. January was always difficult to deal with, even under the best of circumstances. At least December had the holidays, and February had the hope that spring was not far off. January, however, had nothing positive to offer. Despite the cold and darkness, I coped quite admirably. The more time that passed with Ellen's doing well on the experimental therapy, the more hope I found. It helped that I was staying busy with writing, and it also helped that the Bears were having a very good year—the Monsters of the Midway were a welcome distraction.

Led by a stout defense, the Bears won their division and finished the regular season with a 13–3 record, earning a bye in the first round of the playoffs and earning home-field advantage throughout the playoffs. They played their first playoff game against the Seattle Seahawks on January 14 in front of a sold-out crowd at Soldier Field. It was a close game all the way, with the Seahawks leading by three heading into the fourth quarter, but the Bears finally pulled it out in overtime, 27–24.

"Much closer than I would have liked," said Jerry, "but a win is a win."

The next game was against the New Orleans Saints. This one wasn't close. Dominating from start to finish, the Bears won 39–14 to advance to the Super Bowl.

"Yes! Yes! Yes!" shouted Jerry at the end of the Saints game. "We're going to the show! We're going to the show!"

I wasn't as vocal about the win as Jerry. I felt more relieved than overjoyed. I was just happy the Bears hadn't blown it. The victory guaranteed me two more weeks of distraction, and I was thankful to have that distraction.

Soon enough, Super Bowl Sunday arrived. I went over to Jerry's to watch the game. We didn't want to go to Al's Pub because we thought it would be too crowded, and we were afraid we wouldn't get a good view of the action. We chose comfort and convenience over the thrill of the crowd. That was not the choice we'd usually make. In past years, we would have claimed our seats at the bar right after it opened, but we were getting older, and the thought of spending all day at Al's was not as appealing.

It was just the two of us at Jerry's. Joyce had no interest in football and was out shopping at the start of the game, and Ellen was going out with Jack to a Super Bowl party at a friend's house. I was glad that Ellen was getting out.

Jack, of course, was rooting for the Indianapolis Colts, the Bears' opponent. Normally, I would have commented to Jerry about how irritating Jack was, but I'd had a change of heart. I was glad that he hadn't abandoned Ellen in her time of illness. I was sure he would, but I was thankfully wrong.

Jerry had chips and guacamole prepared when I came over. He sat in his easy chair, and I settled on the couch, and we turned on the pregame show.

"Remember the 1985 season?" he said. "That was my greatest sports thrill of all time. Nothing even comes close. The Bears lose only one game all year and dominate their way to a Super Bowl victory. That was amazing."

"I agree," I said, trying to sound enthusiastic but probably not succeeding. It wasn't that I didn't find the topic of discussion interesting—I certainly did—it's just that given my state of mind, I found it hard to truly get excited or feel pleasure. "That was a good year. The only other time I came close to feeling that way was when St. John's won the National Championship in 2003."

"Yeah, I remember that," said Jerry. "You drove up to Collegeville, Minnesota, to catch a couple of games that year."

"Yep, I was there when St. John's beat Bethel, making John Gagliardi the all-time winningest coach in college football history."

"Isn't he the coach with the Rule of No's?" Jerry asked.

"He's the one," I said. "He has a very unorthodox coaching style. No tackling in practice; no warm-up drills; no playbooks; no whistles; no clipboards; no grading films; no blocking sleds or tackling dummies; no yelling at players; no practice in rain, extreme heat, or cold; no meetings; no cheerleaders; no trash talk; and no rules—except the Golden Rule."

"That's a lot of no's," said Jerry.

"It is," I said, "but it works for him. That 2003 season was really a storybook season. Not only did the coach set the record, but St. John's went undefeated, including a stunning upset of the nation's number-one team. If what they did had happened at the Division I level, instead of the Division III level, it would have gone down as one of the greatest stories in the history of sports. The team they played in the championship, Mount Union, was the Goliath of Division III football. They came into the game with a fifty-five–game winning streak and had crushed all of their opponents that year. As a matter of fact, Mount Union won the semifinal game, 66–0. Although St. John's was a very good team, they squeaked by in a few of their victories and were in no way a juggernaut like Mount Union. Mount Union had a lot of transfers from Division I schools. Their players were much bigger and faster than the players for St. John's. Yet that didn't matter. In the end, the game wasn't even close. St. John's routed Mount Union, 24–6. Their toughness and intelligence was enough to overcome the physical superiority of their opponent."

"I remember seeing highlights from that game on ESPN," said Jerry. "The anchors at ESPN kept commenting on how big the Mount Union players were compared to the St. John's players. They emphasized how monumental the win was because with Mount Union's loss, the longest active winning streak in college football had been snapped. At the end of the broadcast, they did a segment on your coach and 'Winning with No's.'"

"It's unusual for Division III schools to get any coverage on national TV," I said, "but that was a special team. Yep, that team and the 1985 Bears were the teams that brought me the most joy in sports. I hope this year's Bears team will be added to that list."

"We're due for a football champion in this city," said Jerry. "We're past due. It's gotta happen. I can just feel it. I know it's going to happen."

The Super Bowl began well. The Bears led 14–6 at the end of the first quarter, and Jerry was cheering like crazy. His enthusiasm was unbridled. He jumped up from his easy chair several times and paced back and forth, bellowing in excitement at the TV set, as if the players could actually hear him. While Jerry shouted at the top of his lungs, I watched with hopeful anticipation. I so wanted my pleasant diversion to end on a positive note. When the Bears stopped an Indianapolis drive at the 36-yard line, forcing a punt, it looked like everything was going their way, but things took an unfortunate turn for the worst after that. Plagued by turnovers and an anemic offense, they scored only three more points the rest of the game and ended up losing, 29–17.

"Pitiful!" Jerry shouted at the TV screen at the conclusion of the game. "That effort was pitiful! The Bears need a new quarterback. They need a real leader like Peyton Manning. That was just pitiful! How can a team of professionals go out there and perform like that? They looked like a bunch of clowns. They should be ashamed. Grossman should be fired! Pitiful!"

I sat there subdued while Jerry ranted and raved. Sadly, my diversion was over. Just like that, the Bears' loss was added to my ever-growing list of frustrations and disappointments. I didn't stay long after the end of the game. I just felt like going home and being alone. I wanted to collect my thoughts.

"We'll get 'em next year," I said to Jerry, right before I left. I didn't really believe that at all, of course, but it's what fans say when their team isn't doing well.

"Yeah, I know. I know. We say that every year," he said, still pacing in frustration over the loss. "And it never happens! I swear I'm going to give up watching football. It's too incredibly frustrating! All it leads to is disappointment. It's like pounding your head against a wall, over and over again. Why do we do it? Why? I swear, I'm giving up football!"

"You say that every year, too, and it never happens," I said with a forced wink and a smile. "The sun will still come up tomorrow. You'll see."

With that, I left and drove home. I was not in my car long before a series of dark thoughts started to take control of my mind. I ruminated about Ellen's health and about the lawsuit. All at once, everything seemed so complex and so overwhelming. Prior to the game, I had been teetering on the brink of major depression, and the Bears' loss tipped me over the edge. Nevertheless, I tried to remain strong.

"I've pulled myself out of depression before," I whispered to myself. "I can do it again. I just have to gain control of my mind."

Unfortunately, it was not that easy to gain control. The dark thoughts were like a rapidly approaching thunderstorm—in the blink of an eye, they clouded everything. Searching for a ray of light, I tried to rationalize, but my rationalizations just led to more ruminations. Negatives were followed by more negatives, and my mind was left spinning in a whirlpool of despair and doubt.

Once I got home, I started pacing back and forth nervously. My heart began pounding, and I developed a splitting headache. It was my own version of a panic attack. I hated the feeling of pure anxiety. "I wish I drank," I said to myself, "because I could use a good strong drink."

I had been a teetotaler all of my life; I didn't really have a reason. Initially, I didn't drink because the peer pressure I received in high school and college had the opposite effect on me. The more people urged me to drink, the more I wasn't going to do it. Then later, I didn't drink because being a teetotaler was part of who I was. It had become part of my identity.

It's probably good I don't drink, I reasoned, *because given my level of anxiety, I'd end up an alcoholic.*

Later that night, I thought back to my conversation with Jerry that preceded the game.

Maybe I should try to simplify things, I thought. *Maybe I should have my own rule of no's.*

I sat for a while and pondered. Filled with pessimism and self-pity, I came up with only two—"No more hope" and "No more happiness."

Sighing in frustration, I started to pray.

"Lord Jesus Christ, please don't let me fall to the lure of self-pity. Please don't let me be overcome by depression. I'm at the end of my rope. Show me the way, oh God. Be my shepherd. Be my guide. Please help me. Please help us."

Chapter 15

FLOWERS ON THE GRAVE

THREE TIMES A year I would take a short trip out to Saint James Cemetery, where Tina was buried. I would go there on her birthday, on the day we first met, and on the day she died. I always brought a bouquet of tulips with me. Tulips were Tina's favorite flower. Seeing them would always make her smile.

"Heaven must be filled with tulips," I remembered her saying.

"Heaven must be filled with smiles like yours," I now whispered to myself.

It was February 12, Tina's birthday. As I drove to the cemetery, with the tulips on the car seat next to me, I recalled the first time I discovered Tina's love of the flower. The episode occurred a long time ago, on a beautiful day in May. Taking advantage of the weather, the two of us decided to visit Long Grove one afternoon. Tina and I had never been there, but we had heard wonderful things about the place. We were not at all disappointed. The charming old town had tulips planted everywhere, rows and rows. The colors were magnificent: red, orange, yellow, pink, and purple. The tulips surrounded the quaint shops, some of which were painted in colorful tones themselves. In many ways, the scene looked unreal; it looked like a dream. I recalled Tina saying that the colors were so vibrant that it reminded her of Munchkinland from *The Wizard of Oz*. I had to agree. Tina was so inspired by the tulips in Long Grove that she insisted on going to Amsterdam in the springtime, once we retired.

She used to say, "I need to see the tulips in Holland before I die."

Unfortunately, we never made it to Holland, but I always brought the tulips to Saint James.

Saint James was a beautiful cemetery, with a chapel near the entrance. In front of the chapel was a large stone with an inscription from the epitaph of Thomas Gray's "Elegy Written in a Country Churchyard." The inscription was moving. It read:

> Here rests his head upon the lap of Earth
> A youth to Fortune and Fame unknown.
> Fair Science frown'd not upon his humble birth,
> And Melancholy mark'd him for her own.
>
> Large was his bounty, and his soul sincere,
> Heav'n did a recompense as largely send:
> He gave to Mis'ry all he had, a tear,
> And gain'd from Heav'n ('twas all he wish'd) a friend.
>
> No farther seek his merits to disclose,
> Or draw his frailties from their dread abode,
> (There they alike in trembling hope repose)
> The bosom of his Father and his God.[10]

After stopping briefly to read the inscription, I walked along the roadside until I came to her headstone. As I stood there, a deep sadness came over me, one that always came over me when I visited the cemetery. With tear-filled eyes, I gently laid the tulips on her grave. I then knelt on the frozen ground and said a prayer. My feelings of sorrow were stronger than ever that day. I was sad not only for my wife but also for my daughter and myself. Life had turned so hard. There was so much turmoil. I was desperate for a reprieve. I prayed for peace. "Lord, please bless my family and me. Please deliver us from harm. Please deliver us from anxiety and sadness. Please grant us mercy."

During my prayer, a dark black raven landed on the ground next to me. It looked exactly the same as the raven I had seen in the forest preserve weeks before.

"You're back," I whispered.

The presence of the black bird along with my melancholy spirit again reminded me of Poe's famous poem. There is a line in the poem that asks the question, "Is there balm in Gilead?" (Is there happiness in heaven?) I myself pondered that very question. In the poem, the raven answers, "Nevermore."

Turning to the jet-black raven standing by my side, I asked, "Is there … is there happiness in heaven?"

---

10 Adapted from URL: http://en.wikisource.org/wiki/Elegy_Written_in_a_Country_Churchyard. Downloaded 1-31-09.

The raven stood silent, not uttering a sound. It simply stood there, facing Tina's grave, just as I was. If I were crazed, I would have sworn it was mocking me. I chose to ignore the bird, and I continued my prayer. I prayed for Tina. I prayed for Ellen. I prayed for mercy. I concluded with the Lord's Prayer. The raven finally broke its silence and shrieked out as I whispered "Amen." Just then, I heard a sound like footsteps from behind. The raven seemed startled and quickly flew off. I looked around to see if anyone was there.

I was surprised to see an old man with snow-white hair and quarter-inch–thick glasses. He looked to be in his late seventies. He was carrying several bundles of flowers. The old man walked up to me, peered sympathetically into my sorrow-filled eyes, and said, "Life is hard sometimes, very hard. There are days when it seems like you're alone in the woods with the devil. But the human spirit is strong, and it is never long before hope comes knocking at your door."

The old man then set down his flowers and extended his hand to me. "Hello. I'm Anthony Woewucki," he said. "Call me Tony."

He seemed familiar. I was almost certain that I had met him before, but I could not place where or when. I shook his hand and replied, "Nice to meet you, Tony. My name is Fred Sankt."

I definitely thought it was odd to be approached by a stranger in a cemetery, especially one who approached with such a greeting, but one look at him told me that he was harmless. My first impression was that he was slightly senile, but after conversing with him a while, I decided that he was just a lonely old man with an unusual manner who was trying to be friendly. He explained that he came to the cemetery often. He was a war veteran who was there to decorate the graves of his old war buddies.

"These were great men," the old man said of his deceased friends. "The greatest of men. They weren't rich or famous. Most of them struggled to just get by, but they worked hard and were honest. More than that, they were family men. Each and every one of them put God and family above everything else. That's what makes men great, not fame or fortune." The old man then started reciting a poetic verse:

"Let not Ambition mock their useful toil,
Their homely joys, and destiny obscure;
Nor Grandeur hear with a disdainful smile
The short and simple annals of the poor.

"The boast of heraldry, the pomp of pow'r,
And all that beauty, all that wealth e'er gave,
Awaits alike th' inevitable hour.

115

The paths of glory lead but to the grave."[11]

"That's eloquent," I said. "Where is it from? I know I've heard it recited before."

"Thomas Gray. It's part of his 'Elegy Written in a Country Churchyard,' just like the epitaph on the stone near the entrance to this cemetery. It's a grand poem. If you've never read the entire thing, you should."

"I will," I said. "I certainly will."

Even though it was a cold winter's day, Tony and I stood outside and talked for quite a while. He told me stories of his war buddies. His bond with them was admirable and uplifting. I told him about Tina. He listened well. I found it very easy to spill my troubles to him. Before I knew it, I had told him about Ellen's melanoma and the lawsuit. The experience was cathartic for me. There were no negative consequences to telling this stranger my problems. I did not have to worry about emotions or what he thought. He was simply a kind stranger who was willing to listen.

---

11   Adapted from URL: http://en.wikisource.org/wiki/Elegy_Written_in_a_
     Country_Churchyard. Downloaded 1-31-09.

Chapter 16

THE BOOK OF PATRICK

SEVERAL WEEKS PASSED, during which I spent my days at work and my nights writing. Writing continued to be the only thing that got my mind off of my troubles. I wrote of Basil the Great, the Bishop of Caesarea, who said:

"A tree is known by its fruit; a man by his deeds. A good deed is never lost. He who sows courtesy reaps friendship, and he who plants kindness gathers love."

Basil was one of the most influential theologians of his era, if not all time, and therefore, in my opinion, warranted a spot in *The Third Testament*. A learned man of high morals, Basil dedicated his life to God, sowing courtesy and planting kindness with his preaching. The words he spoke inspired Christians for generations and led many away from the lure of evil. Using his God-given talents, Basil boldly fought against the heresies of his day and was rightfully honored as a Doctor of the Church. The good bishop was best known for his stance against the Arians and for his promotion of monasticism, but it was another one of his beliefs that caught my attention most. In researching Basil, I came across an interesting fact—the fourth-century saint strongly condemned abortion. He said it was a grave sin, "no matter if the fetus was formed or unformed."

Remarkable, I thought. *That's the same argument that is debated today. In over sixteen hundred years, not much has changed.*

As the Bible has always served as a source of societal morality, I believed it was only appropriate to include moral issues in *The Third Testament*, and I intended to do so as much as I could. Abortion was certainly a major moral issue of the modern era, and it was clear that the Church opposed it, even as early as the third century. After reading Basil's statement—and countless others like his—I temporarily toyed with the idea of including all moral statements on a particular subject, such as abortion, in one section, regardless of when the statements were made, but quickly decided that it was better to keep things in chronological order.

The chronology of events needs to be preserved for historical integrity, I resolved. *The moral issues will be sufficiently addressed as these subjects are brought up again and again over the historical timeline.*

Focusing on the noteworthy saints of the fourth century, I wrote of the great compassion of Saint Nicholas, the legendary bishop from Myra who secretly tossed three bags of gold through the open window of a peasant man's home in order to save the man's daughters from a life of slavery. Nicholas' good deed was the basis for Clement Clarke Moore's famous poem, "A Visit from St. Nicholas," more commonly known as "'Twas the Night before Christmas." The kindhearted bishop was a popular saint before the poem was ever written but became even more so as the poem became a Christmas institution. He easily ranked as one of the top ten most renowned and beloved figures in Christian history and was certainly one of my favorite saints. I wrote:

> In the city of Myra there lived a man of modest means who had three beautiful young daughters. He loved his daughters more than anything in the world, and they loved him. The man was a goodhearted soul who worked hard and worshiped the Lord. He and his daughters had a good life together. Unfortunately, the man fell on to hard times. Work in Myra became scarce, and he was forced to spend every cent he had just to feed his family. Despite his hardships, the man kept a good attitude. He continued to eagerly work at any job that became available, and he continued to keep the faith, but he was just barely able to get by. Time passed, and soon his daughters reached the age of courtship and marriage. However, the man had no money for dowries, so his daughters were without suitors. It deeply saddened the man to see his daughters passed over because of his poverty. Likewise, the daughters were deeply saddened to see their father struggle so. During one particularly harsh winter, the man's financial situation reached its lowest point. He barely ate at all, as he saved whatever food there was for his children. The three girls knew they had to do something. Regrettably, there was only one way for women to earn money in Myra—prostitution. The girls prayed and prayed to the Lord that their father would find work, but it seemed as if there was no hope. Resigned to their fate, the girls one evening laid plans to start their appalling new profession. They did their best to muffle their tears so their father would not hear. Although their father on earth

did not hear their sorrowful cries, their heavenly Father did. Late that same night, after they had finally fallen asleep, the girls were suddenly awakened by a loud thud. They were so startled by the noise that they jumped up from their beds in a panic. "What was that?" they exclaimed. When they looked around, they realized that someone had tossed a cloth bag filled with rocks through their window. Within seconds their father came rushing in to make sure his daughters were all right. He looked at the bag on the floor curiously. "What can this be?" he said. "Why would someone throw a bag of rocks into our home?" He then opened the bag and found that it was not filled with rocks but with shimmering gold. The man and his daughters rushed to the window to look outside, but no one was there. Overcome with emotion, the man dropped to his knees and began to thank God for the great blessing. Equally moved, his daughters cried tears of joy. On the subsequent two evenings, the family was again blessed with bags of gold flung through their window by a mysterious stranger. Three daughters, three bags of gold, three dowries, and three brides—the family's prayers were fulfilled.

The man and his daughters never were able to see who it was who had thrown the gold through their window. If they had only been faster to the scene, they would have caught a glimpse of an old man with a white beard, riding furiously away. The old man was none other than the benevolent bishop of Myra, better known to the world as Saint Nicholas.

He may not have worn red or climbed down chimneys, but the spirit of the man was consistent with Moore's benevolent old elf, I reasoned. He came in secret, in the darkness of the night, bringing gifts to the good, purely for the sake of kindness—that is the essence of the tradition.

Throughout his life, Nicholas was credited with many miracles and was named the patron saint of children, sailors, fishermen, repentant thieves, and of many cities. For centuries, his good deeds were celebrated by Christians from around the world, especially in Holland and Germany. The Dutch pronounced his name as *Sinterklaas*, which eventually evolved into the more familiar Santa Claus.

"Jolly old St. Nicholas ..." I crooned to myself as I typed.

After completing the brief section on Saint Nicholas, I wrote of Saint Athanasius and Saint Ambrose. The former was a great champion against heresy, and the latter was a gifted orator. It was Ambrose who coined the phrase, "When in Rome, do as the Romans do."

I then wrote of Saint Augustine of Hippo and of his many words of wisdom. Augustine, a great theologian and Doctor of the Church, pursued the pleasures of the flesh in his youth, rejecting God and ridiculing those of faith, but he miraculously converted to Christianity in the year 386. The story of his conversion was truly biblical in nature.

One day, while walking alone in a garden in Rome, Augustine experienced a spiritual crisis. Pondering the criticisms of his saintly mother, Monica, he began to question the merits of his life and the sinful ways in which he lived. He soon was in torment, torn between hedonism and Christ. He did not want to give up his life of pleasure, but he knew in his heart that it was wrong. He wept from the anguish that plagued his mind and cried out to God. As he cried out, he heard children in the distance chanting the words "*Tolle et lege, tolle et lege*," meaning "Take and read, take and read." At that moment he turned and saw a Bible on a nearby table in the garden. He picked up the Bible and read the first passage that caught his eye:

> "Not in rioting and drunkenness, not in chambering and wantonness, not in strife and envying, but put on the Lord Jesus Christ, and make not provision for the flesh to fulfill the lusts thereof."[12]

It was then and there that Augustine dedicated his life to Christ and went on to become one of the most prominent Christians of all time.

I included several excerpts from Augustine's autobiographical work, *Confessions*, in *The Third Testament*, recounting his conversion and eventual baptism. In reviewing *Confessions*, I was particularly impressed with Saint Monica, a truly moral and compassionate woman who was terribly troubled by the waywardness of her son. She impressed me because never once did she give up on him, no matter how horribly he behaved or how viciously he mocked her Christian faith. A devoted mother, she followed him around the ancient world, incessantly praying and pleading with him to reconsider his ways. She persevered and prayed not merely for thirty minutes, or thirty hours, or thirty days, or thirty weeks but for thirty years—such was her faith and determination. Disappointed time and again, she came to realize that she could not persuade him on her own and therefore looked to the clergy to help her. Regrettably, most priests saw her struggle as a hopeless cause and turned her away. One clergyman, however, did console her, saying:

> "It is not possible that a son of so many tears should perish."

---

12   Peter Brown. *Augustine of Hippo*. Berkeley and Los Angeles, California: University of California Press, 2000, p.101.

By divine Providence, that clergyman was Saint Ambrose, who, after much time in prayer himself, triumphantly baptized Augustine on Easter eve in the year 387, thus completing the greatest conversion in the history of the Church.

After his baptism, Augustine traveled from Rome to the city of Hippo in North Africa, where he was appointed bishop. During his time there he worked untiringly to spread the word of God. He preached with fervor and wrote volumes of theological texts. Unambiguous and well expressed, his thoughts served as a cornerstone of Christian doctrine for centuries. A far different man than he was in his youth, Augustine came to know God in ways that few others did, and in doing so, he came to understand the mysteries of the universe. In the post-Resurrection era, only Saint Thomas Aquinas would match his wisdom as a theologian.

> Augustine said: "Trust the past to God's mercy, the present to God's love, and the future to God's Providence."

> He said: "Pray as though everything depended on God. Work as though everything depended on you."

> He preached of faith: "Faith is to believe what you do not see; the reward of this faith is to see what you believe."

> He preached of humility: "It was pride that changed angels into devils; it is humility that makes men as angels."

> He also preached of sin and forgiveness. It was Augustine who coined the phrase, "Love the sinner but hate the sin."

Augustine's most famous work was *City of God*. The book was a defense of the Church against those who claimed that Christianity led to the decline of Rome. In the book, the City of God represented the Church, and the City of Man represented Rome. Augustine said:

> "Two loves have built two cities: the love of self, which reaches even to contempt for God, the earthly city; and the love of God, which reaches even to contempt for self, the heavenly city. One glories in itself, the other in God."[13]

---

13   Adapted from URL: http://www.ereader.com/product/book/
excerpt/1403?book=The_City_of_God. Downloaded 1-15-06.

Augustine prophesized that the City of Man would inevitably collapse because its leaders and citizens were plagued with the curse of original sin— the empty promise that "you will be as Gods." Alternately, he prophesized that the City of God, filled with citizens who placed their hopes only in the Lord's Providence, was destined to last until the end of time.

I included multiple passages from *City of God* and from Augustine's other works in *The Third Testament*. In all, it took me several days to summarize his many contributions to the Church.

After completing the section on Augustine, I wrote of the wisdom of Saint John Chrysostom, the greatest of the Greek Church fathers. Chrysostom preached against envy, saying: "As a moth gnaws at a garment, so doth envy consume a man."

And I wrote of Saint Jerome and the cataclysmic fall of the Roman Empire to the barbarian invaders. It was Jerome who proclaimed: "The lamp of the world is extinguished, and it is the whole world which has perished in the ruins of this one city."

Continuing on, I wrote of Saint Leo's encounter with Attila the Hun in the year 452 and how an apparition of Saint Peter saved the Church from destruction. Attila the Hun was a ruthless tyrant who proclaimed himself the "Terror of the World" and the "Scourge of God." After the fall of the Roman Empire, there were no military legions left to protect Rome from pillage, and Attila set his sights on sacking the defenseless city. With Attila and his army fast approaching, Pope Leo embarked on a journey to confront the warrior king and plead for mercy. He was accompanied by only two companions, as few had the courage to face the barbarians. Most Romans, including the emperor, believed that it was futile to confront men of their ilk. They believed that the mission was an act of senseless desperation, and that Leo and his companions would surely be killed. But by the grace of God they were wrong. I wrote:

At the very time when Emperor Valentinian prepared to flee the city in terror, Pope Leo I, the wise and pious bishop of Rome, set out with Avienus and Trygetius to confront the king of the Huns.

Leo was long in years. His hair was gray and his posture stooped, but his spirit was strong. He must have known that a confrontation with Attila would almost certainly result in death, but Leo was a holy man with great faith in the Lord and was not afraid to die. Leo believed in his heart that he could negotiate with the tyrant. He believed he could persuade "the Scourge of God" to show mercy. Reason alone could not have led him to draw such a conclusion—Leo was inspired from above.

On a fateful morning in the year 452, Leo, armed only with his faith, faced the leader of the Huns in Mantua. Yet the king of the Huns had no mercy. He was a cold-blooded killer who did not respect the meek. He only respected the sword. By his nature, he certainly would have called for Leo's head. By his nature, he certainly would have ordered the destruction of Rome and of the Church. Attila certainly would have done these things by his nature, had he not witnessed something most unnatural. With Pope Leo, the forty-fifth bishop of Rome, humbly kneeling at his feet, the king of the Huns had a vision. He saw before him an apparition of Saint Peter, the first bishop of Rome. Attila stood silently in awe as the apparition issued a stern warning: "Heed the plea of the good bishop who kneels before you, or face the fury of the Creator."

The vision of Saint Peter put fear into the heart of the tyrant warlord. The "Terror of the World" timidly retreated when confronted with the wrath of God. Attila looked Leo in the eye and bowed his head. He said: "This is a battle I cannot win. Pray for me to this Lord you serve." He then instantly gathered his army and withdrew. Thus, by the grace of God, Rome and the Church were saved from pillage.

Having used his faith to overcome the greatest of odds, Leo walked away victorious. The citizens of Rome were sincerely grateful for his efforts, for he did what the emperor would not. They praised the good bishop for his bravery in confronting the fearsome Huns and rightfully honored him with the title "Leo the Great."

Now that's definitely a biblical story, I thought. *That's one that could easily become a Sunday school favorite.*
Finally, at the end of a long week, I wrote of Saint Patrick, the patron saint of Ireland. Of all the saints in the history of the Church, Patrick was perhaps the most well known. Only he and Valentine had feast days that could be easily picked out on a calendar by common laypersons, and of the two, only Patrick was associated with widespread evangelization. Few other saints single-handedly converted as many to the faith, and few other saints performed as many miracles—or as great of miracles. Because he had such a profound impact on the Church, I spent a lot of time reviewing and recording his history. I was impressed by all he accomplished. After reading

pages and pages of ancient Celtic texts, it became clear to me that Saint Patrick was as important a character in Christian history as Elijah or any of the other prophets of the Old Testament. In the end, I decided that it was only appropriate that one of the books of *The Third Testament* be named after him—"The Book of Patrick."

Patrick was a Briton, called Patricius at birth, who was kidnapped by Irish druids and enslaved in Ireland during his youth. Suffering many hardships, Patricius grew close to God during his time of enslavement and prayed constantly; he prayed that he would one day be released from his bonds. In answer to Patricius' prayers, the Lord appeared to him in a dream and showed him the way to freedom. The young Briton's journey to freedom was a difficult one, but with the Lord at his side, he overcame every obstacle he faced. I wrote:

> There were many who spread the word of Christ throughout the Roman world, but it was not until the fifth century, on an island at the outskirts of Europe, that the word of God reached beyond the confines of the empire.

> In the year 387, in Kilpatrick, Scotland, a child was born to Calphurnius and Conchessa, a husband and wife of high rank in the Roman Briton society. The child, named Patricius, was raised by his parents to worship and honor Christ. Patricius' grandfather Pontitus was a Christian priest, and the Christian faith was strong in his family. Yet despite his parents' efforts, young Patricius did not follow in the ways of the Lord. He neglected prayer and thought only of himself. Preoccupied with his youth and his family's wealth, Patricius did not see a need for God in his life. He believed he could find true happiness through other means. He was blinded by the promise of original sin. This all changed in the year 405, when at the age of sixteen, Patricius was kidnapped by Irish marauders who were raiding the western coastal villages. The pagan Irish druids forced the young Briton into a life of slavery. It was a difficult and lonely existence, devoid of comfort or pleasure. Patricius was initially stunned and despondent, but he eventually learned to accept his fate. For the next six years, he served a master near the forest of Fochlat in Connaught, tending pigs and sheep.

> During his time in slavery, Patricius began to embrace the lessons taught to him as a child. He now sought the path he once rejected. He called on Christ for strength and guidance, and he yearned for fellowship with the Holy Spirit. His call was answered and with each passing day,

through prayer, he grew to know and love the Lord. He later wrote of the experience:

"And his fear increased in me more and more, and the faith grew in me, and the spirit was roused, so that, in a single day, I have said as many as a hundred prayers, and in the night nearly the same, so that whilst in the woods and on the mountain, even before the dawn, I was roused to prayer and felt no hurt from it, whether there was snow or ice or rain; nor was there any slothfulness in me, such as I see now, because the spirit was then fervent within me."[14]

After six years of slavery, and six years of prayer, Patricius heard the voice of God in a dream. It was a dream that would change his life forever. The Lord Almighty, creator of heaven and earth, told Patricius that his faith would be rewarded and that his time served as a slave would soon come to an end. "But how?" Patricius questioned. "How will I make my escape?" Miraculously, his questions were instantly answered. A vision of a small ship appeared to the young saint. It was the ship that would carry him to freedom. God said to Patricius, "Behold, thy ship is ready."

After he awoke from the dream, Patricius heeded God's message and departed for the coast at once. His heart was filled with hope and excitement, yet such an escape seemed impossible. Patricius was a four days' journey from the nearest seaport, and he had not a cent to his name. But with God, anything is possible. Guided by the Holy Spirit, Patricius safely made it to the coast, where he was allowed passage on a ship loaded with a cargo of Irish wolfhounds. The ship's crew consisted of unscrupulous drifters who ridiculed Patricius for his faith in Christ. They called him a fool and laughed at him. They were brazen and obstinate, and their insults were incessant. Yet in time, their ridicule turned to praise and awe. One day, when the ship landed in a desolate area devoid of food, Patricius fervently prayed to the Lord for assistance. The crew mocked him as they had never mocked him before, for they were angry and afraid. They questioned that if God were so powerful, why were they lost and starving? Patricius disregarded their taunts and assured them that God would provide. Just at that moment, a herd of pigs miraculously appeared from nowhere, and the men feasted. The food was overflowing in abundance, and the men's stomachs were filled

---

14   URL: http://www.newadvent.org/cathen/11554a.htm. Downloaded 4-4-09.

to contentment. Never before had they had such a grand meal. From that day forward, the crew no longer doubted the young saint. They begged for forgiveness and converted to Christianity. Conscripted into the fellowship of the Holy Spirit, they gave up their unscrupulous ways, and devoted their lives to God.

As promised, Patricius returned safely to Briton but was later called by God to come back to Ireland to convert the pagan druids. Heeding the Lord's call, Patricius changed his name to the Celtic "Patrick" and returned to the Emerald Isle. Soon after his return, Patrick came under attack from the fearsome druid warlord Dichu. Surrounded and unarmed, Patrick was about to be killed, but he prayed to God, and Dichu's right arm was temporarily paralyzed. I wrote:

> Now there was a druid chieftain called Dichu, a giant of a man with serpent tattoos and a fiery red beard, who was feared by all. One day this serpent worshipper came upon Patrick in the city of Ulster. He angrily threatened the good saint for preaching a religion foreign to his land. Showing no mercy, the mighty chieftain grasped his sword in his right hand and prepared to strike. Faced with death, Patrick did not run. He did not beg for mercy. He simply stood before the druids and prayed. He prayed serenely, with no concern that he would be harmed. Such was his great faith in the Lord.

> As Dichu raised his sword upward for the fatal blow, an astonishing event occurred—the chieftain's right arm became rigid as a statue. Try as he might, he could not move it at all. Those around him stared in fear and amazement. "Behold the miracle!" they cried out. Having witnessed the act of God, the druid Celts of Ulster converted to the Christian faith. Dichu was the first to convert, and with his conversion his arm was, by the grace of the Lord almighty, fully restored.

After the conversion of Dichu, Patrick traveled throughout Ireland, preaching to the masses and teaching them the mysteries of the Church. Among his many teachings, he described the Holy Trinity, using the shamrock as an example. He taught that the three leaves represented the Father, the Son and the Holy Spirit, and the stem signified that they were of the same origin. Empowered by his devotion to Christ, Patrick was successful in converting many pagans to the Christian faith.

Despite the many conversions, the majority of the druids in Ireland still opposed Patrick. One day, King Loaghaire, leader of the druids, summoned all of the pagan warlords to a great feast at his castle at Tara to muster support against the growing Christian influence. As part of the ceremony, Loaghaire decreed that no fire should be lit throughout the land until a signal blaze was lit at Tara. Although the king's word was law, the decree was nevertheless defied. Early in the evening, while Loaghaire and his men caroused, they saw a great blaze of fire in the distance on the Hill of Slane. It was a Pascal (Easter) fire, boldly lit by Patrick. In response to the distant flames, the dismayed druid chieftains confronted Loaghaire with an ancient prophecy: "This fire, lighted in defiance of the royal edict, shall blaze forever in this land unless it is extinguished this very night." At once, Loaghaire demanded that the fire be put out. Heeding Loaghaire's order, the druids tried to extinguish the fire, but were unsuccessful—it blazed throughout the night. In fulfillment of the ancient prophecy, Patrick went on to convert all of Ireland to the Christian faith. Thus, the pagan druid religion, symbolized by the serpent, was forever driven out of Ireland.

In the Gospel of John, Christ proclaimed that those who believed in him would do miraculous works like him, and greater works also. Patrick truly believed in Christ, and through him, Patrick performed countless miracles while converting the pagan Irish. The ancient manuscripts extolled Patrick's exploits. I quoted them in *The Third Testament*:

> "For the blind and the lame, the deaf and the dumb, the palsied, the lunatic, the leprous, the epileptic, all who labored under any disease, did he in the Name of the Holy Trinity restore unto the power of their limbs and unto entire health; and in these good deeds was he daily practiced. Thirty and three dead men, some of whom had been many years buried, did this great reviver raise from the dead."[15]

Patrick's most noted miracle involved the raising of a pagan prince and princess from the dead. It was a miracle that changed the course of history—certainly the history of Ireland. Although not an Irishman, I nevertheless found it inspiring. I wrote:

> One day Patrick came to a small village where there was great sorrow. The pagan ruler of the village, Aphismus, had lain to rest his only son and daughter. The son had passed of an unknown illness, and the daughter, Dublina, deeply beloved by all, had drowned while bathing in a river. Her lifeless body was found by fishermen in a riverbed on the outskirts of the town. For the people of the village, it was truly a time

---

15   URL: http://olrl.org/lives/patrick.shtml. Downloaded 1-20-06.

of suffering and sadness. Soon after Patrick's arrival, Aphismus and his forlorn nobles came to greet the good saint. They greeted him with much anticipation, for word had spread of the miraculous healings he performed in the name of God. They beseeched Patrick for assistance. They told him of their sorrow and that they were desperate to lift the despair that bound them unremittingly like a vice. With tears in their eyes, the entire village promised to be baptized in the name of Christ if the good saint would restore the prince and princess to life. Patrick looked into their souls and felt their sincere sorrow. He experienced their pain as if it were his own. "Take me to the children's tombs," he said to them. Heeding his command, the villagers took Patrick to the melancholy tombs, and he began to pray. The good saint prayed with great fervor. He prayed so that his hands shook and tears fell from his eyes. In the name of Christ, he freed the brother and sister from the clutches of death and, in doing so, converted the entire village. Deeply moved by the miracle, the townspeople became fully devoted to Christ and the fellowship of the Holy Spirit. Witnessing this devotion firsthand, Patrick prophezied that the small village would someday become great. Years later, the village was named Dublin in honor of the beloved princess who Patrick, through his fervent prayers to the Lord, raised from the dead. And just as the good saint prophezied, Dublin became a great village indeed.

Patrick was truly a remarkable saint, not just for the Irish but for all Christians, I thought as I typed.

Late that evening I allowed myself to smile, for I realized that I had really accomplished a lot in a relatively short period of time. My writing was quickly becoming a part of who I was. I looked forward to the day when I could share my work with others. Yet there was still so much more work to be done.

Chapter 17

BIOCHEMOTHERAPY

IT WAS NOT long before it was time for Ellen's appointment with Dr. Gudmundson. Ellen was feeling positive about the treatment. She noted that her energy level had been improving. "The treatment must be doing something," she rationalized, "because if the tumors were growing, I don't think I'd feel this good."

I went with her to her appointment with Dr. Gudmundson. She'd had CAT scans two days prior to see if the treatment was working, and we were both very anxious to get the results.

The waiting room in Dr. Gudmundson's office was busy. We sat down next to a friendly woman who appeared to be about seventy years of age. She smiled at us and said, "The doctor is running behind today. They just called my Charlie ten minutes ago, and we'd been waiting close to an hour and a half."

"He must be busy," I said in reply. Ellen just smiled politely and picked up a magazine.

The woman went on speaking. "My Charlie has melanoma," she said. "He's been getting treatment from Dr. Gudmundson for over a year now. He's doing really well."

The word "melanoma" caught my attention, and I could tell that it caught Ellen's interest also because she promptly set aside her magazine.

"Do you mind if I ask what he is being treated with?" I questioned.

The sweet little lady replied, "He's getting an experimental therapy that shrinks blood vessels. He's been on it for months now, and his tumors have been slowly shrinking. Dr. Gudmundson says Charlie is doing really well."

Oh, those were words of joy to our ears.

"That's wonderful," Ellen said. "That's really wonderful. You must be so thankful."

"We are," said the little old lady. "We pray to God all the time. And we're so thankful to have Dr. Gudmundson as our doctor. He's such a great man."

"Yes, he is," Ellen said.

I nodded in agreement.

It was actually not too long before Ellen's name was called. I could tell that the sweet lady was surprised to see that Ellen was the patient. I think she had assumed that I was the patient.

"Good luck, and God bless you," she said as we walked toward the doorway leading to the exam rooms.

The nurse brought us back to an empty room. She took Ellen's vital signs and asked a few questions. Then we waited for Dr. Gudmundson to come in and give us a report.

"That was promising news to hear," I said to Ellen. "That woman's husband is getting the same treatment you are, and he seems to be having a good response."

"It was nice to hear," Ellen agreed. "I just hope that it works for me. Oh, it would be so wonderful if it works for me. I just want the doctor to walk in and give us good news. I want that so badly."

Soon there was a knock at the exam room door, and Dr. Gudmundson walked in. He greeted us, sat down in a chair opposite us, and opened up Ellen's chart. He pulled out a couple of papers and held them in his hands. "Ellen, I have your CAT scan reports here," he said. "Unfortunately, the tumors are still growing. The therapy did not do what we hoped it would. We'll have to look into other options."

My heart sank. I looked over at Ellen. Initially, she seemed to handle the blow. There were no tears, no signs of sadness, but with each passing moment, it became clearer that she was afraid.

"How much have the tumors grown?" she asked.

"The tumors in your liver have grown by two to three centimeters," he said. "The tumors in your lung are about the same size as they were before, but there are two new lesions."

"How big are the new lesions?" she asked.

"They are small," he said. "Only one to two centimeters."

"So would you say the melanoma is growing very quickly?" she questioned.

"Ellen," he said, "the tumors have not grown by a large amount, but not that much time has passed. I wouldn't say that they are growing quickly, but

I wouldn't say that they are growing slowly, either. In any case, we need to find another treatment for you."

"What are the treatment options?" I asked.

"The only things I have to offer are standard chemotherapy, which doesn't work very well, and interleukin-2," he said. "In my experience, interleukin-2 is much more likely to kill you than to cure you. It is a highly toxic therapy that benefits very few patients. I would certainly not recommend that. Your best approach is to try another experimental drug. Unfortunately, I do not have any other experimental protocols for melanoma here at my clinic. I recommend that you go back to see Dr. Greenspan at the Chicago Cancer Institute. He is one of the world's experts in melanoma, and he will certainly have several options for you."

Ellen then asked a final question. "Dr. Gudmundson ... Dr. Gudmundson, how much time do you think I have? I know you said before that there is no way you can tell me for sure, but you must have some sense of it. You must at least have a guess. It's important for me to know."

Dr. Gudmundson sighed. I could tell that he was uncomfortable with the question. I know that I was uncomfortable with the question, and I certainly did not want to hear the answer.

"Ellen," he said, "I would really only be guessing, and I'd rather not guess. I really cannot tell you how long you have to live. But since you've asked, I will tell you the timeframe that the average patient with your extent of disease can expect—it can be measured in months. It is unlikely that it would be only weeks, and it is also unlikely that it would be years."

"Months," she whispered. Ellen paused for a moment, then sorrowfully said, "Thank you for your honesty, Doctor."

We promptly made an appointment to see Dr. Greenspan at the Chicago Cancer Institute. He was able to get us in just two days later. Although we did not particularly care for Dr. Greenspan's bedside manner, we were appreciative of the fact he was able to see us on such short notice.

"Ms. Sankt," Dr. Greenspan said, "your tumor is aggressive, and you need aggressive treatment. We have a clinical trial that you would fit into just perfectly." Dr. Greenspan went on to explain a long and complex trial that involved several steps.

"The first part of the treatment combines several chemotherapy drugs with other drugs that work to boost the immune system," he said. "This combination is called biochemotherapy. You will be on this therapy for several months. It is an aggressive therapy, and it has a lot of side effects, but you are young and should be able to handle it. Assuming that your tumors shrink or are at least stable in size, this will be followed by radiation to your brain. We do this because melanoma frequently spreads to the brain, and the chemotherapy does not do a good job at preventing brain tumors from forming. Once melanoma spreads to the brain, there is nothing that can be done. The prognosis is dismal. One moment, a patient will be up and talking and the next thing you know, he or she is on the floor, unconscious from a seizure. It is horrible to witness. By giving the radiation, we hope to prevent the melanoma from spreading to the brain. This will be followed by low doses of the drugs used to boost the immune system, which you will continue indefinitely."

"What side effects can I expect?" Ellen questioned.

"During the first part of the therapy, your hair will fall out," he said.

"All of my hair?" Ellen questioned.

"Yes, all of your hair." He continued with a long list of side effects. "You will lose your appetite. You will feel quite fatigued. You will not be able to work. It is likely that you will experience nausea and vomiting. Your blood counts will drop low, and you will be at increased risk of infection. It is important that you have a thermometer at home to check your temperature. If you develop a fever, it is important that you call us immediately, as infections in this setting can be life-threatening. You may develop depression. You may develop nerve damage and possibly kidney damage from the therapy, but most patients do not. There is also a risk of developing leukemia, but that is highly unlikely. Patients who get leukemia from chemotherapy don't develop it until years later, and we'd be very happy to get you to that point."

"That sounds ... terrible," Ellen said.

"Melanoma is terrible," Dr. Greenspan said bluntly. "Unfortunately, there is more. The radiation to the brain also has side effects. It can lead to problems with cognition. It primarily affects your memory, but it may affect your balance, too. The immune therapy that follows the radiation may leave you chronically fatigued and possibly depressed."

"Do people really make it through all of that?" I asked.

"Young, otherwise healthy patients can make it through," he said. "Melanoma is an aggressive cancer, and I believe that it needs aggressive treatment. This is the most aggressive treatment available, but because it is so aggressive, it comes with side effects. There is even a risk of death from the therapy itself."

"Does this therapy cure anyone?" I asked.

"We do not know that yet," Dr. Greenspan said. "That's why we are doing the study. I will say this—I believe it is more likely to help you than any other therapy that currently exists."

"What are the other treatment options?" Ellen inquired. "There has to be something with fewer side effects."

"There are therapies with fewer side effects," Dr. Greenspan said. "But I think the potential benefits also will be fewer. We do have an experimental pill, called MM314, that may help you. The pill targets a receptor called the epidermal growth factor receptor. Tumors need this receptor to grow. By blocking the receptor, we may be able to stop the growth of the melanoma. It is a very promising therapy, but we know less about it than we know about biochemotherapy."

"What are the side effects of that pill?" she asked.

"There are very few side effects," he replied. "Some patients develop a rash that looks like acne, but other than that, patients do very well."

"Do we know for sure that the aggressive therapy you told us about is better than the pill?" I asked.

"That's a good question," Ellen concurred. "Unless the aggressive therapy is definitely better than the pill, I think I'd like to try the pill. I'm feeling good right now, so why should I do something that is going to make me very sick? If the pill doesn't work, I can always do the more aggressive therapy later."

"We have no way of knowing if the biochemotherapy is better than the pill right now," Dr. Greenspan explained. "If you are concerned about the side effects of the biochemotherapy, it would be a reasonable option to try the pill first, and if it doesn't work, then to take the more aggressive approach. If it were up to me, I'd just do the more aggressive therapy now and get it over with, but it is your choice."

Ellen decided to try the experimental pill first. She said to me, "Dad, I'm realistic. It isn't likely that anything is going to cure this. If I'm feeling good right now, why should I compromise my quality of life with a treatment that is going to make me miserable and may even kill me? If the pill doesn't work and the tumors continue to grow, I'm sure I'll start to have symptoms from the cancer. At that point, I'll try the more aggressive treatment because if I get really sick, I can always tell myself that without it, I'd be sick from the cancer anyway. Does that make sense to you?"

"Yes, sweetheart, that makes a lot of sense," I said.

Hearing my only daughter rationally discuss the likelihood of her death was something I'd never thought I'd have to do. It was heartbreaking.

Sometimes God asks too much of us, I lamented.

Chapter 18
NICHOLAS C. HUGHES

WITH THE NEWS that the cancer was getting worse, our greatest fears were realized, and we regressed emotionally and psychologically. Panic and despair once again set it. The torment was insufferable. Thankfully, Ellen soon began therapy with the experimental pill MM314. It was much easier to cope with the problem when we felt we were doing something about it, and the start of the new therapy brought us hope and helped to calm our nerves. The emotional trauma eventually wore away, and within a few weeks, we returned to our baseline state of anxiety. Life went on. It was certainly not a happy life, but it was not one of utter misery either. The typical everyday ups and downs were still there. The ups were simply not as high, and the downs had the potential to get awfully low. It was like looking at life through a veil. I could still distinguish the brightness of the morning sun from the blackness of the night, but everything was a shade darker than it should have been.

I continued writing. It was the one thing that brought me even the slightest sense of contentment.

Focusing on the fifth through the ninth centuries, I wrote of the Basilica of Mount Gargano, the oldest shrine in Western Europe dedicated to Saint Michael the Archangel, the greatest of the angels in heaven.

Like so many biblical stories, the story of the basilica began with a holy apparition. In the year 493, Saint Michael, on a mission from Christ, appeared to Lawrence, the bishop of Sipontum, and told him to transform a cave used for Mithras worship into a Christian shrine. The angel said:

> "I am Michael the Archangel and am always in the presence of God. I chose the cave, which is sacred to me. There will be no more shedding of bull's blood. Where the rocks open widely, the sins of man may be

pardoned. What is asked here in prayer will be granted. Therefore, go up to the mountain cave and dedicate it to the Lamb of God!"[16]

A holy man of faith, Lawrence obeyed and brought a group of workers to the mountain cave to build a church there. The workers were at first skeptical of the reports of the apparition. Then, as they entered the cave, they were met with a miraculous surprise. I wrote:

> When Saint Michael appeared to Lawrence, he promised him a sign so that others might believe. He said, "Enter this cave and celebrate the Resurrection of Christ. I will show you how I have consecrated this place." Although at first fearful, Lawrence ultimately obeyed. Determined to do the Lord's bidding, he brought workers to the mountain cave to erect a Christian shrine. When he arrived with the workers, they were astounded to see that the cave had, in fact, been consecrated, not by human hands but by the defender of divine glory. A vibrant purple cloth was already in place, covering what appeared to be a natural altar. The cloth was more beautiful than anything they had ever seen. They said to each other, "It must be from heaven." Their suspicions were confirmed moments later when they saw the archangel's footprints embedded in the rock near the altar. The rock was very old and very hard, and no ordinary man could have left an imprint in it. Witnessing the miracle, the workers dropped to their knees in awe and gave praise to God. Not long thereafter, a basilica was erected, and the cave that once served as a site of sacrilege was transformed into a sanctuary of Christ. As per Saint Michael's command, there was no more shedding of bull's blood.

I was pleased to include the brief passage about Saint Michael. Religious references to Saint Michael dated back thousands of years. He appeared in the Old and New Testaments and also appeared in ancient Jewish and Islamic manuscripts.

It is appropriate that he will also be referenced in The Third Testament, I decided.

Although it was not first composed until centuries later, I included the Prayer to Saint Michael at the end of the story of the apparition. I then switched subjects and wrote of Saint Benedict, founder of the Benedictine Order. He was a remarkable man who, by the grace of God, performed countless miracles, the most noteworthy of which included the freeing of an

---

16   URL: http://www.smcenter.org/apparition1.htm. Downloaded 1-20-06.

innocent prisoner from his unjust bonds and the raising of a young child from the dead. Yet as noteworthy as the miracles were, they were not Benedict's most important contribution to the Church. In the early sixth century, Benedict overthrew the temple of Apollo at Monte Cassino and established a monastery there. It was at the monastery that he wrote the Benedictine Rule, the founding principle for Western monasticism. In my opinion, Benedict's efforts at Monte Cassino—specifically, his devotion to the monastic way of life—preserved the Church from ruin and, in doing so, changed the course of history.

Christianity would have never survived the Dark Ages without monks and monasteries, I rationalized. *And there would have been no monasteries, had it not been for Benedict.*

Continuing to focus on the early pillars of the Church, I wrote of Saint Gregory the Great, the "Servant of the Servants of God." Gregory was a devoted, early medieval pope who greatly influenced the spread of Christianity throughout Europe, including the conversion of the Anglo-Saxons. Along with Ambrose, Augustine, and Jerome, Gregory was considered one of the four great Latin fathers of the Church.

I also wrote of Saint Boniface and the felling of Thor's oak. The felling of the oak was a magnificent story. Boniface, in order to convert the pagan people of Hesse, cut down a giant oak at Geismar on the summit of Mount Gudenberg. The oak was believed to be sacred to the Norse god Thor, and the pagan Norsemen cursed the saint as he took an axe to the tree. Bolstered by faith, Boniface ignored their warnings and swung his axe with no ill consequences. I wrote:

At Geismar, near Fritzlar, on the summit of Mount Gudenberg, in the primeval forest of mystic wonders, there stood a tall oak, taller than any other tree in all of Hesse. The heathens there believed the oak to be sacred to Thor, the pagan god of thunder. Much as Yggdrasil was the heart of the mythical Norse universe, the oak at Geismar was the heart of paganism in Hesse. When the moon was full, the pagans gathered around its thick trunk and engaged in ritualistic ceremonies. They honored the Norse gods in primordial fashion, making sacrifices and chanting rhythmic oaths, just as their ancestors had done for centuries before them.

By the start of the eighth century, the heathens in Hesse had heard of the marvels of Christ, but they resisted conversion. They deeply feared the wrath of their pagan gods, especially the fiery thunder god, should they accept the Christian faith.

"Thor has a temper like no other," they said. "With a bolt of lightning, he will vanquish those who betray him."

In the year of the Lord 722, a sainted preacher came to the heathens of Hesse. His name was Wynfrith, but he was later called Boniface, the apostle of the Germans. Boniface dedicated his life to the conversion of the northern peoples. "Fear not your pagan gods," he said, "for there is only one true God—Christ, the Lord Almighty." He proved this to them by venturing to the summit of Mount Gudenberg to the primeval forest, where he took an axe to the sacred oak at Geismar.

The fateful day was a dark and foreboding one. The skies were covered with tempestuous clouds, and the heathens of Hesse feared the worst.

"No, you fool!" cried the onlookers as Boniface struck at the oak. "You will bring doom to us all!"

Boniface did not heed their warning; he continued to swing his axe. He struck and he struck, each blow stronger than the last. He struck at Thor's towering oak until it came crashing to the earth. Boniface then stood on the trunk, before the fearful pagans, and boldly proclaimed, "How stands your mighty god of thunder now? The God of Light is stronger than he."

The heathens held their breath, waiting for a bolt of lighting to come down from the heavens and strike the apostle dead. But instead of lighting, the clouds that had darkened the day parted, and the sun's rays brightened the skies above all of Hesse.

When the great oak fell, it split into four and crushed all of the other trees in its vicinity, all except a single, sturdy fir tree. Draped in sunshine, Boniface stood by the fir and said to the heathens, "Much as the oak was the tree of Thor, let this fir be the symbol of Christ. This humble tree's wood is used to build your homes; let Christ be the center of your households. Its leaves remain evergreen in the darkest days; let Christ be your constant light. Its boughs reach out to embrace and its top points to heaven; let Christ be your comfort and your guide."[17]

---

17 Adapted from URL: http://www.stboniface.org.uk/whowas.htm. Downloaded 1-22-06.

After seeing the thunderous clouds miraculously part, the heathens took heed of Boniface's words and were instantly converted to a life in Christ. In celebration of the great conversion, Boniface used the wood of the felled oak to build a Christian church near Fritzlar. He dedicated the church to the holy apostle Peter and worshiped there with great fervor for the remainder of his days.

The story of Boniface and the sturdy fir became the basis for the Christmas tree tradition that began in Germany and spread throughout the world. It was a tradition that I truly cherished.

What would Christmas be like without the tree?

– – – – – – – – – –

Working at a feverish pace, I wrote of Charles Martel, the man who saved Christian Europe from radical Islam. As both a student and professor of Christianity, I had spent a lot of time researching radical Islam, even before writing about Martel. It was my long-standing belief that in order to understand the saga of Christianity, it was necessary to also understand the threat of radical Islam and of the Jihadist movement.

Islam began in the year 570 with the birth of Mohammed in Mecca. Mohammed was a descendant of Ishmael. At a young age, he was proclaimed as a prophet by Bahira, a Christian monk. Later in life, Mohammed himself proclaimed to be not just a prophet of God but the greatest prophet of God—greater even than Christ. A persuasive orator, Mohammed developed a strong following. Raising an army, he conquered Mecca in the year 630 and united the Arabian people. Once in control, he firmly established his new religion, which he detailed in the Koran, and worked untiringly to spread his teachings across the face of the earth. He did this not by peaceful persuasion but by military means. Much as Christianity was preached by the lamb, Islam was preached by the sword. Thus, the word "Jihad" ("Holy War") came to be.

After succeeding in his ambitions, Mohammed fell ill and died at Medina in 632, but his legacy of Islamic expansion continued on long after his death. Like a swarm of locusts in the desert, Mohammed's successors swept rapidly across the Middle East and North Africa. Their march of conquest was terrifying:

- In the year 633, the Muslims advanced into Syria and Iraq.
- In the year 635, they conquered Damascus.
- In the year 636, they conquered Edessa.

- By the late 630s, all of Syria was in the hands of the Muslims.
- In the year 637, Ctesiphon, capital of Persia, fell under Muslim control.
- The holy city Jerusalem fell in the year 638.
- In the year 641, the Muslims conquered southern areas of Azerbaijan, Daghestan, Georgia, and Armenia.
- Mosel and Babylon fell to the Muslims in the year 641.
- In the year 642, the great library of Alexandria was burned to the ground by the followers of Mohammed.
- Tripolitania fell in the year 647.
- Persopolis fell in the year 650.
- In the year 653, Muawiya led an Islamic raid against Rhodes, taking the remaining pieces of the Colossus of Rhodes, one of the Seven Wonders of the ancient world, and shipping it back to Syria to be sold as scrap metal.
- Cyprus was overrun by Islam in the year 654.
- By the year 656, Islam reigned in all of Iraq and Egypt.
- The Muslims attacked Sicily in the year 667.
- Chalcedon fell in the year 667.
- By the year 674, the Muslim conquest reached the Indus River.
- The Muslims reached Morocco in the year 669.
- Carthage fell in the year 698.
- Tunis fell in the year 700.
- The Muslims captured Tangier in 707.
- In the year 711, the Muslims began the conquest of Sindh in Afghanistan.
- Islamic warriors invaded the Iberian Peninsula in 711 and captured Gibraltar.
- Lisbon and all of Spain fell under Islamic control in the year 716.

The Muslim conquerors ran unchecked until they faced Charles Martel. Most people I knew had never heard of Martel, but he did as much to shape the current world as any man in history. Truth be told, his contributions to Christian civilization cannot be overemphasized. Had Martel faltered at the epic Battle of Tours in the year 732, then all of Europe would have been overrun by the Jihadists, and Christianity itself would have been extinguished. I wrote:

> By the beginning of the eighth century, the entire Mediterranean region was either controlled by or at conflict with radical Islam. Feeling

invincible, the Islamic invaders advanced into Gaul, the last Christian stronghold on earth. Driven by the call to Jihad, the Mohammedans made it their quest to bring terror to the followers of Christ and to forever replace the Bible with the Koran.

In the year 724, the Christian cities of Carcassone and Nimes were mercilessly sacked. Churches and monasteries were targeted in the raids; holy objects were stolen and clerics were enslaved or murdered. In 730, Narbonne and Avignon fell, after which the Mohammedans set their sights on the city of Tours. There was a cathedral at Tours, dedicated to Saint Martin, that the Muslims coveted.

The Frankish kings of the eighth century were ineffective leaders and incapable of mounting a defense against the Muslims. They ruled as no more than figureheads. There was, however, one man in Gaul with the courage and skill to face the militant followers of Mohammed. His name was Charles, mayor of Austrasia.

Charles was the illegitimate son of Pepin, a prominent Frankish nobleman. Throughout his youth, Charles struggled to gain political power in Gaul, and in doing so, he learned the art of war. He commanded a well-trained and battle-tested army of Merovingian knights. The Merovingians did not fear death, and they did not fear the Muslim threat.

In the fateful autumn of 732, Charles led his men to meet the formidable Islamic forces at Tours. For six days, the two armies camped opposite each other outside of the city limits. For six days, there were only minor skirmishes between the two adversaries. For six days, the people of Tours prayed to Christ, the Risen Lord. For six days, they waited with apprehension. On the seventh day the great conflict commenced.

The fighting at Tours was ferocious. There was horrific bloodshed, and by midmorning the battlefield was covered with the bodies of dead warriors. The Merovingians fought bravely, but it appeared that the radical sons of Islam, privileged with superior numbers, would prove victorious. Then, late in the day, a false cry arose in the ranks of the Mohammedans that the Christians were plundering their camp and reclaiming the treasures stolen during previous battles. Compelled by avarice, several squadrons of Arabs rode off to their tents in disarray to save their precious spoils of war. Abd-er-Rahman, the fearsome leader of the Jihadist forces, tried to curtail the chaos and lead his men back to battle, but in the confusion he found himself surrounded by a regiment of brave Christian knights. The knights hurled their spears through the air, piercing Abd-er-Rahman's flesh. The evil warlord fell dead on the spot, and for a brief moment in time, all was still at Tours.

With the Jihadist commander slain, the tide of the epic battle turned, and the Islamic invaders fell into full retreat. Thousands upon thousands were slaughtered as they tried to gather up their stolen treasures. One by one, they were destroyed by their own greed. By the grace of God, the once seemingly unstoppable army was brought to its knees.

When the Christian forces assembled the next morning to prepare for another day of battle, they found the enemy camp deserted. Charles was triumphant. He had done what all other European leaders had failed to do—he led the way to victory over the militant Muslims. He fought with such rage that he earned the name "Martel," meaning "the Hammer."

After finishing the summary of Martel, I went on to chronicle the life of his grandson, the great Frankish king Charlemagne. Charlemagne established a Christian Camelot in Western Europe and was crowned the first Holy Roman Emperor on Christmas Day in the year 800. He was called the "new David" because like David of the Old Testament, he was a warrior king and great champion of God's people. The title was certainly fitting. Yet it was not David but another famous king with whom I more strongly associated Charlemagne. In my opinion, Charlemagne was the closest king to the legendary Arthur who ever lived. For a brief shining moment in time, he brought hope to a world that had become clouded in darkness.

I had always had a great interest in the King Arthur legends. When I wrote about Charlemagne, I drew as many comparisons to Arthur as I could. After doing some research, I was pleasantly surprised to find that there were many such comparisons. Included among them were the twelve paladins of Charlemagne's court, led by Roland, Charlemagne's heroic nephew. The brave and loyal paladins championed goodness and were akin to the knights of the Round Table. Also included among the comparisons was the brilliant monk Alcuin, who paralleled Merlin. Alcuin was Charlemagne's lead scholar and advisor. An indefatigable proponent of Christian learning, he invented cursive script as a way to more efficiently copy religious manuscripts.

Charlemagne was a remarkable man who surrounded himself with other remarkable men, I thought. *Like Arthur, he was the epitome of a Christian king.*

I wrote:

On Christmas Day in the year 800, Pope Leo III did the unexpected. During the Mass at Saint Peter's in Rome, Leo walked forward toward Charlemagne, placed a crown on the king's head, and proclaimed that he was the peace-bringing emperor of the Romans. The proclamation astounded all those in attendance, and the children of God rejoiced. They were filled with a sense of hope—after centuries of barbarism and disorder, a new Roman emperor had been crowned. Leo's actions had far-reaching effects. With the coronation, the world was forever changed. The Holy Roman Empire came to be; it was an empire that would last one thousand years. In Arthurian fashion, Charlemagne imposed altruistic reforms to the Church and society, and his reign was known as the Carolingian Renaissance. The warrior king became an emperor of kindness and enlightenment. Charlemagne legislated for agriculture, industry, finance, education, and religion, as well as for government ethics and morals. He fought to protect a free peasantry against spreading serfdom. He gave praise to God and championed justice. Under his watch, hope and goodness prevailed. Yet just as Camelot came to an end with the passing of Arthur, giving way to a barbarous age, the Carolingian Renaissance came to an end with the death of Charlemagne. The "new David" died in 814 on the twenty-eighth day of the first month. He was succeeded as Holy Roman Emperor by his son, Louis the Pious. Louis was weak and indecisive and allowed the empire to be divided among his quarreling sons. Although Christendom survived for one thousand years, Charlemagne's golden age of Christian enlightenment came to an end as Europe was engulfed with fear from the marauding Muslims and Vikings.

"For a brief shining moment in time," I whispered, echoing the theme of Camelot as I completed the passage. "Let it never be forgot ..."

Finally, at the end of a long day, I wrote of the unequaled charity of the good king Wenceslaus. Wenceslaus, the tenth-century ruler of Bohemia, was a saint in the truest sense of the word. Strongly embracing the fellowship of the Holy Spirit, he was always a Christian first and a king second. His compassion and devotion to the poor were legendary. He fed the hungry, clothed the naked, gave shelter to the homeless, and bought freedom for the slaves. His most noted act of benevolence involved an episode in which he walked barefoot in the snow to bring alms to a troubled peasant—the event that inspired the hymn for which he is famous. To his people, Wenceslaus was considered not a monarch but the "father of all the wretched."

The reign of Wenceslaus in Bohemia was one of peace and harmony. It was a time of goodness, but it was not to last. In the year 935, Wenceslaus was tragically murdered by his brother, Boleslaus, and his henchmen on the steps of the church of Alt Bunziau. Boleslaus lusted for power and killed the kindhearted saint in an effort to gain control of the kingdom. The murder took place as Wenceslaus was on his way to morning Mass to celebrate the feast of Saint Cosmas. It was an event that brought immeasurable sorrow to all those who had been touched by his kindness.

Soon after his death, the people of Bohemia began to report miracles at Wenceslaus' tomb. According to their reports, the sick and the lame were healed, and prisoners were inexplicably released from their shackles, all through the good king's intercession. News of the miracles spread, and it was not long before Christians from all of Europe traveled far and wide to visit the holy grave. I included a story of one of the miracles in *The Third Testament*:

Following the death of the good-hearted king, there was a period of great sadness. During this time, the pious Christian people of Bohemia, countless in number, paid tribute to the fallen saint by visiting his tomb. They came to mourn and to pray—Wenceslaus had given so much to them during his brief reign. One day, a poor woman, who was blind and crippled, came to mourn at his tomb. Years earlier, she had cried tears of joy when the good king, in a true act of kindness, brought food to her starving family. Now, all of her tears were tears of sorrow. The poor old cripple fell to the ground in front of his grave and prayed as she wept. Numerous other villagers from the city were at the burial site, paying tribute also. They all knew the old woman and felt sorry for her. "It is a sad day," they said. One of the villagers began to walk over to comfort her when something inconceivable happened. There, in front of the crowd of mourners, the old woman rose to her feet without assistance and began to walk. She walked without any hesitation in her step, for not only had her limp vanished but after decades of living in darkness, her sight had returned. The onlookers were astonished. They stared at each other in amazement. "How can this be?" they said. There was only one explanation for the extraordinary phenomenon—a miracle had occurred at Wenceslaus' tomb.

Over time, there were many such miracles reported at Wenceslaus' tomb. Fearful of the wondrous happenings, Boleslaus repented and, in an act of devotion, had his brother's remains transferred to the Church of Saint Vitus in Prague, where they remain to this day.

Both in life and in death, Wenceslaus was a righteous man. His kindness and infinite generosity left an indelible mark in the hearts of the people of Bohemia, and his spirit touched Christians throughout the world, myself among them.

"Therefore, Christian men, be sure, wealth or rank possessing/ Ye who now will bless the poor, shall yourselves find blessing," I crooned as I typed.

- - - - - - - - - -

One afternoon while I was working in my office, I received a phone call from my lawyer's secretary.

"Good afternoon, Mr. Sankt," she said. "Mr. Jacobson would like to set a date for your deposition. What does your schedule look like in March?"

I quickly got out my calendar and discussed potential dates. We decided on March 15. She then informed me that I would meet privately with Mr. Jacobson for an hour at his office, and then we would take a cab over to the Thomas, Thomas, and Hughes firm for the actual deposition.

"Do I need to meet with Mr. Jacobson prior to the fifteenth to prepare for the deposition?" I asked.

"No," she said. "Mr. Jacobson will go over everything when he meets with you on the day of the fifteenth."

An hour of preparation did not seem as if it would be enough, but I was confident that Mr. Jacobson knew what he was doing.

On the morning of March 15, I put on my best suit and wore a conservative tie. When I arrived at Mr. Jacobson's office, I was greeted with a warm hello from his secretary; I took a seat. After about a twenty-minute wait, Mr. Jacobson called me into his office. He closed the door behind me as I entered.

"Have a seat, Mr. Sankt," he said, gesturing to the chair in front of his desk. "Have you ever sat through a deposition before?"

"No, sir," I said. "This will be my first and, I hope, my last."

"OK," he said. "There are a few simple points that you need to understand, and a few simple rules that you need to follow. The first point is that the law is nothing more than a game of words. The words you use can be twisted and manipulated to your disadvantage. The more you say, the more likely it is that you will say something detrimental to your case. There is no penalty in this game for pausing before you answer a question. Take a deep breath and think about what you want to say, and when you do answer, give only the information that was specifically requested. If possible, it is best to answer every question with a simple yes or no. Do you understand?"

"Yes, I do," I said.

"Good," he said. "Let's go on to the second point, which relates to the first. The second point is that you must know and understand your opponent. Please heed my words, Mr. Sankt. The opposing attorney for this case is Nicholas C. Hughes. Nicholas Hughes is widely regarded as the best injury attorney in this state, if not the country. He has been a rapidly rising star in the legal industry. He is brilliant. He speaks nine languages fluently. He is witty, charming, and persuasive. His appropriate use of humor is masterful. He can talk almost anyone into saying or doing almost anything. He is smooth. He never hesitates or misspeaks. Beware!"

The more I listened to Mr. Jacobson, the more anxious I became.

He continued, "Most people who sit through a deposition are nervous. I suspect that you, Mr. Sankt, are nervous. Well, Nicholas Hughes will try to make you feel at ease. He will try to make you feel like you are talking to a friend. He will try to fool you into thinking that you are simply having a cordial conversation. Mr. Sankt, what you are about to go through is no cordial conversation. It is an inquisition! At no point must you forget that. I cannot stress enough how important it is for you to try to limit your answers to a simple yes or no or I cannot recall. Do you understand?"

"I understand," I said.

Mr. Jacobson and I went over the details of the case one last time, and then we caught a cab over to the Thomas, Thomas, and Hughes law firm. It was only a five-minute cab ride, but it seemed like an eternity. Nervous about the deposition, I wasn't really paying attention to where we were going. My eyes half-closed, I looked down at my hands, watching my twiddling thumbs. They remained that way until we turned down Dearborn. Then my eyes popped widely open as we stopped in front of a fifty-story black building—the 66 North building.

"Is this where Hughes' office is?" I asked in disbelief.

"Yes," said Mr. Jacobson. "You seem surprised."

I was more than surprised; I was shocked—the 66 North Dearborn building was the building from my second strange dream, the building that was on fire.

This can't be, I thought. *What are the chances?*

As we sat there in the stopped cab, I began having flashbacks from my dream. I instantly recalled the sinister orange flames, the black smoke rising upward, the horrific shrieks of agony, and the intolerable odor of burning flesh.

It was horrible, I remembered as I agonized over the flashbacks. *It was literally a nightmare.*

At that moment, one nightmare merged with another. I was briefly overcome with vertigo as I realized that the cab had stopped in the very spot where I had met with my friend in my dream.

What are the chances? I asked myself again.

It seemed like an incredible coincidence, but I wasn't about to try to explain it to Mr. Jacobson.

How can I possibly tell him that I had a vision that this place was a wretched inferno?

I knew that I had to come up with another explanation for the expression on my face. "I'm just surprised because I used to pass by here all the time," I told him. "I simply wasn't expecting it to be this building."

"Mmm-hmm," he murmured, looking at me like I was crazy.

You have no idea how crazy this is, I thought.

As we exited the cab, we were met with a terrible stench. City workers were doing sewer work in the area, and the fumes permeated the air. It was an awful odor that made me wretch. Surprisingly, it didn't seem to bother Mr. Jacobson.

"Are you OK?" Mr. Jacobson asked as we made our way toward the door. "You look sick."

"I'm a little queasy," I said. "But I think I'll feel better once we get inside."

Even after entering the building, however, I still felt like I needed to throw up. That may have been partly due to my nerves, which were getting worse by the second. My heart was rapidly pounding as we rode up the elevator, and I could feel a warm dampness of the sweat coming out of my pores. Feeling my hands start to quiver, I invoked the name. "Victor Petrov," I softly whispered. *Oh, the treachery of Satan ...*

Just at that moment the elevator stopped, and the large metal doors swiftly slid open.

The law firm office was on the twenty-first floor; the deposition took place in a room that likely was a conference room. An elongated oval table was in the center of the room, surrounded by leather chairs. Mr. Hughes' secretary showed us in. A court reporter was already seated in the room to record my testimony. She cordially introduced herself. Within a few minutes, a tall, distinguished-looking man entered. I knew in an instant that it was Nicholas Hughes. He was handsome and carried himself with a sense of purpose. He looked like a young Rock Hudson. His brown hair was conservatively cut, and there was not a hair out of place. He wore a black Armani suit and had a Rolex on his left wrist. His shoes were perfectly polished. He extended his hand to me and introduced himself with a warm smile. He offered me coffee or any other beverage of my choosing. I politely declined.

The deposition involved an extensive series of questions. I concentrated on what Mr. Jacobson had told me and tried to be as brief as possible with my answers—and that was hard at times. He asked many questions that required a protracted explanation. Still, I did the best that I could to be succinct.

Mr. Hughes never took his eyes off of me during the questioning. His degree of focus was impressive. His questions were delivered in a cordial manner, just as Mr. Jacobson had described, but I felt intimidated nonetheless. He did not use any notes, and he never hesitated with his next question. He used perfect grammar and enunciated every syllable of every word. If this was a game, then he was surely in control.

Stay calm and stay focused, I told myself.

Each question Hughes asked seemed to lead me down a path of distortion. Each cordial suggestion was laced with deceit. It was clear that he was trying to get me to paint a different picture of the event than what actually had occurred. He was trying, in a cunning manner, to make me look irresponsible and uncaring.

I can't let him do that, I thought.

While Hughes rattled off his well-plotted succession of misrepresentations, I found myself looking down at the table, as if afraid and ashamed. I realized that I had no reason to be ashamed. Regardless of whether I was at fault, it was an accident. My intentions were never in the wrong place. I meant no harm and wished no ill will. Of all the people in the room, I certainly was not the villain. Pulling myself together, I held my head up and looked him straight in the eye.

You're the one with ill intentions, Mr. Hughes. You're the one who should be ashamed. In the eyes of God, what you do for a living is abhorrent.

After over an hour of questioning, Nicolas Hughes rested, and then Mr. Jacobson asked me a few questions that were more in my favor.

I felt shaken after the entire thing was over. My head ached, and I again felt like throwing up. I was surprised when Mr. Jacobson told me that I had done an excellent job.

"What happens now?" I asked.

"For you," he said, "there is more waiting. We still need to get the deposition from Sylvester Jones and his doctor. After that, I will review everyone's testimony, as will Mr. Hughes. That is when the negotiations begin. We either settle or go to court."

"I don't want to settle," I said. "I don't feel that I've done anything wrong. Sylvester Jones and his lawyer are trying to swindle me. I don't want to settle!"

"We will cross that bridge when we get to it," Mr. Jacobson assured me. "If this case goes to jury, anything can happen. Settling can be a good option. Sometimes the known is better than the unknown."

Chapter 19
JERRY'S REPORT

WHEN I GOT home from the city, I wrote for a while. I had not gotten very far when Ellen called to find out about the deposition. Trying to stay positive, I neglected to say that the whole experience had made me feel sick. Instead, I simply answered, "It went very well, sweetie. My lawyer said I did an excellent job. That Nicholas Hughes didn't seem so tough."

"Oh, thank God," she said. "I was so worried about you. I was praying all afternoon."

"You shouldn't worry about this," I said. "It will work itself out. I am 100 percent confident that justice will prevail. We shouldn't even discuss it. More important, how are you feeling today?"

"I feel good, Dad. That's what's crazy. If they hadn't told me I have cancer, I'd never know it. The only thing I have is the rash on my face from the treatment—even that is a little better. The cream that Dr. Greenspan prescribed seems to help."

I was impressed with how well Ellen was coping with the entire situation. It certainly helped that she was feeling good. She no longer cried, and never once did she complain or feel sorry for herself. She did her best to stay positive. In that regard she reminded me of Tina. Tina was always a much more positive person than I was.

Later that evening, Jerry stopped over. I filled him in on Ellen's condition and gave him the full details of the deposition. I told him how angry I was that Sylvester Jones and his lawyers were trying to swindle me.

"I can't imagine what it is like to be going through what you're going through," he said. "If there is anything I can do—anything at all—just ask."

"You've been very supportive. I truly appreciate that. You've been a good friend. There is nothing more I can ask."

Jerry nodded in acknowledgment. He looked as if he was going to say something, but instead paused. He took a deep breath, held it for a second, and then exhaled, as if to relieve the tension.

"What is it?" I asked.

"Fred ..." he said hesitantly. "I've been keeping a close eye on Sylvester Jones. For the past several weeks, when I wasn't busy at work, I followed him around. He has such a scandalous history that I thought for sure that I'd find that he was making up this entire thing. I mean, it was the logical conclusion because the guy is definitely a crook. My God, he scammed money from innocent old people. You can't get more crooked and sleazy than that."

I was pretty sure that I knew where Jerry was heading with his story, and I braced myself for the truth I did not want to hear.

Jerry continued, "I thought for sure that I'd find that he wasn't really in pain. In my heart I believed it was a scam. But ..."

"But he really is disabled," I said, finishing for him.

Jerry sighed deeply. "Yes, Fred, it appears that he really is disabled. He does appear to be in pain. If he's faking this, then he is doing an awfully good job of it. He isn't letting down his guard, not even for a second—at least, not out in public." He shrugged helplessly, and then said, "I'm so sorry. I know that isn't what you wanted to hear. I feel like this is my fault. I shouldn't have gotten your hopes up. I should've waited until I had evidence before I even brought it up."

In an instant my anger toward Sylvester Jones and his lawyer turned to self-blame. This time I sighed. "No, Jerry, there is absolutely no reason for you to apologize. You were just being a friend. I thank you for going through all of the trouble you went through. It isn't your fault that Sylvester Jones turned out *not* to be a crook."

"Whether or not Sylvester Jones is disabled, he's still a crook," Jerry insisted, "and what he is putting you through is still wrong."

"Do you really believe that?" I asked. "Do you really believe that I'm the victim here? Don't you think that maybe I was driving too fast, in bad weather, and an innocent man is crippled because of it?"

For a moment, there was silence.

"Sylvester Jones is no innocent man," Jerry retorted, breaking the silence. "He is an evil man. Maybe you were driving too fast on a slick winter's day, and maybe the car crash really did cause Sylvester Jones' disability. I have no way of knowing. But you're certainly not the first person to drive a few miles over the speed limit in December. People make mistakes. That's why they have car insurance. What Sylvester Jones and his big-shot lawyers are doing to you is wrong. They are acting out of avarice. They're trying to take everything you have and ruin your life—and for what? Because you're human, and you made a mistake? Where is the justice in that? There is no justice in that! With God as my witness, I believe that Sylvester Jones is an evil man, and so is his sleazy lawyer."

I truly appreciated Jerry's passion and that he would stand by me, his friend, no matter what. I certainly did not want him to feel guilty about breaking bad news, so I tried to diffuse the situation with some humor. "With God as your witness?" I said with a wink. "Jerry, you don't even believe in God."

He exhaled slowly and then broke out into a smile. "I guess I always am calling God as my witness. Well, maybe that's why the world is so screwed up, because God is wasting all of his valuable time watching me."

Jerry is really a good egg, I thought after he left that night. Years ago, it used to bother me that he was an agnostic because it is written that only those who believe in Christ will have eternal life. I'd wonder how a good person like Jerry could be denied eternal life.

Then, somewhere along the way, I came to an important realization, which over the years became a strong conviction. Who was Christ, other than goodness in human form? And what better way to show that someone believed in and supported something than to actually do what he believed? It was easy to form the conclusion: those who do good believe in goodness. Because Christ is goodness, those who do good also believe in Christ.

Therefore, even though Jerry didn't go to church, I still believed he would be saved because he was a genuinely good person.

Chapter 20

The Book of Francis

Several weeks passed, during which time Jerry came up with a new theory—that Sylvester Jones had not become disabled from the car accident but through some other means, and he was only blaming the car accident so he could make a buck. He cited the fact that there was so little damage done to the car, and that Sylvester Jones waited almost two years to file the suit.

"It just doesn't add up," Jerry said. "The fenders of the cars were barely dented. It would have taken a much larger collision to cause the disability he is claiming. There's something rotten there. And why would he wait so long to file the law suit? Did he just suddenly decide that he needed help with his medical bills? He's asking for far more than he would need to pay his bills. The amount he is suing for is ridiculous."

I agreed that it did not all add up, especially considering that Sylvester Jones was a known con artist. I had always been an internalizer, blaming myself for everything. Still, in my gut I sensed that something was not right about the lawsuit.

- - - - - - - - -

I was making decent progress with my writing. It had taken me several months but I had covered the history of the first millennium of the Church. Proceeding onward, I started writing about events from the beginning of the second millennium. I began with the Great Schism, the titanic divide between the Western and Eastern Church that occurred in 1054. As recorded by Christian scholars in the Catholic Encyclopedia, for several centuries leading up to the Great Schism, there was a brewing tension between the

Church in the West, led by the Pope in Rome, and the Church in the East, led by the Patriarch of Constantinople. The tension heightened with the crowning of Charlemagne as Holy Roman Emperor and boiled over when Michael Caerularius, the Patriarch of Constantinople, disparaged the Western Church in the middle of the eleventh century. Seeking conflict, Caerularius rudely repudiated the Pope's ambassadors, who had journeyed to Constantinople in an attempt to improve relations. The Pope's ambassadors responded in dramatic fashion. After three months of fruitless dialogue, they left a bull of excommunication on the altar of the church of Constantinople. Outraged, Caerularius retaliated by excommunicating the Pope. With the excommunications, the first great schism came to pass. The Catholic Church became the church of the West, and the Orthodox Church became the church of the East. It was, unfortunately, just the beginning of many schisms for the Church.

The Great Schism was a tragedy, I thought. *It was a triumph of the devil to see the Church so divided. What a sad day for Christianity. What a sad day for all mankind.*

Changing my focus to something more positive, I wrote of Saint Bernard of Menthon and of the Alpine pass for which he is famous. Bernard was a kindhearted monk who established a hospice to house weary travelers as they made their way across the frigid Alps on pilgrimage to and from Rome. The hospice was located near the Pennine Pass, which led from the valley of Aosta to the Swiss canton of Valais. The pass, situated high in the mountains, eight thousand feet above sea level, was covered with snow even during the spring and summer months. When weather conditions became treacherous, as they often did, Bernard would go out in the snow and ice and guide stranded pilgrims to shelter. He did this with no concern for his own safety. His only concern was to do the Lord's work; to watch over God's lambs. He served God in this way for all of his days. Centuries later, the priests of the hospice trained dogs to help find travelers who were lost in the snow. Risking their own lives, the dogs saved countless pilgrims from the elements. They brought them food and drink and led them to safety. Appropriately, the noble beasts were called St. Bernards in honor of the blessed eleventh-century monk.

St. Bernards ... there are so many aspects of everyday life that have been touched by the saints, I thought.

It did not take me long to complete the brief section on Bernard. I then wrote of Thomas Becket and his great friendship with King Henry of England. Beckett's was a sad but noble tale. A man of great wealth, he was appointed Archbishop of Canterbury, the highest ecclesiastical position in all of Britain, in 1161. After the appointment, he gave up his life of luxury to serve God. Unfortunately, he soon faced a great personal crisis. In order to fulfill his duties, he found that he had to oppose the ambitions of the king, his best friend. Without hesitation, Becket placed God above friendship and staunchly denounced the anticlerical pursuits of King Henry. For this he was hunted down and murdered on the cold stone floor of Canterbury Cathedral. He died a martyr for Christ and to this day is held in highest regard by the people of Britain.

T. S. Elliot's poetic drama *Murder in the Cathedral* was based on Becket's story. I had never read it but, intrigued by the archbishop's martyrdom, I ordered a copy of it from Amazon.com before I went to bed that night.

The next morning I awoke early and wrote of Saint Francis of Assisi, the blessed founder of the Franciscan Order. I had always been a great admirer of Francis. All things considered, he was my favorite saint. His compassion and devotion to the poor were legendary, and the miracles he performed were nothing short of astounding. A student of history, I often compared him with the most prominent of the ancient prophets, especially Moses. It was my heartfelt belief that his holy deeds were just as important to God's people as were the deeds of Moses in the Old Testament. Like Moses, Saint Francis knew the Lord face to face and obediently followed his plan.

Both were great servants of God, I reasoned.

Born in the year 1181 at Assisi in Umbria, Francis was the son of Pietro di Bernardone, a rich cloth merchant, and his wife, Pica, a French aristocrat. As is true of many of the saints, Francis did not begin his life on a path to God. He grew up in a time of knights in shining armor and chivalry and had aspirations to find glory as a knight. Throughout his youth, his only concerns were worldly concerns. He spent all of his time carousing with his friends and dreaming of great adventures. He drank and cursed and sought pleasures of the flesh. Until the age of twenty-five, he truly lived a life of sin. Yet the lure of darkness could not hold him—he was called to a different path. In the year 1206, Francis began to hear the voice of Christ and changed his ways. Christ said to him:

> "Francis! Everything you have loved and desired in the flesh it is your duty to despise and hate, if you wish to know my will. And when you have begun this, all that now seems sweet and lovely to you will become intolerable and bitter, but all that you used to avoid will turn itself to great sweetness and exceeding joy."[18]

Heeding the message from Christ, Francis rejected his unscrupulous past

---

18 URL: http://www.americancatholic.org/Features/Francis/Who_Was.asp.
    Downloaded 1-28-06.

and embraced a life of piety and poverty. However, the Lord's plan for Francis did not stop there; the King of kings had a great task in store for the young Assisian. In a dark age of cruelty and hardship, Christ chose Francis to rekindle the love of God in the world. Just as God called out to Moses from the burning bush, summoning him to lead his people, Christ called out to Francis. The historic call to service occurred one day while Francis was praying in the wayside chapel at Saint Damian's. Instead of a burning bush on a mountain, Christ used a crucifix in an abandoned church to communicate his wishes to the saint. The effect was the same; like Moses centuries before him, Francis was moved in untold ways by the Lord's powerfully spoken words. A well-known and much admired event, Francis' call to service at St. Damian's has been recounted by numerous Christian authors over the years. Having read several accounts, I particularly appreciated Reverend Candide Chalippe's version of the miraculous episode, written in the eighteenth century, and I included it in *The Third Testament*:

> "The Servant of God, walking and meditating one day out of Assisi, near the church of St. Damian, which was very old and falling into ruin, was moved by the Holy Spirit to enter it to pray. There, prostrated before the crucifix, he repeated three times the following words, which gave him great interior consolation, and which he subsequently made frequent use of: 'Great God, full of glory, and Thou, my Lord Jesus Christ! I entreat you to enlighten me and to dispel the darkness of my mind, to give me a pure faith, a firm hope, and an ardent charity. Let me have a perfect knowledge of Thee, O God, so that I may in all things be guided by Thy light, and act in conformity to Thy will.' He then cast his eyes, filled with tears, upon the crucifix, when a voice came forth from it, and he heard distinctly these words repeated three times, not interiorly, but loudly pronounced: 'Francis, go and repair my house, which thou seest is falling into ruin.' So wonderful a voice, in a place he was alone, alarmed him greatly, but he felt immediately the salutary effects of it, and he was transported with joy."[19]

Upon hearing the words, "Go and repair my house, which thou seest is falling into ruin," Francis at first thought that Christ was referring to St. Damian's, which was dilapidated. But later, Francis realized that Christ was referring to the universal Church. With all his heart and soul, Francis obeyed

---

19   Rev. Candide Chalippe. *The Life of St Francis of Assisi*. New York: D & J Sadler Company, 1889, p. 47.

Christ's command. He repaired Christ's house with his words and deeds, humbly serving the Lord as no man had done before. It is written:

> "Shining like a morning star in the midst of a dark cloud, he enlightened by the bright rays of his pure doctrine and holy life those who lay in the darkness and shadow of death, and thus guided them onwards by his bright shining to the perfect day."[20]

Even though I associated Francis with Moses and the prophets of the Old Testament, in many ways the Assisian's extraordinary life story read more like an excerpt from the Gospels of the New Testament, especially his life story, as recorded by Saint Bonaventure, the primary source for Francis' words and deeds. Graced by the Holy Spirit, Francis had a remarkable power to heal. He used this power to do great good. Following in the footsteps of Christ, he went about the countryside, tending to the neglected or infirm. He restored sight to the blind and strength to the crippled. He cured lepers and cast out demons. He did these things in the name of the Lord so that others would know the Lord's goodness. Before long, word of his heavenly power spread far and wide, and the people began to see him as a true messenger from God.

I included the story of one of his miraculous healings in *The Third Testament*.

> There was a man from Spoleto whose face was being eaten away by leprosy. Desperate for a cure, he went to see countless physicians, but not one could help him. He then set out on a pilgrimage to visit the shrines of the apostles in search of a miracle but found none. On the way back from visiting the shrines, he encountered Francis, preaching on the street. Having heard of Francis' goodness, the man dropped to his knees and crawled forward to kiss the saint's feet. A humble man, Francis at once implored the leper to rise. Looking upward to heaven, the Lord's servant said a prayer and then selflessly kissed the loathsome face of the one who wished to kiss his feet. To the amazement of all those in witness, at the very moment of Francis' holy kiss, every sign of the disease suddenly vanished, and the leper returned to the perfect health he so longed for.

---

20 Cardinal Manning. *The Life of St. Francis of Assisi, from the "Legenda Santa Francisci" of St. Bonaventure*, eighth ed. London: Burns, Oates and Washbourne Ltd., 1867, p. 5.

Such was the heavenly power of Saint Francis, and such was his humility.

Humility will raise the humblest soul to the throne that was lost through pride, I thought, moved by the story of the leper.

Humility was certainly one of Francis' defining characteristics. It is said that the theologians of the era did not know which to admire more—the Assisian's incredible humility or his extraordinary power to heal. It was evident to me that the two were intricately connected.

Francis' humility and great compassion extended beyond the realm of man. A true lover of life, the good saint had a special devotion to all of God's creatures, and they had a special bond with him. This bond with nature—or as Francis would say, "brotherhood," with nature—was another of the saint's defining characteristics. It certainly was unique. When Francis preached in the groves surrounding his beloved Portiuncula Chapel in Assisi, the birds would gather in silence, as if listening to his words. As soon as the saint was done with his sermons, the birds would resume their singing and go about their business. And when Francis went out into the woods, as he often did, the beasts, too, would pay homage to him, heeding his commands with absolute obedience.

Working feverishly, I described one of Francis' more noted animal encounters:

> In the village of Gubbio, there was a vicious wolf that fed on the flocks of the people there. It was so ferocious that none of the villagers dared go near the woods where the wolf lived. One day Francis passed through the village and heard the people's plight. Wanting to help the villagers, he set out to the woods to meet the wolf. Several people of the village went a short distance with him, but they soon became too frightened to go any further. Francis then went on alone, unafraid. Deep in the woods, he confronted the wolf. The wolf charged at him, showing its saber-sharp fangs. Still, Francis did not fear; he trusted in God. Making the sign of the cross, he ordered the beast to desist. He said, "Come, Brother Wolf. In the name of Christ, I order you to cease your aggression." Hearing these words, the wolf halted in its tracks, lowered its head, and gently rested at the saint's feet. Francis told the townspeople that the wolf would do no harm if they fed him every day. From then on, the townspeople fed the docile beast as it went from door to door.

Inspired by Francis' miraculous deeds, and even more so by his devotion to God, others soon began to follow him. Like Francis, these followers took a vow of poverty. They all wore long, rough tunics of undyed wool and preached among the sick and the poor. In the year 1209, Francis and eleven of his followers, whom he called brothers, ventured to Rome to seek Pope Innocent III's official approval of their simple rule of life. Innocent, a pensive man with conservative ways, was hesitant at first to accept the new brotherhood, but then he had an extraordinary vision. In the vision he foresaw a catastrophe; it appeared that the Church of Rome was about to crumble and fall. The top of the edifice trembled and swayed. The trembling grew worse and worse until suddenly, it stopped. "Why did it stop?" the good Pope wondered as he looked up at the steeple. Then Innocent gazed downward. There he saw Francis, standing alone, holding up the pillars of the Church. As a result of this dream, Innocent approved Francis' rule and gave Francis and his followers permission to preach throughout the land. The Franciscan Order was thus established.

The Franciscans remain a buttress for the Church to this day, I reflected as I wrote about Pope Innocent and his prophetic dream.

Although he valued deeds more than words, Francis was a gifted speaker and writer. Like Christ, he often spoke in proverbs and told parables. In doing so, he was able to connect with the common man in ways others could not. Utilizing his oratory skills, Francis converted many to the faith—many who had previously heard but not believed.

I recalled that when I was very young, my grandfather told me one of Francis' parables. A Church historian like myself, my grandfather told me countless stories about the saints, most of which I had long forgotten, but this particular parable stuck with me. It was deep and inspiring and provided a life lesson that, over the years, I had found to be quite valuable. Whenever I would think of it, and I often did, it was almost as if I could still hear my grandfather's gruff but loving voice.

"One day a fellow clergyman, Brother Leo, came to Francis and questioned him about the meaning of true joy," the parable began. "Brother Leo asked if converting princes and kings to the faith is true joy, and Francis answered, 'No.' Brother Leo asked if knowing the answers to the secrets and mysteries of the universe is true joy, and Francis answered, 'No.' Brother Leo then asked if curing the sick and lame, or even raising the dead, is true joy, and Francis answered, 'No.' Confused, Leo then begged that Francis tell him what true joy is. Francis explained with a story. He described a scenario where he was returning from a long journey, and it was freezing cold outside. In the scenario, he was barefoot with blood-stained feet. Completely exhausted, starving, and truly miserable from the horrid weather conditions, he went to the monastery and asked to be let in, but he was turned away by a friar who did not recognize him. Francis pleaded with the friar, but his pleas were met with ridicule. Not wanting to be bothered, the belligerent friar called Francis a fool and callously banished him into the dark and cold."

"That's terrible," I remembered saying to my grandfather. "Francis must have really been mad." At that time, I had no idea how the parable was going to end or how it was going to relate to true joy.

"It does seem terrible, but it is very important that you remember what Francis said next," my grandfather instructed.

I've never forgotten.

At the conclusion of the parable, Francis turned to Brother Leo and said, "If I had patience and did not become upset, true joy, as well as true virtue and the salvation of my soul, would consist in this."[21]

Thinking that it would make an excellent addition, I included the parable of Francis and the coldhearted friar in *The Third Testament*.

"You can't have a biblical book without parables, and that was a memorable parable," I said aloud.

Throughout his life, Francis went about doing the Lord's work. He tended to the sick and championed the poor. In everything he did, he tried to emulate Christ. Near the end of his life, while on pilgrimage at Monte La Verna, Francis was blessed with the mystical stigmata. After several weeks of fasting and prayer on the mountain, an archangel appeared to him and showed him a vision of Christ on the cross. When the vision ended, Francis found that he was miraculously anointed with the marks of the crucifixion. He carried the holy marks with him for the remainder of his days. I wrote:

> In the summer of 1224, Francis was led by divine Providence to Monte La Verna, where for forty days he fasted and meditated in preparation for the feast of Saint Michael the Archangel. During this time, he pondered the Passion of the Lord and the depth of Christ's suffering. While deep in meditation, an archangel appeared to him. Per the Lord's command, the seraphim granted Francis the greatest of privileges. He revealed to Francis a vision of Jesus on the cross, the very foundation of the salvation of man. Seeing the vision, Francis was overcome with emotion. At once, tears filled his eyes, and he dropped to his knees in reverence. Miraculously, when the vision ended, the saint found that his body had been marked with the stigmata of the crucifixion. He had black excrescences on his hands and feet and a wound on his side that oozed blood. The marks were imprinted on him by the glorious power of the Risen Lord, the God of Light, Creator of the heavens and earth.

21   Teresa De Bertodana. *The Book of Catholic Wisdom*. Chicago: Loyola Press, 2001, p. 190.

"September 17," I blurted out as I wrote about the stigmata. "I think it is September 17."

Curious to see if my memory served me correctly, I grabbed a Catholic charities calendar from one of the drawers in my desk. Opening the calendar to September, I saw that on the seventeenth, there was a notation in small print:

"The Feast of the Stigmata of St. Francis of Assisi"

I thought that there was a feast day on the liturgical calendar commemorating the stigmata. Why doesn't the Church make a bigger deal out of this? It seems like something that everyone should know about.

After receiving the blessed stigmata, Saint Francis lived for two more years, before passing at the age of forty-four. During that time he composed his most famous prayer to God, the Canticle of the Sun:

> Most High, all-powerful, all-good Lord,
> All praise is yours, all glory, all honor, and all blessing.
> To you alone, Most High, do they belong,
> No mortal lips are worthy to mention Your name.
> Be praised, my Lord, through all your creatures,
> especially through my lord Brother Sun,
> who brings the day; and you give light through him.
> And he is beautiful and radiant in all his splendor!
> Of you, Most High, he bears the likeness.
> Be praised, my Lord, through Sister Moon and the stars;
> in the heavens you have made them bright, precious and beautiful.
> Be praised, my Lord, through Brothers Wind and Air,
> and clouds and storms, and all the weather,
> through which you give your creatures sustenance.
> Be praised, My Lord, through Sister Water;
> she is very useful, and humble, and precious, and pure.
> Be praised, my Lord, through Brother Fire,
> through whom you brighten the night.
> He is beautiful and cheerful, and powerful and strong.
> Be praised, my Lord, through our sister Mother Earth,
> who feeds us and rules us,
> and produces various fruits with colored flowers and herbs.
> Be praised, my Lord, through those who forgive for love of you;
> through those who endure sickness and trial.

Happy those who endure in peace,
for by you, Most High, they will be crowned.
Be praised, my Lord, through our Sister Bodily Death,
from whose embrace no living person can escape.
Woe to those who die in mortal sin!
Happy those she finds doing your most holy will.
The second death can do no harm to them.
Praise and bless my Lord, and give thanks,
and serve him with great humility.[22]

Francis died in peace on October 4, 1226. He spent his final moments near the sacred Portiuncula Chapel, surrounded by those closest to him. As he wished, he died simply, lying on the ground, covered by an old habit. It is said that at the time of his passing, great flocks of larks came and circled the roof of the chapel, as testimony to the glory of the saint.

A true man of God, Francis would go down through history as one of the greatest shepherds in the annals of the Church. Saint Bonaventure summarized his blessed life best. He said:

> "Like a hierarchic man, he was lifted up in a fiery chariot, as will be seen quite clearly in the course of his life; therefore it can be reasonably proved that he came in the spirit and power of Elijah. And so not without reason is he considered to be symbolized by the image of the angel who ascends from the sunrise bearing the seal of the living God."[23]

"Francis was no ordinary man," I murmured to myself. "As Bonaventure said, he was an angel sent from heaven to guide the Lord's lost sheep."

After completing the summary of Saint Francis, I wrote of Saint Anthony of Padua and of Saint Dominic. Both lived around the time of Francis, and both were holy men who were granted miraculous powers by the Lord. Saint Anthony, in particular, was known for his heavenly deeds. He was called the "wonder worker" for all of the miracles he performed. In the name of Christ, he went around curing the sick and casting out demons; he retrieved things lost and stolen; and he converted even the most obstinate of heretics.

One of Anthony's more noted miracles involved a temperamental young man named Leonardo, who one day, in a fit of anger, kicked his own mother.

---

22 Adapted from URL: http://en.wikipedia.org/wiki/Canticle_of_the_Sun. Downloaded 1-31-09.

23 Adapted from Bonaventure. *The Life of St. Francis*. Mahwah, NJ: Paulist Press, 1978, p. 2.

Soon after the incident, the volatile youth felt a deep sense of remorse for what he had done. Repentant, he confessed his fault to Anthony, who admonished him, saying:

"The foot of the son who kicks his mother deserves to be cut off."

The impulsive and imprudent lad took the good saint's words literally and cut off his own foot. Learning of this, Saint Anthony brought the amputated foot to the unfortunate youth and, praying to Christ, miraculously healed him. The young man was forever grateful and, heeding the instructions of the saint, mended his ways and went on to live a life in Christ.

Another noted miracle involved Anthony's psalm book. One day the book was stolen by a misguided young Franciscan who had deviated from the path of God. The troubled youth fled the Order in hopes of finding riches and adventure. When he left, he took Anthony's cherished psalm book with him. Upon realizing that his book was gone, the good saint prayed to the Lord Jesus Christ that it would be found and returned to him. At the moment of Anthony's prayer, the troubled youth, who by this time was miles away from the friary, came to realize the error in his ways. At once, his soul felt abject emptiness, the emptiness one feels when he rejects God. The boy quickly returned to the Franciscan Order and gave Anthony his book. He felt deeply sorry for what he had done and begged for forgiveness. Under Saint Anthony's direction, the boy was forgiven and went on to become a humble and virtuous friar.

Anthony's numerous heavenly deeds were lauded by his contemporaries, no more so than in the "Miraculous Responsory," a brief verse written centuries ago:

If then you ask of miracles
Death, error, all calamities,
The leprosy and demons fly,
And health succeeds infirmities.

The seas obey, and fetters break,
And lifeless limbs thou dost restore,
Whilst treasures lost are found again
When young or old thine aid implore.

All dangers vanish at thy prayer,
And direst need doth quickly flee.
Let those who know thy power proclaim,

Let Paduans say—"These are of thee."[24]

Anthony's most famous miracle involved a sermon to the fish of the Brenta River. One day, while preaching in Rimini, Anthony came across a large group of heretics who refused to listen to his words. Anthony tried for nearly a week but made no progress with them. Clinging to their worldly joys, the heretics were irreverent and pigheaded and would not be swayed. At last, inspired by God, Anthony ventured down to the shores of the river and began to preach to the fish. It was not long before multitudes of fish raised their heads above the water, giving the wonder worker their absolute attention. Anthony blessed the fish, for even though they were animals without reason, they honored God more than the sinful heretics. While Anthony preached, the number of fish increased, such that never before had so many been seen in the sea or river. The people of the city, hearing of the miracle, made haste to go and witness it. With them also came the heretics, who were so stunned by the multitudes of reverent fish that they instantly threw themselves at Anthony's feet and converted to the faith.

Saint Anthony's sermon to the fish was eloquently recounted in a passage from the fourteenth-century book *Little Flowers of St. Francis*. I included the passage in *The Third Testament*, and then proceeded to write about Saint Dominic.

Saint Dominic, like Saint Anthony, was a remarkable man who greatly inspired the people of God. He founded the Order of Preachers, better known as the Dominican Order. He also began the tradition of praying the Rosary. I took particular interest in the story of Dominic and the Rosary; it was certainly biblical in nature, and it certainly impacted modern society.

As the story goes, one night in the year 1208, while Dominic was residing at the chapel of Notre Dame de la Prouille, the Virgin Mary appeared to him in a dream and showed him a heavenly wreath of roses. Supported by the Holy Spirit, the roses hovered in the air next to where the Blessed Virgin was standing. They were radiant, like the sun, and emitted an unparalleled sweet fragrance. Dominic described them as being more beautiful than any flowers he had seen in his entire life. It was obvious to the saint that they were arranged by the hand of God. It was also obvious that Mary had an important purpose in revealing them to him. The roses, greater than fifty in number, served as a representation of the angelic psalter, also known as the Rosary—the Lord's chosen instrument of reform. As Dominic watched in

---

24 Deymann Clementinus. *Devotion to St. Anthony of Padua*. San Francisco, CA: A. Waldteufel, 1888.

awe, Mary gestured toward the heavenly wreath with her right hand and, with the gentle voice of a loving mother, instructed him to pray the Rosary.

"Teach it to all who will listen," she said. "One day, through the Rosary, I shall save the world."

Dominic reverently obeyed, and the devotion to the Rosary spread across the earth, thanks to the dutiful saint.

I came to realize that the twelfth and thirteenth centuries, a period when kings and popes utterly failed the Church, were guided by some of the most remarkable saints to ever walk the earth.

God definitely is watching over us, I thought.

Chapter 21

FEDERAL DISTRICT COURT VERSUS GONZALES 1881

ELLEN CONTINUED ON the experimental pill MM314. Her two-month checkup showed that the tumors had not shrunk at all, but on the upside, they had not grown at all either. Dr. Greenspan encouraged us to continue with the treatment. He said that without treatment, a cancer will always grow, so the fact that the tumors had not grown was a sign that the therapy was working. We were pleased with his assessment, but when we asked how long we could expect the experimental drug to keep the tumors in check, all he said was "Only time will tell."

The legal issues in my life were becoming more of a problem. Mr. Jacobson recommended that I seek a settlement. I was unhappy with that decision, but he warned me that letting a jury become involved would put me at risk for losing everything.

"You don't want to see what can happen after Nicholas C. Hughes misleads the jury with his charm and legal illusions," he said.

After much discussion, I agreed to seek a settlement. The problem was that my accusers were not looking to settle. Nicholas Hughes and his client, Sylvester Jones, were conspiring to take everything. If their plot were to succeed, my home would be gone, my life savings wiped out, and my wages garnished. I would be left with absolutely nothing. The crazy thing was that I really did not care about being left with nothing. All I cared about was Ellen. I would have gladly given up all of my possessions if it meant that Ellen would be OK. And if Ellen were to die, all the treasures in the world could not suppress my sorrow. So the potential of losing my home and savings did not trouble me. What did trouble me was the absence of justice.

How can an immoral crook and his slick predator lawyer get away with this? I asked myself. Never in my life had I intended to harm anyone in any way. I had lived a good life. I prayed to God. I went to church. I contributed to charities. I never cheated in my life. There was not an ounce of malice in my heart. Yet I was being hunted like a criminal. *Where is the justice?*

My frustration with the legal system reached a climax on the morning of May 25. I recall the day exactly because it was the anniversary of the day when Tina and I first met. It was a slow morning, and I was flipping channels on TV while eating breakfast. One of the local news stations was doing a story on Vincent Rocca, the famous Chicago mob boss who murdered his wife in cold blood but got off on a legal technicality. They reported that he was writing a book, which they expected would be a best-seller. The reporter interviewed Rocca as he was playing golf. Superficially charming, Rocca laughed and smiled throughout the interview. He seemed to be carefree and full of life. The scene made my blood boil.

"This monster is responsible for the death of his former wife, and yet he walks the streets free, without a care in the world," I grumbled. "He walks free while I sit and suffer, besieged by venomous predators." Overflowing with anger, I abruptly shut off the television and threw down the remote control. "Incredible!" I fumed. "Incredible! What a messed-up society we live in."

Later that day, after cooling off a little bit, I drove up to Saint James cemetery to visit Tina's grave. I always visited on the anniversary of the day we met. It was a day that changed my life forever. I remembered it fondly. I was a senior in high school at the time. On Friday nights, Jerry, Joe, and I would go to Sammy's to hang out. Sammy's was more or less a club for teens—a pizza parlor and bowling alley with an arcade and dance floor. It was very popular. Kids from all of the local high schools would gather there on weekends. The three of us would go there in the hope of meeting girls. Joe was very much a ladies' man, but Jerry and I were more introverted. We spent most of our time playing games in the arcade while Joe was off flirting. There were many days that I wished I was more like Joe. In particular, there was one girl I had my eye on, but I was not brave enough to approach her. "She's too beautiful," I lamented. "She would never go for a guy like me." I put her out of my mind and focused on trying to get to know a couple of other girls that Joe had introduced to us. Unfortunately, I did not have much success and was feeling down. One day, Joe told me that he had met a girl who was interested in me. "Let me introduce you to her," he said. I agreed and he led me to where she was sitting. Together, we walked from the arcade over to the pizza area. As we approached the tables, I nudged Joe and said, "Hey, there's the girl I've been telling you about."

Seated at one of the tables was the beautiful girl that I was too shy to meet.

I pointed her out to Joe. Erupting with enthusiasm, Joe instantly turned to me and said, "No way! No way!"

I was confused by his reaction until he explained that the girl I had pointed out was the same girl he was bringing me to meet. That girl was Tina.

The memory of the day we met burned brightly in my mind as I passed through the entrance of Saint James cemetery.

"Those were better times," I murmured. "Those were better times."

As always, I brought a bouquet of tulips with me to the cemetery. Filled with tension, I clutched them tightly in my hand. I was still quite upset with the legal system as I stood in front of Tina's gravesite.

"What an unjust world you left me in, my darling," I whispered over her tomb. "As much as I need you now, I am thankful that you are not here to witness the sadness in this life."

I looked up to the sky and then back down to the earth. I shook my head in frustration. Sighing, I placed the tulips on Tina's grave and knelt to say a prayer, but my thoughts were racing, and it was difficult to concentrate. Inside of me there was an unsettled feeling—a feeling of anxiety, and anger, and emptiness, and sadness, all fused into one emotion. I searched my mind for a soothing thought but could find none. I sighed a second time. "Lord, please have mercy," I said aloud. "Please show me justice."

I then reached my hand into my pocket and pulled out a rosary. I clutched the beads and began praying, hoping that the rhythm of the Rosary would soothe my soul. Despite my efforts, the disquieted feeling remained. I sighed a third time.

Getting up to leave, I bowed my head. "There is no justice on earth," I said. I then began to walk slowly back to my car. Again, I looked up to the sky, and as I lifted my head, something caught my eye in the distance. It was the figure of a man. He seemed to be carrying something. When I stopped to get a better view, I realized that it was the old man I had seen there before, Anthony Woewucki, the war veteran. He was carrying several bundles of flowers. I walked over to greet him. I did not expect him to remember my name. I was actually quite impressed with myself that I remembered his.

The old man surprised me. "Fred!" he called out with a smile as he saw me approaching.

"Tony," I called back with a nod and a wave.

Setting down the flowers, he extended his hand to greet me. "It's good to see you, Fred," he said.

"It's good to see you, too," I replied.

He asked how Ellen was doing—I could not believe that he remembered her name. That was truly remarkable. He seemed very interested to hear how her therapy was going. I explained that she had been to two different oncologists and was currently being treated with an experimental drug.

"Has she been to see Dr. Kruntzel?" he asked.

"Who?" I didn't recognize the name.

"Dr. Thomas M. Kruntzel," he said. "He's an outstanding oncologist at Northwestern University. She should go to see him. If he can't help her, no one can."

Right after Ellen was diagnosed with her cancer, I thoroughly researched all of the melanoma experts in the country. I did not recall seeing the name Thomas M. Kruntzel.

"Is he a melanoma expert?" I asked.

"Dr. Kruntzel specializes in several different types of cancer," he said. "Melanoma is one of them. Ellen should definitely go to see him."

"Well, thank you," I said. "We can certainly use all of the good advice we can get."

Tony then asked me how my legal problems were going.

I groaned in reply to his question. "There's no justice," I said.

"With God, there is justice," he replied with assurance.

I went on to tell him my woes and related how angry it made me to see a man like Vincent Rocca living such a happy life while I was suffering legal persecution.

Tony could see how frustrated I was. He said, "Fred, trust God. Justice will be served! And it will be a more profound justice than you can ever imagine."

I sighed and smiled skeptically.

Sensing my doubt, Tony said, "Let me tell you a story. Back in 1881, when I was still a young man"—with that, he winked—"there was a cold-blooded killer in New Mexico named Jose Gonzales. Jose Gonzales was a sheepherder who turned into a murderer. Vicious and evil, he killed his victims by slashing their throats. He was also arrogant and foolhardy. He thought he could escape the law, but he was wrong. Jose Gonzales eventually was apprehended and brought before a judge of the Federal District Court. The judge found him guilty of murder and handed down the following sentence, which I quote verbatim:

'Jose Manuel Miguel Xavier Gonzales, in a few short weeks, it will be spring. The snows of winter will flee away, the ice will vanish, and the annual miracle of the years will awaken and come to pass, but you won't be there.

'The rivulet will run its course to the sea, the timid desert flowers will put forth their tender shoots, the glorious valleys of this imperial domain will blossom as the rose. Still, you won't be there to see.

167

'From every treetop some wild woods songster will carol his mating song, butterflies will sport in the sunshine, the busy bee will hum happily as it pursues its accustomed vocation. The gentle breeze will tease the tassels of the wild grasses, and all nature, Jose Manuel Miguel Xavier Gonzales, will be glad but you.

'You won't be there to enjoy it because I command the sheriff, or some officers of the county, to lead you out to some remote spot, swing you by the neck from a knotting bough of a sturdy oak, and let you hang until you are dead.

'And then, Jose Manuel Miguel Xavier Gonzales, I further command that such officer or officers retire quickly from your dangling corpse, that vultures may descend from the heavens upon your filthy body until nothing shall remain but the bare bleached bones of a cold-blooded, throat-cutting, sheepherding, blood-thirsty, murdering, evil-hearted, son of Satan.'"[25]

Tony completed his discourse, and we both stood there for a moment in silence.

"That's poetic justice if I've ever heard it," I quipped. "They sure don't make judges like that anymore. We could probably use a few more judges like that in this crazy world."

I was in awe of the way Tony could rattle off quotations like he was reading them straight from a book. For an old man, he had a sharp mind. He certainly did have an unusual manner, though. Looking into his eyes, I could see he was very serious and passionate about every word. I still was not sure how his story related to my situation, but then he spoke further.

"Fred, the harsh sentence handed down by the judge to this cold-blooded killer cannot even approach the condemnation that God has in store for those who sin against his people. To equate the two would be like comparing the flicker of a candle to the fire of the sun. Do not be concerned with the courts. Do not be concerned with the deceitful words of lawyers. The law will do what the law must do, but beware to the sinners of the world, for there is a God, and he *will* bring justice. It will be profound and awesome. This is a truth that cannot be denied, not even by the devil himself. Have faith, and believe."

---

25 Adapted from United States of America vs. Gonzalez, United States District Court, New Mexico Territory Sessions, 1881.

Chapter 22
THE EPIPHANY

"COMING UP DURING our next segment, a new breakthrough for melanoma," announced Nancy Kwon, a channel 5 news reporter, during the 11:00 AM newscast.

The announcement instantly caught my attention, and I anxiously sat on the couch in front of my forty-one-inch television set. "I've got to hear this," I said. I grabbed the remote control and turned up the volume extra loud. I also grabbed a pen and notepad in case there was anything I needed to write down.

After what seemed like an eternity of senseless commercials, Nancy Kwon came back on and reported the effects of turmeric, the potent spice found in yellow curry, on melanoma.

"Turmeric demonstrated dramatic results," Kwon reported. "It has potent anticancer powers, causing the melanoma cells to stop proliferating and pushing them to commit suicide. Researchers at M. D. Anderson Cancer Center in Houston, Texas, are continuing to study this promising new therapy."

Finally, some good news! I thought. *Oh, thank God*.

My spirits were uplifted. I immediately called Ellen and told her the news. She quickly got on the Internet and looked up turmeric. What she found made each of us very hopeful.

Ellen read aloud from an article on the M. D. Anderson Web site. "This says that turmeric 'blocks virtually every tumor marker we have tested.'" The article confirmed the report of dramatic results and potent anticancer properties. "This is wonderful. It sounds so promising," Ellen said. "This is really good news."

"We were due for some good news," I said.

"I'm going to ask Dr. Greenspan about it the next time we see him," Ellen said.

"It certainly can't hurt to see what he has to say," I said. "If it is in yellow curry powder, it can't be toxic. It sounds like it's a really amazing breakthrough."

The good news was a nice respite from the cloud of dread that had hung over us for the past several months. It was like a temporary reprieve from a jail sentence. I was happy to have a reason for optimism, but at the same time, I was afraid that being optimistic would lead to more disappointment. Overall, the happiness won out, and I began to do more things that I enjoyed; for the first time in a long time, I began to live and breathe again. In an effort to get into better shape, I started jogging and eating better. I also started taking small steps toward being more social. I went out to dinner with Jerry and Joyce at least once a week, and Jerry and I even made plans to join a bowling league. I still spent a lot of time writing, as writing had become not only an escape and enjoyment but an obsession.

It's a magnificent obsession, I realized.

— — — — — — — — — —

On Sunday, June 12, while seated in the second-to-last pew in the back of St. Mary's Church, I began to contemplate the conclusion of *The Third Testament*. My writing was nowhere near finished, but I nonetheless questioned, *How should it end?* Remarkably, I had not thought about it, focusing instead on the chronology of events without concern about a stopping point. Now, the time had come for me to consider the ending.

There are plenty of biblical events in the twentieth century to choose from, I mused as I stared upward at the ornate cathedral ceiling. *Maybe the second Vatican Council?* With that thought, my eyes turned from the cathedral ceiling to Father Tom, who was facing the congregation and speaking in clear English. *No Latin, thanks to Vatican II.* I glanced at the choir, which was accompanied not by organ music but by a guitar and drums. *Ugh*, I grimaced. *So much for tradition.* Finally, scanning the church, I saw that it was less than two-thirds full; I came to a quick decision. *No, that won't do. That won't do at all.* Although Vatican II was a monumental change for the Church, it remained to be seen whether or not it was a change for the better, and I did not want to end with a question mark.

Maybe Medjugorje, I pondered as my eyes gazed back up at the beautiful ceiling. At first Medjugorje seemed perfect—the appearance of the Virgin Mary in modern-day Europe, encouraging the world to pray and to receive

Holy Communion. *A well-documented miracle in the 1980s—that's a definite possibility.*

It only took a minute, however, before I found fault with my own idea. My main concern was that the apparitions at Medjugorje had not been authenticated by the Church. *What if, in the end, the Church finds that the claims are fraudulent?*

I continued to search for alternatives. *Perhaps the establishment of the state of Israel in 1948.* The establishment of Israel was certainly a biblical event. In the early twentieth century, Christian Zionists professed that the establishment of Israel was a necessary event prior to the End of Times and the Second Coming of Christ. They cited passages from the Bible's prophetic books as proof to their claim.

The herald of the Second Coming. Hmmm. The Second Coming would, of course, have been the perfect conclusion to *The Third Testament*, but since it has not yet occurred, that was not an option. However, picking an event leading up to the Second Coming seemed to be an excellent choice. *I think I'm on to something here.*

Just then, my stream of consciousness was broken by the lector reading a passage from the Second Epistle of Peter:

> "Know this first of all, that in the last days, scoffers will come to scoff, living according to their own desires and saying, 'Where is the promise of his coming?' From the time when our ancestors fell asleep, everything has remained as it was from the beginning of creation. They deliberately ignore the fact that the heavens existed of old, and earth was formed out of water and through water by the word of God. The world that then existed was destroyed, deluged with water. The present heavens and earth have been reserved by the same word for fire, kept for the Day of Judgment and the destruction of the godless. But do not ignore this one fact, beloved, that with the Lord one day is like a thousand years and a thousand years like one day! The Lord does not delay his promise, as some would regard 'delay,' but rather he is patient with you, not wishing that any should perish but that all should come to repentance. But the day of the Lord will come like a thief. The heavens will disappear with a roar; the elements will be destroyed by fire, and the earth and everything in it will be laid bare."[26]

With the Lord, one day is like a thousand years, and a thousand years like one

---

26   Adapted from "2 Peter 3." URL: http://www.tedmontgomery.com/bblovrvw/ NIVBible/Pet_2.html. Downloaded 2-26-06.

day. I repeated the passage in my mind. I had heard it many times before but never took note that it originated from Saint Peter. I found it curious that the lector read a passage about the End of Times at the very moment that I was thinking about the End of Times. *Maybe God is trying to tell me something.*

When Mass ended, I walked out to my car, a black Volkswagen bug that looked more gray than black because it had not been washed in a very long time. I had a backpack on the passenger's seat, filled with bottles of water and snacks; I was planning to take a long hiking trip later that day. I had been thinking about taking a hiking trip for quite some time, but previously had been too down to actually do it.

Living in the Chicagoland area, there were a few interesting places to hike. In the northwest corner of Illinois, just three hours from Chicago, was the town of Galena. Situated along the bluffs of the Mississippi River, Galena had something that few towns in Illinois had—hills. The rolling landscape was truly quaint and made for a pleasant drive through pastoral farmland. There were not any state parks or forest preserves for hiking in Galena, but the Chestnut Mountain Ski Resort had several hiking trails that were open to the public. The trails curved along the slopes of a 500-foot bluff overlooking the Mississippi, and in a few spots, the views were fantastic. Autumn was the best time of the year to go because the fall colors produced a brilliant panorama.

For a longer hike, I liked to drive up to Wisconsin to Devil's Lake. A three and a half hour drive from Chicago, Devil's Lake provided the closest thing to mountain scenery in the area. The 360-acre glacial lake was surrounded by two 600-foot pine-covered bluffs that climbers enjoyed. Near the top of one of the bluffs were some very unusual rock formations that made for great photos. One of the formations, called Devil's Doorway, ranked among the most unique formations in the continental United States. The way the rocks balanced seemed to defy the laws of physics. It was a very popular site. I usually tried to go up to Devil's Lake midweek during my vacations because it was always crowded on weekends.

A third place I enjoyed was the Warren Dunes in southwestern Michigan. Just a two and a half hour drive from Chicago, the 250-foot dunes towered above Lake Michigan, offering phenomenal views of the great lake. The best time to go was in midsummer, when the air was hot, allowing the landscape to masquerade as a Caribbean paradise. From time to time, I would see people hang-glide there; that was not something I was used to seeing in the Midwest. The gentle lake breezes and acres of warm sand made me feel like I was thousands of miles away from the city.

Of all the places in the area that I liked to hike, my favorite by far was Starved Rock State Park, nestled near the small town of Utica, Illinois, just an hour and a half from Chicago. Starved Rock consisted of a series of limestone bluffs and canyons situated along the Illinois River. Several of the canyons had waterfalls that flowed strongly in spring but quickly dried up by midsummer. The park derived its name from a Native American legend dating back to the 1760s. According to the legend, Pontiac, chief of the Ottawa tribe, was slain by an Illiniwek while attending a tribal council in southern Illinois. Seeking revenge, the Ottawa tribe and their allies, the Potawatomi, attacked the Illiniwek. During one of the battles that ensued, a group of Illiniwek sought refuge atop a 125-foot sandstone butte that jutted out into the Illinois River. It was a fatal mistake. Surrounded by the Ottawa and Potawatomi, the hapless Illiniwek eventually starved to death atop the rock.

Many of my friends had been to Starved Rock, but few could understand my love of the area. They said it was OK, but nothing spectacular. Their problem was that they hadn't gone to the best parts of the park. There was a charming lodge at Starved Rock, located near the main bluff that gave the park its name. Most people who visited the park ate at the lodge and then climbed the main bluff and two or three of the adjacent bluffs. The views were nice but admittedly, they were far from breathtaking. In between these frequented bluffs were a few rather uninteresting canyons. Getting to the best parts of the park required a longer hike into areas that were not easily accessible by car. The paths were often muddy, and few casual visitors ever made it that far. They really missed out.

LaSalle Canyon at Starved Rock was the crown jewel of the park and in my opinion was the most beautiful spot in Illinois, if not the entire Midwest. The sandstone walls of the canyon rose approximately 120 feet, surrounding a stream that cascaded down the rock until it emptied into the Illinois River. There were several waterfalls along the canyon that were separated by shallow rapids and pools. Unlike most water in Illinois, which was muddy-brown like the Mississippi, the pools in spring were a vibrant green, much like pools seen in Hawaii and other tropical places.

Years before, I had tried to photograph the canyon but without success. The curves of the canyon wall and the shade from the high rocks made it impossible to adequately capture its magnificence on film. Perhaps that was for the best—I never ceased to be amazed when I experienced it firsthand.

I arrived at Starved Rock State Park a little after noon. It was a beautiful day, not a cloud in the sky, and I felt a rush as I made my way over to the head of the trail that led to LaSalle Canyon. The path was muddy, as there had been a lot of rain in the previous two weeks, but I did not let it deter me. As I walked along, I thought about *The Third Testament*. Again, I considered the possible conclusions to the story. I liked the idea of using the establishment of Israel as the conclusion, but the problem was that if I ended it there, I would be leaving out some of the most important people of the twentieth century, including Mother Teresa, Reverend Billy Graham, and Pope John Paul II. I had already started writing chapters on the three and was determined to include them. In addition, I wanted to include President Ronald Reagan's famous "Evil Empire" speech. The history-changing speech, given on March 8, 1983, to the National Association of Evangelicals, was filled with references to God and was truly biblical in nature. In my opinion, it was the most important spiritual oration in modern times.

I can't leave all of these things out of the story, I thought.

After about a twenty-minute hike, accompanied by much pondering, I made it to the mouth of LaSalle Canyon, where the canyon stream emptied into the Illinois River. The muddy riverside path changed to a more easily trod limestone path, and I picked up my pace in anticipation of what lay ahead. The path went up and down, left and right, following the curves of the southern canyon wall until it came to a 90-degree bend. Turning the corner, I could hear the rush of water flowing over the largest waterfall in the canyon. My heart raced when I heard the sound, for I knew that I was about to be greeted with a spectacular sight. A few more footsteps, and there it was—the glorious center of the canyon. The moss-covered limestone walls arched in such a way as to make it look like a natural amphitheater. At the front of the theater were the great falls that flowed into a large pool of sea-green water.

"The Garden of Eden," I whispered to myself. *How truly beautiful.*

I had always found truth in the quote, "Life is not measured by the amount of breaths you take, but by the moments that take your breath away." There were several times in my life when my breath was truly taken away by nature. The most memorable time was in August 1987, when Tina and I visited Chateau Lake Louise in the Canadian Rockies. The aquamarine lake surrounded by snowcapped mountains was incredible, and the constant fragrance of pine was enchanting. I always said it was the closet thing to heaven on earth.

Maui was also incredible. I recalled how the first time we visited Maui, Tina and I walked along the beach one morning and saw two rainbows out over the ocean. It was unreal. The lush green mountains and the warm ocean breeze were indescribably perfect. It was truly amazing.

The majesty of Caribbean-blue water surrounding the Mayan ruins along the shores of Tulum in Mexico was also amazing. "There's no blue like Caribbean blue," I recalled Tina saying to me. It was literally breathtaking.

The only place in the Midwest that ever made me feel that way was LaSalle Canyon at Starved Rock. I will never forget our first visit there. Tina and I were dating at the time, and we decided to take a day trip to get away from the city. It was a very hot day in June, but we nonetheless spent a lot of time hiking. We did not know a thing about Starved Rock, certainly not about the waterfalls, and simply followed the trail that coursed along the bluffs adjacent to the river. After about a two-mile hike up and down the bluffs, we were about to turn back when we came to a sign at the mouth of LaSalle Canyon, stating that it was one mile to the waterfall. Although hot and exhausted, we were curious to see the falls, and so we continued onward. After several twists and turns along the limestone path, we eventually came to a spot where we could here the thunder of the falls ahead. It was an exhilarating sound. One more turn around the giant limestone canyon walls, and there it was—the center of LaSalle Canyon. It surpassed anything we ever would have dreamed of seeing in the state of Illinois. The natural amphitheater with its sea-green pool and thundering falls was spectacular. Filled with joy, we both stood underneath the cool water of the falls and took in the glory that surrounded us. It was an ethereal experience.

The moments that take our breath away bring us closer to God, I thought as I recalled my first visit there with Tina. *Those spectacular moments are God's gift to us; a small taste of the Eden that was lost because of our desire for the fruit of the Tree of Knowledge.*

"Forbidden knowledge," I whispered as I walked deeper into LaSalle Canyon. "What a shame to lose all this."

Looking ahead at the shimmering falls, my eyes were temporarily blinded by a brilliant light that reflected off the water cascading over the rocks ahead. Feeling euphoric, I was not the least bit bothered by the blinding light. Rather, I found it as beautiful as the surroundings. Stirred by the beauty, my mind began to race, not in a haphazard way but with unusual clarity. All at once, I felt as if I was flooded with wisdom; it was a sensation I had never felt before.

The Garden of Eden … forbidden knowledge … the End of Times. The rush of thoughts was mesmerizing. *Satan … the fall of man … Jesus Christ.*

Standing in front of the glorious falls, surrounded by the magnificent moss-covered canyon walls, I experienced an epiphany.

It all makes sense. Incredible! It all makes perfect sense.

"Oh, great Lord," I whispered.

Shaking my head in amazement, I quoted the words of Christ: "Upon this rock I will build my Church, and the gates of hell shall not prevail against it."

Then and there, I knew how *The Third Testament* would conclude.

Chapter 23 ———
The Seven Stages of Death and Dying

Scholars contend that there are seven stages of death and dying. The first stage is shock. This is followed by denial, which is followed by anger, then bargaining, and then depression. Depression is followed by acceptance. The seventh and final stage is death itself. Not all of the seven stages are equal in length or depth, and the stages do not necessarily come in exact order. I witnessed Tina go through the stages. It was painful to watch. Her time spent in denial and anger was brief. The bargaining and depression stages were the longest and most dramatic. It seemed as if the stage of depression lasted forever. Near the very end, when life was filled with nothing but suffering for her, she accepted and welcomed death. It was not the type of acceptance that they write about in fictional books. There was no state of enlightenment achieved. It was more of a sad realization that the best way to heal the pain was to cease to live. The macabre affair was horrible to witness.

After Tina's death, I began saying a prayer each night for all the mourners in the world. I never dreamed I would have to go through that hell again myself, but I was wrong.

Ellen called me one Tuesday morning in October. "Dad, I think I must be coming down with a virus. The past several days I just haven't felt well."

"What's wrong, sweetie?" I asked. "What's bothering you?"

"I just haven't had very much energy for the last few days," she said. "And I don't have an appetite."

"You've been under a lot of stress. Stress can really wear you down. Have you been sleeping OK?"

"I've been sleeping just fine," she replied. "If anything, I've been sleeping too much. Each afternoon I take a nap. I don't think it's stress. I think I have some sort of stomach flu. The right side of my stomach has been bothering me, and I feel a little queasy. I've also been coughing quite a bit."

"I think the stomach flu has been going around," I said to reassure her. "Give it a few days, and I'm sure you'll feel better."

I did not have the heart to say what was truly on my mind. I did not have the courage to tell her that the description of her symptoms was terrifying to me. Part of me wanted to say the obvious—to tell her to make an appointment with Dr. Greenspan as soon as possible. It was much simpler, however, to bury my head in the sand and pretend I hadn't heard the grim report. My cowardice did not matter, though, because Ellen came to the obvious conclusion herself.

"Dad, I'm frightened," she said. "I called Dr. Greenspan's office this morning and made an appointment."

Oh, thank goodness she's seeing the doctor. "When is your appointment?" I asked.

"It's not for two weeks," she said. "Dr. Greenspan is out of town. The appointment was the soonest I could get. His nurse practitioner arranged for me to have CAT scans just before I see him to make sure the tumors haven't grown."

I didn't want to alarm her, but two weeks seemed like a long time for us to wait and worry. Hesitating at first, I finally voiced my concern. "Do you want to try to go back to Dr. Gudmundson in the meantime?"

"Do you think I should?" she asked. "I really think I just have a case of the stomach flu. Do you think it's the cancer?"

"No, I'm sure it's not the cancer," I lied. "But until you are seen by a doctor, I'm sure we'll worry about it, and there is no need to carry that burden any longer than we need to. It makes sense for you to see a doctor to make sure everything is OK."

Ellen agreed and made an appointment to see Dr. Gudmundson.

Later that evening, she developed a fever. She called me on the phone and was actually overjoyed to have the fever. "I knew it was just the flu," she said. "The melanoma wouldn't cause me to have a fever. Thank God it's just the flu."

The next day I went with her to see Dr. Gudmundson. Ellen looked ill. It had been several days since I had last seen her, but she looked weak and fatigued. The nurse at the clinic took her temperature.

"You are burning up," she said to Ellen. "Your temperature is 102 degrees." She brought Ellen some Tylenol and then walked out of the room, saying, "Doctor Gudmundson will be in shortly."

Dr. Gudmundson greeted us perfunctorily when he came into the exam room and asked Ellen how she was doing. He noted that Ellen had swollen lymph nodes on the right side of her neck that he had not noticed before. After listening to her lungs, he also said that it sounded as if she had pneumonia. Dr. Gudmundson sent her to the laboratory to have her blood drawn and then for a chest x-ray.

When Ellen was done with the tests, we returned to the exam room and waited for Dr. Gudmundson to give us the results. He walked in and slowly closed the door behind him, making sure it was all the way shut. He sat down in a chair across from us, looking quite somber. "I have some bad news," he said. "The x-ray shows that the tumors in your lung have increased in size. One of the tumors is compressing your airway and causing pneumonia. That is why you have a fever."

"How much have the tumors grown?" Ellen asked, her voice trembling.

"It appears that the tumors you had previously are at least somewhat larger, and in addition, there are several new tumors. The x-ray is not the best test to assess how much the tumors have grown. You will need CAT scans. Given your pneumonia, I'd like to admit you to the hospital for intravenous antibiotics. While you are in, we can order the CAT scans of your chest, abdomen, and pelvis. We should also check an MRI of your brain just to be certain the melanoma hasn't spread there." Dr. Gudmundson then paused for a moment, looking Ellen directly in the eye before he said, "I'm very sorry, Ms. Sankt. I realize how difficult this must be for you. Once we get your pneumonia under control, we can get you back to see Dr. Greenspan for further therapy."

"Thank you, Doctor," Ellen said. "Where do I go now?"

"Wait right here," he said. "The medical assistants will be here in a few minutes to escort you to your hospital bed."

I temporarily left Ellen's side and followed Dr. Gudmundson out of the exam room. "I heard about a major breakthrough for melanoma on the news a couple of weeks ago," I said. "I was wondering if that would be something that could help Ellen."

"Oh, the sensationalist news," Dr. Gudmundson said with a sigh. "They always make every new discovery, no matter how preliminary, sound like an earth-shattering advance. I'm assuming you're referring to the report about turmeric that they had on NBC."

"Yes, Doctor," I said. "That's what I'm referring to."

"Mr. Sankt, the studies on turmeric were done in a petri dish, not in humans. Unfortunately, many of the drugs we test seem to work in the lab but then show no benefit when we test them in people. It must have been a really slow news day because that data on turmeric is not even new. M. D. Anderson first reported that information a couple of years ago."

"Is there even a possibility it could help Ellen?" I asked.

"Mr. Sankt," Dr. Gudmundson said, "I wouldn't put your hopes in turmeric. It will still be years before we know if it has any significant benefit in humans. Unfortunately, it is not something that is going to help Ellen."

"Oh, that's too bad," I said. "Thank you, Doctor."

I walked away deeply dejected and returned to Ellen's side.

Ellen spent seven days in the hospital and had several tests done. The CAT scans showed that the tumors in her lungs and liver had gotten significantly larger.

At least it has not yet spread to her brain.

A pulmonologist arranged for laser therapy for Ellen's lung, to keep the tumor from collapsing her airway. With the antibiotics and the laser treatment, Ellen's fever improved, but she still felt weak. Her appetite remained poor, and she began losing weight. We were both shocked at how quickly things were changing. Psychologically, Ellen was struggling. I could see she was going through the stages. Ellen began to talk about going back to work once she got out of the hospital. It was evident to me that she was in a state of denial. Dr. Gudmundson said that it was best not to try to refocus her on reality. He said the state of denial was a useful defense mechanism for her. I listened to the doctor and told Ellen that she would be back to work in no time. It was hard for me to tell her such things when I saw how weak she really was, but I wanted to do what was best for her.

– – – – – – – – – –

After what seemed like an eternity, the day of Ellen's discharge finally arrived. I stayed with her for the first few days that she was at home. Thankfully, she did regain some of her strength, as Dr. Gudmundson had predicted she would, once the pneumonia was treated. Focusing on the future, we both anxiously awaited her appointment with Dr. Greenspan at the Chicago Cancer Institute. We knew her next round of treatment would be very difficult, but we were desperate to do something.

Jerry and Joyce visited us each evening. They were very supportive. Ellen's friends stopped by throughout the day, and Jack was there as often as he could come. The display of human compassion was moving. Cards, flowers, and gifts poured in.

"Look at how many there are," Jerry commented. "I don't think I even know so many people."

"I have a lot of people praying for me," Ellen replied. "I need all of the prayers I can get."

Jerry looked downward, nodding silently.

At the end of the week, I went with Ellen to see Dr. Greenspan.

Psychologically, we both were ready to start the next phase of treatment. Ellen, in particular, was anxious to get started. She was in a fighting mood and was looking forward to hearing what Dr. Greenspan had to say. She was desperately in search of hope; of something positive. Unfortunately, when Dr. Greenspan entered the room, the first thing he did was make a negative comment about the amount of weight Ellen had lost.

"Don't you have an appetite?" he asked.

"Not a very good one," she answered. "I've been taking protein supplements the last several days. I'm hoping that will help me regain some of the weight I've lost."

"Perhaps," Dr. Greenspan answered. After reviewing the current state of Ellen's cancer, he went on to paint a grim picture—more grim than we'd expected.

"I do not think you are strong enough to endure biochemotherapy in your current state," he said. "It is too aggressive at this time. I think it would do more harm than good."

In lieu of the biochemotherapy, Dr. Greenspan suggested that Ellen enroll in another clinical trial that used an investigational drug that was "less toxic." He admitted that the experimental drug also was likely to be less effective but said that it was necessary to sacrifice efficacy for safety. His attitude frustrated Ellen. I could see the tension build up in her face.

It was almost déjà vu. We had been down this exact path before, but the roles had completely reversed. When Ellen was feeling good, she didn't want to suffer through an aggressive therapy that would make her really sick, even though that was what Dr. Greenspan initially suggested. Now that she was feeling sick from her tumors, Ellen wanted to be as aggressive as possible. She felt she had nothing to lose. I could not argue with her.

"I'm not ready to give up!" she exclaimed. "Why choose something safe if I'm going to die anyway? I'd rather go down fighting! Give me a chance! I deserve a chance."

Dr. Greenspan coldly replied, "There is nothing we can do now to change the ultimate outcome of this disease. I will not give you a therapy that is only going to make you sicker."

Ellen began to cry. I, too, felt overwhelmed.

"I don't believe this," Ellen wept in frustration.

"I'm sorry," Dr. Greenspan replied, "but the primary rule of medicine is 'first, do no harm.' It wouldn't be right for me to offer you an aggressive therapy in your condition. If I were you, I would strongly consider the other option." With that, Dr. Greenspan got up from his chair and left the room. It was very clear that he did not want to deal with Ellen's emotions.

Deeply disappointed, Ellen and I gathered up our things. Our exit felt as solemn as a funeral procession. We silently took the elevator down to the first floor, too stunned to speak. The silence was disheartening—it was an indication that neither of us had the strength to comfort the other. Yet as disheartening as it was, it was not nearly as troubling as Ellen's words that finally broke the silence: "What am I going to do, Dad?"

Chapter 24
THE MAGNIFICENT OBSESSION

I WAS DEEPLY distraught. I spent the entire night searching the Internet for a new path. I scanned the Web pages of the Mayo Clinic, Massachusetts General Hospital, M. D. Anderson Medical Center, Sloan-Kettering, and UCSF. I even searched the sites of cancer centers in other countries. I was looking for a melanoma expert who could offer us hope. I jotted down notes about clinical trials and wrote down numbers to call. I didn't sleep a wink. The next day, I started making phone calls. For the most part, I met with frustration. The people in Boston said that Ellen did not fit their trials. The people at M. D. Anderson and Sloan-Kettering said that Ellen would have to move to their cities for a period of weeks to months to get treatment there. I knew that was something that Ellen would not want to do. All of her friends were in Chicago, and she loved her home. I continued down the checklist of cancer institutes. My phone calls to UCSF and the Mayo Clinic were promising at first. They each put me directly in touch with a physician. The problem was that after I discussed Ellen's case with them, they told me something I did not want to hear—they each recommended that we go to see Dr. Greenspan at the Chicago Cancer Institute. Their recommendations made me want to yell out with frustration. The last call I made was to the National Cancer Institute in Bethesda, Maryland. I spoke with a woman named Judy, who was quite sympathetic.

"We have several trials for which your daughter would be eligible," she said. "I will mail out information to you this afternoon. You can look it over and if you're interested, you can schedule an appointment."

"Thank you," I said. "Thank you so very much! You've been very helpful."

I immediately called Ellen. I could tell that she had been crying. Her voice was hoarse and cracking. She also seemed groggy, as if she were drugged.

She must be groggy from the pain pills, I thought.

Ellen had started taking a pain medication prescribed by Dr. Gudmundson to relieve the discomfort from the tumors in her liver. The medication was a form of morphine, and Dr. Gudmundson said it would cause Ellen to be sleepy.

"What's wrong, Dad?" Ellen asked in answer to my call.

"There's nothing wrong, sweetheart," I said. "I've been making some phone calls this morning, talking to people from cancer centers throughout the country. I think I've found something to be hopeful for. Would you be willing to travel to the National Cancer Institute in Bethesda?"

Ellen's reply to my question was one that I was not prepared to hear. "Dad, I'm thirty-one years old, and I'm dying of cancer. I'd travel to the moon if I thought it would help, but what are they going to do for me there? What can they possibly do?" Ellen began coughing. Each cough was a deep cough, and she had several in succession. The sound made me shudder. Her despondency also made me shudder. I had never before heard her speak like that. Physically and emotionally, my daughter was deteriorating—that much was obvious—and I didn't know what to do. The feelings of helplessness and hopelessness were overwhelming. Before I could say anything she again had a succession of coughs. *Her lungs must be getting worse*, I thought. At the end of the string of coughs, Ellen took a deep breath. I, too, took a deep breath and then told her, "The woman I spoke with—the woman from the National Cancer Institute—is going to mail us information about their trials. She said there were several trials you would be eligible for."

"Oh, wonderful," Ellen sniped. "I can be a guinea pig for some other mad scientist. They don't care about us. They don't care about the patients. They just want to do their research so they can publish their papers in their little journals and then go around the country giving speeches so they can feel important. We're just toys for them to play with. We're their pitiful, dying rag dolls who are supposed to cling to their sliver of hope—and a false hope, at that." She paused and took another slow, deep breath. "Why did God do this to me? Why?"

How do I respond to that? I wondered. I felt so useless, so frustrated.

Looking for solace after Ellen and I ended our call, I turned to the words of a well-known saint. In his infinite wisdom, Saint Augustine once said that God had one child without sin but never one without suffering.

All humans suffer, I rationalized. *On the cross, even Christ begged, "My God, my God, why have you forsaken me?" Christ's death for our salvation was more than a physical death. It was a death that required the separation of Son from*

Father. How terrible it is to feel abandoned by God. How hard it is for a father to see a child suffer so.

Ellen's despondency was enough to push me over the edge and drive me completely insane. Yet I knew that I must hold together for her.

We'll weather this storm, I resolved. *We* must *weather this storm*.

- - - - - - - - - -

I once again turned to writing as a temporary respite from the cruel reality that held me prisoner. That night, I sat in front of my computer in despair and wrote about Frederick II, Holy Roman Emperor and self-proclaimed king of Jerusalem. He was a man most people had never heard of, and yet he held an infamous claim to fame. He was the only man throughout history to be officially branded by a pope as the Antichrist. The title of Antichrist seemed to fit him well. Frederick was a bizarre and immoral man with fiery red hair and eyes that were "green, like those of a serpent."[27] Obsessed with power, he made it his quest to topple the Church and took steps to establish a new world order, in which he would be hailed as the secular messiah, replacing Christ. He was devious and ruthless and would let nothing stand in his way. Chillingly, his quest came close to succeeding.

Frederick was born on December 26, 1194, in Jesi near Ancona. His father was Emperor Henry VI and his mother, Constance, was the queen of Sicily. In order to eliminate any doubt about his origin, the already forty-year-old Constance gave birth to the child publicly, in a marketplace, surrounded by throngs of onlookers. Frederick's unusual birth was a source of much fascination; travelers came from far and wide to Jesi to see him. Many came bearing gifts, including gifts of incense and gold.

Frederick's parents died during his youth, and he was raised on the streets until Pope Innocent III became his guardian. Under Innocent's direction, Frederick was educated in Rome and took great interest in science and economics. He was the finest of students and could speak nine languages. He lusted for knowledge and used his brilliance as a weapon to combat his foes. Many considered him a genius. His contemporaries called him "Stupor mundi," or "the Wonder of the World." Frederick used his cunning and political skills to vault himself into positions of great power. He was crowned king of Germany in 1212, and Pope Honorius III crowned him Holy Roman Emperor in 1220. Yet despite his many successes, he still wanted more.

Frederick coveted the fame and adoration of Christ. In the year 1225, the

---

27   URL: http://en.wikipedia.org/wiki/Frederick_II,_Holy_Roman_Emperor.
     Downloaded 1-29-06.

German monarch married Yolande, the heiress to the kingdom of Jerusalem. From that time on, Frederick viewed himself as the rightful ruler of Jerusalem and blasphemously declared himself king in 1229. The unholy coronation was held in the Church of the Holy Sepulcher, located on the hill of Cavalry where Christ was crucified. The Patriarch of Jerusalem refused to crown Frederick, so the fiend placed the crown upon his own head. The idea of ruling the Holy City enthralled the bizarre beast. It raised his demonic passions to unequaled heights and fueled his already pathological conceit. In his own misguided mind, Frederick believed he was greater than Jesus, and he sought to prove his greatness by presiding over the land in which the Savior of the earth once roamed.

During his reign, Frederick embraced the Muslims, praising Islam over Christianity, and used deceit and torture to try to undermine the papacy. Unfortunately, there was no one in his kingdom to stand in his way. His subjects feared him, for at any moment he could burst into wild rage and execute horrific deeds. On one occasion, Frederick, in a fit of lunacy, had two captives fed at different hours and then disemboweled them so that he could see how the digestive system works. On another occasion, he had a man sealed alive in an airtight barrel, wishing to show that the soul perishes with the body. On yet a third occasion, he cut off the thumb of a notary who had mistakenly spelled his name as Fredericus instead of Fridericus.

As much as he was known for his temper, Frederick was equally infamous for his perversion. Finding ecstasy in debauchery, he rejoiced in the company of Muslim slave girls and defiled innocent young boys.

Taking heed of Frederick's actions, Pope Gregory IX, the reigning pontiff at the time, condemned the tyrant, issuing an encyclical:

> "Out of the sea rises up the Beast, full of the names of blasphemy who, raging with the claws of the bear and mouth of the lion and the limbs and likeness of the leopard, opens its mouth to blaspheme the Holy Name and ceases not to hurl its spears against the tabernacle of God."[28]

A great struggle evolved between Frederick and the Pope, which in due time escalated to all-out war. It was a war that would determine the future of the Church. The self-proclaimed king of Jerusalem commanded the most powerful army in Europe, and it seemed as if he could not be stopped, but by the grace of God, he failed. Frederick was inexplicably overcome with illness at the very moment he was about to succeed. He died on the thirteenth day of

---

28 Thomas Bokenkotter. *A Concise History of the Catholic Church*. New York: Doubleday, a Division of Random House, Inc., 2004, p. 176.

December, the darkest month, sacrilegiously wearing the habit of a Cistercian monk. It appeared that with his death, the world had rid itself of his evil, yet that was not the end of his story. After his death there arose an ominous prophecy that he would come again and fiendishly establish a Thousand-Year Reich. According to the prophecy, Frederick was not truly dead; he was merely asleep in the Kyffhäuser Mountains and would one day awaken in a second coming. It was a haunting prophecy that was passed on from generation to generation. Parents warned their young children to beware the day that the beast would rise. Yet as years became decades, and decades became centuries, fewer and fewer took heed until it was all but forgotten.

I remember my grandfather telling me this legend when I was a child, I thought as I wrote about Frederick. *Back then, I presumed it was just a good ghost story, but maybe there was more to it.*

The prophecy of Frederick's thousand-year reign was made in the mid-thirteenth century, but now it seemed eerily similar to a twentieth-century prophecy. After doing some research, I could not help but wonder—*was this the same Thousand-Year Reich that Hitler promised to establish*? Intrigued by the Hitler comparison, I wrote:

> In the year 1250, on the thirteenth day of the twelfth month, Frederick II of Germany, the licentious, malicious, most unholy Holy Roman Emperor and self-proclaimed king of Jerusalem, died and was buried in a dark-red porphyry sarcophagus, thus ending the diabolical reign of the man Pope Gregory IX had titled Antichrist. Upon the loathsome murderer's death, a dark prophecy was made that the demon in Frederick would one day awaken in a second coming and would establish a Thousand-Year Reich. Over six centuries later, a man just as ambitious and just as wicked as Frederick came to power in Germany. His name was Adolf Hitler, and in the year 1933, he boldly proclaimed the establishment of a thousand-year Reich.

There were many who believed that, like Frederick, Hitler was the Antichrist. Hitler was born in 1889 at Braunau am Inn in Austria-Hungary. In 1913 he moved to Munich and when World War I broke out in 1914, he enlisted in the German army. In 1916, Hitler was wounded in battle in France. It has been said that it was at this very time—666 years after the death of Frederick II—that the demon took control of Hitler's soul, as payment for his return to health. While most men of faith believed this was nothing more than a myth propagated by the misguided, it is true that not long after his recovery, Hitler, who previously had been a model soldier, was described as dangerously psychotic by his superiors in the German military.

A malevolent reincarnation? I mused. *Now that's a story of biblical proportions.*

The sensational musing captured my interest and inspired me to work even harder.

- - - - - - - - - -

Over the next few weeks, I immersed myself in writing. I wrote of the Crusades and of the Inquisition. These were two of the blackest marks in the history of the Church. I also wrote of Saint Thomas Aquinas, the most remarkable theologian of all time. In his youth, Thomas was called a dumb ox because of his large build and quiet nature. He proved his detractors wrong—he became the most brilliant thinker of his age. He composed the *Summa Contra Gentiles* and, more significant, the *Summa Theologica*, the greatest Christian manuscript outside of the Bible itself. Many Church scholars believed that, like the Bible, the works of Saint Thomas Aquinas were divinely inspired. Aquinas did seem to be filled with the Lord's wisdom. He said:

> "When the devil is called the god of this world, it is not because he made it but because we serve him with our worldliness."

He also said:

> "Three things are necessary for the salvation of man: to know what he ought to believe; to know what he ought to desire; and to know what he ought to do."

Never afraid to tackle the most difficult and controversial subjects of the day, Aquinas wrote in defense of just war and capital punishment. He also wrote of free will. He said:

> "God neither wills evil to be done, nor wills it not to be done, but wills to permit evil to be done, and this is good."

Aquinas spent his entire life teaching and writing about God. He wrote homilies and disputations and hymns. He even wrote an essay on the existence of God. In the essay, widely known as the *Quinque viae,* he firmly avowed that God's existence can be rationally proven in five ways.

Aquinas also wrote prophecies. In an era ruled by kings and despots, he foretold that governments based on a system of representative democracy would, in due course, preserve the virtues of the fellowship of the Holy Spirit and, in doing so, would uphold the divine will of God. He said:

> "The best form of government is a state or kingdom wherein one is given the power to preside over all, while under him are others having governing powers; and yet a government of this kind is shared by all, both because all are eligible to govern, and because the rulers are chosen by all. For this is the best form of policy, being partly kingdom, since there is one at the head of all; partly aristocracy, in so far as a number of persons are set in authority; partly democracy, i.e. government by the people, and the people have the right to choose their rulers."[29]

Perhaps the most significant aspect of Aquinas' life was not what he said or wrote but rather what he saw. Late in his life, while in prayer, Thomas was blessed with a magnificent vision of heaven. After that moment, he stopped writing. When asked why he stopped, Thomas replied:

> "I cannot go on. All that I have written seems like straw compared to what I have seen and what has been revealed to me."

Aquinas was a fascinating man, I thought as I typed.

Aquinas was truly fascinating in many ways. Given my legal problems, I took particular interest in his comments on unscrupulous lawyers. In the *Summa Theologica*, Aquinas unequivocally maintained that if a lawyer unknowingly advocates an unjust cause, then it is to be excused to the extent that ignorance is excusable. However, if a lawyer knowingly advocates an unjust cause, as many do, then it is, without doubt, a grievous sin.

"A grievous sin … it's unfortunate they don't teach that in law school," I said to myself.

Continuing on in chronological order, I wrote of Saint Catherine of Siena. She lived in the fourteenth century and was a great shepherdess to God's people. A deeply religious woman, Catherine began her adult life in contemplative seclusion. She was a hermit who prayed constantly and was content to be alone. However, in the year 1366, she was called by God to public life. One night, in a dream, she experienced a spiritual espousal to Christ. Moved by the dream, she offered her heart to the Lord and vowed to courageously uphold his will, which she did with saintly eloquence. Leaving behind her life of seclusion, she went out into the world and became a heroic

---

29 Excerpt from the *Summa Theologica*. URL: http://biblestudy.churches.net/ CCEL/A/AQUINAS/SUMMA/FS/FS105.HTM. Downloaded 1-30-06.

leader and devoted spiritual author. Her writings were unquestionably biblical in nature. She authored *Dialogue of Divine Providence*, which to this day remains a Christian masterpiece. I already owned it but took note that there were several copies of it on sale at Barnes & Noble and at Borders. It was no surprise that it was still selling so well because it truly was an amazing work.

I included several excerpts from *Dialogue of Divine Providence* in *The Third Testament*. After recounting her words, I could not help but come to the conclusion that Catherine was a modern-day prophet. Throughout the *Dialogue*, she spoke authoritatively, as if she were a messenger of God. She instructed the people of the world to hope and trust in the Lord's goodness. She explained that although we do not see him, God is very near to us. Above all else, she implored that we heed his words. In truth, many of the passages in *Dialogue of Divine Providence* were his words.

Just as God spoke through the prophets in the Old Testament to the Israelites, God spoke through Catherine to the Christians.

Working diligently, I came to appreciate that there were many noteworthy religious events during the Middle Ages, and I tried to include as many as I could in my writing. I wrote of Martin Luther and his legendary Ninety-Five Theses. Luther, an Augustinian monk from Wittenberg, Germany, was deeply concerned with the state of the Church in the early sixteenth century. It is true the Church of that time was plagued with many vices. The practice of simony—the selling of Church goods and offices—was widespread, even though it was condemned by pious souls as immoral. Regrettably, there was no leadership in the Church at the time to bring an end to the corruption. Most of the Church offices were held by secular nobility who had no interest in theology. The greatest sin of the Church was the selling of indulgences. Indulgences were spiritual pardons bestowed by the Church for acts of good work. The greed of the Church leaders led to the practice of granting indulgences in exchange for money. The people of God were misled to believe that for a proper fee, they could absolve themselves—and their loved ones in purgatory—from punishment for sin. The most notorious peddler of indulgences was Johann Tetzel, a Dominican in the diocese of Mainz. Tetzel blasphemously chanted in the streets:

"As soon as a coin in the coffer rings, another soul in heaven springs."

Fed up with the corruption of the era, Luther posted Ninety-Five Theses, which promoted reform, on the door of the town's chapel. Luther's actions sparked the Protestant Reformation, and the Church was soon splintered into many sects.

I proceeded to list each of Luther's Ninety-Five Theses in *The Third Testament*:

> I. Our Lord and Master Jesus Christ, when He said Poenitentiam agite, willed that the whole life of believers should be repentance.
>
> II. This word cannot be understood to mean sacramental penance, i.e., confession and satisfaction, which is administered by the priests.
>
> III. Yet it means not inward repentance only; nay, there is no inward repentance which does not outwardly work divers mortifications of the flesh.
>
> IV. The penalty, therefore, continues so long as hatred of self continues; for this is the true inward repentance, and continues until our entrance into the kingdom of heaven.
>
> V. The pope does not intend to remit, and cannot remit any penalties other than those which he has imposed either by his own authority or by that of the Canons...[30]

I then spent the next several days detailing the many events and key characters of the Reformation, including Jean Calvin, the father of predestination; John Knox, founder of the Presbyterian Church; King Henry VIII, founder of the Church of England; and Thomas More, the renowned statesman and martyr.

The Reformation was a tragedy, I decided as I wrote about the titanic division of the Catholic Church. *Luther simply wanted to reform the Church. He never intended to break it up into fragments.*

Moving on to a more inspirational subject, I wrote of the appearance of the Blessed Virgin Mary to Juan Diego at Guadalupe in Mexico and of the miraculous *tilma* (poncho) that bears the likeness of the Mother of God.

The story of Guadalupe was one of the best-known stories in all of Mexican literature. It began in the year 1531, when the Virgin Mary appeared to a lowly Indian man named Juan Diego as he was walking alone along a mountain trail. The Blessed Virgin instructed him to have a Christian shrine built outside of Mexico City. A humble and obedient man, Juan Diego intended to do her bidding, but no one believed him, for he was a mere peasant. The Spanish clergymen in Guadalupe insisted that they would not follow his instructions without proof in the form of a miracle. Juan Diego tried again and again to convince them but without success. He soon became despondent, believing that he was a failure, unworthy to carry out the mission of the Blessed Virgin. His despondency only worsened when his beloved uncle, Juan

---

30 URL: http://en.wikisource.org/wiki/95_Theses. Downloaded 11-6-09.

Bernadino, became gravely ill with the plague. With his uncle only hours from death, Juan Diego set out to find a priest to give his uncle the last rites. While he was walking along the mountain path in search of the priest, the Blessed Virgin again appeared to him and told Juan Diego not to fear. She explained that she would care for all of his needs. Like a child cradled in his mother's arms, Juan Diego found comfort in her words. He then humbly asked the Mother of God for the miracle the clergymen had demanded, and she granted his request. Mary said to him:

> "Go to the top of the hill, my son. There among the rocks you will find a field of flowers. Gather them. The flowers are the sign thou shalt take to the bishop. Thou shalt tell him in my name to see my will in them. Thou shalt be my emissary, full worthy of my whole trust."[31]

As instructed, Juan Diego proceeded to gather a bundle of beautiful Castilian roses from the mountainside. It was the winter season, a time when no roses bloomed in the region. Thus, Juan Diego was pleased as he wrapped up the miraculous flowers in his tilma to bring to the clergymen. Standing before the bishop and several priests, Juan Diego opened his tilma to release the roses. The clergymen were truly stunned but not by the roses. They stared in amazement at the tilma itself, for on the tilma was an exact likeness of the Blessed Virgin. Beholding the divine image, the clergymen instantly came to believe. Filled with the Holy Spirit, they reverently dropped to their knees and gave praise to the Lord.

Although only a meek and humble peasant, Juan Diego had accomplished his mission, just as the Virgin Mary had said he would. He was indeed a trustworthy emissary, and he was rightly blessed. When he returned home later that day, he found his uncle in perfect health, healed by the Mother of God.

In fulfillment of Mary's request, a shrine was erected in the town, and millions of indigenous Indians converted to Christianity. Housed in the shrine, the miraculous image on Juan Diego's tilma came to be called the Lady of Guadalupe.

The account of Mary's encounter with Juan Diego was transcribed in an ancient Indian document called the *Huei tlamahuiçoltica*. I included a translation of the document in *The Third Testament*.

After completing the section of Guadalupe, I wrote of Saint Ignatius of

---

31   Adapted from URL: http://www.udayton.edu/mary/meditations/guadalupe. html. Downloaded 2-3-06.

Loyola, Saint Teresa of Avila, Saint John of the Cross, and Saint Martin de Porres. Saint Teresa's words were particularly memorable for me. She said:

"Christ has no body now on earth but yours, no hands but yours, no feet but yours, yours are the eyes with which he looks with compassion at the world, yours are the feet with which he is to go about doing good, and yours are the hands with which he is to bless us now."

Also memorable was a parable involving Saint Martin de Porres, the pure-hearted seventeenth-century Dominican friar from Lima, Peru. I wrote:

One day Saint Martin saw an unclean beggar lying helplessly in the street, covered with sores. Saddened by the sight, he brought the poor man back to the friary and gave him his own bed. Angered that an unclean beggar was being housed in the pristine friary, one of the other Dominicans reproached Martin for having gone too far with his charity. Always composed, Saint Martin calmly said:

"Compassion, my dear brother, is preferable to cleanliness. Reflect that with a little soap I can easily clean my bed covers, but even with a torrent of tears I would never wash from my soul the stain that my harshness toward the unfortunate would create."

I then wrote of the miracle of Oberammergau, and the origin of the Passion Play that is held in the pastoral German village every ten years. I had been looking forward to writing about Oberammergau for quite some time. The miracle there was one of the main events that inspired me to start writing *The Third Testament* in the first place. It was a miracle that was very personal to me. When I was a young man, my grandfather took me on a trip to Germany one summer. As part of the trip we stopped in Oberammergau and took in the Passion Play. It was an extraordinary experience. From a religious perspective, it moved me in ways I had seldom been moved, before or since. After seeing the play, for the first time in my life, I came to truly appreciate Christ's incredible sacrifice for us; I came to know and understand the Passion. Poignantly, the cross on that stage changed me. In a world that was rapidly becoming secular, it opened my eyes to God. Since then, I've maintained that the trip to Oberammergau marked my true baptism into the Christian faith.

Like many of the stories from the Old Testament, the story of Oberammergau began with the ravages of a horrible plague. In the seventeenth century, the bubonic plague, better known as the Black Death, spread quickly throughout

Europe, generating a great fear among the people. The plague, carried and spread by rats, was a rapidly fatal disease. More than any war and more than any earthquake or flood, it decimated the population. In the larger cities, thousands upon thousands horrifically succumbed. The cause of the plague was unknown at the time. Its origin was shrouded in superstition. In morbid fashion, a popular children's nursery rhyme evolved from the superstition:

Ring around the rosey,
A pocket full of posies,
Ashes, ashes,
We all fall down

The leading medical thought at the time was that posies would purify the air of its bad humors. "Ring around the rosey" referred to the pinkish circle that would form on a victim's body prior to its turning black. "Ashes, ashes" referred to burning those things that belonged to a person who had died of the plague, in hope of stemming the spread of the disease. The concluding line of the morose rhyme, "We all fall down," was the grim concession that death would overcome all.

Oberammergau was a small village high in the Bavarian Alps and was a safe haven from the plague. Tragically, the sanctuary was broken when Kasper Schisler, a farm laborer and native of Oberammergau, returned to the village after spending time working in a nearby town. Kasper Schisler brought the Black Death with him, and soon Oberammergau was ravaged by the pestilence. In order to save themselves, the surviving villagers made a covenant with God. As an act of devotion, they promised to perform a reenactment of the final days of the life of Christ, a Passion Play, every ten years for eternity. In the year 1634, on a makeshift stage overlying a field of graves, the villagers performed the first Passion Play. Miraculously, from that moment onward, the Black Death took no more lives in the village. I wrote:

One day a young farm laborer named Kasper Schisler, a native of Oberammergau, attempted to return home after spending time at work as a harvester in the nearby town of Eschenlohe. He wanted to spend the Feast of the Dedication of the Church with his family, but the young man was prohibited from entering Oberammergau by the village guards because of the fear of the plague. He pleaded with them. "Please let me in," he said. "I miss my home, and I miss my family." The guards felt deeply sorry for the young man, but they also felt honor-bound to their duty and turned him away. The next day the young man returned again to plead with the guards. "Please," he begged, "I will give you all of my earnings if you just let me in." The guards patiently explained to the young man the reason why they could not help him, and again they denied his request. The young man did not give up. He was so homesick that in desperation, he concocted a dangerous plan to steal into the village. In the darkness of the night, he risked life and limb, traversing rugged terrain, and entered the village in a location where no one would spot him. His mission was successful. He made it home, and his family welcomed him with open arms.

Several days after Kasper Schisler returned home, tragedy struck. The young laborer began to feel ill. He was stricken with fever, and his abdomen ached. Over the next several days, his fever worsened and the glands throughout his body began to swell. His breathing grew weak, and he coughed up blood. The young man's family summoned a physician, but there was nothing anyone could do to help him. His glands swelled more and more, and a rose-colored rash developed on the young man's limbs. The rash grew darker as each day passed, until his arms and legs were cold and black. Within a mere twelve days of the onset of the illness, Kasper Schisler was dead. The Black Death had come to Oberammergau.

A wave of panic spread throughout the village. The city fathers cautioned all to remain calm. Having never before seen a victim of the plague, they were not even sure if the young man's demise was due to the dreaded disease. "There is nothing to fear," they said. "Go about your business." Several days went by, and the villagers waited with apprehension. Then, just when it seemed as if the threat had passed, their greatest nightmare came true. Two other villagers fell ill with fever. Like the young man before them, they, too, developed a rose-colored rash that evolved into blackness and death. There was no doubt now that the plague had shattered the sanctuary of Oberammergau. Frightened, the villagers locked themselves behind closed doors and avoided all contact with their neighbors. Despite their efforts, the march of death continued on. Within twelve weeks, eighty-four lay lifeless, each and every one an innocent victim of the plague. The victims' bodies were buried in a secluded field on the outskirts of town. It became commonplace to see new graves being dug in the macabre field. It was a field of sadness. It was a field of darkness. It was a field of death.

The city fathers gathered together on the Feast of the Apostles Simon and Jude in an attempt to find a solution to the crisis. The city fathers were pious, God-fearing men, and they quickly reached the conclusion that only the Lord could save them. They summoned all of the villagers to meet in the center of the town, where they unveiled their plan. "In exchange for God's mercy," they said, "we villagers must perform an act of devotion. We shall all take part in a Passion Play, a holy reenactment of the final hours of Christ's life. We and our descendants shall repeat this act of devotion every ten years until the end of time."

The good people of Oberammergau agreed to the plan and together, they made a solemn vow to the Lord that they would perform the Play of the Suffering, Death, and Resurrection of Our Lord Jesus Christ every ten years, forever and ever. As a community, they put their trust in Christ and in the fellowship of the Holy Spirit. Thus, in the thirty-fourth year of the seventeenth century, at Pentecost, a Passion Play was performed. It took place in the field overlying the graves of those who had died before the vow. The field of death became a field of faith and a field of hope. Each and every villager, whether young or old, took part.

Placing their lives in the Lord's hands, the people of Oberammergau performed the play with heavenly passion in their hearts. God was witness to their great act of devotion. The Author of Life was pleased. He smiled down upon the village. Miraculously, from that moment forward, the plague took no more lives in the town. Those who had previously been afflicted were healed. After months of darkness and despair, the horrible nightmare was over. The fear of death was overcome, and the villagers began to live again. Filled with gratitude, the people shouted in the streets, "Alleluia! Let us rejoice and be glad!"

Now that's a biblical story if I've ever heard one, I thought as I completed the passage. I was certainly not the only one to find the story biblical. In researching Oberammergau, I came across a powerful quote that, in my opinion, aptly summarized the true significance of the event:

"Not since Moses lifted up the brazen serpent in the wilderness had there been such divine deliverance from mortal illness on such simple terms."[32]

---

32   URL: http://www.birmingham.gov.uk/GenerateContent?CONTENT_
ITEM_ID=51552&CONTENT_ITEM_TYPE=0&MENU_ID=5396.
Downloaded 8-20-06.

- - - - - - - - - -

Incessantly working, I wrote of the siege of Vienna, the second great Islamic threat. In the seventeenth century, the Jihadists again sought to end Christian civilization. Kara Mustafa, an avaricious Muslim warlord, led an army of Islamic militants through southeastern Europe and laid siege on Vienna. The threat was dire, for Vienna was all that stood between Mustafa and the heart of Christendom. A ruthless and cunning commander, Mustafa appeared as if he would succeed, but the tide of the war changed when John Sobieski, the brave king of Poland, entered the battle. Marching under the banner of the Virgin Mary, in whom they placed their absolute trust, Sobieski and his forces routed the Jihadists. After the victory, Sobieski proclaimed, "Veni, vidi, Deus vicit" ("I came, I saw, God conquered.") The devout Christian warrior was later hailed by the Pope as the savior of Western civilization. The praise was well deserved, for had it not been for the Polish king, Christendom would have been decisively overrun by radical Islam.

I then wrote of Saint Vincent de Paul and of his miraculous appearance to Saint Catherine Laboure many years after his death. A disciple of Saint Francis de Sales, Vincent was the Lord's greatest servant of the seventeenth century. Kindhearted and compassionate, he strove to help the poor and downtrodden. In the year 1625, Vincent founded the Congregation of the Mission, devoted to helping peasants in France. In 1633, together with Saint Louise de Marillac, he founded the Sisters of Charity. Throughout his hallowed life, Saint Vincent relentlessly labored for Christ and his Church, establishing seminaries, hospitals, and orphanages. It is said that there was no human suffering he did not seek to relieve.

Vincent died in Paris in 1660, but he appeared to Saint Catherine in a dream over a hundred years later. Seeing that Catherine was unsure of her path in life, he instructed her to follow Christ and to dedicate her life to those who suffer. Catherine heeded his words and became a great saint in her own right.

Next, I wrote of John Newton, one of the most remarkable men of the eighteenth century. For much of his life, Newton was a wretch who had lost his way. Although raised by a devout Christian mother, he became a great sinner and blasphemer who loved no one. Working on the slave ship *Greyhound*, Newton faced death one day when his ship was caught in a horrible storm. At first, Newton scoffed at the threat of death, but as the situation grew more dire, he was overcome with fear and regret. Surprising even himself, Newton spontaneously looked to heaven and begged God for mercy. The date was May 10, 1748, and the time was nine o'clock in the morning—a date and time Newton would forever remember. Always merciful, the Lord heard his call and, with amazing grace, saved him in more ways than one. Thankful that he had been saved, Newton repented and devoted the remainder of his life to good. He took to preaching and became the foremost hymn writer of modern times.

Newton was best known for composing the hymn *Amazing Grace*, but his hymn *I Saw One Hanging on a Tree* was the most inspiring to me.

It is a beautiful hymn:

> "I saw One hanging on a tree,
> In agony and blood,
> Who fixed His languid eyes on me,
> As near His cross I stood.
>
> Sure, never to my latest breath,
> Can I forget that look;
> It seemed to charge me with His death,
> Though not a word He spoke.
>
> My conscience felt and owned the guilt,
> And plunged me in despair,
> I saw my sins His blood had spilt,
> And helped to nail Him there.
>
> A second look He gave, which said,
> 'I freely all forgive;
> This blood is for thy ransom paid;
> I die that thou mayst live."[33]

Still not finished, I wrote of the evils of Voltaire and the French Revolution. Much as the early Christians praised Christ, the New Age atheists praised Voltaire. To the atheists, Voltaire was a brilliant prophet who enlightened the world. They saw him as such because the eighteenth-century philosopher championed their cause. Voltaire dedicated his life to the promotion of societal secularization, and in many ways he succeeded. He wrote countless criticisms of religion, which had a profound impact on the course of history. In France, Voltaire's derisive anticlerical rhetoric led to an uprising against the Church. His words fueled the chaos of the revolution—a revolution not of good but of evil. In the end, Voltaire's legacy was one of utter tyranny. Because of him,

---

33 Adapted from URL: http://en.wikisource.org/wiki/I_saw_One_hanging_
    on_a_tree. Downloaded 1-31-09.

thousands upon thousands of good people were persecuted and murdered under the false pretense of enlightenment. I wrote:

> Voltaire was a deist, one who believes that God created the universe but then chose to neglect his creation. To the deist, God is but a distant observer. Like other deists, Voltaire believed in human reason and science but not in faith. A philosopher and satirist with a quick wit and a savage bite, Voltaire viciously attacked every aspect of Christianity, from the Holy Trinity to the Virgin Mary. Fueled by the devil, his fame grew to great heights, and an entire society changed because of his wicked words. No one man was more strongly associated with the Age of Enlightenment than he. Lamentably, many "enlightened" souls fled the faith because they marveled at his wit. The irony is that when Voltaire was confronted with the limits of his own life, he desperately grasped for the very faith from which his wit had driven so many. On his deathbed, Voltaire found no use for the marvels of human reason. He found no solace in praying to a distant God. He found no hope in science. On the contrary, when faced with his own mortality, Voltaire begged for forgiveness from Christ and from the Church. It was only at the very end that Voltaire found true enlightenment.

> *Mock on, mock on, Voltaire;*
> *Mock on, mock on; 'tis all in vain!*
> *You throw the sand against the wind,*
> *And the wind blows it back again.*[34]

After briefly recounting the blasphemy of Voltaire, I chronicled the story of the Carmelite nuns of Compeigne—how they died by the guillotine during the French Revolution because of their unwavering faith. Their story was tragic but moving. I wrote:

> In the fateful year 1789, the common people of France overthrew King Louis XVI and formed a revolutionary government. It was revolutionary in that it promised to bring about a better world through faith in man. It was revolutionary in that it attempted to create a new world order, an order in which only revolution itself was cherished. It was revolutionary on many levels, not the least of which was its depth of cruelty. The new

---

34 Adapted from William Blake's "Mock on, Mock on, Voltaire, Rousseau."
URL: http://en.wikisource.org/wiki/%22Mock_on,_Mock_on,_Voltaire,_
Rousseau%22. Downloaded 11-6-2009.

French government, deeply influenced by the philosophy of Voltaire, strongly opposed the Church. By means of devious propaganda, public opinion was swayed, and the Church was portrayed as an opponent of progress. A great persecution of the clergy ensued. Church lands were confiscated and sold. Thirty to forty thousand priests were murdered or driven into exile. Christian holidays were abolished and replaced with atheistic feast days commemorating labor, reason, virtue, genius, rewards, and the Revolution itself. Sunday was eliminated from the calendar, as it was seen as a day of God. All references to the birth of Christ were dropped by establishing a new era, dating from the start of the French Revolution. Priests who were not murdered or exiled were forced to leave the priesthood and take wives. It was truly a dark time.

In 1792, the religion of reason became the faith of France, replacing Christianity. Churches were turned into "temples of reason," and a statue of the Goddess of Reason was erected in the Notre Dame Cathedral in Paris. Streets named after saints were renamed for revolutionary heroes. Church bells and chalices were seized and melted. France, a nation with a rich history of faith in the Lord—a nation with a rich history of support of his Church—changed drastically in the blink of an eye. Seduced by the devil, the lost sheep of France rejected Christ, and the sins of a godless people became manifest. The Reign of Terror began, and the cross, symbol of salvation, was replaced by the guillotine, symbol of damnation.

At the outbreak of the French Revolution, there lived a group of twenty-one Carmelite nuns in a monastery at Compeigne. They maintained a simple and holy life of devotion to God, spending their days working for the greater good of man and praying that their nation would find peace. During the dechristianization of France, their convent was closed, and they were ordered to leave. It was at this time that, by government decree, it became a crime to be a priest or a nun.

In accordance with the law, the nuns left the convent and took ordinary jobs. They wore ordinary clothes. They ostensibly lived ordinary lives. Yet they were far from ordinary. Sixteen of the twenty-one continued to meet in secret and pray together to the Lord Jesus Christ. These sixteen had faith so strong and hearts so pure that they were like flakes of pristine snow, standing out against the background of dark, cold, barren soil. Surrounded by chaos and human filth, these sixteen devotedly prayed that the tyranny in France would come to an end. But the influence of the devil had grown too strong, and it was not to be. Word spread of their clandestine meetings and the nuns were arrested. A farce of a trial was held, in which they each were found guilty of treason against the Revolution. Unjustly, the sixteen Carmelites were sentenced to death.

It was not long before the fateful day came—the day of execution. It was in the seventh month, and the heat was sweltering. A mass of people gathered in the town square in Compeigne. The hellish heat drove them mad with passion—their eyes were wide, and their brows furled with anger and hate. As if possessed by demons, they cried out for blood. Lamentably, the scene had become all too commonplace. Every day they gathered in the square—every day—for in the middle of the square was the ominous guillotine, with blade so sharp and consequence so final. They gathered to scorn those found guilty of treason and to watch as the devilish blade fell onto the necks of its victims. They gathered like a satanic cult.

A woman in the crowd counted each death that the guillotine wrought. She shouted out so that all might hear, and the crowd rejoiced with each death. "Long live the Republic!" they cried out.

Men in the crowd mocked the nuns as they were brought forth that day.
"We introduce you to Saint Guillotine!" they shouted.
"Traitors! Traitors!"
"Ignorant fools! How stupid they are!"
"Murder the traitors!"
The cries of the maddened masses were deafening.

Surrounded by pandemonium, the nuns serenely sang out, in pure, confident voices, unafraid of the fate that awaited them. Each of the sixteen sang:

"Hail, Holy Queen,
Mother of Mercy
Our light, our sweetness, and our hope."

The commotion of the crowd was so great that at first, few could hear the song of the women. The masses were too caught up in the frenzy to notice; they were too possessed by hatred to care. But as much as the masses did not notice the sixteen, the sixteen did not notice the masses, and they calmly sang on.

The first of the nuns stepped up to the guillotine. She did not try to resist in any manner; rather, she took her place as if it were routine. She continued to sing with the rest of the sisters as she rested her neck over the beam. Within seconds, the demonic blade came speeding down. The woman in the crowd shouted out, "One!" The masses rejoiced. "Long live the Republic! Death to the traitors! Blessed is Saint Guillotine!"

The second nun stepped forward. Like the first before her, she showed no signs of fear. She made no attempts to resist. She simply sang the melody.

"Two!" the woman shouted.

The third stepped forward, then the fourth and the fifth and the sixth. The woman counted on, louder and louder with each number. The crowd jeered the Carmelites; then cheered with each fall of the blade. The sweat poured down their crazed brows in the summer heat.

It was at this point, after the sixth was gone, that some of the members of the crowd began to take note of the song sung by the nuns. "Look at them, and listen to them," they said. "Have they no fear of death?" Others said, "We have never seen anything like this before." Rumblings spread quickly throughout the masses. Many of the eyes, so wide with hateful passion, now squinted with confusion; many of the brows furled by anger now furled with puzzlement.

"Seven!" the woman in the crowd shouted out.
The remaining nuns sang on.

"Hail, Holy Queen,
Mother of Mercy
Our light, our sweetness, and our hope."

The clamor of the crowd grew weaker, and more and more hushed to listen to the nuns' song.

"Eight!" the woman cried out. The remaining eight continued their song, unfazed by their surroundings; unfazed by the earthly fate that awaited them.

"I have never seen such bravery," remarked one of the men in the crowd. "I have never seen such faith," remarked another, and as he turned and walked away, the woman in the crowd shouted, "Nine!"

Ten, and eleven, and twelve—the guillotine blade never tired, but with each death, the clamor of the crowd grew softer until there was nothing but a murmur.

"Hail, Holy Queen,
Mother of Mercy
Our light, our sweetness, and our hope."

Many in the crowd began to feel ill at ease. Clearly, the devil was losing his grip on the souls he possessed. The crowd began to turn. "This is not right," they said. "These are not traitors. What have they done wrong? What have we done?"

"Thirteen" and then "fourteen"—the woman no longer had to shout to be heard. She looked about in confusion, and then she looked up at the final two. For the remaining Carmelites, there was no confusion. They embraced their fate as they continued to sing.

"Fifteen!" the woman shouted again after the blade fell, hoping to rouse the diminishing crowd, but she stirred no response.

One of the men still in the crowd turned to a woman who had most viciously mocked the nuns and said to her, "May God have mercy on your soul. May God have mercy on all of our souls."

The final Carmelite nun, the Mother Superior, stepped up to the dreaded machine and placed her neck on the beam. Her song was the only sound filling the air, and her voice was sweet and pure. The blade came crashing down one final time on that hot and humid day, and then—stillness.

"Sixteen," the woman whispered as the remaining onlookers stood in total silence. The final numeral was uttered so softly that none could hear, not even the devil himself.

I am the Resurrection and the Life, saith the Lord; he that believeth in me, though he were dead, yet shall he live; and whoever liveth and believeth in me shall never die.

Marie Claude Brard, Madeline Brideau, Marie Croissy, Marie Dufour, Marie Hanisset, Marie Meunier, Rose de Neufville, Annette Pebras, Marie Anne Peidcourt, Madeline Lidoine, Angelique Roussel, Catherine Soiron, Therese Soiron, Anne Mary Thouret, Marie Trezelle, and Elizabeth Verolot—sixteen sang all the way to the guillotine; sixteen sang all the way to eternal life.

Pausing briefly from writing, I pondered what it would be like to live in such a strife-filled era. I was appalled by the malice of a society that would murder innocent nuns. I quickly concluded that the French Revolution was the darkest period in the annals of humanity. *It wasn't the best of times and the worst of times; it was just the worst of times. Thus was the legacy of secularization—a world without God, a world of abject tyranny. Sadly, we didn't learn our lesson.*

Finally, I began to write about the extraordinary yet misunderstood nineteenth-century prophet Lamennais. Prior to the start of *The Third Testament*, I had never heard of Lamennais, but after coming across his name on several occasions while doing research for the book, I became intrigued by the man. Lamennais was a French priest and visionary who foresaw the future of the Catholic Church with remarkable clarity. He constantly pushed for Church reform, and many of the reforms he championed, although vehemently rejected in his day, eventually came to pass. In actual fact, by the late twentieth century, a distinct majority had come to pass. So great was his foresight that one ecclesiastical scholar went as far as to say that all the directions of contemporary Catholicism originated with him.

A true-to-life modern-day prophet, I thought. *But why is there so little written about him?*

There was some information about him on the Internet, but I wanted to know more. Unfortunately, I had a very difficult time finding more information. The most frequently referenced book about him was *Prophecy and the Papacy*, written in the 1950s by Alec Vidler, but when I searched Amazon.com, I found that it was no longer in print. I could not find a copy of it. I tried the public and university libraries but had no luck.

I've got to get that book, I thought obsessively. *I've got to include a chapter on Lamennais.*

Sadly, obsession had become an integral part of my life, and as my depression worsened, writing had turned from a magnificent obsession into a pathologic obsession. I was determined, if not desperate, to finish my task. It was all I thought about, day and night. It was my only defense mechanism against the profound sadness that engulfed me.

I've got to find Prophecy and the Papacy.

There was one person I knew who I thought might have it—Professor Erlichman.

Chapter 25

THE NUTTY PROFESSOR

PROFESSOR ERLICHMAN WAS my colleague at the Catholic college where I worked. An immigrant from the former East Germany, he had a guttural German accent and was quite eccentric. His hair was never combed and his face appeared unwashed, and aside from his lectures, he kept to himself. Despite his odd behavior, he was a brilliant and well-read man. Unfortunately, he was better known for his eccentricities than for his abundant knowledge. Foremost among his unusual behaviors was his insistence that students rise and say the Pledge of Allegiance at the start of each 8:00 AM class. That was certainly unique. I was quite sure that there was no other place in the country where college students were led in the Pledge of Allegiance by one of their professors. His devotion to America was somewhat understandable, even if his disheveled appearance was not. He had come to the United States late in 1954 as a refugee from the Communist Bloc and was one of the last immigrants to actually enter through Ellis Island. He never said what led him to escape East Germany, but it must have been terrible, because even after fifty-plus years, he still gritted his teeth when he said the word "Soviets."

Professor Erlichman had a large collection of books. His office was filled, wall to wall and floor to ceiling, with old religious texts and magazines. Although we had been colleagues for many years, I had only visited his office on two other occasions, and I am certain that he had never visited mine. My first visit to his office left me with quite an impression. Upon opening the door, I felt like I had walked into a bizarre shrine. Multiple pictures of the Virgin Mary and the Statue of Liberty were everywhere—on the door to the office, the bookshelves, the windowsills, his desk, and on the floor. Anyplace where there wasn't a book, there was a picture or a statue.

I recalled that my eyes popped wide open in awe the first time I saw the unusual exhibition. Yet the pictures and statues were not all that was unusual that day. Sitting at his large oak desk, Professor Erlichman observed my reaction to the icons and proceeded to reveal to me an outlandish belief.

"You know, Frederick," he said, "they are one and the same."

Confused, I looked at him with a puzzled expression. "Who is one and the same?" I questioned.

"The Mother of Exiles and the Blessed Virgin are one and the same," he said. "The Statue of Liberty is a representation of the Blessed Virgin."

Again, I gave him a puzzled expression.

"The statue's crown is a nimbus—a halo," he explained. "She is obviously wearing a gown and sandals, just as the Blessed Virgin would have worn, and she is carrying tablets. The Blessed Virgin is often depicted holding tablets. Not only that, but the Blessed Virgin has been called Santa Maria della Liberta, or Saint Mary of Liberty. She has also been called the Mother of the Forsaken, which is just another way of saying the Mother of Exiles, who stands there in the harbor, watching over this great country of ours, this nation under God."

I did not want to start an argument with him, but I could not let such a seemingly ridiculous statement go unchallenged. "You do know that the sculptor was a freemason who despised the Church and patterned the statue after the Roman goddess Libertas," I said in the least antagonistic tone I could muster. "And Emma Lazarus, the author of the famous inscription on the bronze plaque inside the statue, was Jewish."

Logic and facts were not about to deter him.

"My dear Frederick, while I agree that what you have said is true, I hold firm to my statement," he said. "Right now, you are only looking at the superficial facts. To understand, you need to look deeper and view this from a wider scope. What I'm saying is that there is a true-to-life Lady Liberty—not a symbol but a reality; a true Mother of Exiles, a true Mother of the Forsaken. She is the Blessed Virgin, and although the creators of the statue and the poem did not intend this to be the case, they nonetheless found the path to truth. That statue is a depiction of the Mother of God, placed there by divine Providence, just as this nation was founded by divine Providence. The words on that inscription—'Give me your tired, your poor, the wretched refuse from your teeming shore'—are the words of Mary calling out to those troubled in the world and promising them hope. Search your heart, Frederick. Who else could the Mother of Exiles be but the Mother of God? If you look at the history of this nation, founded on Christian principles, you will understand."

I didn't buy his argument, but I was astounded by his imagination. *The nutty professor*, I thought.

As nutty as he was, he was admired by his students. Year in and year out, he won the college's Best Teacher award. Upon first meeting him, most students would be amused by his eccentricities, but it was never long before they became captivated by his zeal. Even though he kept to himself, when he did speak, he spoke with great passion, and his depth of knowledge was remarkable.

One late Friday afternoon, after I was finished lecturing for the day, I made my way over to Professor Erlichman's office to see if he owned a copy of Vidler's *Prophecy and the Papacy.*

"Good afternoon," I said as I poked my head inside his partially opened door.

"Frederick, please come in. To what do I owe this pleasure?" the elderly professor said in his thick German accent.

"I'm searching for a book," I said. "I know you have quite a collection, and I thought you might have it."

"Which book are you looking for?" he asked. "I will help you find it."

"Prophecy and the Papacy by Vidler," I answered.

"Ah, the prophet Lamennais," he said. "He was extraordinary—a truly brilliant man; a man before his time."

"So you own it?" I asked.

"Yes, I own it," he said. "It is here in this office some place. You will find it fascinating." He then put on his glasses and gingerly stood up from his desk, visibly slowed by arthritis. "Let me find it for you."

The hunchbacked professor hobbled across the room and began scanning his shelves. While he was searching, I gazed around the room, taking note of all of the icons and books. New to his office since the last time I had visited was an irregularly shaped stone on his desk. I knew in an instant what it was. Several years earlier, Professor Erlichman had journeyed to Berlin to visit his relatives. He returned with a piece of rock from the Berlin Wall. I had heard that he had gone to great lengths to get it. The stone was placed in the center of an opened rosary on his desk. The rosary appeared to be handcrafted and quite expensive, and it surrounded the stone in a carefully arranged manner. I did not understand the significance of the ornate display, but fearing a long and drawn-out explanation, I was not about to ask.

Also new since my last visit was a 10 x 12-inch color photograph of Pope John Paul II, shaking hands with former president Ronald Reagan. The framed photograph was prominently displayed in the center of one of his bookshelves. Based on its location in the room, it was clearly something that Erlichman valued. Inscribed on the lower border of the frame were the words "Holy Alliance." Just like the rosary, I did not understand the inscription's significance, but knowing the professor, I was sure that there was a fanciful story behind it.

To the immediate left of the photograph on the shelf was a small stack of *Time* magazines. When I looked down at the cover of the top magazine in the stack, I saw that it was an issue from February 24, 1992. The headline on the cover read "Holy Alliance," just like the inscription on the photograph. Intrigued, I picked it up and read the subtitle: "How Reagan and the Pope conspired to assist Poland's Solidarity movement and hasten the demise of Communism."

This could have some useful information for my book, I thought.

"Here it is," the professor said as he pulled *Prophecy and the Papacy* from the shelf. As he turned around with the book in his hand, he saw me paging through the *Time* magazine issue. He instantly seemed pleased, as if he was happy that I had shown interest in his possessions. "That was the greatest story since the coming of Christ," he said.

"Which story is that?" I asked, not sure if he was referring to the *Time* magazine headline or the book in his hand.

"The Holy Alliance," he said. "The fall of the evil empire."

"The greatest story since the coming of Christ?" I asked cordially. "That's quite a claim. How do you figure that?"

Professor Erlichman smiled warmly and gestured toward a chair. "Please sit down, Frederick. Let me tell you the amazing saga of the rise and fall of Satan's empire."

I was tired and simply wanted to get the book and go home, but to appease the wishes of the nutty old professor, I sat in the chair and listened.

"Communism is said to have begun with Karl Marx in the late 1800s," he began. "But really, it is far older than that. It originated in the garden of paradise, when the serpent made the promise 'you will be as gods.' You see, Communism is Satan's religion. From its inception, Communism falsely promised that man could achieve an earthly salvation if he hoped in himself instead of hoping in God. More specifically, Communism said that Christianity was holding man back from achieving true greatness, the greatness of gods. Marx brought the evil religion to the forefront of the world's attention, but he only did so when Satan thought the world was ready. Satan, of course, prepared for a long time before he thought the world was ready. He first went to great lengths to convince the world that he did not exist. He did this by preying on man's conceit, convincing man that everything in the universe could be explained by human intellect."

Peering at me over the top rim of his glasses, the professor shook his head, indicating his displeasure with man's gullibility. "The theory of evolution is the perfect example of man's misguided faith in the human intellect," he said.

"It is a deeply flawed theory, and yet it is accepted as absolute, unquestionable gospel by the 'experts.' According to these experts, there is no Creator and there is no plan. There is only time and natural selection. According to the experts, there is no good, and there is no evil. There are only chemical imbalances in the human brain.

"Taking his plot one step farther, Satan fostered secularization and atheism in our classrooms and news outlets, making it politically incorrect to speak of spiritual matters in public. Manipulating members of the clergy, he even cultivated disbelief among certain religious Christians. As you know, today there are many Christians who believe in God but not in Satan."

"Yes, I know," I lamented.

"William Booth, the pious founder of the Salvation Army and contemporary of Marx, warned us against Satan's plot. He said the chief dangers of the coming century would be 'religion without the Holy Spirit, Christianity without Christ, politics without God, and heaven without hell.' Unfortunately, his warning largely fell on deaf ears, and Satan was able to hide in a world where there was 'heaven without hell.' Frederick, Satan's cleverest trick was to convince the world that he does not exist. With all of my heart, I believe this is true. It was his cleverest trick in that it allowed him to carry out his devious plot without being suspected. After all, how could he establish a religion on earth if he never existed? Many were fooled but not all. Many, to this day, are still fooled, but don't you be. Satan was absolutely behind Communism. If you analyze it closely, you will have to agree that what Marx proclaimed in the 1800s—that the human material life would be emancipated, at which point religion would whither away—was really just another way of saying what the serpent said to Eve in the Garden of Eden. There is no denying this fact. Look at the words, and look at their context. It is explicitly clear. Thus, it is also clear that Communism is the second oldest religion, the religion where man sees himself as God."

I nodded, not so much to indicate that I was in agreement as that I was listening carefully to what he was saying.

"Did you know, Frederick, that Marx was a Satan worshipper?" the professor asked.

"I know that his close friend, Mikhail Bakunin, was," I replied. "Bakunin praised Satan as being the eternal rebel, first thinker, and emancipator of worlds. But I know of no documents that suggest that Marx himself worshipped Satan."

"Of course Marx was!" the professor retorted with a jovial chuckle. "If his closest friends were, do you really believe he was anything else, especially given his life's ambitions? Look at how he worded his famous *Communist Manifesto*: 'A specter is haunting Europe ...' and 'A Holy Alliance has formed to try to exorcise the specter.' Why do you think Marx used the term 'exorcise'? Do you really believe he chose the word by chance? Certainly he didn't. The specter was Satan."

"Perhaps," I said, humoring him.

"With Marx as his gardener," he said, "Satan planted an evil seed late in the nineteenth century, and that seed took root in the nation of Russia. He targeted Russia for a reason. We in the West have little knowledge about the Orthodox Christianity of the East, especially the Russian Orthodox Church, but the history of Christianity in Russia is a very important history, a history that has determined the destiny of the earth."

Here comes another outlandish theory, I thought.

"In the year 1510," he explained, "Filofey, a Russian monk and prophet, proclaimed that Russia was the third Rome, the heart of Christian truth. You see, after Christ's Resurrection, Rome became the center of Christianity and took the lead in spreading the word of God around the world. When Rome became corrupted by politics and fell to the barbarians, the center of Christianity moved to Constantinople, the second Rome. When Constantinople fell to radical Islam in 1453, the center of Christian truth moved to Russia, the third Rome. Filofey proclaimed there would not be a fourth, meaning that Russia would complete the destiny of spreading Christianity to every corner of the earth. In the eighteenth and nineteenth centuries, Russia was, in fact, a champion of the Christian cause. It was the main defender of Christian civilization from its greatest threat—Islam. Catherine the Great led the nation of Russia to astounding victories over the Muslims in the War of 1768 and again in the War of 1787, freeing thousands upon thousands of pious souls from Islamic persecution. Russia's involvement in the War of 1828 led to the emancipation of the Greek nation, and its involvement in the War of 1877 led to the emancipation of Bulgaria and Serbia. In the twentieth century, at the onset of World War I, the Russians prevailed in several decisive battles against the Ottoman Empire. Their success was such that if they had continued their string of conquests, they would have reclaimed Constantinople for Orthodox Christianity. But then Satan's plan began to unfold. Marx's evil seed took root and a tragedy of greatest proportion followed."

"The Bolshevik Revolution," I said.

"Yes, the Bolshevik Revolution," he said. "Guided by the eye of Satan, Marx knew of Russia's providence. He knew Russia was destined to spread its beliefs around the entire world, but because of his efforts and the efforts of demons like him, it was not Christian beliefs that Russia spread around the world—"

"It was Communism that was spread around the world."

Professor Erlichman's eyes were wide with enthusiasm. "Indeed! The next chapter in the story brings us to another famous minion of Satan—Grigori Rasputin. His role in history cannot be over emphasized. The evil empire would have never come to be if it were not for him. As you know, Rasputin was a dark mystic who rose to prominence in Russia through acts of deception and black magic. He proclaimed himself a holy man and prophet, but he was the farthest thing from holy. He gained the trust of the czar and czarina by healing their beloved son Alexei of hemophilia, but his intentions were impure. While living in St. Petersburg, Rasputin practiced the occult and preached blasphemy, claiming that grace could only be reached through sinful actions. He used this claim to seduce the innocent and ignorant. He cut locks of hair from all the virgins he slept with and buried the locks in his garden."

"I remember reading about that, years ago," I said. "When his home was razed in 1977, authorities unearthed numerous boxes containing long locks of women's hair."

"Yes," the professor concurred. "He was utterly diabolical. Some say he communed face to face with Satan himself. This much is true: his efforts directly led to the foundation of the Soviet Union. Having achieved a place of influence by healing the czar's son, Rasputin cunningly spent his days currying favor from the Russian aristocracy, and he hedonistically spent his nights soliciting prostitutes and drinking himself into a stupor. He then patiently waited, like a lion in the bush, for his chance to seize ultimate power, and that chance came quickly. After the First World War broke out, Rasputin claimed to have had a revelation that the Russian armies would only be successful if Czar Nicholas personally took command of them. Nicholas, unfortunately, heeded Rasputin's words and left St. Petersburg to take command of his military. Nicholas' decision had dire consequences. While the czar was away at the war front, Rasputin's influence over Czarina Alexandra grew immensely. He became the czarina's confidant and personal advisor. Using his charm and persuasive powers, he gained total control over all critical governmental policy decisions. The web he wove was thus complete. In short time, it became clear that Russia was on a path to doom. Under the command of Czar Nicholas, the Russian army suffered one humiliating defeat after another at the hands of the advancing Germans, and because of the evil, manipulative ploys of Rasputin, the Russian economy began to crumble.

"As the turmoil in Russia reached immeasurable heights, Rasputin did nothing but intensify the controversy by bragging about the profound influence he had over the czar and czarina. By the year 1916, the Russian people began to strongly turn against the czar, and the czar began to turn against Rasputin. Sensing betrayal, Rasputin cursed Czar Nicholas and the entire Romanov family. He proclaimed:

'Czar of the land of Russia, if you hear the sound of the bell which will tell you that Grigori has been killed, you must know this: if it was your relations who have wrought my death, then no one in the family, that is to say, none of your children or relations, will remain alive for more than two years.'[35]

"Just as Rasputin predicted, a Romanov did plot his death. Czar Nicholas' first cousin, the politically driven Grand Duke Dmitri Pavlovich Romanov, had Rasputin murdered, and Rasputin's curse against the czar and his family came to pass. Within three months of the demon's death, Nicholas II and the Romanov dynasty were overthrown by Lenin and the Bolsheviks, and within nineteen months, the czar and his family were all dead. Thus, the intricate work of Satan became clear—Rasputin's sinister deeds paved the way for the Russian Revolution and the establishment of the Communist state. Indubitably, Satan's garden of evil was growing."

"Rasputin was certainly one of history's most notorious characters," I agreed.

"He was a demon in human form," the professor said matter-of-factly. "With the czar and his family out of the way, there was no one to oppose Lenin in Russia. The sinister leader of the Bolsheviks thus commenced his plot to eradicate Christianity and spread Communism around the world." Professor Erlichman paused in his story to ask me a childish question. "Have you ever seen the portrait of Lenin with horns sticking out of his head?"

"Yes," I said, "I'm sure I have. At least, I think I have." I could not place exactly where, but I recalled seeing an old anti-Communist propaganda poster depicting him as the devil.

"The horns naturally suit him, don't you think?" the professor said. Smiling, he then continued with his saga. "The next chapter in the story brings us to Poland. After the bloody Bolshevik Revolution, Poland was all that stood between the Communists in Russia and the heart of European Christian civilization. In the year 1919, the Communists in Russia set out to conquer the world and began with an invasion of their neighbor to the west. The Poles were outnumbered and were routed in the early battles but then came the Miracle on the Vistula."

The Miracle on the Vistula? I had never heard of it.

"Have you seen the painting by Polish artist Jerzy Kossak?" Professor Erlichman asked.

"No, I have not," I said.

"Ah, I must show it to you." The professor slowly pulled himself out of

---

35   URL: http://en.wikipedia.org/wiki/Rasputin. Downloaded 2-17-06.

his chair and hobbled over to one of his bookshelves, where he grabbed an art book off the shelf. Paging through it quickly, he found an image of the painting and showed it to me. The painting, titled *Miracle on the Vistula*, was of a war scene, filled with soldiers with rifles and bayonets. In the background of the scene was a majestic woman, high in the clouds, overlooking the battle. I did not know its significance, but the professor proceeded to explain it to me.

"The Vistula is a river in Poland, just outside of Warsaw," he said. "In August of the year 1920, after achieving a devastating succession of victories, the Communist forces gathered along the river in preparation for the battle that would lead to their final, triumphant march through the Polish capital. Prior to the battle, a group of pious Christians in Poland prayed in front of the Black Madonna for victory over the Communists, but most Poles—and most of the world—believed that the war was already lost. Then came the miracle. As the Russians began their attack, they saw a vision of a woman in the clouds, wearing a blue and white gown, with a golden crown on her head. It was the Virgin Mary. Seeing the miraculous vision in the clouds, the Russians became afraid and confused and were routed by the outmanned Polish forces. Because of the miracle on the Vistula, the course of history dramatically changed."

"Dramatically changed?" I questioned, thinking I had found a factual flaw in his outrageous argument. "How is that? The Soviets gained control of Poland just twenty years later."

"True," he replied. "In 1939, Poland became the devil's playground. The poor nation was split in two, one half controlled by the Nazis and the other by the Soviets, and after the war, it fell firmly into the hands of the Soviets. As you have pointed out, it would seem to the eye of evil that the miracle on the Vistula was but an empty last hurrah by the overwhelmed pious in Poland; it would seem to the eye of evil that hell's victory was complete. Yet what the eye of evil could not see was the birth of a child just three months prior to the miracle. The child born was no ordinary child; he was exceptional. Filled with the Lord's grace, he would grow up in a Christian state and would devote himself to the fellowship of the Holy Spirit. He, like his Polish brethren, would spend countless hours in prayer to the Blessed Virgin and through his fervent prayers and heavenly devotion, he would one day lead to the downfall of the evil empire. He would do this because the victory at the Vistula allowed him to grow up free and Christian."

"Karol Wojtyla," I said, figuring out to whom the professor was referring.

"Yes, the future Pope John Paul II," he said.

Although I thought his theory was raving mad, I became deeply intrigued nonetheless. It truly was an amazing story. Yet what he had said thus far could not compare with what was to come next.

"The next chapter in the story brings us to the rising of the beast," he said.

"The beast?" I questioned.

"Yes, the beast—the dragon, the man of sin, the son of perdition," he answered.

"Do you mean the Antichrist?" I questioned.

"Yes, Frederick, the Antichrist," he said.

This I've got to hear, I thought.

"The world has seen many evil men over the centuries, but none could compare with the evil of Stalin," he said. "Sure, there was Hitler, but Hitler failed in his evil quests; Stalin did not. Stalin was Satan's favored son. He was the Antichrist. What he did was abominable. He put over forty million innocent victims to death, and he brought hell to earth by cultivating the gulag system."

"Professor Erlichman, I know Stalin was evil, but the Antichrist?" I said. "Don't you think that maybe you're going a little overboard?"

"I tell you he was the Antichrist," he said with conviction. "He was a monster who was born and reared in the image and likeness of evil. The words he spoke were evil. He diabolically proclaimed 'Gratitude is a sickness suffered by dogs,' and 'the death of millions is a statistic.' Using deception and brutality, he came to power and made it his quest to poison the earth. He successfully promoted the spread of Communism around the world, and with its spread came unprecedented death and despair." The professor then began to go over a litany of Stalin's atrocities:

"During the Russian Revolution, Stalin invited local officials to meet with him on a barge moored on the Volga. When he was not convinced of their loyalty to the Communist cause, he had them shot and thrown in the river.

"Between the years 1932 and 1933, five million peasants died of famine in the Ukraine and lower Volga regions because of Stalin's agricultural policies that were specifically put into place to destroy the peasant factions that opposed him.

"Between the years 1936 and 1938, millions of Stalin's opponents were executed by firing squad during the Great Purge. Countless others suffered the dread of the gulags. The victims of the Purge were put through mock trials and brutally forced to confess to crimes they did not commit. Many were tortured and beaten before being put to death. Thousands of women were raped. It was a tragic time in a godless land.

"The perilous decade of the 1930s also saw the extermination of an entire social class of people in the Soviet Union. The kulaks, the upper-class peasants, were seen as opponents to the Communist cause. The kulaks were good people who worked hard and through their hard work, they came to own their own farms. They were a threat to Communism because they did not rely on the government. As a class, they were hated by the Bolsheviks. To promote the spread of evil, they needed to be eliminated. Stalin instituted class warfare, a ploy created by Satan himself, to rid Russia of its hardest-working landowners. During the reign of the beast, tens of thousands of kulaks were executed—men, women, and innocent children—simply because of their social standing. Hundreds of thousands of other families had their property confiscated and were deported to the gulags to serve as slaves. They were packed into trains and sent to the remote regions of the empire. Many died of cold and starvation along the way."

The professor's eyes grew wider and wider, and he gritted his teeth more and more as he continued on with the litany of atrocities. "In 1940, Stalin signed an order to brutally execute thousands of Polish prisoners of war in what became known as the Katyn massacre.

"During the war with Hitler's Germany, Stalin decreed that any Russian soldier who retreated without order should be shot on the spot, and thousands were. In addition, millions of prisoners of war were sent to the gulags to labor until their death.

"All along, Stalin plotted to undermine Christian civilization, specifically targeting America. He said, 'America is like a healthy body, and its resistance is threefold: its patriotism, its morality, and its spiritual life. If we can undermine these three areas, America will collapse from within.'

"Near the close of the Second World War, Stalin pretended to befriend Roosevelt and Churchill at the Yalta Conference. The two Western leaders made a deal with Stalin that allowed him to be guardian of the East.; it was a deal with the devil. Stalin proceeded to turn the East into an earthly hell surrounded by an iron curtain."

Concluding the litany, he said, "After the war, Stalin promoted the spread of Communism to China and Southeast Asia, where millions more were put to death by tyrannical Communist despots like Mao Zedong and Pol Pot." Looking at my expressions, the professor could tell that I was not buying his argument, so he argued further. "Stalin did everything in his power to undermine religion," he said. "He mandated the teaching of atheism in schools. By his order, churches were closed and converted into theaters. Religious icons were melted down, and religious meetings were banned throughout the country. The slogan 'religion is the opium of the people' was displayed everywhere. Members of the clergy were brutally executed. Christians were forced to go underground in order to hide from Soviet brutality. Shortly after his rise to power, Stalin created the League of the Militant Godless.

The purpose of the League was to propagate atheism. It ridiculed, harassed, and humiliated people of faith. It transformed monasteries into antireligious museums. It published newspapers and promoted films supporting science and atheism over religion. It organized demonstrations and parades in an attempt to convince the Russian public that the worship of God was harmful. It referred to religion as superstition. The League went as far as to stage contests to show the superiority of godless fields—agricultural plots that used modern soil and plant science over those of religious peasants who prayed to the Lord for a good harvest. The reign of Stalin was truly a tragic period in the annals of man."

"Maybe he was the Antichrist," I said, not because I believed it but because I was impressed with the professor's argument. He had obviously spent a lot of time thinking about it and had a lot to say, but he was still not done.

"Stalin employed repression, deception, and propaganda to manipulate the Russian people and promote his status to that of a deity," the professor said. "He became the focus of massive adoration and worship. He was hailed by cultists as a 'shining sun,' 'the staff of life,' a 'great teacher and friend,' and the 'hope of the future for the workers and peasants of the world.' Numerous cities and villages were renamed after him. Through years of oppression, he brainwashed the masses. In the end, the Orwellian horror was true—they loved Big Brother."

"He did have them brainwashed," I agreed. "As the saying goes, the Holy Trinity was replaced with a new Communist triune godhead—Marx, Lenin, and Stalin."

"Stalin eventually died, but his evil spirit did not," the professor continued. "Communism continued to spread around the globe. It seemed unstoppable. Poland, Latvia, Estonia, Lithuania, East Germany, Czechoslovakia, Bulgaria, Hungary, China, Albania, Yugoslavia, Mongolia, Cuba, North Korea, Laos, Cambodia, and Vietnam all fell into the hands of the devil. By the late 1970s, nearly one-third of the world's population was ruled by Communist party-led governments, and the tide of the Cold War had turned decisively in the Soviet Union's favor. Lamentably, the weeds of Satan's garden were choking the life out of the world. The pillars of Christian civilization were weakening. It seemed inevitable that in only a matter of time, the entire earth would fall into the dark hands of the devil. But the Lord, creator of the earth and all that is good, had other plans, and it was a secret alliance between two great pillars of faith that led to the downfall of the evil empire." Tapping his index finger on the cover of the "Holy Alliance" edition of *Time* magazine, he said, "This is the best part of the story. This is where you truly come to understand that God has a plan for us; that he is watching over us."

Opening the magazine to a picture of the Pope and president standing together, he said, "In 1982, Ronald Reagan and Pope John Paul II met and formed an alliance to bring down the Soviet Union. The alliance was a paradox. It was an unlikely union in that no pope had had any formal contact with a United States president in over one hundred years, and yet at the same time, it was a natural union because the two men had so much in common. They each survived assassination attempts, one six weeks from the other. They each had great faith in the Lord Jesus Christ and a great devotion to the Blessed Virgin Mary. They each believed deeply in the power of intercessory prayer, and they each believed they were saved from death by God's Providence for an important future role. That future role was the struggle against the Soviets. They each vowed to use all of their power and might to bring down Communism. They saw this as God's will. Indeed, they believed that the fall of the Soviet Union was an inevitable fact, not based on economics or politics but on a divinely inspired plan."

"Is this where Fatima ties in?" I asked.

"The Virgin Mary's promise was fulfilled, was it not?"

"That it was," I agreed.

"It couldn't be more straightforward," he said. "In the very year that the Communists murdered Czar Nicholas and came to power, the Virgin Mary appeared to three shepherd children in faraway Portugal and delivered a message that was uncharacteristically stern. She told them that because of man's misdoings, Russia would spread unprecedented terror around the world, but that the terror would end when the world was consecrated to her heart. Decades later, Pope John Paul II heeded her message, consecrated the world, and soon thereafter, against all odds, the Soviet Union fell."

"I once read a book about Fatima by Renzo Allegri, one of Pope John Paul's chief biographers," I said. "Allegri explained that prior to the consecration, John Paul had a desperate purpose about him; he believed the world was in grave danger and spoke in apocalyptic tones. Allegri made it clear that the Pope was acting as a modern-day prophet, urging the world to save itself through Christ."

"Yes, I have Allegri's book," the professor said as he shuffled over to the bookcase and pulled it from the shelf. "Everything about Fatima was apocalyptic, even the Miracle of the Sun, and John Paul did, in truth, act with a sense of dire urgency. He implored the world to pray the Rosary, just as the Blessed Virgin had instructed. He then did everything in his power to bring the bishops of the world together for the consecration. When the world was at last consecrated, Lucia de Santos, the last of the three shepherd children of Fatima still living at the time, acknowledged the Pope's efforts and said, 'Christ will keep his promise.'"

"It was an incredible series of events," I said, nodding my head in affirmation of each statement.

"At its core," the professor continued, "the conflict with the Soviets was a spiritual conflict between good and evil. It follows, then, that the Pope and president's battle against the Soviets centered around a very basic message— the message that good is greater than evil." Turning to a picture of Pope John Paul II preaching in Poland, he said, "The Pope's role in the clandestine plot was to remind the people of the East that they were inherently good, and Reagan's was to demonstrate to the world that Communism was abjectly evil ... *and* to stand strong against that evil."

That's a clever theory, I thought as I shifted in my seat.

"In fulfillment of his role in the pact," the professor said, "Pope John Paul journeyed into an earthly hell—he went on a pilgrimage behind the Iron Curtain and said to the people of the East, 'Do not be afraid. You are not who they say you are. Let me remind you who you are.' It was an extremely important message because he was telling them that they were children of God and that they had a future in Christ. And while the Pope preached a message of hope and change, Reagan boldly declared to the world that the Soviet Union was the focus of evil on the earth. He did not cloud his words in metaphor; he was absolutely clear with his message. He said, 'Let us pray for the salvation of all of those who live in that totalitarian darkness—pray they will discover the joy of knowing God. But until they do, let us be aware that while they preach the supremacy of the state, declare its omnipotence over individual man, and predict its eventual domination of all peoples on the earth, they are the focus of evil in the modern world.' Reagan then made it equally clear that he would not back down to evil. In speech after speech, he implored the people of the West to join him in the fight against Communist tyranny. He said, 'You and I have a rendezvous with destiny. We will preserve for our children this, the last best hope of man on earth, or we will sentence them to take the first step into a thousand years of darkness. If we fail, at least let our children and our children's children say of us, we justified our brief moment here. We did all that could be done.' Like Pope John Paul, Reagan fully understood the gravity of the situation, and he was therefore steadfast in his mission. Rallying this great nation, this shining city on the hill, he engaged the Soviets in an all-out arms race that crippled their economy." A great smile then broke out on the professor's face. "It is the irony of justice that Satan used a theory of economics—communism—to cloak his evil attempt to poison the world, and yet it was economics that largely contributed to his failure."

Again, clever, I thought.

"Frederick, now comes the conclusion of my story. By the 1980s, the situation in the world looked bleak; the Communists were definitely winning;

no one can argue that fact. But in the darkest hour, when all seemed lost, the light of Christ shined through. By the grace of God and with the help of the Virgin Mary, the Pope and president's efforts to win over the minds and souls of the people miraculously penetrated beyond the Iron Curtain. The first crack in the iron occurred in the Pope's homeland, Poland. Thanks to the untiring efforts of John Paul II, the Polish people held free elections in the middle of 1989. The Communists were decisively routed in the elections; they completely lost control of the Polish government."

"Then all of Eastern Europe followed suit," I said.

"Yes, Poland was the domino that led to the fall of the evil empire," he said. "After Poland's conversion, the grip of Communism was decimated in Eastern Europe. Hungary underwent vast reforms and opened its border with Austria. Independence demonstrations erupted in Lithuania, Latvia, and Estonia. Demands for freedom spread to East Germany, Czechoslovakia, Bulgaria, and Romania. Walls crumbled and gates opened. It was truly amazing. Bolstered by the prayers of millions, the spiritual message of the Pope and president even reached the leader of the Soviet Union himself, who met with the pontiff in 1989. When Soviet General Secretary Gorbachev introduced his wife, Raisa, to the Pope, he said to her, "Raisa, I introduce you to His Holiness John Paul II, the highest moral authority on earth.""

"Did Gorbachev really say that?" I questioned. It seemed hard to believe.

The professor nodded his head yes. Then, looking me straight in the eye he solemnly said, "Thus, my dear Frederick, the spiritual war was won. The prophecy of Fatima came to pass exactly as Mary said it would. Russia was converted. Satan's plot was foiled. The Berlin Wall fell. Nations were freed. Against all odds, the evil empire—the greatest threat in the history of the Church—crumbled before our very eyes, and peace was restored. As Reagan himself said, in the end, 'the power of prayer proved to be greater than the power of kings.'" With that statement, the professor placed his left hand on the stone on his desk and made the sign of the cross with his right. "That is the end of my story—my story of God's Providence."

"Well," I said, "that is quite a story."

"It is," he said, "but now we await the future, a future clouded with uncertainty. Will man turn to God or turn to sin? Will we find peace in our time or find ourselves faced with an even greater evil? Those are the ever-so-crucial questions."

"They are the questions that will define our era," I wholeheartedly agreed. "They will define the future of America and all free people. I can only hope that we are up to the challenge."

Pausing briefly to contemplate the significance of the challenge, I came up with a Reagan quote of my own. "If we ever forget that we are a nation under God, then we will be a nation gone under."

"True," the professor said. "Oh, so very true."

Looking at my watch, I saw that it was already late, and I got up from my chair. "Thank you for the book," I said.

"I hope you enjoy it, Frederick. Take a copy of the magazine also. Read it, and see what you think."

"Thank you," I said. "I will return it when I'm done."

"No need; it is yours."

"Thank you," I repeated. I headed for the door, but just as I was about to step out of his office, Professor Erlichman said one final thing.

"There is Providence, Frederick," he said. "Everything happens for a reason. Even our meeting tonight happened for a reason."

- - - - - - - - - -

When I got home later that night, I started reading *Prophecy and the Papacy*. Just as Professor Erlichman had said, it was fascinating. I came to have an even greater appreciation of Lamennais' role in the world and realized that he truly was a man before his time.

Lamennais lived by the motto "God and Freedom," and he boldly proclaimed:

> "The Church is being suffocated beneath the weight of the fetters which temporal power has put upon it; and liberty which has been called for in the name of atheism must now be demanded in the name of God."[36]

He further proclaimed:

> "The world is in a great crisis: everywhere it is trying to detach itself from a past out of which the life is gone, and to begin a new era. Nothing will stop this magnificent movement of the human race—it is directed from on high by Providence; but it is being held up by several causes. The welfare of society rests on two principles, which, rightly understood, comprise all its laws: 'No liberty without religion' and 'no religion without liberty.'"[37]

---

36 Alec Vidler. *Prophecy and the Papacy*. New York: Charles Scribner's Sons, 1954, p. 153.

37 Alec Vidler. *Prophecy and the Papacy*. New York: Charles Scribner's Sons, 1954, p. 222.

Lamennais was misunderstood by his contemporaries and was ultimately rejected by the Church that he had toiled so hard to support. The "Pilgrim of God and Liberty," as he was called, believed that freeing the people of the world from the bonds of tyranny was necessary to fulfill God's plan. He promoted democracy and universal suffrage. He also petitioned to free the Church from the corruption of the state. Lamentably, his quest to link God and freedom was denied by Pope Gregory XVI; the infamous denial occurred in 1832. Having witnessed the great chaos and anarchy that the French Revolution had brought to God's people, Pope Gregory XVI was fearful of any revolutionary philosophies. Instead, he staunchly supported the old system, where the Church and the monarchies worked together to lead the people of the world.

Although devastated by the rejection, Lamennais never abandoned his most heartfelt beliefs. To his dying day, with all of the conviction in his soul, he preached the message that was central to his ministry:

> "An immense liberty is indispensable for the development of those truths which are to save the world."

Lamennais' words would prove to be prophetic indeed.

Chapter 26
THE NEW PATH

ONE DAY, AFTER writing, I met Jerry at Al's Pub. The pub was unusually crowded, and we grabbed the last table in the place. Al either had a good sense of humor or a poor sense of taste because he'd mounted the back end of a moose on the wall, just above the fireplace. The display was quite the sight and always drew a lot of humorous comments. Jerry and I had heard them all over the years. Unfazed, we sat just underneath the moose's hindquarters, picked up our menus, and settled in for lunch.

Reaching for a basket of popcorn, I noticed that there was a young man at a table by himself just behind us. He was sitting quietly, reading *A Tale of Two Cities*. He seemed out of place in the dark and smoky pub. He was reading so intently that he seemed more appropriate for a library. I doubted that Jerry even noticed him.

Jerry grabbed some popcorn for himself. "How ya holdin' up, Fred?"

"I'm at the end of my rope," I said. "Ellen is so despondent right now. She doesn't want to talk about further therapy. She doesn't want to talk at all. I'm so afraid. This all seems to be happening so fast."

"I'm so sorry. Is there anything I can do?"

I shook my head. "I don't think there is anything that anyone can do."

Jerry nodded sympathetically. Despite his gruff, tough-guy exterior, he was a good man, filled with compassion.

"I've been calling cancer centers around the country," I said. "The National Cancer Institute in Bethesda has several melanoma trials. Memorial Sloan-Kettering in New York, and M. D. Anderson in Houston also have trials. The problem is that Ellen is so emotionally overwrought right now that she won't discuss traveling. I'm not sure that traveling is even the right answer. Her disease seems to be so aggressive. I'm afraid that by the time she gets established with someone out-of-state, it will be too late. I'm afraid she'll be too sick. We need a miracle, Jerry."

"Aren't there any other melanoma specialists around here that she can see?" Jerry inquired.

"No, Dr. Greenspan is the only one, and Ellen is so frustrated with him that she won't go back. I don't blame her. He basically told us that the trial he had wouldn't have any major impact. He just said, 'At least it shouldn't make you any sicker.' He didn't want to be aggressive. He said she's already too sick to be aggressive." I sighed, and then Jerry sighed, too.

Lately, I found myself sighing ever so often. In the 1961 movie *Breakfast at Tiffany's*, Holly Golightly, played by the unforgettable Audrey Hepburn, complained of a state of mind worse than the "blues," a state of mind she referred to as the "mean reds." The "mean reds" was a state of inconsolable agitation. It was a state of pure misery. It seemed that I was constantly plagued by the "mean reds," and my only defense mechanism was sighing. My mind would race, and I would sigh. When I was cornered by anxiety, I would sigh. When it seemed that there was no good conclusion—when it seemed like there was nothing else that could be done—I would sigh.

How many sighs does it take to end the pain? I wondered.

"Jerry," I said, "I know you don't believe in God, and you'll probably think that I'm crazy, but I'd like to take Ellen to Lourdes." I paused a second to make sure Jerry understood what I was saying. I could see in his eyes that he was familiar with Lourdes and understood exactly what I was saying. "There have been unexplainable cures there—amazing cures, Jerry. I'd really like to take her there, but I don't think she'd ever agree to go. And besides, I'd be afraid to even give the suggestion for fear that she would see it as a sign of desperation."

For a moment there was silence. "Regardless of what I believe, Fred, if the doctors are telling you that she needs a miracle, neither I nor anyone else can fault you for looking for one. And if you're looking for a miracle, Lourdes would be the logical place to start. I don't think you're crazy."

"Thanks, Jerry. I just wish there was an easy solution to this, a solution we could get to quickly."

"I just can't believe, with all of the major academic medical centers in the area, that there isn't another melanoma expert around town," Jerry said.

"I've looked. I'd love to find another local melanoma expert. Dr. Greenspan is the only one. For as common as melanoma is, you'd think that there would be more. You'd think that in a city as large as Chicago, there would be several. There's not ..."

My train of thought was broken by the young man at the table behind us. Unexpectedly, he put down his book and waved his hand, shouting out, "Yo,

Tony!" I turned around and saw that he was waving a friend over to where he was sitting.

"Tony," I whispered under my breath.

"What's that?" Jerry asked. "Did you say something?"

"You know, Jerry," I said, "there actually *is* a local doctor we were referred to. I had almost forgotten because his name doesn't appear in any of the lists of melanoma experts on the Internet, but I met this quirky little old man who gave him the highest level of praise. The old man insisted that this doctor could help—he's an oncologist at Northwestern. I can't remember his name, but I know it begins with a K."

"Maybe you should call Northwestern and find out. At least it's close by. Just 'cause his name isn't on the list of experts doesn't mean he can't help."

I took Jerry's advice and called Northwestern's Department of Oncology, asking for the name of a doctor who treated melanoma. They gave me the name Dr. Thomas M. Kruntzel.

Thomas M. Kruntzel—that was the name Tony had mentioned. I took the liberty of scheduling an appointment for Ellen. *If she isn't interested, we can always cancel*, I thought.

"Your daughter has an appointment to see Dr. Kruntzel on Wednesday morning at 8:30," the Northwestern receptionist said. "Please bring in a copy of her melanoma reports and scans, and also bring in her pathology slides for review here at Northwestern."

I called Ellen and told her that I had scheduled an appointment for her. She seemed indifferent but said she would go. I, of course, would go with her.

The Northwestern physicians had a beautiful office building; it appeared more like a fancy hotel than a hospital clinic. The oncology offices were on the twenty-first floor. Ellen and I sat patiently in the waiting area for about forty-five minutes before she was called back to a room. A nurse took her weight, height, and blood pressure, and then we waited for the doctor. After a few more minutes, a young man dressed in a long white coat entered the room. He was thin, had dark brown hair, and wore glasses. He looked much too young to be a doctor. He cordially introduced himself but I didn't catch his name. He said he was the oncology fellow. We had learned at the Chicago Cancer Institute that an oncology fellow is an oncologist in training. Doctors spend four years in medical school, followed by three to four years of residency training. Then some doctors go on for further specialty training, which can take another two to four years. That further specialty training is called fellowship.

The young man asked detailed questions about Ellen's cancer. He recorded all of her previous therapies and asked to see the reports from her CAT scans. When he was finished, he said he would discuss the case with Dr. Kruntzel and return with him in a few minutes. Less than ten minutes passed before the young man returned with Dr. Kruntzel. Dr. Kruntzel had gray hair but otherwise appeared young. He had an air of confidence about him. He asked Ellen several questions about how she was feeling, and then he examined her.

"Well, here's the situation," he said when he was done with the examination. "You have melanoma that has spread throughout your body. Melanoma is a very difficult type of cancer to treat once it has spread. Unlike certain other types of cancer, melanoma really doesn't respond to chemotherapy. The best therapy to treat melanoma is immunotherapy—therapy designed to help the body's immune system fight off the cancer itself. The most effective immunotherapy available is interleukin-2, also known simply as IL-2. Have you heard of it?"

"Yes," Ellen replied, "but my understanding is that it is very toxic and not very effective. None of the other doctors I've seen have recommended it."

"It is true that high-dose IL-2 has a lot of side effects, but most of the side effects are short-lived; they resolve quickly once the therapy is stopped. It is also true that IL-2 helps only a very small percentage of patients. Perhaps one out of every twenty patients will have their tumors disappear. Those aren't great odds, but they're odds worth taking because if you're one of the lucky few patients for whom the tumor completely disappears, the chances are that it will never come back, and no other therapy has the potential to cure this disease once it has spread."

"Are you saying that there is still a chance that I could be cured?" Ellen asked. For the first time in a long time, I could see hope in my daughter's eyes. My spirits were lifted at the sight.

"I don't want to falsely raise your hopes," Dr. Kruntzel replied, "but yes, there is a very small chance that with IL-2, your tumors will disappear and never come back."

"Why does the interleukin-2 help such a small percentage of patients?" I inquired.

"That is a true mystery. Physicians and scientists have been trying to find the answer to that question for many years, but even with all of the advances in medicine and technology, we haven't a clue why only a small subset of patients does well. Maybe it's divine intervention," he said with a smile.

"Will the IL-2 therapy be too toxic for me?" Ellen asked. "The doctor at the Chicago Cancer Institute said I was too sick for aggressive therapy."

"There certainly are risks involved," he said, "but I've treated other patients in your condition, and they've made it through just fine. It won't be easy, though." Dr. Kruntzel then went on to list the side effects from the therapy. They sounded dreadful. "The IL-2 is given every eight hours for a total of fourteen doses over a five day period," he said. "You will spend those five days in the hospital. Starting approximately two hours after each dose, you can expect to develop fever, with shaking chills, nausea, and vomiting. The side effects get worse with each subsequent dose. Your blood pressure will drop, and you may have to go to the intensive care unit to receive medication to help keep your blood pressure elevated." He paused for a second to see if we had any questions and then continued. "You can expect to retain fluid. Your ankles will swell, and there is a chance that your lungs could fill with fluid. Many patients experience diarrhea. Many patients become confused. Some hallucinate. If you develop changes in your mental status, then we will have to hold the therapy. The one symptom that tends to persist for a few weeks is the skin rash. It is the equivalent of a sunburn, and your skin will likely peel as it heals."

"Sounds wonderful," Ellen scoffed.

"It certainly is not a pleasant experience, but patients make it through. Once you've completed the first week of therapy, you get nine days off. After that, you come in for a second five-day treatment."

"Two bad weeks, and then it's over?" Ellen asked.

"Yes, two bad weeks, and then it's over," Dr. Kruntzel said.

"When do we find out if it is working?" I asked.

"We'd repeat CAT scans approximately eight to ten weeks after the completion of the treatment."

I looked over at Ellen, wondering what she would say. After momentary pause, she said, "I'll be very honest with you Dr. Kruntzel. I'm afraid. I'm afraid because with each day, I feel that I'm getting weaker. I'm afraid that if I don't find something to help soon, it will be too late. This IL-2 treatment you've described sounds awful, but if there's a chance it could help, even if it is a small chance, I'd like to try. I feel that my time is slipping away, but I'm not ready to give up."

"I agree that we should get started right away," Dr. Kruntzel said. "Right now, I think you're healthy enough to tolerate the treatment, but in a few weeks, you might not be."

"How soon can I start?"

He closed her file and stood up to usher us from the room. "You can start on Monday."

Chapter 27
A Not-So-Difficult Decision

I RECALLED THAT both Dr. Gudmundson and Dr. Greenspan had reservations about IL-2. It was not simply a matter of not recommending the therapy; they seemed to be strongly opposed to it. The recollection made me uneasy about Ellen's decision to proceed with treatment with Dr. Kruntzel. Sure, Dr. Kruntzel seemed like a reasonable man. He certainly was straightforward and very confident when he spoke. But if Ellen had only one option left—and given her declining state of health, I believed that was all she had left—then I had to question if IL-2 was the right option.

I decided to call Dr. Gudmundson's office. He had always been kind and helpful. I wanted to better understand why he opposed IL-2 therapy. I left a message with his secretary, who said he was with a patient but would return my call when he had a free moment. Surprisingly, within an hour the busy doctor phoned me back.

"Hello, Mr. Sankt," he said in his gentle baritone voice.

"Hello, Doctor. Thank you for returning my call."

"It's my pleasure. How is Ellen doing?"

"She's having a rough time, emotionally," I said. "There are far more bad days than good. Her energy seems to be decreasing, and her pain seems to be increasing."

"I'm very sorry to hear that," he said. "I know this must be a very difficult time for the two of you."

"It is."

"Is there anything I can do?" he inquired.

"Well, Doctor, there is. I just wanted to pick your brain for a second. Ellen went to see a Dr. Kruntzel at Northwestern University. He recommended that she undergo treatment with high-dose interleukin-2. I just wanted to get your opinion about that."

I could hear him take a deep breath. "Oh, Mr. Sankt," he said, "I really don't want to complicate matters for the two of you, but I would advise against that."

"Why is that?"

"IL-2 therapy is extremely toxic, and there is a very small likelihood that Ellen will derive any benefit whatsoever from the treatment."

"Well, that's what I wanted to talk with you about. Dr. Kruntzel said that in a small percentage of cases, IL-2 can be curative. If there is really any chance for cure, even a small one, we would like to try it."

"Mr. Sankt, although it is true that there are reports of cures from IL-2, I certainly have never seen it, and I've been in practice a very long time. Besides, those patients in the reports who were said to be cured by IL-2 had tumors that were very different from Ellen's tumors. Their tumors were often confined to the skin or to the lungs. Patients with disease confined to the skin and lungs have a much better prognosis than patients like Ellen, whose melanoma has spread all over."

"Has there ever been a patient like Ellen who was cured with IL-2?" I asked.

Dr. Gudmundson sighed. "Yes, there probably has, but it is extremely rare. Mr. Sankt, I really don't think that the IL-2 is going to have any positive effect on her disease. And more than that, given her weakened state of health, I'd be afraid that the IL-2 would kill her."

I was deeply disappointed by Dr. Gudmundson's response. Based on previous conversations, I expected him to have negative comments about the IL-2, but I did not expect him to be quite so blunt. The words "would kill her" seemed to hang in space for me. It was as if time temporarily stopped, and I saw my life flash before my eyes.

I saw my youth. I saw my parents. *What wonderful parents they were.* I saw them smile as they watched me grow. I saw Jerry. I saw us laughing together. *We had so many good times.* I saw Tina. I saw our wedding day and how beautiful she looked. I saw the true meaning of love in her eyes. *Oh, they were beautiful eyes.* I saw Ellen. I saw Tina rocking her to sleep as a baby. It was a poignant sight. *My little girl.* I saw Ellen playing as a child. She was so full of life. I saw her grow up into the exquisite woman that she now was. *She makes me so proud.* I saw so many wonderful things. I wanted to hold on to all of them, never to let them go for all eternity, but in an instant—a wretched instant—they were gone. They were gone, and I was left with nothing but a somber vision of my only child in the grave.

"Doctor, is there any other therapy you've heard of that might help her?" I asked.

"Unfortunately, melanoma is a very difficult disease to treat. There certainly isn't any standard therapy that can help her. I hope she can find an experimental therapy that is less toxic than IL-2."

"Thank you for your time and candor. I truly appreciate it."

"Call me any time you have questions, Mr. Sankt. My thoughts and prayers are with you and Ellen."

Later that evening, I called Ellen. I told her about my conversation with Dr. Gudmundson and asked that she think about what Dr. Gudmundson said.

Her answer to my request caught me off guard, not so much for what she said, but for the calmness and certainty with which she said it. "Dad, I spent my entire day bargaining with God to send me a miracle. It's amazing what you're willing to do, or to give up, when your life is on the line. By late this afternoon, I came to the conclusion that there is nothing I wouldn't do to be able to live. There is nothing I wouldn't give up to return to the life I knew before this dreaded disease attacked my body. But Dad, I'm realistic, and I'm not so sure God will be sending any miracles my way. So if I'm going to die anyway, I'd like to go down fighting, and that's why the threat of death from IL-2 doesn't scare me so much."

- - - - - - - - - -

At midnight, hours after I had drifted off to sleep, I awoke from a dream. In the dream I'd seen a vision of a woman. It was the teary-eyed woman I had greeted months before at the Feast of All Souls Mass at St. Mary's parish, the woman who was deeply mourning the loss of a loved one. Just as she had been in real life, the woman in my dream seemed to be hopelessly engulfed by despair. The sadness in her dark brown eyes was profound and mesmerizing. Staring into her pupils, I saw nothing but loneliness and suffering. Indeed, her pupils were an abyss of sorrow. In my dream I pitied the poor woman.

"What a miserable existence," I said. "She would have been better off if she had never been born."

The longer I stared, the more her tear-filled eyes gripped my soul and left me with a feeling of emptiness. I had the sensation of being drawn slowly, against my will, into the sorrow-filled abyss. It was an unsettling sensation, like helplessly sinking into quicksand. Although it was not real, it was one of the most disturbing sensations I had ever experienced.

As the despair deepened, the color of the woman's eyes mysteriously changed, turning from dark brown to blue. The change in color was the only change—her tears remained, as did the incomparable sadness.

"Oh, what a miserable existence," I whispered again. "What a cursed life. Lord, please grant mercy to this poor unfortunate soul! Please grant mercy ..."

There was more I wanted to say, but I could not speak further, as I was overwhelmed with grief. I realized then that the change in color was not the only change after all. At that wretched moment, I recognized that the mournful blue eyes into which I was staring were, in fact, my own, and the miserable existence of incomparable loneliness and suffering, which I so pitied, was solely and utterly mine.

The dream of the mournful woman was poignant but not nearly as poignant as the dream that immediately followed.

My second dream was of Tina singing a lullaby to Ellen when she was just a baby. Tina was sitting in a rocking chair in the family room of our home in Riverside, gently cradling Ellen in her arms. She looked so beautiful and so happy as she sang. The lullaby was a tender melody that I had not heard in years. The dream seemed so real. It was almost as if I could still hear Tina's voice:

Wynken, Blynken, and Nod, one night sailed off in a wooden shoe;
Sailed off on a river of crystal light into a sea of dew.
"Where are you going and what do you wish?" the old moon asked the three.
"We've come to fish for the herring fish that live in this beautiful sea.
Nets of silver and gold have we," said Wynken, Blynken, and Nod.

The old moon laughed and sang a song as they rocked in the wooden shoe.
And the wind that sped them all night long ruffled the waves of dew.
Now the little stars are the herring fish that live in that beautiful sea;
"Cast your nets wherever you wish; never afraid are we!"
So cried the stars to the fishermen three—Wynken, and Blynken, and Nod.

So all night long their nets they threw to the stars in the twinkling foam.
'Til down from the skies came the wooden shoe, bringing the fisherman home.
'Twas all so pretty a sail, it seemed as if it could not be.
Some folks say 'twas a dream they dreamed of sailing that misty sea.

But I shall name you the fisherman three—Wynken, Blynken, and Nod.

Now Wynken and Blynken are two little eyes and Nod is a little head. And the wooden shoe that sailed the skies above is a wee one's trundle bed.[38]

Awaking from the dream, I felt overrun with emotional pain. "That was such a wonderful time," I whispered. "I'd like to go back to that time."

As the clock ticked on that night, the pain was eventually replaced with numbness, and the numbness ultimately gave way to emptiness. Blanketed with the emptiness, I rolled over and fell back into a restless sleep.

38　Adapted from URL: http://en.wikisource.org/wiki/Wynken,_Blynken,_and_ Nod. Downloaded 1-31-09.

Chapter 28

THE THERAPY BEGINS

OVER THE NEXT several days, I wrote and wrote—it was my only relief. Unfortunately, my breaks from reality were transient. At the very moment that I would stop typing, my fears would return. With the decline in Ellen's condition, my anxiety had turned to terror. When Ellen was first diagnosed with melanoma, I knew all of the horrible consequences that might ensue, but this was the first time that I felt her death was near. She was getting weaker every day. There was no denying it; no escaping it. Her precious life was fading, and I was going insane with fear and doubt. My thoughts haunted me.

"Isn't there any hope?" I would whisper in my darkest moments. "Does she even have the strength to survive the therapy?"

These were truly grim questions, but they were not nearly as macabre as the more sinister question that plagued my soul—"When will be the day, and the cursed hour, that the sun shall set, never to rise again?"

- - - - - - - - -

On Monday, January 7, the coldest day of the year, Ellen checked into Northwestern Memorial Hospital to begin the treatments. I took off work for the entire week to be at her side. We were both very nervous. Although Dr. Kruntzel had explained the process in detail, we still did not know exactly what to expect. We knew that Ellen was going to get sick; we just didn't know *how* sick.

The first day passed uneventfully. In the morning, Ellen and I stopped by the admissions desk on the second floor and then proceeded up to her assigned room on the fifteenth floor. We were pleased to find that all of the rooms at Northwestern were private.

"A private room is a definite plus," Ellen said.

Ellen's room was very nice—nicer than the rooms in many hotels. Most hospital rooms I had visited in the past had made me feel claustrophobic, but this one was not at all confining. Not only was the room spacious, but from the window on the east side we could see Lake Michigan.

"You have quite a view," I said to Ellen.

"I certainly do," she said. "I guess if a person has to be sick, this is a good place to be. It must be pretty in summer when the lake is blue."

Soon after eight o'clock, a cheerful young nurse named Heather stopped by and drew Ellen's blood. Approximately an hour later, she came back to administer the first dose of IL-2. Prior to starting the drug, she outlined the treatment plan and explained many of the expected side effects of IL-2, just as Dr. Kruntzel had done.

"You will get three doses each day, every eight hours," she said. "You can expect to get fevers and chills and shakes. Most patients develop diarrhea, and some develop confusion. As the treatments go on, your blood pressure will likely drop. If your blood pressure drops too low or if you are feeling too sick, we will skip the dose."

Ellen developed mild nausea after each IL-2 infusion that day and had a low grade fever with some chills at one point, but all in all, she did very well. Tuesday morning brought more of the same. By Tuesday afternoon, I began to think that things might not be so bad; I began to breathe easier. Then came Tuesday evening. Two hours after her fifth dose of IL-2, Ellen developed the chills.

"Dad, can you cover me with another blanket? I'm cold," she said.

"Of course, sweetheart."

Soon thereafter, she began to shake all over.

The nurse took Ellen's temperature. It was 103°F. "I'll bring her some Tylenol to try to bring her fever down," the nurse said.

Before the nurse could bring in the Tylenol, Ellen developed nausea and started vomiting. Things only got worse after that. The chills turned to shakes—shakes that were uncontrollable. The nurse brought in medication, but it did not seem to help. Ellen shook so hard that she could not even speak. Forty minutes passed without relief. Ellen then became confused. She did not recognize where she was. She started speaking nonsense. She again started to throw up, but there was nothing left in her stomach, and she simply dry heaved. The nurse summoned the resident doctor. It was several minutes before he came to the room. I was so frightened. I held Ellen's hand and prayed. I feared she was going to die. Everything seemed to be happening so fast. Then, as quickly as it began, the episode subsided. By the time the doctor got to the room, the worst was over. The doctor reassured me that all of her symptoms were attributable to the IL-2 therapy and were expected.

"Will she have to go through that with each dose she gets?" I asked.

"I'm afraid so," the doctor said. "Often, patients do really well with the first one or two doses, but as the week goes on, things get much more difficult."

Things got more difficult indeed. Two hours after Ellen got her IL-2 dose on Wednesday morning, she developed the shakes again, and she shook uncontrollably. She threw up three times. She again became confused—for a period of time, she thought she was in her bedroom at home; later, she thought she was at work. It broke my heart when, in a state of delirium, she asked, "Is Mom coming by to see me?" I could not help but wonder if at that moment, deep in her subconscious, she thought she was close to seeing her mother. I had read that patients often know when they are about to die; they can somehow sense it. The thought put a shiver down my spine. I grabbed Ellen's hand and began to pray. "Please Lord, God of mercy, help us now."

On Wednesday evening, Ellen's blood pressure dropped, so she skipped her IL-2 dose. She received her next dose on Thursday morning and again became violently ill. This time, her blood pressure dropped severely low. The nurse called the doctor on duty, who promptly came to examine her. He took Ellen's blood pressure himself. "We are going to have to start a medicine to help keep her blood pressure elevated," he explained. "If she requires too much of this medication, we will have to transfer her to the intensive care unit."

"Is she going to be OK?" I asked.

"She'll be OK," he reassured me, "but we'll probably have to skip her next couple of doses of the IL-2. If everything works out well, we will give her two doses on Friday and then stop for this week."

With the doctor's plan, Ellen's blood pressure soon returned to normal, and after missing two doses of the IL-2, she was feeling better. She was still weak, but her confusion resolved, and she even was able to get up and walk a little.

"Are you sure you want to continue this?" I asked.

"Yes, I'm sure. I'm very sure," Ellen replied.

When Dr. Kruntzel stopped by on Friday morning, he reiterated what the resident doctor had told us the day before.

"Let's try to get in two more doses today, and then you'll have the entire week to recover," he said to Ellen. She agreed.

Ellen actually did pretty well with the first of the two doses. She only experienced the shakes, mild confusion, and a small drop in blood pressure. The second dose was a different story. She again became violently ill. She threw up seven times in succession, and her blood pressure dropped. Once again, the nurse called the resident doctor to the room.

"Let's give her some IV fluids," he said to the nurse, "but not too much. I don't want to flood her lungs. And let's start the dopamine."

Dopamine was the medication used to try to raise patients' blood pressure.

"Mr. Sankt," the doctor said, "I'm going to transfer Ellen to the intensive care unit. She's pretty sick right now, and they will be able to monitor her more closely there."

"Is she going to be OK?" I asked.

"She will be OK," he reassured me, as he had before.

I was not so certain. In my heart I feared that she was going to die.

Ellen never did get transferred to the intensive care unit. Shortly after the doctor left the room to speak with the physician in intensive care, Ellen's blood pressure started to rise, and her symptoms improved. When the doctor came back to check on her, he decided that she didn't need to be transferred. Ellen spent the next two days in the hospital—time spent just regaining her strength—and then was discharged home.

She was still very weary and slept most of the way home from the hospital. Her face looked like an angel's as she slept. To me, she was still the little girl I used to cradle in my arms, yet she was withering away. I knew that it would not be long. The horror of her disease was too much to bear. Tears filled my eyes as my mind was plagued with yet another grim question—"How will I ever face the sad good-bye?"

Chapter 29
VICTOR PETROV

I MADE ARRANGEMENTS to stay with Ellen at her apartment. She could do little more than sit on the couch and watch television. I did my best to encourage her to eat, but she had almost no appetite. Tina went through the same process. I knew that cancer took away the appetite and that it did no good to try to force cancer patients to eat. Too much food would make them feel sick. Doctors suggest that instead of two or three big meals each day, patients should eat several small meals of things they really like. I brought Ellen all of her favorite foods, but she only picked at them.

Ellen spent much of her day napping. She hadn't had a lot of sleep during her week in the hospital, so she needed to catch up. I hadn't had much sleep that week, either, but despite my being exhausted, I still slept very little at night. I would doze off but then wake up at 3:00 AM, unable to fall back to sleep. I had gone through the same thing after Tina died; I knew it was a sign of depression. I eventually got over the depression after Tina passed, mainly because I had Ellen. Without Ellen, I knew there would be nothing but despair—lonely, empty, never-ending despair. The thought of it was overwhelming.

"Poe said it best," I lamented aloud. "'And my soul from out that shadow that lies floating on the floor; shall be lifted—nevermore!' Nevermore," I whispered. "Nevermore."

- - - - - - - - -

Always supportive, Jerry and Joyce stopped by several times each week. A few of Ellen's other friends stopped by also, although not as many as before.

I think they knew she was reaching the end, and some people just can't deal with that.

Jack hadn't been by in a while. I could tell that it bothered Ellen that he wasn't there. She didn't say anything, but it was clear that she was fond of him. Her hopes visibly heightened with each ring of the phone, only to be dashed when the call was not from him.

The stress was too much for him, I surmised. *I doubt he'll ever come back.* Contrary to my past feelings, I had no animosity in my heart toward Jack. He'd stuck around far longer than I would have ever guessed. I just felt sad for Ellen. *How much can one person take?*

On Wednesday, Jerry and Joyce stopped by while Ellen was napping. I must have looked more dejected than usual because Jerry immediately put his hand on my shoulder. He looked me straight in the eye and, whispering so he wouldn't wake Ellen, said the name that I had been hearing in my own mind more and more; the name I wished I would never again need to hear—"Victor Petrov."

I looked downward and replied, "Victor Petrov."

Then, there was silence.

Standing just several feet away, Joyce's puzzled expression conveyed her confusion. "Who is Victor Petrov?" she asked.

I was somewhat surprised that she had never heard of him. After all those years, I would have thought that we'd have mentioned him at some point, but evidently we had not told her.

"That's a long story," I said, waving my guests into the kitchen where we could talk without disturbing Ellen. We sat down at the kitchen table, and I began to recite the story of Victor Petrov. "Joyce, as you know, Jerry and I were neighbors growing up," I said. "We lived on a dead-end street lined with elm trees that made a canopy over the road. It was a middle-class neighborhood—the lots measured about a quarter-acre and most of the homes on the street were modest. There was one home, however, at the very end of the street that had an enormous three-acre lot. Most of the lot was free of trees so it made a perfect place to play tag with our schoolmates."

"We had some great times there," Jerry chimed in. "Some days, we would spend five or six hours playing, taking breaks only to get snacks and go to the bathroom."

"The owner of the lot was a middle-aged man named Greg Peters," I continued. "He was a friend of our parents, and he granted us free rein to play there as we pleased. Greg Peters was married but didn't have any children of his own. He and his wife were good neighbors, overall ordinary people who lived ordinary lives, but there was one peculiarity about their property. At the southwest corner of their three-acre lot stood an unusually shaped shed. It was kept locked, and we never saw anyone go in or out."

"It had no windows so we couldn't see in," Jerry added. "We often wondered what was in there, but no one ever told us."

"True," I said. "We didn't learn about the purpose of the strange shed until one day when I asked my parents a question that they never expected me to ask. I can still remember the day clearly in my mind. It was September 1961, and I was eleven years old. Sitting at the dinner table, I turned to my mother and asked, 'Is there going to be a nuclear war?' It was the height of the Cold War at the time, and all the kids at school were talking about the Soviet Union and the end of the earth. Based on what they were saying, World War III seemed like a real threat—and an imminent one at that. I remember being more afraid than I had ever been before. It was a terrible feeling."

"Everyone was frightened back then," Jerry concurred. "People brought up the possibility of doomsday all of the time. To most of us, it wasn't a matter of 'if' but of 'when,' and most of us believed that the 'when' would be sometime in our lifetimes. It was easy to think that way. There was constantly something about the A-bomb in the news, and the radio was filled with songs about nuclear war. Do you remember Simon and Garfunkel's 'Now the Sun Has Come to Earth'? Boy, that was a depressing song."

"I think you mean 'The Sun Is Burning in the Sky,'" Joyce corrected him. "'Now the sun has come to earth' is just one of the lines of the song, not the title."

"I think you might be right," Jerry conceded. "But anyway, it was a scary time to live."

"My parents could tell I was scared and did their best to alleviate my fears," I said. "They sat down with me after dinner that evening and explained that even if there were such a war, we would be safe. It was then that they revealed that Greg Peters' strange, locked shed was the above-ground opening to a nuclear bomb shelter."

"I remember hearing about people building bomb shelters," Joyce said, "but I never knew anyone who actually had one. I always thought it was crazy that people were obsessed with digging holes in the ground."

"Well, this wasn't just your run-of-the-mill hole in the ground," I continued. "Greg Peters spent his entire life's savings building an elaborate six-room shelter that was over one hundred feet underground and was fully supplied with food rations that would last at least a decade."

"It was incredible," Jerry added. "He showed it to us, once when we got older."

"There were a lot of things that were revealed to us as we got older," I said. "When we were teenagers, we came to understand what drove him to build such a structure; we came to understand the history of the man. You see, Greg Peters' birth name was Grigoriy Petrov. He was born in Leningrad, the son of Victor and Alexandra."

"Ah, now we get to Victor," Joyce said.

"Yes," I said, "Victor Petrov was a loving father and an outspoken member of the Russian Orthodox Church. When Stalin came to power in Russia, the Church was harshly persecuted, and Victor sent Alexandra and Grigoriy to the United States, where he knew they would be safe. He planned to eventually join them but stayed behind to finish some business with his younger cousin, Leonard. Well, Victor never made it to the States. One night, a group a Soviet thugs broke into his home and arrested Victor and Leonard, falsely accusing them of conspiring against Stalin. They sent them to a labor camp in Totma, where the two were beaten and placed in small wooden boxes with nails sticking through the sides. The Soviets commonly did this to break the will of their prisoners. Victor was treated with particular cruelty because he refused to renounce his faith in Christ. Day after day, he was kicked, ridiculed, and spat upon. This went on for 451 days, at which time Victor and Leonard were separated. Leonard was transferred to a gulag in Tobolsk—he eventually was released during World War II, thus allowing him to tell this story to his family. Victor, however, was not so fortunate. Because he was a staunch Christian, he was sent to the worst of the gulags, a horrific place in Siberia called Kolyma."

"I've heard of Kolyma," Joyce said. "I don't remember where, but I've definitely heard of it."

"You've probably heard me refer to it as a frozen hell," Jerry said.

"Maybe," Joyce said. "I know that in the back of my mind it has a very dark connotation."

"After departing for Kolyma, Victor was never heard from again," I said. "The conditions at Kolyma were notoriously bad, so it's not hard to imagine his fate. During the long winters, the average temperature in Kolyma was negative 70 degrees Fahrenheit. The overworked prisoners were not given coats and were not allowed to build fires, and the majority eventually froze to death, if they did not starve first. Not only that, but unlike most gulags, where virtually all of the prisoners were learned political opponents of the Soviets, Kolyma was half-filled with murdering, maniacal thugs, who were there to make life all the more miserable for the innocents."

"That sounds horrible," Joyce said. "It even sounds worse than the Nazi concentration camps."

"It was the epitome of horror," I said. "Can you imagine working eighteen-hour days in the frigid cold, having absolutely no contact with your loved ones, and being brutally beaten almost every day?"

"Knowing this, it was not hard to understand why Greg Peters built his elaborate bomb shelter," Jerry said. "He fully grasped the unfathomable depths of Soviet tyranny."

"Death must have been a blessing for Victor," Joyce suggested.

"Exactly," I said. "Hearing the story of Victor Petrov, Jerry and I came to realize that there are fates much worse than death. From that time on, anytime we thought we were faced with a hardship, we would remind ourselves of Victor Petrov. Saying his name was a way of saying that things could be worse—much worse."

"That's how things were until Tina was diagnosed with melanoma," Jerry explained. "Then the name Victor Petrov took on a second meaning for us."

"Yes," I agreed, "it took on a second meaning. When Tina became ill, and I was miserable, day in and day out, the name Victor Petrov came to represent empathy. It was as if he was a kindred spirit in suffering. Saying his name was a way of acknowledging the pain."

The three of us sat and talked for another hour. By that time, I was exhausted. Jerry and Joyce could tell that I needed to get some rest—I'd sighed more and more as the afternoon wore on. Prior to their leaving, Joyce touched my hand and looked at me with sympathetic eyes—eyes that also glistened with a hint of tears. In a faltering voice, she gently whispered, "Victor Petrov."

- - - - - - - - -

Later that evening, Ellen awoke and came out to the living room to lie on the couch. She carried a blanket and pillow with her and still appeared groggy.

"Jerry and Joyce stopped by this afternoon," I said. "You were sleeping peacefully, and they didn't want to wake you."

"It is nice that they stop by so often," she said. "They are really good people."

"Well, they're like family," I said.

"They *are* like family," she agreed.

After arranging the pillow just to her liking on the couch, Ellen asked, "Did I get any phone calls while I was sleeping?"

"No, sweetheart, there were no calls," I said, hating the answer I had to offer.

"Oh." She looked downward, clearly saddened because she hadn't heard from Jack.

It broke my heart to see the disappointment in her eyes. "What would you like for dinner?" I asked, changing the subject.

"I'm really not hungry, Dad. If I get hungry, I'll snack on something later."

"I'm going to need to run back home sometime tonight to gather my mail and pay some bills," I said. "Are you sure you don't want me to pick up anything while I'm out?"

"No, I'm really not hungry, but thank you."

"OK," I said, "But let me know if you change your mind."

I read for a while as Ellen watched TV. I hoped that if I waited long enough, she would work up an appetite, but she didn't. Around eight o'clock she turned to me and said, "If you are going to run out, you should probably get going. They keep on having news flashes about the weather on TV. They are predicting quite a snowstorm tonight, and you don't want to get caught in it."

"I wasn't paying attention to the television. How many inches are they predicting?"

"Ten to fourteen."

"That's quite a lot. I suppose I should get going," I said. Getting up slowly from my chair, I went into the kitchen to get a glass of water.

"Would you bring me a glass of water, too?" Ellen asked.

"Of course, sweetheart."

After quickly gulping down my water, I filled a glass with ice for Ellen and then grabbed a lemon from the refrigerator. I cut a thin slice and dropped it into Ellen's drink—she always liked lemon with her water. I brought her the water; then got my coat and hat. As I opened the door, I turned, intending to ask Ellen one last time if she wanted food, but she was looking right past me, staring intently into the hallway outside. I turned to see what had caught her attention and was startled by a man standing there in a long black coat, his hand poised to knock on the door.

"Hello," Jack said, his eyes fixed sympathetically on Ellen.

"Hello," Ellen replied, with a weak smile; it was all she had the strength to muster. As weak as it was, it was genuine and joyful, and it was the first smile I had seen on her face in a long, long time.

He showed up, I thought, with a sense of both disbelief and pleasant relief. *Thank the Lord he showed up.* Nodding my head to greet him, I said, "Jack, if you'll excuse me, I was just leaving."

As I stood in front of the elevator doors, my eyes slowly welled up with emotion. The picture of Ellen's feeble smile was firmly imprinted in my brain, and the thought of it was too much for me to hold in. I was heartbroken to see my child in such a state, but was deeply touched by her simple expression of joy. It was just a small positive, but at that moment, it meant so much.

God bless the sick, God bless the weary, and God bless you, Jack Murphy, for coming to see my dying daughter.

Chapter 30

THE ENCOUNTER

ON WEDNESDAY NIGHT, long after I had left Ellen's apartment, I sat down at my computer, opened the file titled *Third Testament*, and reviewed my recent work. I had spent a lot of time on the Middle Ages, and with good reason, for there was a lot to cover. There was one thing I had consciously left out, however, and it began to bother me that I had done so. The most famous prophet of the modern era lived during the Middle Ages, yet I'd made no mention of him in my book. *How can I leave out Nostradamus?* I questioned.

Nostradamus was an apothecary and mystic who used ancient divinations to foretell the future. He was a celebrity in his own time, popularizing astrology and the occult in the era of Christendom—an unlikely feat, given the threat of the Inquisition. Like so many who become famous, his path to glory was a dark one. In his youth, Nostradamus studied medicine at the University of Montpellier. Later in life, he developed an interest in Islamic mysticism. He read *The Elixir of Blissfulness* by Sufi master al-Ghazzali, and he studied *De Mysteriis Aegyptorum*, a book on Chaldean and Assyrian magic. He also studied the *Kabbalah*, a book of Jewish mysticism. Swayed by his studies, Nostradamus began to use black magic and the occult to tell the fortunes of Europe's aristocracy. In doing so, he rejected God and all that was holy.

In 1555, Nostradamus published the book *Les Propheties* and instantly developed an enormous cult-following. *Les Propheties* consisted of a series of cryptic quatrains, or four-lined verses, that purportedly predicted the future if interpreted correctly. In total, Nostradamus wrote over one thousand quatrains, some of which have been successfully deciphered; some of which have not. Since the Book of Revelation, no single man has been more strongly associated with prophecy than he.

How can I leave him out? I questioned again.

There was the obvious answer—Nostradamus was Satan's prophet, not God's, but the problem was more complex than that. I did not want to glorify the insights of Satan's seer, but at the same time, I wanted to accurately recount the story of God's people and their triumphs and tribulations, and it was impossible to recount their tribulations without detailing the acts of Satan's servants.

The product of demonic communion, most of Nostradamus' divinations dealt with darkness. The malevolent prophet told of the coming of plagues, of bloody wars, and of horrific religious persecutions. Astonishing the masses, he precisely detailed the death of King Henry II of France, who was killed freakishly in a jousting match. His most famous prophecy was particularly disturbing—he foretold that the Apocalypse would occur in the year 1999, in the month of July.

He was wrong about that one.

Although Nostradamus lived in France in the sixteenth century, his practices and prophecies greatly impacted the twentieth century. Using the black arts as his guide, he foresaw the coming of three Antichrists. One was Hitler, whom he described by name and deed, averring "the son of Germany obeys no laws." Another was Stalin, whom he described as the "Great Red One." He correctly told how Stalin would annihilate his enemies, exile the righteous, and spread red hail (Communism) around the globe. The identity of the third Antichrist is not known.

Perhaps he is yet to come.

After a brief deliberation, I decided that even though he was a prophet of evil, Nostradamus should be included in *The Third Testament*.

His prophecies give important insights into the Church's titanic struggle against Satan, I concluded.

I proceeded to write a chapter detailing his sacrilegious divinations. I stayed up very late writing. I couldn't sleep anyway, and writing was a good way to pass the time.

- - - - - - - - - -

On Thursday, Jerry stopped by Ellen's just before noon. Ellen was feeling slightly better and was much more talkative than she had been the previous few days.

"Dad, why don't you and Jerry go out for lunch?" she said. "You've been by my side constantly since I got home from the hospital. It would do you good to get out. I'm doing OK."

I really didn't care to go out, but I thought that perhaps Ellen would appreciate a little time to herself. After a brief discussion about where we should go, Jerry and I got in my black bug and drove to Al's Pub. It was a dark and cloudy day, with a steady, cold rain falling; the day could not have been any drearier. In every way, my mood matched the dreariness of the surroundings. More so than ever, I felt as if I was on the brink. Jerry could sense my despair. We did not talk too much on the way over, but that changed as soon as we were seated, face to face, at the table at Al's.

"You look terrible, Fred. Have you been getting any sleep?"

"Very little," I replied.

Jerry nodded in sympathy. He knew that Ellen's dying was tearing me up inside. His nod of sympathy acknowledged my pain.

For a moment, we sat there in silence. During that moment, I thought that I might be able to pull myself together and have a normal conversation, but I was wrong. All at once, my emotions got the best of me. I tried to hold it back—I sighed three times in succession, but it was no use. My eyes filled with tears. With faltering voice, I asked him, "How do you say good-bye to a child?"

Jerry had no reply. What *could* he say? There was no answer to the question. I wasn't really looking for an answer, anyway—it was just my emotions taking control.

Jerry responded in the best way he could—his eyes also filled with tears.

At about the same time that I was breaking down, four men at the table behind us broke out in loud laughter. At first, I was too caught up in my own pain to take notice, but then they became quite boisterous. I couldn't tell exactly what they were laughing about, but I did catch part of a crude comment. Jerry turned around to face them, but when he did, something clearly startled him—he looked as if he'd seen a ghost.

"What is it?" I asked. "What's wrong?"

Jerry just shook his head, unable to answer, but I knew there was something not right about the raucous men. They definitely were not choir boys.

"Are those men crooks?" I whispered.

At that moment, we overheard the men exchange several perverted remarks, followed by more boisterous laughter.

"Do you see the man in the black leather jacket?" Jerry asked. "The one with the loudest laugh?"

I carefully took a closer look at the large man in black. "I see him."

"That man is Sylvester Jones."

Before the words even left Jerry's lips, I had figured it out for myself. At first I hadn't recognized him because his back was to me, but then it became clear. The bald head with curly black hair on the sides and back, pulled into a short ponytail; the neck as thick as a tree stump; the gigantic torso—it was without a doubt Sylvester Jones.

For a moment I did nothing but stare at him. His enormous frame shook violently with each bout of laughter.

Seeing my accuser there, in such good spirits, was surreal. I felt numb inside. There was no other way for me to feel—I was too depressed to be angry and too exhausted to feel self-pity.

As I sat there, speechless, another perverted remark poured forth from Jones' lips, this one about their waitress. It was followed by still more laughter.

"I don't think I can eat," I said to Jerry.

"I understand," Jerry said. He waved over our waitress to let her know we were leaving.

I could still hear Sylvester Jones happily laughing as we walked out the door.

Chapter 31
THE MISSED GOOD-BYE

BY FRIDAY, ELLEN was feeling stronger, but her overall condition was still that of wasting away. I had deep concerns about her ability to survive another week of IL-2. For better or worse, Ellen herself remembered little of the gruesome details from her week in the hospital, but I remembered every distinct moment, and the memories made me shiver with fear.

If she goes back into the hospital, she will surely die, I thought. Deep in my soul, I knew that I must confront Ellen with my fears.

"Ellen," I said to her, "may I speak with you in earnest?"

"Yes, Dad. What is troubling you?"

"I know you don't remember a lot of the details from last week. It was a rough week, for sure. There are just some things about this IL-2 therapy that worry me. I'd like to discuss them with you, if I may."

Ellen nodded her head in agreement.

"Sweetheart, you became very ill in the hospital—*very* ill. The therapy caused you to shake uncontrollably. You threw up again and again. On several occasions, your blood pressure dropped to dangerously low levels. I was hoping that you would recover more of your strength during this week off, but as I watch you here at home, I see that you're still very weak, and you're not eating. I'm just worried that this therapy is too much for you. I'm worried that you are too weak to undergo another round of treatment."

For all of her physical weakness, Ellen was strong emotionally. Just a few weeks prior, she had struggled with her emotions, but now, she seemed to have reached a level of acceptance. Although she was still fighting, she had accepted her condition, and she had accepted the consequences of that condition. She answered me with courage and conviction.

"Dad, I know you're worried that the therapy is going to kill me," she said.

246

"It certainly sounds as if it came close to that. But if the therapy came so close to killing me, maybe it came equally close to killing the tumor. My only hope is that I am stronger than the melanoma. If this therapy brings me to the edge of death, then so be it. And if this therapy leads to my death, then it's God's will. It will only be a brief period before the melanoma kills me anyway. I see no choice—for me, there is no decision to be made. On Monday, I'll check back into the hospital to continue the IL-2." She paused for a moment to peer into my eyes; then she continued. "You've been the most wonderful father anyone could ever ask for. You've taught me how to love, and you've taught me how to live. You've given me so much ..."

Ellen stopped. Looking deeper into my eyes, she saw that I was not ready to have that conversation; that I was not prepared to say good-bye. She was so very right. I was not ready. When Ellen began telling me what a wonderful father I was, every muscle in my entire body contracted and tightened, to the point that I was actually in physical pain.

Later that evening, I was overcome with a great sense of guilt. My only daughter, faced with dreadful circumstances, had wanted to tell me good-bye, but I had not been strong enough to face it. I felt like the furthest thing in the world from a wonderful father; I felt like a true coward.

Chapter 32

THE HUMBLE SERVANT

ALTHOUGH UTTERLY DEJECTED, I continued to work on *The Third Testament*. Everything I had written thus far had been purely historical; there was nothing original; nothing that was solely mine. I'm not sure what inspired me to do so, but late that Friday evening, I decided to include my own parable. I guess I just had something to say and wanted to say it. My thoughts flowed spontaneously. Without actual planning, I wrote a short, simple parable. By early Saturday morning, it was done:

> One day a humble servant of the Lord lost a very dear friend to the scourge cancer. The humble servant felt great sorrow and prayed that he would someday see his friend again. After much time in prayer, the humble servant was confronted by a demon. The demon said to him, "Why do you waste your time in prayer? There is no proof that God exists."
>
> The humble servant answered, "I have faith, and that is why I pray."
>
> The demon then said to him with disdain, "Faith is no more than superstition. On what do you base this 'faith'?"
>
> The humble servant answered, "I base this faith on trust."
>
> "Trust in whom?" the demon retorted. "In whom do you have such trust that you would ignore the laws of probability and the laws of science?"
>
> "I trust in Christ," the humble servant replied.

"In Christ!" the demon exclaimed. "In Christ! Name one thing that Christ has done to earn your trust. Tell me, please, what has he ever done to earn your prayers? I dare you to name one miracle that he has ever performed that science has proven to be true. Name it! Name it!" he taunted with glee.

The humble servant stood patiently and then answered with three simple words: "The Church exists."

"What?" the demon declared in confusion. "What do you mean, 'the Church exists'? Please tell me how this relates to trust. Please tell me how this justifies your wasted time in prayer."

The humble servant calmly explained his answer. "Jesus Christ made a promise—the simple promise, 'Upon this rock I will build my Church, and the gates of hell shall not prevail against it.' And now, after two thousand years, the Church still endures. It endures despite a history of heresies and persecutions. It endures despite the tyranny of despots. It endures despite the laws of probability and the laws of science. What greater miracle is there than this—that the son of a simple carpenter, who lived a life of poverty and dwelled with the lowly, who never ventured more than a hundred miles from the town of his birth, and who died a criminal's death on a cross, would establish a great and holy Church, and that the teachings of this Church would be spread throughout the world by twelve simple men—men who hid in fear after the crucifixion? Yet in a mere three days after this lowly criminal's death, these twelve sprang forth, and proclaimed his word, and gave up their lives so that his promise would ring true. And over the centuries, thousands of others gave their lives also, so that the Church would go on. The most powerful kings and most menacing armies stood against it, but the Church did not falter. For two thousand years this Church has withstood the test of time, overcoming the greatest of odds, again and again. It surmounted the insurmountable. It beat the unbeatable foe. It prevailed through the harshest of storms. This Church has shattered the very laws that you exalt. It defied the laws of probability, and it humbled the laws of science.

"The existence of this Church is not a myth. The existence of this Church is not a legend. That this Church exists is an undeniable fact. That Christ's promise was kept is an undeniable fact. And if he kept this promise, then how can there be any doubt that he will keep his greatest promise—the promise that was central to his ministry, the promise that said 'If you believe in me, and eat of this bread, and drink of this cup, you shall live forever'? So when you ask why I have faith, I tell you it is because I have trust, and nothing that your fair science can offer can break that trust. This is why I pray, so that someday, I will enjoy that most sacred covenant of all"—the humble servant paused briefly and then added with solemnity and conviction—"together with my friend!" He then looked the demon right in the eye. "What good can your science and probability offer that is greater than this?"

With those words, the demon turned away, never to bother the humble servant again.

Chapter 33

THE BOOK OF LOURDES

"One day, when I had gone with the two girls to collect wood by the bank of the River Gave, I heard a sound. I turned toward the meadow and saw the trees were not moving at all. I looked up and saw a grotto. And I saw a lady wearing a white dress with a blue sash. On each foot was a yellow rose; her rosary was the same color.

"When I saw her, I rubbed my eyes. I thought I must be mistaken. I put my hands in my pocket, where I kept my rosary. I wanted to make the sign of the cross, but I could not lift my hand to my forehead; it fell back. Then the lady crossed herself. I again tried and although my hand was trembling, I was eventually able to make the sign of the cross. I began to say the Rosary. The lady slipped the beads of the rosary through her fingers, but she did not move her lips. When I finished the Rosary, she immediately disappeared.

"I asked the two girls if they had seen anything. They said no and asked what I had to tell them. I told them I had seen a lady wearing a white dress, but I did not know who she was. But I warned them to keep silent about it. Then they urged me not to go back there, but I refused. I went back on Sunday, feeling drawn by an inner force.

"The lady spoke to me a third time and asked me if I was willing to come to her over a period of a fortnight. I replied that I was. She added that I must tell the priests to have a chapel built there. Then she told me to drink from the spring. Not seeing any spring, I was going to drink from the River Gave. She told me that she did not mean that, and she pointed with her finger to the spring. When I went there, I saw only a little dirty water. I put my hand in it, but I could not get hold of any. I scratched and at last, a little water came for drinking. Three times I threw it away; the fourth time I was able to drink it. Then the vision disappeared, and I went away.

"I went back there for fifteen days, and each day the lady appeared to me, with the exception of a Monday and a Friday. She reminded me again to tell the priests to build a chapel, asked me to wash in the spring and to pray for the conversion of sinners. I asked her several times who she was, but she gently smiled at me. Finally, she held her arms outstretched and raised her eyes to heaven and told me that she was the Immaculate Conception."[39]

—Saint Bernadette of Lourdes (1844–1879)

On Sunday, I awoke early to get ready for Mass. Ellen was too weak to attend, so I planned to go alone to pray for her. It was a cold, blustery winter's day. Undeterred by the weather, I threw on my parka, got in the car, and drove to St. Mary's Church. I arrived several minutes before the start of the service. Few people were there, in large part because it was cold and early on a Sunday morning. Usually, I would have attended the fully packed ten o'clock service, but during the period of Ellen's decline, I exclusively attended the early Masses. I found a greater sense of peace at church in the early hours. It certainly seemed quieter at that time.

After entering the church, I walked up the aisle, sat in a pew to the right of the altar, and began to pray. I started with the "Our Father" followed by the "Act of Contrition" and a "Hail Mary." I then asked the Lord for mercy and for deliverance from harm. With all my soul, I prayed for a reprieve from our misery, and I prayed for redemption.

Please, Lord, help us through this. Please grant us a miracle. Please let Ellen live. Please forgive us our sins and protect us from sadness. Protect us from suffering. Protect us from all evil. Please grant us peace.

Although deep in prayer, I noticed that a figure had walked up next to where I was sitting. *There are so many empty seats*, I thought, without looking up. *Why would someone come to sit next to me?* I then looked up and was stunned by who I saw.

"Hello, Fred."

---

39   St. Bernadette of Lourdes. From a letter of St. Bernadette of Lourdes to P. Gondrand, 1861.

For a moment, I thought I was hallucinating. "Jerry," I said with a mystified tone.

Jerry had not been to Mass in many years. Living in a secular society, he found it easy to abandon religion, and he had—for over three decades. Sure, he'd attended Tina's funeral Mass, but he spent the entire time pacing at the back of the church and did not participate in the ceremony whatsoever. He made it clear that he had no desire to know God, and he believed that God had no desire to know him. I never dreamed that I'd see Jerry come back—never. He would sometimes make light of his staunch agnosticism, saying, "I'll return to church when the Chicago Cubs win the World Series. A miracle of any lesser degree simply won't suffice."

I was truly stunned. *Why had he come?* I wondered. "Jerry, what are you doing here?"

"I'm here for the same reason everyone else is here," he said. "I've come to pray with a friend."

With that, he sat next to me. With his right hand, he made the sign of the cross. He then began to pray—silently, with hands clasped tightly and eyes closed—until the opening hymn.

- - - - - - - - - -

The topic of Father Tom's sermon that day was suffering. He preached of Christ's suffering. He preached of how the martyrs suffered. He preached how every day, innocent people suffer.

"Blessed are those who suffer," he said. "The kingdom of heaven is theirs."

His sermon was refreshingly honest and sincere.

"Do you know why good people suffer?" he asked. "That is truly one of the great unanswered mysteries on earth, isn't it? Saints and prophets and popes and politicians have tried to answer that question but without success. Yes, it would be easy to say that suffering leads people to greater faith in the Lord. For some, that is certainly true, but for others, it seems to lead to nothing but sorrow. In many instances, suffering seems to be senseless. When an innocent child dies in a car crash; when a pregnant woman miscarries late in term; when a senior citizen passes day after day, helpless and alone, in pain and sorrow, with no one to care for him; you may ask, *Why?*"

Father Tom then paused, and the church was silent. I felt as if Father Tom was addressing me, personally. In fact, I felt as if we were the only two people in the church. Deep inside the inner workings of my mind, I desperately wanted an explanation. I desperately wanted to know the reason why.

Why must people suffer? I must know. There must be a reason. Why?

Finally, after what seemed like an interminable lull, the priest gave his answer. "I do not know why good people suffer," he said. "I haven't a clue. Logic cannot seem to explain it. Science cannot seem to explain it. I realize many of you find that unsatisfying. You feel a need to understand. I'm sorry. I'm sorry because I just don't know." Slowly and clearly, he repeated, "I just don't know. But let me tell you what I do know. I know that God's greatest servants suffered. Yes, those closest to God suffered. The saints and the martyrs suffered miserably. They were belittled, tortured, beheaded, and crucified. They were spat upon and beaten. They were betrayed and abandoned by friends. I know this because it is recorded in the annals of history. History is something that I do have the capacity to understand.

"Keeping this in mind," he said, "let me suggest that we ask a different question. Instead of asking why the good suffer, maybe we should focus on asking, 'What does God have in store for them?' This is something we know, with certainty, for Christ himself proclaimed:

> 'Blessed are the poor in spirit, for theirs is the kingdom of heaven.
> Blessed are those who mourn, for they will be comforted.
> Blessed are the meek, for they will inherit the earth.
> Blessed are those who hunger and thirst for righteousness, for they will be filled.
> Blessed are the merciful, for they will receive mercy.
> Blessed are the pure in heart, for they will see God.
> Blessed are the peacemakers, for they will be called children of God.
> Blessed are those who are persecuted for righteousness' sake, for theirs is the kingdom of heaven.
> Blessed are you when people revile you and persecute you and utter all kinds of evil against you falsely on my account.
> Rejoice and be glad, for your reward is great in heaven.'"[40]

Father Tom took a deep breath and looked out over the congregation. "Do you know of a good person who suffers?" he questioned. "Do you yourself suffer? If you do, I suggest that you don't ask why. Instead, have faith in an ancient covenant, and ask a different question. Ask the question, 'What does God have in store for me?' Because if you remember the answer—and there is an answer—then your reward will truly be great."

— — — — — — — — — —

---

40   Adapted from Matthew 5:3–11. ESV. URL: http://www.gnpcb.org/esv/ search/?q=Matthew+5. Downloaded 1-29-09.

On Sunday evening I sat at my computer and began writing about the town of Lourdes. Like so many Christians, I was deeply moved by the story of Lourdes and the Grotto of Massabielle. It was truly a wonderful story—a story of hope, a story that made it easier to have faith. Of all of the miracles of the past few centuries, the miracles at Lourdes were the hardest for the skeptics to disregard. The happenings at the grotto were inexplicable to science or logic. They could only be explained by belief in a higher power. In the last 150 years, many "learned men" tried to refute the wondrous things that took place there, but none came close to succeeding. None could find truth in a world without God. Indubitably, the events of Lourdes were best summarized by the memorable lines at the opening of the movie *The Song of Bernadette*, a 1943 award-winning film about the famous grotto.

> "For those who believe in God, no explanation is necessary. For those who do not believe in God, no explanation is possible."[41]

The miraculous events of Lourdes began in the year 1858 with Bernadette Soubirous, a poor, illiterate, fourteen-year-old from southern France. Bernadette was a sickly child, crippled by severe asthma, who, despite the best of intentions, was unable to help her family overcome their abject poverty. Desperately wanting to be of use, Bernadette one day insisted that she accompany her sister on a mission to gather firewood. Her mother reluctantly agreed, and Bernadette ventured out into the cold, along with her sister and another companion. After walking a ways, they eventually stopped near a grotto in Massabielle. While the other girls wandered around the grotto, Bernadette was distracted by a mysterious gust of wind. Immediately thereafter, she saw a strange light emanating from an alcove in the grotto. Looking closer at the light, she was surprised to see an apparition of a beautiful woman standing in the alcove. The woman spoke to her but did not give her name. Bernadette listened carefully to what the woman had to say and soon, she found herself in another world, a better place. She later told her friends of the experience, and her friends told others, until everyone in Lourdes came to know. I wrote:

> On the seventh day of the first month of the year 1844, Bernadette Soubirous, a pious servant of the Lord, was born in Lourdes, a small village hidden at the foot of the Pyrenees Mountains in the south of

---

41   URL: http://www.americancatholic.org/Features/SaintOfDay/default. asp?id=1288. Downloaded 2-10-06.

France. She was born in a mill, the Boly Mill, which also served as her family's place of residence. At that time, few in the world knew of Lourdes and even fewer knew of the Soubirous family. Francois Soubirous, a miller by trade, and his wife, Louise, were very poor. They had nine children, but five of the nine died in infancy. Bernadette was their eldest child. She was a good and obedient daughter who cherished her family and was cherished by them. Although surrounded by love, her childhood was not an easy one. Because of her family's poverty, she was uneducated and illiterate. She could not even speak French; rather, she spoke only an obscure dialect. Her lack of education was not the greatest difficulty that she faced. Bernadette was a sickly girl. She suffered terribly from asthma. At times, her lungs would tighten, making it hard for her to breathe. The symptoms were at their worst when she would catch cold; her breathing would become so restricted that she would almost suffocate. It is said that the battles she fought to breathe in her youth were perhaps necessary to prepare her for the struggles that she would face throughout her life here on earth, for her struggles were many.

In the year 1854, crops were poor, and France was cursed with famine. All of the villagers of Lourdes fell on hard times, and the Soubirous family was particularly afflicted. They were turned out from the Boly Mill and left to wander from boarding house to boarding house. This went on for some time, until finally, in 1856, they found themselves utterly homeless. Out of pity, their cousin Sajous granted them residence in the Cachot, a one-room former prison that was below human living conditions. It was a damp and cold room, heated by burning twigs in a single fireplace. The room overlooked a stable yard that contained livestock, and a stench incessantly filled the air. The tiny room was cramped—it was not suitable to house six people, but the Soubirous family had no other choice. They were grateful just to have shelter over their heads, even if that shelter was a miserable, unused jail.

Francois and Louise took whatever menial jobs were available, just to get by. Unfortunately, work was scarce, and even when there was work, wages were meager. These were very difficult times. The cold winter months were the most difficult, especially for Bernadette, who truly felt imprisoned. She so wanted to help her family, but her health was unsteady. The smoke from the burning twigs and the dampness of the cell worsened her asthma, leaving her sick and infirm. It pained her to see her family struggle while she helplessly watched. At times, she felt like she was nothing but a burden to them. She prayed for her family; she prayed to God to let her help, even if it was in the simplest way.

On the eleventh day of the second month of 1858, Bernadette set out with her sister Toinette to collect firewood. At first, her mother forbade her from going out into the cold, but Bernadette pleaded to be released from her confinement.

"Please let me go with Toinette," she said.

"Not in this cold," her mother answered. "What about your cough? You must think of your health."

"I will be fine, Mother," she said. "It will do me good to get some fresh air. And besides, we will be able to gather more branches if I go."

Her persistence paid off. Louise Soubirous conceded and allowed Bernadette to accompany her younger sister to gather twigs for the fire. The two met a third girl, Jeanne Abadie, who was their friend. Together, they set out to the banks of the River Gave, where they hoped to find ample firewood. In the dampness and cold, the three made their way through town, then down a hill toward their destination. When they approached the river, they saw the Grotto of Massabielle. The grotto was a natural cavern, valued by no one. It was a muddy area filled with driftwood that had washed up from the river. Toinette and Jeanne crossed the small stream that was there. The stream's water was frigid, and Bernadette was hesitant to cross, for fear that she would catch cold and exacerbate her asthma, but after Toinette and Jeanne pestered her to follow, she decided to try to brave the passage. She initially tried to cross without taking off her stockings but found that this would not work, so she walked back toward the grotto. By this time, the other girls had already run ahead. Determined, she hurried to take off her stockings so she could catch up with them. As Bernadette took off her first stocking, she heard the sound of rushing wind, but when she looked up at the trees, she saw no movement of the branches. All was still. She reached for her second stocking and again heard a rush of wind. Bernadette stood motionless for a moment, bewildered by the phenomenon. Then, suddenly, she was startled by an intense, shimmering light that emanated from the cave. She was so taken by the brilliance of the light that she dropped to her knees in awe. There, in an alcove to the right of the grotto, was a radiant woman who bowed her head in greeting. Bernadette could not believe her eyes. She even rubbed her eyes, but she still saw the same image. The woman wore a beautiful white dress and held a rosary in her hands. At first, Bernadette was frightened. Her hands trembled and heart pounded as she reached for her own rosary. While Bernadette tightly grasped the beads, the radiant woman in the alcove of the grotto made the sign of the cross and began to pray. Bernadette, too, began to pray. Her feelings of fear turned quickly into feelings of warmth and perfect tranquility as she gazed in amazement at the spectacular woman. When Bernadette finished praying, the woman disappeared.

Bernadette's encounter with the apparition in the grotto set off a series of events that would prove to be as amazing as any since the Resurrection of Christ. Inspired by the Holy Spirit, the sickly young visionary returned to the grotto several times over the next few weeks to see the beautiful woman. Soon, crowds began to gather as people from Lourdes became curious. Only Bernadette could see the woman, but the crowds were nonetheless moved by the fact that Bernadette appeared to be in a state of perfect tranquility during the encounters. Even the most skeptical onlookers were moved; some were profoundly moved. I wrote:

> On the twenty-third day of the second month, Jean-Baptiste Estrade, a wealthy tax collector, brought a small group with him to the grotto to mock Bernadette and those who believed in her. He was a proud and pompous man, who looked with disdain upon the lower classes. "Look at their gullibility," he said. With contempt in his heart, Estrade watched as Bernadette knelt in the grotto. Once again, she appeared to be in a state of perfect tranquility. To Estrade's surprise, she appeared as one would be expected to appear if approached by a messenger from God.

> While Bernadette prayed, she held a candle in her hand. At one point, the hot wax spilled onto her, but she did not flinch; she did not even notice. Miraculously, her skin was unharmed. Estrade stared in amazement. He had expected to find a spectacle and a circus at the Grotto of Massabielle, but instead, he found something hallowed and magnificent. He was deeply moved. Despite all of his pomposity and bravado, he came to believe. With veneration, he described Bernadette's appearance saying, "She was like an angel in prayer, reflecting in her features all of the glory of the heavens."[42]

---

42   Therese Taylor. *Bernadette of Lourdes: Her Life, Death and Visions*. London: Burns and Oates, 2003, p. 87.

At each encounter, the beautiful woman requested that a chapel be built at the grotto and that people do penance and pray for sinners. Bernadette relayed the message, but many doubted her. One day, when a particularly large crowd had gathered, the woman instructed Bernadette to drink from a spring. Bernadette was confused, as there was no spring in the vicinity. Seeing only a puddle of muddy water, Bernadette began to dig in the mud. Working determinedly, her hands and clothes and face became covered with soil. The crowd immediately gasped at the sight. They were shocked by her behavior and many viciously mocked her. I wrote:

The twenty-fifth day of the second month was cold and rainy. The sky was overcast, and the wind was brisk. Despite the miserable weather, a crowd again gathered at dawn to watch the meeting between Bernadette and the mystical lady. The day began with a request that Bernadette made to the woman. The head of the clergy in Lourdes, Cure Peyramale, had insisted that Bernadette ask the woman for a miracle. He wanted the woman to make the rosebush at the grotto bloom roses, even though it was the dead of winter. Bernadette relayed the message, but the radiant woman ignored the priest's request. Instead, she, in return, had a message. As Bernadette knelt by the grotto, the woman said to her, "Pray the Rosary and ask for peace." She then said, "Kiss the ground, as penance for sinners."

Bernadette obeyed the woman's request and kissed the ground. What was to happen next would change the lives of thousands upon thousands. The woman said to Bernadette, "Go drink at the spring, and wash yourself in it."

Bernadette was confused. *What spring?* she thought. There was no spring there. Bernadette walked toward the River Gave, thinking that the lady must be referring to the river. The radiant woman redirected her, saying, "No, not the Gave."

The woman pointed to an area next to a rock, but there was no spring there; there was only a puddle with mud. Wanting to show obedience to the woman from heaven, Bernadette searched for the spring. She began scratching and digging in the mud by the rock where the lady had pointed. She vigorously dug but to no avail. No spring appeared;

there was only the puddle. After much effort, she cupped her hands to take in what little water was there. The onlookers were shocked and horrified to see the young girl crawling and digging in the mud. Many lost faith. Laughs and jeers poured forth from the crowd. Even members of Bernadette's own family lost faith in her. Her aunt came up to her and slapped her in the face, and her mother spoke sharply to her as she grabbed Bernadette by the arm and pulled her out of the mud. Seeing the people jeer, Bernadette was horribly dejected. Tears ran down her face. One onlooker commented that she seemed to carry all the sorrow of the world.

After the episode in the mud, some accused Bernadette of being insane; others accused her of being a fraud, but she insisted her story was true. Several days later, one of the villagers from Lourdes discovered that a spring of water had, in fact, emerged from the very site where Bernadette had been digging. The emergence of the spring was a miracle of God and was rightly recognized as such. Instantly, the villagers regained faith in Bernadette, and crowds again appeared to witness her meetings with the beautiful woman, who they believed was an angel. Taking interest, the local clergymen insisted that Bernadette find out the woman's name. Bernadette repeatedly asked but time and again, the woman only smiled in reply. Then one day, Bernadette determinedly asked the woman her name, four times in a row. After the fourth request, the beautiful woman revealed her identity, saying, "I am the Immaculate Conception." I wrote:

> Like her most holy Son, Mary was conceived without the mark of original sin. She lived a life of pure devotion to the Lord, and after her time on earth was complete, she was assumed into paradise by the hand of God, where she was hailed by all of the prophets and angels as the Queen of Heaven. For many years, there were those who did not believe that Mary was free of the chains of sin. Blinded by Satan's prejudice against women, they did not accept that a woman would be granted such a grace, nor did they accept that a woman could hold such a place of power as to be called "Queen of Heaven." Because of this, the truth of the nature of the Blessed Virgin went unconfirmed for centuries. It was not until the year 1854, when Pope Pius IX established the doctrine Ineffabilis Deus, that the absolute purity of the Mother of God was made Church dogma. In the doctrine, Pope Pius IX proclaimed that Mary was "preserved immune from the stain of original sin"—that she was conceived immaculately. Among the inner circles of the clergy, the Pope's proclamation was known as the Doctrine of the Immaculate Conception.

Bernadette was a simple, uneducated girl. She had no knowledge of the Pope's proclamation and, until the twenty-fifth day of the third month of the year 1858, she had never heard the words "Immaculate Conception." Other than Cure Peyramale and several other members of the clergy, no one in Lourdes had ever heard the term. That would soon change in a dramatic way. The twenty-fifth day of the third month was the Feast of the Annunciation, the celebration of the day that an angel from heaven came to Mary and announced that she would give birth to the Savior of the world. Bernadette experienced a divine impulse on this day. She awoke suddenly in the early hours of the morning. It had been three weeks since she had been to the Grotto of Massabielle, but Bernadette felt compelled to go back. She jumped out of bed, threw on shoes and a coat, and ran furiously to the grotto. Several people already were there, praying, by the time she arrived. The people were excited to see her return. Some of them ran to spread the word throughout the town, and it was not long before a crowd gathered.

Bernadette knelt by the spring, and the radiant woman appeared to her. This time, Bernadette was determined to find out her name. She stubbornly begged three times, "Madame, would you be so kind as to tell me who you are?"

Each time the lady only smiled in reply. Then, Bernadette asked a fourth time. With the fourth attempt, there was no smile. The radiant woman raised her eyes to heaven and held her arms outstretched. Bernadette's soul overflowed with anticipation. The morning sky had been covered with dark and dreary clouds, but at that moment, the sky opened and the sun glowed brilliantly, illuminating the grotto. At last, the woman revealed her identity. She said, "I am the Immaculate Conception." After her announcement, the woman disappeared.

Just as quickly as Bernadette had arrived that morning, she hurried away to see Cure Peyramale, the entire time repeating the words "Immaculate Conception" so that she would not forget. When Bernadette told the cure what the lady had said, the clergyman stepped backwards in shock. "You must be mistaken," he said. "This cannot be." He turned pale and went to sit in a chair. "Do you know what that means?" he asked. Bernadette shook her head. Cure Peyramale explained it to her. "That woman is not just an angel from heaven," he said. He then paused as his hands started to quiver and his eyes filled with tears. With a faltering voice, he said, "The Immaculate Conception is the Mother of God, the Blessed Virgin Mary."

"The Immaculate Conception," I whispered to myself as I contemplated the magnificence of that moment. "For those who believe in God, no explanation is necessary. For those who do not believe, no explanation is possible."

Fortified by the Blessed Virgin's grace, the water from the spring in the grotto had the heavenly power to heal. Word spread far and wide of the water's power, and in short time, Lourdes became a place of pilgrimage for Christians everywhere. The consequences were far-reaching; the small French village had a profound impact on the Church. In an era that focused on human achievement over religious devotion, the sanctuary at Lourdes revived the Christian spirit. In many ways, the spring at the grotto became a baptismal fountain for a world that had lost its faith.

Over the decades, numerous astounding miracles occurred at Lourdes, and many were scrutinized again and again by reputable medical doctors. One of the more notable miracles involved a child named Francis Pascal. I recounted his story in *The Third Testament*:

In the year 1937, at the age of three, Francis Pascal was afflicted with meningitis, a severe infection of the lining of the brain. He was left blind and paralyzed. His legs were flaccid—they had no strength whatsoever. His parents took him to see several physicians, who told them that there was nothing that could be done; the condition was permanent. "Francis will never walk, and he will never see," they said. The doctors' words left the child and his parents in deep sorrow.

Francis' father was a man of faith. He prayed to the Lord for guidance. After much thought and prayer, he decided to bring his son to Lourdes. In 1938, Francis and his parents boarded a train for a journey to the holy city. Francis' mother was somewhat skeptical, but she was desperate and willing to try anything that might help her son.

When they placed him in the celestial water the first time, Francis shivered from the cold. Seeing her sickly child shiver made his mother feel ill at ease. Her faith was not strong, and she began to see the trip to Lourdes as nothing more than a hopeless act of desperation. She decided she wanted it to end. When the child emerged from the water, still without his sight and still unable to walk, she said to her husband, "See? This is foolish. We should leave now." The boy's father was deeply saddened to see that his son was still blind and lame, but he did not give up hope. He pleaded with his wife. "Let him go in the waters once more," he said. "We must have faith in Christ and the Blessed Virgin." After much debate, the mother agreed, and Francis again went into the water. The second time, he emerged not only with his sight but with the ability to walk. When the doctors near his home reexamined Francis, they spoke of a definitive cure—an inconceivable cure. "There is no medical explanation for this," they said. For Francis and his family, no medical explanation was necessary.

Another of the miracles involved a young man named Vittorio Micheli, an Italian soldier from Scurelle. He suffered from a malignant tumor that was destroying his iliac bone. The tumor was so large that his left thigh became loose from its socket, leaving his leg limp. Vittorio went to Lourdes in search of hope. There, he found more than hope; he, like Francis Pascal, found a heavenly cure. After his visit to the spring at the Grotto of Massabielle, Vittorio's tumor disappeared, and his severely damaged bone slowly healed over time. The medical community had this to say about his recovery:

"A remarkable reconstruction of the iliac bone and cavity has taken place. The x-rays made in 1964, 1965, 1968, and 1969 confirm, categorically and without doubt, that an unforeseen and even overwhelming bone reconstruction has taken place of a type unknown in the annals of world medicine."[43]

I was inspired by the stories of miraculous cures. Burning the midnight oil, I wrote in detail of Bernadette and of her encounters with the Blessed Virgin. As I wrote, I was impressed with the very difficult life that Bernadette Soubirous led. She suffered miserably. The Blessed Virgin Mary told her that she would. The Queen of Heaven said to Bernadette:

"I do not promise you happiness in this world but in the next."

The words "I do not promise you happiness in this world but in the next" resonated throughout my mind.

So many of the saints suffered, I thought. It was hard for me to think of a saint who had not suffered—I searched and searched but could find none. I then sighed deeply, stared momentarily at my computer screen, and continued writing.

---

43 URL: http://avemaria.bravepages.com/articles/mar/alex.html. Downloaded 2-11-06.

Chapter 34

THE SETTING SUN

SUNDAY PASSED, AND Monday morning arrived, a cold and cloudy day. The winter's gloom was at its height. Getting up early, I accompanied Ellen to Northwestern Memorial Hospital. We checked in at the registration desk, on the second floor by the cafeteria, and within minutes were escorted up to a room on the oncology ward. I watched sadly as patients with bald heads walked the floor, pulling their IV poles along. So many of them looked too young to have cancer. Ellen was too young; that was for sure.

"Why Lord?" I asked. "Why couldn't I be the one afflicted with the tumor? Why did it have to be Ellen?"

Within minutes of getting settled into a room, Barb, one of the oncology nurses, walked in. "Welcome back," she said. "I'll be taking care of you."

Barb was very upbeat and cheerful. She had been Ellen's nurse for part of her previous stay. The nurses on the oncology ward at Northwestern all were wonderful. They were caring and compassionate, and their dedication was extraordinary. To deal with the issues that they had to face, day in and day out, was unimaginable. They stood by each patient through the roughest of times—shaking chills, pain, vomiting, and depression. They helped feed those who could not feed themselves; they helped lift those who could not stand; they helped cleanse those who were infirm; they wiped the tears of those who were sad, and they held the hands of those who had lost hope. They were truly angels.

"Let me get your IV hooked up, sweetie, and then we can start right in with the treatments," Barb said. "We're going to get you through this just fine."

I was hoping Barb's words would prove true, but it was not to be. The first dose of the IL-2 went in without much difficulty, but trouble started soon after the second. Ellen developed a really high fever and shook uncontrollably.

Here we go, I thought.

After just the third dose, her blood pressure started to drop and she began to hallucinate. After the fourth dose, her shaking was the worst I had ever witnessed. It went on for close to two hours. The nurse gave her three injections of a medication called Demerol to try to quiet the convulsions, but it did not seem to help. The Demerol only seemed to worsen her nausea. Ellen threw up twice in succession, and then suffered through several rounds of dry heaves, lasting over half an hour. She appeared miserable. Her mental status was deeply clouded, and she spoke only gibberish. The nurse called the resident physician, who suggested that Ellen skip the fifth dose, which she did.

When Dr. Kruntzel came in the next morning, I told him how Ellen struggled so with the therapy. I explained that she was very weak, and I expressed my concerns about continuing the treatment.

"She may do better, now that she skipped a dose," he said. "I assure you, what she is experiencing is common among patients getting IL-2. We are keeping a close eye on her. I think we should proceed with the treatment. It is her best chance."

"OK," I said. "Seeing her look so ill is just hard for me to take."

"That I can imagine," he said. "Try to hang in there. This is a difficult treatment—difficult for patients from a physical standpoint and difficult for family members to witness. It's natural to be concerned. If Ellen gets to the point where she looks too ill, we will stop. I promise you that."

I appreciated the fact that Dr. Kruntzel took the time to speak with me, and I appreciated the fact that he assured me they would stop the therapy if Ellen got too sick. But to me, she already looked too sick. What I wanted to say—but did not—was, "What if it is too late by the time you stop?" That was my deepest fear. That was haunting me. That, and the melancholy thought tied to the fear—"What if I don't have the chance to say good-bye?"

Ellen went on to get three more doses of IL-2. She started hallucinating again after the first of the three. She did not even recognize who I was. Part of that may have been secondary to the fact that they were giving her higher doses of Demerol to prevent the shakes. Demerol was known to cause confusion. They were also giving her three different medications to prevent the vomiting.

The second of the three IL-2 doses was complicated by a significant drop in blood pressure. The nurse gave her some intravenous fluids and started dopamine to keep her blood pressure elevated.

The true terror started after the third and final dose of IL-2. Ellen's entire body trembled, and she hallucinated terribly. Her blood pressure plummeted as it never had before. The nurse called the doctor, who came quickly. He seemed very concerned and made preparations to transfer Ellen to the intensive care unit.

At that point, Ellen was talking but not making any sense. She seemed deeply distressed. She called out for help several times. I grabbed her hand and held it. I prayed to God. "Please, Lord, grant us mercy. Grant us mercy!" Tears filled my eyes. My hands began to tremble, and I broke out in a cold sweat. I knew that the situation was serious. I could tell by the way the doctors and nurses were reacting—they were panicked by the severe drop in Ellen's blood pressure. I knew that they were afraid she was dying.

Ellen's voice grew fainter and fainter as she babbled incoherently. Then, suddenly, she became calm. Her eyes closed. The grip of her hand in mine weakened. The shaking stopped, and Ellen made one final utterance before losing consciousness. She whispered, "Thank you."

The hospital staff rushed Ellen to the intensive care unit. I was not able to be with her at first, as they made me wait outside. Reluctantly, I sat alone in a waiting area. I was a nervous wreck at baseline, and things only grew worse as I waited. In desperate need of support, I called Jerry, and within an hour, he was there with Joyce. They asked if I had heard any news, but I hadn't at that point. Then, after another forty-five minutes, a doctor from the intensive care unit came to speak with me. He looked somber. Watching him approach was like a nightmare unfolding in slow motion. I feared the worst. I stood motionless, as did Jerry and Joyce.

"Mr. Sankt," the doctor said, "I'm Dr. Stewart. I'm one of the physicians taking care of your daughter, Ellen." He extended his hand in greeting, and I shook it.

"How is she doing?" I asked, unable to disguise my panic.

"She is stable right now. We have her on two different medications to keep her blood pressure elevated, and it seems to be holding up OK. She is sleeping comfortably."

"Can we go into see her?"

"Yes, I think that should be OK," he said. "Just to warn you, she still isn't fully conscious. Only time will tell how long it will be before she regains full consciousness."

"Thank you, Doctor."

Jerry and Joyce followed me into the intensive care unit room to see Ellen. She appeared to be sleeping. She had a needle in the artery of her left wrist, connected to some tubing. The nurse said it was there to continuously measure her blood pressure. When I looked up at the monitor in the room, I saw that the blood pressure reading was 80/50. I had learned enough from her previous hospital stay to know that was abnormally low, especially as she was on two medications to raise her blood pressure.

"Is it OK if we stay here in the room until she wakes up?" I asked in a quivering voice.

"You can be here for now," the nurse answered, "but our visiting hours end at 9:00 PM."

We stayed in the room for three hours.

The first hour passed without any sign of movement from Ellen.

What if she doesn't wake up? I wondered.

After the second hour, she showed signs of movement but still did not open her eyes. Her blood pressure increased slightly to 88/55. I asked the nurse if she was on any medication that would cause sedation; she wasn't. That worried me, of course—it meant that there was no extrinsic factor causing her to be unconscious. She was simply that ill. I sighed heavily.

"Why don't you go to the cafeteria and get a bite to eat?" Jerry said. "You haven't eaten all day."

"I'm really not hungry," I replied.

"You need to eat, or you'll pass out," Joyce said. "We'll stay here with Ellen. You should really go."

I actually did feel like I was on the verge of passing out, so I half-heartedly agreed. "Please come get me immediately if anything changes," I said.

"We absolutely will," Jerry said.

The cafeteria was on the second floor but, not paying attention, I rode the elevator down to the first floor by mistake. When I realized my mistake, I decided to take the escalator up one flight. As I was walking down the corridor toward the escalator, I caught the glimpse of a man I recognized about twenty yards in front of me. His back was turned to me, but I was sure it was Tony, the old war veteran from the cemetery.

What is Tony doing all the way down here? I wondered.

From the looks of it, he was heading toward the exit. I didn't want to shout in the hospital, so I picked up my pace to try to catch up to him before he walked out the door. I wanted to tell him about Ellen. Unfortunately, he made it outside before I could reach him. I stepped out on the street with the intention of calling out his name, but when I got outside, he was nowhere to be seen. The street was crowded with shoppers coming from Michigan Avenue, but there was no sign of my old friend.

A blast of wind started up and for a second, I thought I heard my name called out. I was sure it must have been him. I turned around and looked, but there was no one there. I turned to look in the other direction, but again, there was no one. The windblown whisper had been my imagination. *I'm definitely losing my mind*, I thought.

Shaking my head, I went back into the hospital and ate briefly in the cafeteria. I then returned to Ellen's room in the intensive care unit.

"Any change?" I asked with a sense of desperation as I entered the room. Joyce shook her head no.

"She'll be OK," Jerry reassured me. "Ellen's a tough girl. She's a fighter. She'll be fine."

"I pray that is so, Jerry."

After another hour, Ellen opened her eyes.

"Dad?" she whispered. "Where am I?"

"Oh, thank God," Joyce said, expressing the incredible sense of relief that we all felt.

"You're in the intensive care unit, sweetheart. They have you on medications to keep your blood pressure elevated. How do you feel?"

"Very weak," she said.

"You should just try to rest," I said.

Rest she did—Ellen slept the remainder of the evening.

By the next morning, her blood pressure had increased to 95/68, and the nurses discontinued one of the two blood pressure medications.

Dr. Kruntzel stopped by. "I think we should stop the therapy," he said. "She's too weak to tolerate any more. Right now, we should just focus on getting her strong enough to get home."

"Do you think she got enough treatments to help the melanoma?" I asked.

"It is possible. Only time will tell."

"How much time?" I asked.

"Well, we'll repeat CAT scans in approximately eight weeks."

"Eight weeks seems like a long time to wait," I said.

"That is the standard," he said. "The fact is that we'll probably know before then. If she starts to get stronger, that is a good sign. But if she continues to weaken, or if she develops new symptoms, that is a bad sign."

"What type of symptoms?" I asked.

"The symptoms could be almost anything," he said. "With the melanoma in her lungs, I would be concerned if she had new signs of pneumonia—for example, fever and cough. Also, melanoma has a predilection to go to the brain, so if she develops headaches, you need to let us know right away."

"Thank you for your time, Dr. Kruntzel."

After one more day in the intensive care unit, Ellen was able to come off of all of the medications she was on. They transferred her back to the oncology unit to watch her for another day and then she was discharged to home. Dr. Kruntzel arranged for her to have physical therapy at home in an attempt to rebuild her strength. Ellen was certainly in need of added strength. She had lost even more weight while in the hospital. She looked like a skeleton—not at all as she had looked several months earlier. Given how weak she was, I was not sure if physical therapy would even do any good.

- - - - - - - - - -

Ellen spent most of her first week at home in bed. She took several naps throughout the day, but she did not sleep well at night. I stayed up through much of the night with her. Day was night, and night was day, and the whole experience was exhausting.

Jerry came by to visit every day. He came alone now—Joyce had come down with a case of the flu, but he wanted to give his support.

"How is Joyce doing?" I asked when he stopped by late one afternoon.

"She's feeling a little bit better. She sends her love to both you and Ellen. She's really been praying for you guys."

"We wish her a quick recovery, and we thank her for her prayers," I said.

"She'll appreciate your well wishes," he said. "I'll be sure to pass them along."

"We thank you for your prayers too, Jerry," I added sincerely.

Jerry did not reply with words. Instead, he simply looked me in the eye and nodded assuredly.

Remarkably, that was the only exchange we ever had about his return to the faith. It was the only one we ever needed to have.

- - - - - - - - - -

Ellen's second week at home was a better one. She started showing signs of improvement. She was eating better and seemed to be regaining her strength. The physical therapist who came to the house to work with her was very encouraged by her progress.

"You're doing really well, Ms. Sankt," he said. "I think a few more sessions, and you won't need me anymore."

I started gaining a sense of optimism. Ellen was still weak and still very thin, but she seemed to be improving. She had almost recovered to the point where she'd been before she started the IL-2.

Could it have worked? I wondered. *Oh, Lord, I would give anything if the therapy worked. Anything!*

I could tell that Ellen was feeling optimistic also—I could see it in her eyes and in the way she spoke. At the end of the second week, she confirmed her optimism.

"Dad, I know in my heart that the IL-2 worked. I don't know why, but I just know it. I've felt that way ever since I woke up in the intensive care unit. I can just feel it."

Her words were beautiful music to my ears. It was great to see her feeling so positive. I was truly hopeful, and it was good to have hope. My heart soared but alas, it was short-lived. By the start of the fourth week after her discharge from the hospital, Ellen seemed to grow weaker. It was a Monday—a very black Monday. Ellen had done so well on Sunday. She ate three full meals and was up and walking around more than she had been in weeks. But Monday was very different. She complained of feeling achy and tired, and she lost her appetite completely. The step backwards quickly shattered my newfound hope. I could see that it also troubled Ellen. I rationalized that she might have simply overdone it on Sunday and was suffering the consequences. But my rationalization could not explain the headache she developed on Monday night.

It was like the nightmare was starting all over again, but this time it was worse. I recalled that Dr. Kruntzel had specifically warned us that a headache was a sign that the melanoma had spread to the brain.

"Oh, good Lord in heaven, please don't let this be. Please don't let this be," I prayed.

On Tuesday morning when Ellen awoke, her headache was worse. She felt extremely fatigued, and I noticed that she had developed a new cough. She didn't have an appetite, and she still complained of generalized body cramps. Plus, she complained of feeling chilled, despite the fact that the thermostat in the house read seventy-six degrees. I was extremely concerned.

"I'm going to take a hot bath," Ellen said. "Maybe that will help me feel better."

"OK, sweetie," I said. "Is there anything I can do?"

"No, Dad," she said. "You've been wonderful. I don't need anything else right now."

I could tell that she was very anxious, and I didn't want to add to that, but I really thought we should call Dr. Kruntzel. He had told us to call immediately if she developed headaches. I planned to discuss the matter with her as soon as she made it out of the shower, but I never got the chance. Just minutes after Ellen finished showering, I heard a loud thud.

I called out to Ellen, "What was that? Are you OK?"

There was no answer. I quickly ran to Ellen's bedroom, where I found her unconscious in her bathrobe on the floor.

"No!" I cried out, shaking her. "Ellen! Ellen, wake up!" Her skin was flushed and felt red hot. Her limbs were limp. "Please, Ellen, wake up!"

I ran to the phone and dialed 911. "I think my daughter's had a seizure," I said to the dispatcher. "She's passed out on the floor. Please hurry! Please!"

"An ambulance will be there within ten minutes," the dispatcher said.

I ran back to Ellen and shook her again. This time, her eyes opened.

"Really ... don't feel well. Head ... really hurts," she whispered, her voice frail.

"Everything is going to be OK, honey," I said. "The paramedics are on their way."

She reached out for my hand and held it to her heart. "I want you to know ... I love you very much. Best father ... in the entire world." She grasped my hand with both of hers, squeezing it with what little strength she had left.

Tears filled my eyes. "I love you, too, sweetheart," I whispered. "I love you, too."

Chapter 35 ---

THE SEVENTH STAGE

THERE ARE SEVEN stages of death and dying. Ellen had gone through the first six stages: shock, denial, anger, bargaining, depression, and acceptance. The time had come for the final stage.

When the ambulance arrived, the paramedics placed Ellen on a stretcher and rushed her to the nearest emergency room. It was at Holy Family Medical Center, a local community hospital located only two miles away. Even though it was close by, Ellen had never been there before, and we did not know what to expect. The uncertainty added to our already intolerable tension.

The emergency room was crowded with patients, causing it to be very loud and seemingly chaotic. All of the workers there were incredibly busy, and everything happened at a fast pace. As soon as the paramedics dropped us off, a young triage nurse came into the exam room and took Ellen's vital signs and started an IV line, and within minutes, a radiology technician was in snapping an x-ray of her lungs.

"You have a high fever," the nurse said to Ellen. "Let me get you some Tylenol. Do you have any allergies?

"No," Ellen replied in a frail voice.

The nurse promptly brought her the Tylenol. "Here is a cup of water to sip it down with," she said. "Let me elevate the head of your bed a little so you don't choke."

"Thank you," Ellen said. Her hands gently trembled as she held the cup to her lips.

"Will the doctor be in soon?" I questioned. My hands were also trembling.

"Yes, he should be in shortly," the nurse replied.

After about twenty minutes, a tall man with a long white coat entered the room. He introduced himself as Dr. Gonzales. He appeared tired but was otherwise strictly professional. He asked several brief questions concerning Ellen's medical condition, and then he examined her. He looked in her eyes, shined a light in her throat, checked her neck for swollen glands, held his stethoscope up to her heart and lungs, and pressed firmly with his hands on her abdomen. He then meticulously tested her reflexes, one by one, with a rubber hammer. Finally, he checked her blood pressure himself, both while she was lying back and sitting up.

"We need to run several tests," he said after completing his exam. "I will be back to speak with you once we have the test results."

With those words, Dr. Gonzales departed the room and did not return again for over two hours. During that time, the nurse came back into the room and drew Ellen's blood, collected her urine, and took a swab from her nostrils. Several minutes later, Ellen was taken away for a CAT scan of her brain. The doctor did not say why he had ordered it, but I was pretty sure I knew why. With Ellen's headaches, he undoubtedly suspected what I suspected—that the melanoma had spread to her brain and that she had passed out from a seizure.

I paced nervously in Ellen's exam room while she was getting her CAT scan. I prayed the entire time. Taking out my rosary, I grasped bead after bead. When I finished going through it once, I started up again. After approximately forty minutes, Ellen rejoined me, and we waited for word from Dr. Gonzales. We both feared the worst, and our anxieties grew with each passing minute. The clamor of the alarms and sirens in the chaotic emergency room temporarily distracted us—but only temporarily. We tried to remain strong but had no viable defense against the overwhelming sensation of impending doom that had engulfed us. It was like standing helplessly in an execution line, hoping for an unlikely reprieve.

Ellen's eyes welled up with tears; the tension was too much for her. My eyes were dry but throbbed painfully from the stress. The clock ticked on and on and on.

I grew frustrated with the long wait. "Where is he?" I asked no one in particular. "Why hasn't he come back to give us the results?" *This is torture*, I thought. *I wouldn't wish this on my worst enemy. Lord, have mercy please.*

I stepped out of the exam room every ten to fifteen minutes to see if I could catch sight of the busy doctor. I did see him a couple of times, but I never got a chance to grab his attention; he was preoccupied with other patients. Then, there was a period of nearly an hour when I didn't see him at all.

Where could he be? I moaned inwardly. *This is so hard. What kind of hospital is this to keep patients waiting so long?*

The nurse stopped by two separate times to reassure us that the doctor was keeping an eye out for the results and that he would be in to talk to us as soon as they were available.

How long can it possibly take? I wondered. The combination of fear and frustration was insufferable.

Finally, after what seemed an eternity, Dr. Gonzales returned. I was certain that he would tell us the melanoma had spread to Ellen's brain. I was certain he would tell us that the tumors in her lungs had increased in size, causing pneumonia. I was certain that the seventh stage was upon us ... and it was.

"I've reviewed the chest x-ray, the blood work, and the brain scan," Dr. Gonzales said. "I do not see anything abnormal in your brain, and your lungs are clear, but ..."

Although he continued talking, I didn't hear another word. I temporarily allowed myself to become fixated on the comment, "I do not see anything abnormal in your brain." I was surprised—happily surprised—that the melanoma had not spread to her brain. I was so sure that Ellen had had a seizure from a tumor in her brain. I knew that if the melanoma had spread to her brain, there would be no hope left. I so desperately needed to hang on to every last ounce of hope. For a brief moment, I felt very relieved by the news.

I took a deep breath but suddenly realized that I had not paid attention to everything the doctor had said. "Wait a minute," I said. "What else did you say?"

Dr. Gonzalez looked puzzled.

"Did you say her lungs are clear?" I questioned.

"Yes, there is no sign of pneumonia," he replied.

"But what about the tumors in her lungs?" I blurted out.

Dr. Gonzales again looked puzzled by my question. He paused for a moment, studying me, and then very clearly said, "There are no tumors in her lungs."

"What?"

"There are no tumors in her lungs," he reiterated.

"That's impossible," I said. "She has several large tumors in her lungs."

"I can show you the x-ray," he said. "Her lungs are clear."

"Are you sure that it is not a mistake?" I asked.

"Nurse, please grab the x-ray and bring it in here," Dr. Gonzales said.

Within seconds the nurse brought the x-ray into the exam room and hung it on the lighted x-ray view box. Dr. Gonzales quickly stepped up to the view box and pointed to Ellen's lungs—first the right and then the left.

"See?" he said matter-of-factly. "There is no sign of tumor anywhere."

"There is no sign of tumor anywhere," Ellen repeated, her voice choked with emotion. "The melanoma is gone?"

Dr. Gonzales did not answer her question immediately. Instead, he seemed to take a step back to contemplate what had just occurred. There, in the pandemonium of the busy emergency room, the overworked, sleep-deprived doctor realized, all at once, that he was a part of something wonderful. Indeed, the news he'd just delivered was beyond wonderful. Eyes widening with joy, he gave his answer. "Yes, Ms. Sankt, it is gone."

Ellen started to cry. She turned to me and grabbed my hand. "It's gone! Dad, it's gone! It's gone! It's gone! It's gone!"

"My God, it's gone?" I said in disbelief. "Oh, Lord of Mercy!" I closed my eyes and took a deep breath. I then looked upward, whispered a simple thank-you, and embraced Ellen.

Dr. Gonzales stood by quietly, watching us. I could tell that he was genuinely happy for us, even though we had just met.

"But how do you account for her symptoms?" I asked.

Dr. Gonzales smiled kindly. "Mr. Sankt, perhaps you didn't hear me the first time. Let me explain … Ellen has the flu. The nasal swab we took confirms this. That is why she has a cough, and headaches, and fever. That is also why she aches all over."

"But why did she pass out?"

"She simply fainted," he said. "That is not unexpected with a fever as high as hers, especially as she had just gotten out of the shower. The heat from the shower, along with her fever, caused her to pass out."

Ellen recovered from the flu over the next several days. When Dr. Kruntzel heard about what happened, he promptly ordered CAT scans of her entire body to confirm that the melanoma was gone—and it was. There was no trace of it anywhere in her body.

- - - - - - - - -

There are not words to express the joy that I felt at that period of time— there is nothing to which I can compare it. Christmas as a child was wonderful. Falling in love was wonderful. Being a new father was wonderful. Yet nothing could compare with the joy of hearing the words, "It's gone!" After months of abject misery, the terror was finally over. After months of struggle and despair, I could breathe freely again. After months of cold and darkness, it was again spring, and I marveled at the beauty of the world. For the longest time, my many prayers had seemingly fallen on deaf ears. Yet by the grace of God, the reprieve came at the final hour. The redemption I so longed for was at last granted, and it was magnificent.

My grandfather used to always say, "With God, things are not always as they seem." My grandfather was very wise. Yes, scholars tell us that there are seven stages of death and dying: shock, denial, anger, bargaining, depression, acceptance, and death itself. They write of the stages in their medical texts. I sadly witnessed Ellen go through the stages. I saw her miserable decline, each step worse than the last. The scholars must have done their research well, for Ellen indeed followed the textbooks to a T—with one glorious exception.

For Ellen, the seventh stage of death and dying was not death. It was life.

Chapter 36
THE HISTORICAL SALVATION OF MAN

"There are many people in the world who really don't understand, or say they don't, what is the great issue between the Free World and the Communist world.
Let them come to Berlin.

"There are some who say ... there are some who say that Communism is the wave of the future. Let them come to Berlin.

And there are some who say, in Europe and elsewhere, we can work with the Communists. Let them come to Berlin.

And there are even a few who say that it is true that Communism is an evil system, but it permits us to make economic progress. *Lass' sie nach Berlin kommen.* Let them come to Berlin."

—President John F. Kennedy, 1963

Over the next several months Ellen regained all of her strength. It was like she had never been diagnosed with melanoma. It was truly a miracle. Each and every day I gave thanks to God.

Instilled with a new spirit, I continued working on my book. The book was like an old friend to me. It had helped me through the most difficult of times. I was glad those times were over. It felt so good to write freely, unencumbered by the feeling of constant despair. I was nearing the end, and the thought of completing my task made me work harder than I ever had before.

With zeal, I wrote of Fatima and the three shepherd children who were visited by the Blessed Virgin Mary in the early twentieth century. I was deeply intrigued by Fatima, as intrigued as I had been about anything I had written thus far. My intrigue was certainly warranted, for the prophecies made there were as astounding as any prophecies in the Old Testament or Book of Revelation. For the Free World and Christian civilization, they were monumental prophecies; so monumental, in fact, that if history books had been recorded by pious religionists instead of atheistic revisionists, an entire chapter would undoubtedly have been devoted to the small Portuguese village and to the incredible events that were foretold there.

The story of Fatima began in the spring of 1916. As the Great War raged throughout Europe and the Middle East, a messenger from heaven came to visit three young shepherd children in the town of Aljustrel, near Fatima, in Portugal, while they were playing pebbles along a hillside. I wrote:

> Early one day, Lucia de Santos and her cousins, Francisco and Jacinto Marto, led a flock of sheep out to graze in the village of Aljustrel. The morning was marked by rain and dreariness, as was common during the spring in that region. To escape the rain, the children took shelter in a cave. They ate there and prayed the Rosary. In the early afternoon, the skies cleared and the sun shone bright. The children came out from the cave and began playing a game with pebbles. While they were playing, they were approached by an angel from heaven. From out of nowhere, the children heard a mysterious blast of wind, the likes of which they had never heard before. Looking out in the distance to the east, they saw a bright light approaching them. As the light came closer, they could see it was radiating from a magnificent man. He introduced himself, saying, "Do not be afraid. I am the Angel of Peace."

The magnificent man was none other than Saint Michael the Archangel. On a mission from God, Saint Michael visited the children on three occasions—once in spring, once in summer, and once in early autumn. In accordance with the Lord's plan, he taught the children how to pray and revealed to them the importance of sacrifice. He also revealed to them the mystery of redemption, one of the great hallowed truths of the world.

Saint Michael's purpose was to prepare the children for the coming of the Blessed Virgin Mary. The Blessed Virgin's purpose was, in turn, to deliver a warning of vital importance. Ever since the time of Voltaire and the French Revolution, man had come to rely on science and human intellect more and more, and in doing so had drifted away from God. This unfortunate drift only worsened during the twentieth century, and its consequences were severe. At the beginning of the twentieth century, over half of the world had faith in the Lord Jesus Christ, but by the end of the century, less than a fourth of the world's population worshipped at his altar. Much of this loss of faith could be attributed to the spread of Communism, which was deeply rooted in atheism. Communism spread the error of original sin and pushed the people of the world to turn their backs to the Lord.

Man's indifference deeply offended the Lord, but instead of sending his wrath, he sent his Mother to lead the world along a new path, which she did with solemn grace.

The Blessed Virgin's first visitation to the three shepherd children occurred on May 13, 1917. As recounted by Lucia de Santos, it was a beautiful, warm spring day. All was still, and there was not one cloud in the entire sky. I wrote:

> Lucia, Jacinto, and Francisco brought their flocks out to the Cova da Iria in Fatima, a short distance from their home in Aljustrel. There, they allowed the sheep to graze on the rolling hills. As the sheep grazed, the children played and ate lunch. After they ate, they prayed the Rosary. While deep in prayer, they were suddenly startled by what appeared to be a bright bolt of lightning in the sky above. They looked up, but there was no sign of a storm. All was calm. They were confused and debated if they should take the sheep home. Erring on the side of caution, the three decided to head down the hillside in case a storm was actually brewing. As they walked down the slope toward the road, they saw another flash of lightning and picked up their pace. After just a few more steps, they saw a shimmering bubble of light, resting gently on a holm oak tree in front of them. There stood a radiant and beautiful woman, who later revealed herself to be the Blessed Virgin Mary. With compassion and kindness, the woman greeted the children, patiently answered their questions, and then made a covenant to meet with them again.

The Blessed Virgin instructed the children to return to see her on the thirteenth day of each month for the next six months, at the very same hour. Moved by her kindness and beauty, the children obeyed, and on the thirteenth day of each month, they came to the Cova da Iria in Fatima and waited near the holm oak tree for her arrival. They waited with their families, friends, and neighbors, who out of curiosity and faith, came with the three little shepherds to witness the encounters.

During her visit on July 13, Mary revealed to the children a series of prophecies that would become famous throughout the world. Historically accurate, one of the prophecies involved the end of the Great War, better known today as World War I. Another involved the start of an even greater war, heralded by a bright light in the nighttime sky. The third prophecy was more mysterious. It involved the assassination of an exalted holy man—a holy man unknown to the children at the time.

The most important of the Fatima prophecies concerned the nation of Russia. It was a dire warning. At the time, Russia was sadly falling under the control of the Bolshevik Communists, a group of atheistic international radicals who boldly sought to rule the world. Led by Vladimir Lenin, the Bolsheviks fostered abject tyranny and brought death to countless innocents, including the good-hearted Czar Nicholas and his family, the most notable Christian martyrs of the modern era. The czar was the head of the Orthodox Church, and his execution, along with the execution of his heirs, on July 17, 1918, symbolically marked the end of Christianity in the East; it was a tragedy of biblical proportion. When the fateful rifles were fired, mercilessly massacring the benevolent Russian monarch and his five young children, a sinister seed was planted. The seed was fertilized by the innocents' blood, and a new garden—a garden of evil—took root. In the garden, totalitarianism and suffering reigned, and prayer was forbidden.

Foreseeing the horrors that the Bolsheviks would bring, not only to the people of Russia but to all mankind, the Blessed Virgin imparted a message at Fatima that was, out of necessity, utterly and disturbingly dark. With solemnity, Mary said:

> "Russia will spread her errors throughout the world, bringing new wars and persecution to the Church. The good will be martyred and the Holy Father will have much to suffer; certain nations will be annihilated."[44]

Unfortunately, Communist Russia did exactly as Mary had said—exactly—and the consequences were dreadful. Over the next several decades, new wars were indeed fought, Christians were indeed persecuted, and entire nations were indeed wiped off the globe.

The Blessed Virgin's warning did not stand alone. With the warning came words of guidance. Speaking through the three shepherd children, Mary asked for repentance and prayer for sinners. She said:

> "I ask that reparations be made in atonement for the sins of the world. When you pray the Rosary, say after each mystery, 'Jesus, forgive us; save us from the fire of hell. Lead all souls to heaven, especially those who are most in need.'"[45]

---

44 URL: http://www.ewtn.com/fatima/apparitions/July.htm. Downloaded 2-14-06.

45 Adapted from URL: http://www.ewtn.com/fatima/apparitions/July.htm.

Mary then called for the consecration of Russia and promised that good would ultimately overcome evil. She said:

> "In the end, my Immaculate Heart will triumph. The Holy Father will consecrate Russia to me, and she will be converted, and the world will enjoy a period of peace."[46]

Analyzing Mary's words, everything seemed to make sense. Russia eventually was converted, not to Christianity but from Communism, and after Russia's conversion, the long and brutal Cold War ended, and peace was restored.

The Fatima prophecies concluded with the extraordinary miracle of the dancing sun. Witnessed by over seventy thousand onlookers, it was arguably the greatest miracle ever recorded in modern times. It also was arguably one of the greatest targets of the modern-day secularization movement. As the secularists and atheists could not refute it, they conspired to ignore it, which they did with much success. Today, outside of Portugal, few discuss the event or its remarkable consequences.

Someday, that will change. I just know it will. It is too important to ignore. It is too amazing.

I described how Mary, during one of her visits to Fatima, made a promise to Lucia de Santos, the oldest of the three shepherd children. She said:

> "Come again to the Cova da Iria on the thirteenth of next month, my child, and continue to say the Rosary every day. In the last month I will perform a miracle so that all may believe."[47]

On the thirteenth day of October in the year 1917, the astonishing miracle occurred. The sun detached from its axis and danced throughout the sky above Fatima. It whirled about wildly, like a wheel of nuclear fire, as the masses watched from below. It painted the earth and sky different colors— vibrant colors—as it whirled. At one point, it raced rapidly toward the earth, leading many to believe that the end of the world was near. Thousands held their breath in anticipation. Thousands of others dropped to their knees to pray and confess their sins. When, by the Lord's grace, the sun was finally

---

Downloaded 2-14-06.

46 Adapted from URL: http://www.ewtn.com/fatima/apparitions/July.htm. Downloaded 2-14-06.

47 URL: http://www.ewtn.com/fatima/apparitions/August.htm. Downloaded 2-15-06.

done dancing, the ground at Fatima, which had previously been soaked by rain, was found to be completely dry, and the sick and the lame, who stood in witness, were instantly cured. I described the event in detail in *The Third Testament.*

On the twelfth day of the tenth month, during the night, it rained. It rained so that the roads leading into Fatima turned into mud. The conditions were truly foul. Yet despite the inclement weather, thousands of pilgrims made their way from surrounding villages to see the miracle of which the three shepherd children spoke. They came on foot; they came on horseback. Others rode bicycles, and a few of the wealthy pilgrims arrived by automobile. Many slept outside in the open that night, awaiting the auspicious day. Their clothes were drenched and covered with dirt, but these were a people of faith who gladly bore the misery. The rain continued to pour throughout the morning of the thirteenth day, as over seventy thousand pilgrims gathered in the fields of the Cova da Iria. It was the largest crowd to gather there, almost triple the size of the crowd that had gathered only a month before. In addition to the pious pilgrims who came to pray and experience a miracle of the Lord, there were many skeptics and nonbelievers who hoped to prove the children were liars. Included among the nonbelievers were several reporters, who mocked the children and all people of faith. They claimed the mystical visitations were nothing but a farce. They came with coldness in their hearts.

As the rain came pouring down from the black clouds covering Fatima, the three shepherd children patiently awaited the arrival of the magnificent woman from heaven. Others in the crowd were not so patient. Shortly after one o'clock in the afternoon, a man who claimed to be a priest spoke to Lucia. He mocked her, noting that the Lady from heaven had promised to arrive at midday but that it was already well past the noon hour. He instructed the crowd to disperse, claiming the entire event was a charade. He then tried to push the children away from the holm oak tree where the Lady had come in the past. His action stirred a great commotion. The commotion lasted until two o'clock in the afternoon. It was at that very hour that the sun was directly overhead—the middle of the day in Fatima. Observing the position of the sun behind the clouds, Lucia pointed to the east and shouted out that the Lady was coming. Just at that moment, she appeared. The radiant woman from heaven took up her position near the hallowed holm oak tree and spoke to the shepherd children. She gave them a message. It was a simple but profoundly important message. She instructed the people of the world to pray the Rosary every day and encouraged them to amend their lives and ask pardon for their sins. The shepherd children took careful note of her words. When she was finished delivering the message, the Queen of Heaven rose toward the east. As she ascended, she lifted her hands in the direction of the blackened sky. At once, the clouds parted, revealing the miracle she had promised. Lucia shouted out, as loudly as she could, to the pilgrims gathered at the Cova da Iria: "Look at the sun!"

Over seventy thousand onlookers gazed up into the sky. The sun was seen like a silver orb, spinning on its axis. It cast rays of various colors that painted the world below—yellow, then blue, then red, then white, then purple. The colors were awe-inspiring and beautiful, as if they had come through the stained-glass windows of a cathedral. To their amazement, the pilgrims were able to stare directly at the beautiful orb without any discomfort to their eyes. People in the crowd shouted out, "It's a miracle!" Then, all at once, the sun stopped spinning. Inexplicably, the brilliant orb seemed to detach from its axis and dance through the sky. It trembled and whirled about wildly, like a wheel of nuclear fire, violating all cosmic laws. The seventy thousand onlookers who witnessed this could not believe what was unfolding. Many were stricken with fear as the sun began to hurl toward the earth. Many fell to their knees in prayer; others wept with emotion. As the sun came closer, the people could feel its great radiant heat. Their clothes, which moments before had been soaked by the rain, were suddenly completely dry, and the ground showed no signs of moisture. It was as if it had never rained at all. The dancing sun and the drying of the ground were not the only inexplicable events to occur. By the grace of God, many who came to the Cova da Iria with ailments that day were cured. After the sun stopped dancing and returned to its proper position in the sky, shouts could be heard from the crowd: "I can see! Thank the Lord, I can see!"

"I can walk! Praise be to Christ and the Blessed Virgin. I can walk!"

The Queen of Heaven had promised the shepherd children a miracle on the thirteenth day of the tenth month, and to the astonishment of the skeptics, the promise came true. Over seventy thousand of God's people had the privilege to witness what came to be known as the Miracle of the Sun. Although there were hundreds of atheists in the crowd that morning, by the midafternoon, there were only believers. Not one of the seventy thousand ever denied the veracity of the event. Not one. People of every age, culture, social class, and faith agreed that what they saw was amazing and without scientific explanation; they agreed that what they saw was biblical in nature. Blessed were they who stood and witnessed the glory and power of God.

In the last several chapters of the book, I focused on the dark and foreboding subject of the Blessed Virgin's prophecy, Communist Russia. In short time, I had come to accept the foundations of Professor Erlichman's theory—it was my belief that Communism was the devil's religion, practiced and enforced by demons. Irrefutably, the goal of Communism was to eradicate Christianity and to convince the people of the world that God does not exist. Through a series of sinister steps, carried out by Satan's minions—men named Marx, Rasputin, and Lenin—Communism came to corrupt the nation of Russia. From Russia, Satan planned to spread his terror throughout the entire world. A more heinous threat man has never known.

By the middle of the twentieth century, Satan's devious plot was coming to fruition—an evil empire was firmly established here on earth. The evil empire was called the Soviet Union, and it opposed all that was good. The Kremlin was Satan's temple, and Stalin was his favorite son. Cultivated by tyrannical despots, the fruits of Satan's empire were utterly monstrous. More people were murdered by Communist regimes in just seventy years than were murdered during the one thousand years of the Roman Empire. More people were persecuted than at any other time in the annals of history. The worst of the persecutions took place in the Soviet gulags; they were harbingers of hell itself—not a hell of smoke and fire but a hell of frigid cold and utter cruelty. The Berlin Wall, the heart of the Communist Iron Curtain, was the earthly representation of the gates of hell. The gulags and the wall were horrible manifestations of what happens when God is excluded from the lives of men. I described the tyranny in *The Third Testament*:

> Many innocent people tried to flee the Communist nations, but they were imprisoned or murdered. It is said that there was an iron curtain around them. In spirit and in truth, the Iron Curtain divided the world of light from the world of darkness. It partitioned hope from despair, freedom from oppression, and good from evil.

> A traveler once noted that when passing through the Eastern Communist nations in mid-December, the earth was dark and cold and barren. There was no cheer. There was no life. When the traveler came upon West Berlin late one evening, however, his heart was filled with joy and hope as he was greeted with the brilliant and colorful lights of Christmas.

The beautiful lights lit up the night sky, for West Berlin was a free and Christian city. Although West Berlin was free, it was lamentably divided from East Berlin by a wall with barbed wire. The wall was not erected to protect the citizens of West Berlin from the Communists; it was erected by the Communists to keep the citizens of East Berlin from fleeing the tyranny that engulfed them. The Brandenburg Gate stood at the center of the wall, dividing East from West. Communist soldiers stood guarding the gate, with orders to fire upon anyone who tried to escape. The gate enclosed a demonic prison of torture and oppression. It encircled a black hole of spiritual poverty, where freedom did not exist and where the poor were left to suffer and die. In the eyes of God, the Brandenburg Gate was the very gates of hell.

Fed by Stalin's treachery, Communism spread quickly, like a cancer, and it posed a dire threat to humanity. What made Communism truly dangerous was that for the first time in the history of the earth, evil had the power to destroy the entire planet. Only faith and prayer would save the children of God from a fiery annihilation. Realizing this, I experienced an epiphany.

In the past, I had questioned why a tree of knowledge would be forbidden to man.

What harm is there in knowledge? I thought. *Why would an all-powerful and loving God forbid his children from having knowledge?*

Then, one beautiful spring day at Starved Rock, I came to understand. With man's creation of nuclear weapons, the evil behind the forbidden fruit was unleashed; knowledge was very dangerous indeed.

In the latter half of the twentieth century, the Soviet Union threatened the world with a nuclear Armageddon. It was a real and terrifying threat; many believed it was inevitable. People lived in constant fear, for they knew that a nuclear war would be like no other disaster in the history of the earth. The unholy consequences of the weapons would be devastatingly rapid—whole cities, whole peoples, wasted in the blink of an eye. The horrific thunder of the bombs would shatter the tranquility of the earth. Buildings would fall. Fires would blaze. Caustic radiation would be spit out into the atmosphere, poisoning the air. The ground would shake. Winds would rage. Black smoke would cover the skies, blocking the sun's rays, and the earth would be shrouded in total darkness. Without the light from the sun, the earth would freeze, and nuclear winter would come to be. The frigid temperatures and the radiation from the bombs would kill the plants and the trees. There would be no birds left to sing; no children left to play. Life on the earth would cease to exist.

In his second letter, Saint Peter the Apostle wrote of the End of Times. He warned his brethren to always be ready, for with the Lord "a thousand years is like one day." In the letter, his description of the End of Times sounded ever so frighteningly like a nuclear holocaust. At Fatima, the Blessed Virgin's message to the shepherd children was equally frightening. Guided by the sinister hand of Satan, the children of God were in danger, the gravest of danger, and Mary was determined to save them, even at the cost of sounding uncharacteristically stern. The Miracle of the Sun was an integral part of her stern message. Undoubtedly, the Miracle of the Sun was more than just a cosmic display. It was a terrifying forewarning of things to come if man did not mend his ways. The descent of the sun toward the earth symbolized the radiant fire of nuclear weapons, weapons that truly contained the power of the sun. The fiery descent symbolized Armageddon.

It became clear to me that Satan's plan was to prematurely bring about the End of Times but that his plan was foiled by Christ through the workings of his Church. All at once, Pope John Paul II's critical role in the fall of the Soviet Union took on new meaning, and all at once, salvation through Christ took on a new form. I realized that Christ lived and died not only to save the souls of man but to save the earth itself. Like never before, Christ's proclamation to Peter rang pure and true: "Thou art Peter and upon this rock I will build my Church, and the gates of hell shall not prevail against it."

At the height of his malevolent reign, Stalin, the most evil of Satan's minions, scoffed at the power of the Pope and of the Church. He derisively proclaimed, "The Pope? How many divisions does he have?" Little did he know that in a mere three decades after his death, a pope, in alliance with a devoutly Christian American president, would lead the way to the collapse of Communist tyranny, thus ending the threat of nuclear Armageddon. Had it not been for Christ, there would have been no Church. Had there been no Church, then the evil of Communism would have gone unchecked, and the world would have been engulfed in a nuclear holocaust late in the twentieth century. Because of Christ, Satan failed in his quest to destroy God's creation.

The historical salvation of man.

"It all fits together so perfectly," I whispered.

I recalled that in the sixteenth century, Nostradamus had foretold that the earth's end would come in the year 1999. I then recalled that three centuries after that foretelling, a Christian prophet boldly brought forth a new prophecy. Lamennais, the misunderstood French visionary, proclaimed that an immense liberty would be "indispensable for the development of those truths required to save the world." The "immense liberty" came in the form of a young nation far across the sea, a nation under God and indivisible. The United States, founded and governed by pious Christians and wholly dedicated to the pursuit of freedom, led the way to the fall of the evil empire.

As I sat in front of my computer, preparing to type, I opened up the 1992 "Holy Alliance" issue of *Time* magazine that was sitting on my desk. Staring at the picture of the Pope and president, the prophetic words of Ronald Reagan echoed in my mind:

> "General Secretary Gorbachev, if you seek peace, if you seek prosperity for the Soviet Union and Eastern Europe, if you seek liberalization, come here to this gate! Mr. Gorbachev, open this gate! Mr. Gorbachev, tear down this wall!"[48]

Filled with a sense of purpose, I fervently detailed the story of the titanic struggle against Communism and of the saintly heroes who, by the grace of God, saved the lives of billions.

– – – – – – – – – –

After just a few more weeks of writing, *The Third Testament* was complete. I had finally fulfilled my task. My only desire was that it would please the Lord. My only hope was that he would take note of my labor and smile a heavenly smile. From the onset, it was my goal to tell the story of his people over the last two thousand years—to recount the good and the bad, the sadness and the joy, the struggles and the triumphs—and to do so as accurately as I possibly could. When I first began this task, I believed that such a work should encompass a history of the Church, the stories of the saints and sinners, an anthology of important Christian writings, and a record of the miraculous events of the past two millennia. Upon completion of the task, I believed I had accomplished all I set out to do.

It was very late at night when I finally finished. I found that fitting because it was very late at night when I had started. It was as if I had taken a long journey and had come full circle. There were a lot of rough spots along the journey, but I ultimately found what I was looking for. There, in the quiet darkness, a feeling of absolute peace entered my heart as I wrote the final words:

> It is a historical fact that, centuries ago, Jesus Christ roamed this earth. And it is a historical fact that, with the help of the apostles, he established a Church here to guide his flocks. And it is a historical fact that, through his Church, he triumphantly saved man from the horrific fires of hell.

---

48   URL: http://www.reaganfoundation.org/reagan/speeches/wall.asp. Downloaded 2-26-06.

This is the story of that triumphant salvation—the historical salvation of man.

After decades of struggle and fear of Armageddon, it was, at last, time for change. The day and the hour were at hand. On the ninth day of the eleventh month in the year 1989, the gates of hell came crashing down. It was an extraordinary day. It was a heavenly sight. The persecuted people of the East rushed the gates and climbed the walls. There were no shots fired. There was no bloodshed. The only tears were tears of joy as the children of the East crossed the momentous divide to greet their brethren in the West. Thousands stood atop the infamous Berlin Wall and rejoiced, for freedom was finally theirs. In the days that followed, the same thousands worked together to raze the wall to the ground. Countless camera crews were on hand to report the event, and soon the entire Christian world was engaged in celebration. It was a celebration for the ages.

Before the collapse of Communism in Eastern Europe, an apocalyptic war between the United States and the Soviet Union was inevitable, but thanks to the prayers of millions, peace was restored. Children no longer went to bed at night, worrying over the horrors that the next day might bring. Parents no longer wondered if their children would live to see children of their own. Scientists no longer debated how many billions would die during the initial strike and how many more would succumb to the radiation thereafter. The fear of seeing fiery mushroom clouds engulf the cities of the world was eliminated. After decades of stress, people could breathe again, free of the terror of a nuclear Armageddon. Such was the significance of the event. Such was the glory of salvation—the devil's most devious scheme ended not with a bang but with the sounds of stones being dismantled from a wall.

It was in the late nineteenth century, when the world was in a volatile state, that Satan began his quest to cultivate an eternal garden of his own, an empire of evil. Working through his minions, Satan nearly succeeded in his diabolical quest. Yet the Church, led by the greatest of all popes, opposed him with strength and spirit, and in the end, Satan utterly failed. To the dark lord's dismay, his treasured Iron Curtain was hurled, in compelling fashion, onto the ash heap of history.

Undeniably, with the fall of the Berlin Wall, Christian civilization had achieved a great victory, but none of it could have been accomplished without prayer. Christ instructed his followers to pray. The message of Lourdes was to pray. The message of Fatima was to pray. The people of God prayed, and good triumphed against the greatest of odds. Let it be known to all mankind that it was divine devotion, not military might, that conquered the most menacing empire on the face of the earth. The fellowship of the Holy Spirit proved to be stronger than Satan and his minions ever imagined.

Long after the Brandenburg Gate was opened, long after the Berlin Wall came crashing down, and long after the worldwide jubilee had come to an end, God offered a sign of hope to his people. He did this not ostentatiously in the streets of Berlin, for that is not the way of the Lord. Rather, the sign was performed discreetly in the remote regions of Russia.

On the fifth day of the tenth month in the year 1990, deep within the desolation of the Ural Mountains, workers erected a cross—the eternal symbol of the Resurrection and the way—as a sign that Christianity had returned to their land. The workers set up the cross where the Ipatiev House had once stood, on the very grounds where Czar Nicolas and his family were brutally executed, the very grounds where, just decades before, Satan and his Communist minions had symbolically triumphed over the Church. After over seventy years, the reign of Satan was finally over. The workers erecting the cross were proof of this.

At the onset of their work, the sky was covered with dark clouds, and snow was falling. But then, miraculously, the clouds suddenly parted, allowing a brilliant ray of light to fall directly on the cross. The light circumscribed a halo around the symbol of the Risen Lord, and no snow fell on that area. There were no reporters to see this, no camera crews, no throngs in celebration. There were simply the workers, diligently performing their duty, in the remote solitude of the Urals. Their hearts were filled with the warmth of the sun, for they knew a truly dark time had ended. The prophecy of Fatima had come to pass. The evil empire was defeated. Hope was renewed. The workers built the cross as an expression of their faith, and the light of heavenly glory shone down upon them. Their souls cried out, "Thanks be to God." The greatest threat in the history of the Church was over.

Blessed is the Lord Jesus Christ, and blessed is his Church on earth, and blessed are the countless souls who joyously sing his praises in heaven. Amen.

"Amen," I said as I beheld my completed work. "Amen." I then sat back in my chair for a moment and marveled at the remarkable history of Christ's long-enduring creation.

Throughout time, the Church has overcome so many threats, I thought. *Contrived by Satan, the threats have been severe; they have been relentless; at times, they have seemed insurmountable. The harassment by the Pharisees, the persecution by the Romans, the barbarian invasions, the spread of militant Islam, the heretics, the corruption, the great schisms, the complacency of man in the age of science, the secularization of society, the plague of immorality, and the unparalleled evils of Communism—no matter how great the obstacle, no matter how severe the storm, no matter how rough the waves, the Church has endured. It has more than endured.*

Although at times, wicked men have used the name of religion to do great wrongs, in its entirety, the story of the Church is a story of virtue. No other institution comes close in compassion and benevolence: the countless schools, the hospitals, the nursing homes, the shelters, the orphanages, the food drives, the unequaled charitable contributions. For two thousand years the Church has done remarkable good. It has done this good despite the obstacles—that is what is so amazing. That is what is truly miraculous. That is how we know God is watching over us.

Certainly, there will be other great threats to come, perhaps greater than any in the past. I, like all Christians, wish this were not the case, but it would be foolish to believe otherwise. No one can deny that there is evil in this world—and a grave evil at that. Until the Day of Judgment, Satan will never cease in his efforts to undermine the glory of God, and he will always have willing accomplices. Yet the Church will go on doing the Lord's work. It will continue to feed the hungry, provide drink for the thirsty, clothe the naked, welcome strangers, and care for the ill. It will continue to call for purity and chastity. It will continue to defend the rights of the helpless and unwanted. It will continue to be a beacon of hope for the poor. It will go on doing good forever and ever. We know this to be true because Christ himself proclaimed it.

"Thou art Peter, and upon this rock I will build my Church, and the gates of hell shall not prevail against it," I ever-so-softly whispered in the dark of the night.

I then shut off my computer and prepared for bed. It was past 3:00 AM, and I was very tired. After saying my prayers, I turned off the bedside lamp next to the picture of Tina holding Ellen as a baby, and I immediately fell into a restful sleep.

- - - - - - - - - -

My life soon returned to normal. Having finished writing, I had a lot more time on my hands. I continued to lecture at the Catholic college, and I did so with renewed vigor. I also continued to take long walks in nature and took them with increased frequency. As before, Jerry and Joyce were a major part of my life. The three of us joined a Thursday night bowling league together. We were on Al's Pub's team and wore red T-shirts with a moose logo on back. We had a lot of fun. Having rediscovered his faith, Jerry accompanied me to Mass every week, although he preferred Saturday service to Sunday. Saturday was fine with me. It freed up all of Sunday for other endeavors. Feeling better than ever, Ellen returned to work full time, and her career blossomed. Her relationship with Jack blossomed also. It was not long before they were engaged. Jack was a changed man from when I first met him. After seeing how he stuck by Ellen during her time of hardship, I was proud to have him as a son-in-law. He certainly made Ellen happy. It was so nice to see her happy and alive again. Her energy was such that she even started training for another triathlon.

As is true for all people, there was still some stress in my life. The lawsuit against me had yet to be settled, but in my heart, I knew justice would be served, if not in this world then in the next. To protect my assets, I placed my home and savings in Ellen's name. I wanted her to have it all anyway; it was only right. All that was mine was hers. She was my life, and Sylvester Jones and his evil lawyer had no power over that.

Everything seemed to be falling into place for me. One Saturday evening during Mass, I recalled the dream that I'd had many months before—the dream that started me on the path to writing, the dream of a very dear friend. For the longest time I could not remember my friend's name. Often, it was on the tip of my tongue, but I could never quite get it out. But on Saturday, July 12, at last it came to me, and I smiled. His name was Tony.

> The world of pure spirits stretches between the divine nature and the world of human beings. Because divine wisdom has ordained that the higher should look after the lower, angels execute the divine plan for human salvation; they are our guardians, who free us when hindered and help to bring us home.

—Saint Thomas Aquinas (1225–1274)

THE THIRD TESTAMENT

The Book of Aquinas
 Saint Thomas Aquinas
 The *Summa Theologica*
 Proof of the Existence of God
 The Hymns of Thomas Aquinas
 The Vision of Heaven
 The Death of Aquinas
 Saint Catherine of Siena
 The Mystical Marriage

The Book of Schism
 Joan of Arc
 The Great Schism
 Johan Tetzel and Indulgences
 Martin Luther
 The Ninety-Five Theses
 The Protestant Reformation
 Jean Calvin
 The Anabaptists
 Sir Thomas More
 The Reformation Expands

The Book of Guadalupe
 The Lady of Guadalupe
 Queen of All of the Americas
 Saint Ignatius and the Jesuits
 Spiritual Exercises
 The Council of Trent
 The False Prophet Nostradamus
 Saint Teresa de Avila
 Saint John of the Cross
 The Wisdom of Saint Francis de Sales
 The Miraculous Cures of Saint Martin de Porres
 The Works of John Donne

The Book of Oberammergau
 The Black Death
 Miracle of Oberammergau
 Saint Vincent de Paul

LaVergne, TN USA
29 October 2010
202773LV00003B/3/P